HER TWO MEN
In Tahiti

What Readers Are Saying

Praise for Her Two Men in London

"This book… this book was everything I wanted it to be and more. It was hot, it was sexy, it was knock your socks off great. I'm ashamed to say I have never read any books by these authors until now, but you can bet that will change. … This book was far more emotional than I was expecting, but aren't all the great ones that way. I sincerely hope you will all check this book out. You will not be disappointed."—Jodi, *Ruby Red Romance Review*

"I have never been so envious and turned on while reading a book in my entire reading existence. …when they came together as a duo or triad it was freaking panty wetting or wet spot worthy. I squirmed, cried, made the dreadful mistake of reading this in public, and so many other TMI moments. To say I am a fan and true promoter of this series of Dana and Kristine duo would be an understatement. The scenes varied, the storyline flowed, and the conflict was there. … This MMF is a downright MUST READ for the summer but be sure to have a man or two on standby."—*Reading By the Book Blog*

"What an amazing new novel that I came across by Dana Delamar and Kristine Cayne! Two new authors that will be on my radar from this fantastic MMF novel that I consumed in a matter of hours! *Her Two Men in London* is scorching, emotional and a breathtaking unputdownable novel that will be on your mind long after you are finished!"—*Up All Night with Books*

"You will definitely need a couple pairs of panties and a new supply of batteries!!! This book should come with a public health warning and its own fire extinguisher. This book is the hottest book I have read in a really long time. … This book set my Kindle on fire and my sheets. This book should NOT BE READ IN PUBLIC or you will drown before you can relieve the burn. I gave this book 5 stars but I'd give it more if I could. If this book was a curry it would have 7 chili peppers!!!"—leopardwolf, Goodreads reviewer

"Wonderful start to the Total Indulgence series by new-to-me authors Dana Delamar and Kristine Cayne that kept me captivated from beginning to end with unforgettable characters and a well-crafted MMF bisexual ménage romance. I loved the instant attraction and skin scorching intimacy… Fans of this genre will love *Her Two Men in London* and I look forward to book two in this hot, sexy series."—Pamela R. Mitchell, Amazon reviewer

"This is my 2nd MMF book. And by God its was freaking AMAZING. Riley and Carter will have you panting with their intense sex scenes. Their love triangle with Paige was so emotional, especially when Riley poured his heart out to Carter. I have cried so many tears with this spectacular book that I want all of my FB family and friends to read what I did with this book. ... Kristine Cayne, boo, thanks for this spectacular wonderful story."—Jackie Marbury, Amazon reviewer

"Ménage fans will just LOVE *Her Two Men in London*. It's a smoking hot and sexy ménage a trois story with as much heart as heat, and a touch of snark as well. Believable characterization tops the list of good things in this smoothly written MMF bisexual romance."—Melanie S, Amazon reviewer

PRAISE FOR HER TWO MEN IN TAHITI

"I am at a loss for words to describe just how much I love this story. I am an emotional reader and I fell in love with every character in this story. Even Damon, Nigel, and Vanessa. While reading this story, I felt everything these characters feel: their joy, their fears, their hope, their heartbreaks. I felt everything. I enjoyed every single second of it. I could not put it down, absolutely addictive. I am truly sad that the story is over and I cannot wait for the next one!"—Gigi, Amazon reviewer

"It only gets better in Book 2, *Her Two Men In Tahiti*! It drew me in from the beginning! I felt so bad for Dev and his family. Then Sky feeling like she might be the third wheel. Then Rod trying to keep his friendship with Dev even though he was in love with him. My heart was breaking for all of them! There were so many emotions in this book. They all had such a great relationship together that I was cheering them on. Thank you for such a great read and I can't wait until Book 3!!"—Donna T, Amazon reviewer

"I loved it. I have always wanted to go to Tahiti and in a sense this read makes you feel as though you are there plus the instant connection with the three characters. The push and pull as well as the electrifying connection between them will leave you not just hot & swooning but begging for more."— Ryan Grey, Amazon reviewer

"After reading Cayne and Delamar's first book, *Her Two Men in London*, I knew I wanted to read this next book. I've been intrigued with the MMF romance trope. Honestly, in my mind, I'm never sure if it will work, and there are plenty of books who do not do it justice. That is not the case with this second offering from these two authors. In fact, I liked this book better than their first book."—Amy D, Amazon reviewer

THE TOTAL INDULGENCE SERIES

HER TWO MEN
In Tahiti

TOTAL INDULGENCE, BOOK 2

DANA DELAMAR
KRISTINE CAYNE

THREE ORCAS PRESS

ISBN (print): 1-949071-03-0
ISBN-13 (print): 978-1-949071-03-0
ISBN (ebook): 1-949071-02-2
ISBN-13 (ebook): 978-1-949071-02-3

Publisher's Note: This is a work of fiction. Names, characters, places, and incidents either are the product of the author's imagination or are used fictitiously, and any resemblance to actual persons, living or dead, business establishments, events, or locales is entirely coincidental.

Cover artwork & series logo design
© 2018, 2019 L.J. Anderson of Mayhem Cover Creations
mayhemcovercreations.com

Cover photos: © DepositPhotos @ Yafimik, @ Dmitry_Tsvetkov,
and @ sasamihajlovic

Dana Delamar author image courtesy of LGImages

Editing, proofreading, and print formatting:
By Your Side Self-Publishing
www.ByYourSideSelfPub.com

ACKNOWLEDGMENTS

Many thanks (once again) to our husbands for putting up with our marathon phone calls, silliness, and shenanigans. We love you!

And many thanks to our readers for your enthusiastic reviews and heartfelt support. You mean the world to us!

Prologue

Three Months Ago

SKY

I awoke slowly to the heaven I'd been in for the past week: smack dab between two hot rock stars, Rod "Hot Rod" Taylor and Dev Stone of King's Cross. *British* rock stars, no less. For some reason, they'd taken a "fancy" to my American accent while we were working together and invited me to take a wild "holiday" with them. Me, Sklyar River, struggling life coach and team-building facilitator.

I didn't know what I was doing here in Palm Springs, other than having the best sex of my life. Rod and Dev were intense and fun and wild—well, Rod more so than Dev. Rod had initiated our little threesome, and Dev and I had eagerly joined in.

Dev was on my left and Rod on my right, both of them nestled against me, Dev's short black hair in disarray, his golden-brown skin so dark against mine. Last night he'd said he was never letting me go, and Rod had echoed the sentiment.

Me. They wanted *me*. Two rock stars, who could have anyone.

I told them I had to think about it. But I was done thinking; I was all in. As crazy as it was, I was falling for them, and I would do whatever it took to be with them, including giving up my business in San Francisco.

1

Rod stirred against me, his right hand still cupping my breast, the one with the little freckle near the nipple. He'd named it Beatrice—the freckle, that is. I'd asked him why and he'd shrugged. "It just looks like a Beatrice."

That was Rod for you—kind of silly under his ultra-glam rock star exterior. He was the kind of guy Adam Lambert took styling cues from. Spiky brown hair with blond streaks, guyliner galore. And oh, could he fill out a pair of leather pants. His thick, hard cock pressed into my hip, Dev's in the same state on my other side. Should I wake them up for round one of today's escapades?

I started sliding a hand along Rod's hip, then stopped myself. My bladder was squealing, and if I'd learned anything about Rod and Dev, it was that once we got started, it would be quite a while before we'd stop. Better zip into the bathroom and freshen up, then initiate the festivities.

I carefully crept out of the hotel room bed and into the bathroom. Might as well brush my teeth and shower while I was there.

When I was done, I tried to run a brush through my tangle of dark brown curls, but it was pretty hopeless—I needed some deep conditioning to sort out this snarl. And they'd just mess it up anyway, one or the other of them winding it around his fist and pulling just hard enough to make me wet and achy. A wave of heat ran through me at the memory of last night—Dev in my mouth, Rod buried in my pussy, me writhing between them.

How had I gotten so lucky?

I walked back into the bedroom and stopped short. Dev was spooning Rod, his cock pressed against Rod's firm ass. Interesting. Rod was openly bisexual—"anything sexual" as he put it—but Dev was adamantly straight, or so he'd said. Was there something more between them, something I wasn't supposed to see?

Rod rolled over so he and Dev were face to face, and Dev nuzzled into the crook of Rod's neck and threw a leg over his hip. What the hell?

They looked hot together, and I certainly didn't object to the idea of the two of them being sexually involved. But… if they were, where did that leave me?

The two of them had grown up together. They'd known each other for almost twenty years. They were as close as two people could be and not be married—though in a way they were, because of the band.

Why were they hiding this from me? Didn't they trust me?

An old memory resurfaced, and I pushed it away. This wasn't the same thing.

Or was it? I'd been lied to before, and the ache in my chest felt the same as it had back then.

Apparently, I was good enough to fuck, but not worthy of being in Rod and Dev's confidence.

Dev exhaled loudly, then he murmured, "I love you."

Rod's eyes snapped open. "Never thought I'd hear you say it." He smiled and closed his eyes again, tightening his arms around Dev, and my stomach dropped to the floor.

Now I understood why Rod had instigated our threesome. He'd wanted me to be the sexual bridge between him and his straight best friend. He'd used me to get what he really wanted. And now he—they—didn't need me.

I'd been the third wheel before, and no way was I going through that again.

My eyes started to burn, but damn it, they didn't deserve my tears, and they didn't deserve my heart.

I quietly dressed and packed my things, the two of them holding each other in their sleep. A lump in my throat, I snuck out and shut the door, already calling for a ride.

I wiped the damn tears away while I arranged for my taxi.

This was the last time I was going to follow my stupid, foolish heart. It never looked before it leapt.

But I should have known better. Three people, one relationship? It had been too good to be true.

Chapter 1

ROD

I wandered into the photographer's studio a quarter hour late and proper shit-faced. Nigel Standen, the bloke we'd hired to manage King's Cross, gave me the stink eye. But what did the bleeding sod expect? The only way I would make it through this fucking nightmare of a photoshoot was to arrive anything but sober.

The photographer, a lush blonde bird with an impressive rack, introduced herself as Zoe while eyeing me up and down. My attire was rock star chic, grungy holed jeans and a leather jacket worn over a ripped and stretched out T-shirt. It was all I'd had time to throw on after an angry call from Nigel pulled me out of the warm arms of Trisha and Tristan.

"Just crawled out of a gutter, mate?" Zoe asked.

"No, just crawled out of a nice, cozy, and still-occupied bed."

"I suppose it'll have to do," she said, wrinkling her nose. "Let's get started."

My bandmates grunted their hellos while she herded us together in front of a mockup of the cover of our new album, *Ultimate Mindf*ck*. "A little closer now, please," Zoe instructed.

I ground my teeth and swung a loose arm around Damon Mercury, the newest member of King's Cross, a Yank guitarist we'd recruited at the label's urging to give the band a harder sound. On his other side, flanked by Mick, Jules, and Tommy, stood Devkinandan Prakesh, aka Dev Stone, the love of my life, former best mate, eternal enemy, and constant knife in my back.

Damon took a whiff of me. "Dude, you smell like sex. Just how many people were you with last night?"

"Twins. And it was this morning."

"Female?"

I grinned. "One of each."

He held up his fist for me to bump. "Dude. You're my hero."

"All right then," Zoe said, after shooting photos from various angles. "Shirts off."

Dev tossed the photographer a shy smile, then tugged his shirt over his head. I barely managed to bite back a groan, and my mouth went dry at the sight of all that smooth copper skin. His muscles flexed and relaxed, rippling under the glow of the photographer's lights. Zoe's eyes brightened, and Dev hammed it up for her, striking poses like some sort of bodybuilder, the fucking wanker.

Not so long ago, all that flesh, those toned muscles, and so much more had been on display for me. Within my grasp. But when I'd dared to take what was so readily offered, Dev had thrown a strop.

Didn't the tosser understand what he'd done to me? How his rejection had flayed my skin and left me bare. Exposed. Destroyed.

He'd pushed me away. Shamed me.

But never again.

"Rod?"

The photographer frowned at me.

"What?" I snapped.

"Your shirt."

I looked around and saw I was the only one still fully dressed. With a grumble, I removed my jacket and tossed my T-shirt into the corner. It landed on top of Dev's. Fucking Christ. Was that as close as I'd get to him now? How pathetic was I that such a small thing had my cock stirring?

Zoe looked us over and positioned Dev and me in the center, with the other blokes around us. As the lead singer, I was the face of King's Cross, and Dev was the lead guitarist—but fuck, he wasn't anymore. He'd stepped back to rhythm guitar and let Damon take his place. Another thing I was pissed about. He'd probably done it just to get away from me. Dev wrote the music and I wrote the lyrics. That was how it had always been.

We were best mates. Emphasis on "were."

These days, Dev didn't talk to me. We hadn't written the songs we needed for the world tour we were kicking off in just two months, not to mention the album we hadn't yet recorded. Nigel was running out of excuses for the delays.

And everyone blamed me.

But was it my fault? I'd always been honest about who I was. My sexuality was out there for everyone to see. And Dev had been my friend throughout it all. Until...

A noise drew my attention. Dev's breath caught in his throat, a sound like the one he made when he came. My eyes shot to his face only to see him transfixed by Zoe. She placed her hand on his shoulder to guide him into position. A flush rose up his chest, then darkened his neck and face. When she smiled at him, his chest puffed out.

"Zoe," he asked in his sexy-as-fuck East Indian accent. "Are you a fan of the band?"

"Of course." She chuckled. "Who isn't?"

Damon held up his arm and flexed his bicep, which made his tattoos seem to come alive. "Who's your favorite?"

Her eyes lingered on Dev before she focused on Damon. "Maybe you're my favorite. That's some right proper ink," she said as she moved around us.

Yeah, right. Her favorite was Dev. A blind man could see it. And as much as I wished it right now, I wasn't blind. Dev wanted her too.

And I wanted everyone to shut up and fuck off. We needed to finish this torture session yesterday. My muscles were shaking, maybe from keeping the position too long, or maybe it was the fucking agonies. What I wouldn't give for a couple dexies right about now.

"Rod, give us a smile," Zoe said.

A corner of my lips rose, and she started to laugh. "That's a snarl, love. Try again."

Nigel lifted his heft off the chair he'd been sitting in and grabbed my chin. "Are you high?"

"Not nearly high enough."

Dev sighed and the sound wrapped around my heart. It was suddenly difficult to breathe. We'd always promised each other we wouldn't let the rock star life take over, but that had been *before*. Now I couldn't make it through a day without indulging in one mind-altering substance or another. And on days like today, where I had to see *him*, it was all I could do not to drown.

Nigel shook his head in thinly veiled disgust and returned to his seat like the gormless worm he was. Having given up on me, Zoe turned to Dev and cupped his jaw. Her thumb touched his bottom lip. His gaze shot to me.

I glared back.

He cleared his throat and looked away. But it was no use. I could feel his heat, smell his arousal, and the urge to scream, fight, or fuck took me over.

I couldn't do this.

I couldn't be this close to Dev and not touch him.

I couldn't stand to see him every day and know that he'd never be mine.

Tearing my eyes from his profile, I stepped away from the group. Slowly at first, but as the distance mounted, so did my speed. I snatched my shirt off Dev's, grabbed my jacket, and stormed out of the room, ignoring the calls of my bandmates, of the photographer, and mostly, of Dev.

A hand gripped my arm and spun me around. I stared at it, the dark on my light.

"You can't leave," Dev said, his stormy eyes the color of a muddy lake bottom.

Once again, I tore my gaze away. I couldn't do this if I looked at him, and I had to do this, before it all killed me.

"I quit," I said softly.

Dev's breath caught, and his fingers tightened on my wrist. "You can't."

Anger rose inside me, a boiling cauldron. I ripped my wrist out of his grasp. "I just did."

"Come on, mate. Don't be a prat. King's Cross is your life."

No, Dev. You're *my life.*

"You'll be fine without me."

Flags of crimson marked Dev's dark cheekbones. "Rod, for fuck's sake. Don't throw everything away just because—"

I lowered my voice so only he would hear. "Because my supposed best mate keeps stringing me along, pulling me closer with one hand, and pushing me away with the other? Yeah." I wasn't worried about myself. I was pansexual and proud of it. But it wasn't my place to out Dev to the world. Hell, he wasn't even out to himself.

"I can't give you what you want." His voice broke and he turned his head away from me.

I closed my eyes. "And I can't stand the sight of you."

I spun on my heel and left the studio, deaf to everything except the sound of my heart cracking.

DEV

I sat at the table in kitchen of my parents' newly renovated Hounslow home, a mid-sized two-story, five-bedroom, three-bath house, as my mother rabbited on about my sister's upcoming wedding.

Our previous home had been a three-bedroom semi-detached house that had been much too small for our seven-member family. My three sisters had shared a room while I'd shared one with my brother. Rod had enjoyed taking the piss about rock star Dev Stone living in his parents' tiny home and bunking with his baby brother. He'd teased me incessantly, asking if I had blue balls from the lack of a private place to jerk off.

He hadn't been wrong.

When I finally grew tired of feeling like Harry Potter living in a cupboard under the stairs, and when living in our home had become too much of a security risk for me, I'd bought both sides of a larger semi-detached and had it completely gutted and refinished. At least now I had my own room, even though I still shared a bath with my siblings.

I'd wanted to purchase some posh place in a gated community, somewhere more upscale than Hounslow, but I'd caved since my parents and siblings wished to remain in our local area, where the Indian community was strong. I always caved.

Truth is, I wished like hell I could grow some bollocks and move the fuck out, get my own flat and be the independent man I wanted to be. At twenty-six and more than financially secure, I had no need to still live with my parents and siblings. But I was like a bird with clipped wings.

My oldest sister, Geena, who was two years my junior, had moved out when she'd married last year. Now I only had to deal with Aahna, the bride to be, who was twenty-three and had just graduated with a degree in engineering; Indira, twenty and studying pre-med; and Patag, who was eighteen and had just passed his A-levels with plans to study law. I was, of course, happily footing the bill for their degrees as well as for Aahna's nuptials, as I had for Geena.

"Devkinandan!" My mother's sharp voice brought my attention back to the discussion of Aahna's wedding.

"Mum?"

She huffed, then seemed to regain her composure, and smiled. "Your sisters and I were discussing the *poonyahvachanam*. You will be seated next to Raj's cousin, Kalini."

Oh joy. Since Aahna's engagement to Raj Gupta, the son of my father's business partner, my mother had been dropping increasingly less subtle hints about Kalini as a prospective bride for me. She was a nice girl, bright and funny, but she wasn't S— No, best not think about her. I flicked a stray crumb off the tablecloth. "Mum, I told you—"

"Oh God. Why must my first-born son always be so difficult?" My mother raised her arms and wailed at the ceiling as though supplicating some divine power. Her eyes lowered to glare at me. "Aahna is marrying in a matter of weeks, and Indira will marry as soon as she completes her bachelor's degree."

Out of the corner of my eye, I glimpsed Indira's grimace, her eyes going hard. Hope rose in my chest that she'd fight back, but then she seemed to rethink opening an old wound and pasted a placid look on her face. My heart sank. *Just wait, little sister, it only gets worse,* I thought, a wave of self-pity crashing over me. The burden seemed so much heavier now that things with Rod were going so poorly. He'd always been my go-to person, my vent-valve when the pressure of conforming to my parents' ideals got to be too much. But now, I was on my own.

King's Cross and our music had always been a sticking point with my family. Good Indian boys didn't parade themselves around on stage. They most certainly were not rock stars with all that the lifestyle entailed. Not that they minded the money it brought, only the lack of control they had over my life.

"It isn't seemly," my mother continued, oblivious to the pain she was inflicting. "It is bad enough you carouse with those"—she scrunched up her face as though she'd smelled something rotten—"rock stars when you are a wonderful classically-trained musician. You could be playing recitals at Royal Albert Hall or be a member of the London Symphony Orchestra."

"What? I'm not to be a physician anymore? Not a brain surgeon?" I asked, bitterness seeping into my tone.

Ignoring me, she folded a dish towel and set it on the counter. "Instead, you insist on creating that noise—"

My fists clenched at my sides and I pushed to my feet, cutting her off mid-sentence. "No one insults my music. Not even you, Mum."

She sniffed and turned her face away. "It is not respectable."

"Perhaps not to you," I said, exhibiting far more calm than I felt. "But to the millions of King's Cross fans, we are far more than that."

Her lips pursed. "That name." She shook her head. "It is the true insult."

Blood drained from my head to pool in my legs. The sheer weight rooted me in place when all I sought to do was escape, run away from this house where my dreams and aspirations were constantly crushed by the fear of disgrace and dishonor. My heart thudded against my sternum and the entire room appeared pink-tinged. "How dare you!"

Aahna rushed to our mother's side, Indira to mine. These were the sides we'd chosen, the roles that had become so ingrained over the years. Why did I continue to put myself through this misery? I did everything I could to be the dutiful son, to honor my parents and my siblings. All I asked for in return was to play my music, my way. It was the only rebellion I'd allowed myself, and despite the fact I gave a large portion of the proceeds to my family, which they gladly accepted, my mother still acted like I was prostituting myself.

Like I wasn't good enough.

Steps thundered down the stairs and all our heads turned toward the doorway that led into the hall. My father's narrow-shouldered frame and scowling face soon filled it. "What is all this yelling?"

"Sorry, Dad," I said, looking at my feet. "We did not intend to disturb your work."

His gaze shifted over to my mother. She raised her chin, confident that he would take her side. And why shouldn't she be confident? He always did. They embodied a united front. It was admirable, really, in the way it had always kept us to heel.

Why couldn't I be more like Rod, unapologetically myself? He'd never given two fucks how others saw him. He did what—and who—he wanted, how he wanted, and when he wanted. And me? I weighed every action against its impact to my family and our standing in the community. I had to make up for not having taken the path my parents had set for me, to be a doctor, marry a good Indian woman, and have a ton of studious, respectful Indian children. That had been my destiny, one I'd craftily avoided.

But maybe, my reprieve was coming to an end.

My shoulders slumped as my spine seemed to dissolve like sugar in a cup of hot tea. I sat heavily in my chair and bowed my head. How much longer could I keep fighting when I didn't have my best friend to prop me up? It was all too much, and after six months of tension, of non-communication, with nothing but harsh words between us, I was completely done in.

"Son?"

I looked up, words of resignation forming in my mind, words of defeat and acquiescence on my tongue.

This was for the best. I would fulfill my contractual obligations to the label while at the same time easing myself out of the band. Due to my close friendship with Rod, the band was more the Rod and Dev show than anything else. We wrote the music and the lyrics. Rod sang the songs and I played lead guitar. The rest of our mates filled essential but nameless roles. But now that Damon, the Yank the label had hired to give the band a harder guitar sound, had joined us and I'd moved to rhythm guitar, the stage was set for a clever retreat. I'd heard Damon had an ear for songwriting. And if that was the case, I'd use the tour to reinforce the working relationship between him and Rod. Once Damon had completely replaced me, I could leave and the band would go on. Rod's life could go on. As for mine?

I'd do what was expected of me.

"I'll... I'll sit with Kalini." I looked at my mum and dad, my sisters. I was doing what would make them happy. So why did I feel like I was dying inside? I wet my lips. "If things go well, I'll—"

My mobile buzzed in my back pocket, cutting me off.

Saving me, at least for now, from committing to a future I'd never be ready for.

I gripped my phone, seizing upon that buoy in the dark waters like a drowning man. It was Nigel. "Please excuse me," I said, my voice a hoarse, desperate whisper. I'd seen the edge of the precipice and it had scared me shitless. "I must take this."

As quickly as my heavy feet allowed, I took the back door into the garden, and made my way to the far end so I'd have a bit of privacy. "Hello?"

"That stupid twat is threatening to quit the band," Nigel spouted in place of a hello.

My heart clenched and I had to grip the fence to keep myself upright. I didn't even have to ask who Nigel meant. I knew. Rod. At the photoshoot, he'd said he couldn't stand the sight of me anymore. Had words ever cut more deeply? I never thought he'd quit the band to get away from me.

"No. Shit. He can't quit. Tell him to stay. I'll leave." I swallowed against the bile rising in my throat. Despite having made this decision a few minutes ago, saying it out loud was like ripping my soul out of my body. No music. No Rod. I blinked back the tears. Leaving King's Cross was worth it. It would make everyone I cared about happy.

Everyone but me.

No one had ever cared about my happiness. Except for Rod, and now he didn't care either. Because if he did care, he wouldn't be trying to take himself out of my life.

"Jesus Fucking Christ. Have you all gone mad? Now listen, here, Dev. No one is quitting this motherfucking band." Nigel wheezed out an audible breath, his fervor having drained him of his energy. "You're all under contract for the album and the tour. Have you forgotten that it begins in eight weeks?"

Without giving me a chance to reply, he barreled on. "The label has convinced Rod to give the band another chance. They've hired an outfit to do some team-building activities with all of you."

I frowned and let go of the fence. "They're cracked if they think a few games and kumbaya chants will fix things."

"It's likely to be a tad more intense than that, eh? Anyway, consider it a bit of a holiday. Pack up your guitar and your trunks. I'll be sending you a plane ticket. You'll be leaving in four days and you'll be gone for a fortnight."

"A fortnight? You know my sister's wedding is then, yeah?" I'd fought hard for everything to be scheduled to finish right before the band began heavy rehearsals for our world tour, which I'd certainly not forgotten about.

"Don't worry. You'll be back to London for the start of the festivities."

"But—"

"Listen, do you want King's Cross to break up? Because if this fails, the label is washing its hands of you lot."

Did I want the band to break up? Of course not. Whether I was a part of it or not, it had to go on. Something of my friendship with Rod, of our twenty-year relationship, had to survive. I couldn't give him what he wanted, but I could give him our music.

I looked back at the house and my parents and sisters milling about. They'd be pissed off that I was leaving so soon before the wedding, but as long as I kept paying the bills, what did anyone really care?

I gripped the phone in my hand and pictured Rod as he'd been the last time I'd seen him truly happy, three months, one week, and two days ago. Not that I was counting.

Before beating a quiet retreat, I needed to see that pure, sunny smile on his handsome face one last time. I passed a hand over my mouth, remembering too much.

"I'll do it," I said, the words at once freeing and terrifying.

SKY

Why had Daniel King, the CEO of Total Indulgence Tours, sent me a plane ticket? Why did he want a meeting with *me*, owner and operator of a tiny business that had nothing to do with travel or event planning? On the phone, he'd claimed to have an offer I couldn't refuse, and given the current state of my business, more floundering than flourishing even after five years of killing myself, I was hardly in a position to reject him outright.

So here I was, on the sidewalk outside the Miami headquarters of Total Indulgence Tours. The low, modern building was located in the quaint community of Coconut Grove and within walking distance of the ocean. Despite it being September, the temperature was still in the nineties, stiflingly humid, and I swore the air smelled of salt and coconut tanning lotion.

Having grown up in California, I was no stranger to heat, sand, and water, but there was something about Miami, about South Florida, that was different in a way I couldn't quite put my finger on. Maybe it was the abundant water supply, the lushness of the flora, or the almost imperceptible *rhythm* of life here. Whatever it was, the result was a sultry, tropical feel that made me want to strip down and relish the breeze as I danced naked on the beach.

I shook my head, chasing away such fantasies and focused on what had brought me here in the first place. I pushed open the glass door and stepped inside. Cool air, just this side of cold, bathed my body, and I inhaled my first refreshing breath since leaving the hotel. Following the instructions in the email I'd received, I took the elevator up to the fourth floor.

As soon as I stepped into an airy modern lobby, a pretty brunette greeted me. "Good morning,"

"Good morning." I approached the woman's desk. "I'm Sky River. I have a 9:30 appointment with Daniel King."

"Of course." She smiled and indicated the cozy seating area behind me. "I'll let Mr. King know you're here. Can I get you something? Coffee, tea, water?"

"Thank you..." I paused, a subtle query for her name.

"Jane."

"Jane. I'll have some water, if it's not too much trouble."

"No trouble at all."

She disappeared somewhere down a hallway, and I took a seat on a comfortable brown and beige U-shaped couch that was not, thank goodness, leather. The walls of the lobby featured beautiful photos of gorgeous locations all over the world. After first hearing from Daniel, I'd done a little online research. TI specialized in custom tours and events, mostly top-of-the-line, luxury excursions for wealthy individuals or corporations. For the life of me, I couldn't imagine what they might want with me. My company organized and led team-building activities for enterprises, both large and small. I taught my clients how to better align their teams for happier and more productive employees.

Most times, we worked in a boardroom with Legos. All that was a far cry from these photos of Paris, London, and Egypt.

Jane returned with my water just as a good-looking, sandy-haired man in his early thirties entered the lobby from a different hallway.

"Oh, there you are, Daniel," Jane said. "This is Sky River."

Daniel held his hand out, a straight-to-business smile on his face. "Thank you for coming to see me, Miss River. This way, please."

I followed him to a large, well-appointed office that occupied one half of the rounded end of the building. The floor-to-ceiling windows made for an amazing view of the coast and downtown Miami. TI appeared to be doing well for itself. My research had revealed that TI was a privately held company, originally founded by Daniel King and Javier Cordero as equal partners. They later added a third partner, Arianna Rodriguez, each partner now controlling one third of the business.

Daniel ushered me into a plush chair, one of two facing his elegant mahogany desk, on which folders were stacked in haphazard piles. It seemed he wasn't a figurehead CEO.

"I'm intrigued by your mention of an offer, Mr. King," I said, opening up the discussion.

"Daniel, please."

"If you'll return the favor."

"Very well, Sky. I see you don't beat around the bush. I like that."

I nodded. There'd been times in my life when being less honest, less straightforward, would have helped. But today was not one of those times.

Daniel steepled his fingers. While he thought about how to make his offer, I sipped my water and admired the view out his windows. He cleared his throat. "My offer is somewhat unusual. Please hear me out before you respond."

I set my water down on his desk. "Of course."

"TI was approached by Reeling Records." They were a label in Los Angeles that provided stateside distribution for recording artists from the UK. "One of their clients is a UK label named Sonic High, and one of the artists on Sonic High's roster is a band named King's Cross. Apparently you've worked with them?"

My brain heard King's Cross and got stuck there.

King's Cross.

Dev.

Rod.

Adrenaline flooded my body, and an intense impulse to flee consumed me. My mouth went dry. I reached for my water and downed half the glass. Daniel's keen eyes narrowed.

"Y-yes. I've worked with them."

He nodded and continued, "They're on the verge of a world tour that has the potential to make them one of the biggest hits of the year, maybe even the decade. Unfortunately, the band seems to be in some difficulty."

"Difficulty?" I asked, my mind racing with a million scenarios.

"The band is falling apart. They haven't written songs for their album that is supposed to be released before the tour, and to top it off, their lead singer is threatening to quit."

My jaw dropped. King's Cross was Rod's life. "Why?"

"He and the lead guitarist"—Daniel pulled a notepad closer and read off of it—"no, sorry, he's the rhythm guitarist now. Anyway, he's the one who usually composes the music while the lead singer writes the lyrics. They had a falling out some months ago, and for some reason everything seems to have come to a head this week."

"Wow." Dev wasn't the lead guitarist anymore? And Rod and Dev had had a fight so serious that Rod was willing to walk away from King's Cross? I couldn't even imagine what must've happened. The last time I'd seen them... when I'd left them in bed... My chest ached at the memory. I'd been certain their connection was the real thing, the enduring kind of love. I'd known then and there that they were meant for each other. Always.

Had I been wrong?

"How does this involve me?"

"Sonic High Records convinced the entire band to commit to a last-ditch effort to save King's Cross. They've all agreed to a two-week intensive retreat to work things out. And we want you to run it."

My mind raced with possibilities as I began to understand where Daniel was going with this.

"We reserved an exclusive resort on the island of Moorea in the French Polynesian islands. It's secluded and very private. There will be no press. No outside help."

"Why me?" I asked. It was the final piece of the puzzle. "I run a small business on the West Coast. I'm honestly surprised you've even heard of me before."

"I hadn't." Daniel stared at me. "The lead singer requested you personally. Actually, he said he wouldn't agree to the retreat if you weren't the one facilitating it. So you see, Sky, the fate of this band rests on you. If they don't resolve their issues before the world tour is set to begin, it's all over, and a lot of people will be hurt. Needless to say, a lot of money has been invested in this band and the tour."

Rod had requested me? Insisted on having me brought into this? It made no sense. Rod had only tolerated me because it got him closer to Dev. Dev was the one who'd liked me, but *Rod* was the one who'd asked for me?

"I-I don't—" I pushed out of the chair and began pacing Daniel's office. Could I do this? The last time we'd all been together, I'd gotten my heart broken. Hell, I couldn't even listen to their music without bawling. It had been three months, and I was only beginning to feel okay again, like maybe my heart was only bruised instead of broken.

No. It was asking too much.

I stopped in front of Daniel's desk. "I can't do this. I'm sorry."

"We could make it worth your while, Sky. There's a million-pound bonus if you succeed."

"One million?" I dropped into my chair. The amount was staggering. I could save my company with that money, I could hire staff, take on bigger contracts. I could finally prove to my parents that my MBA from Berkeley Haas in Management of Organizations had been worth it. That I was meant for more than just working in a shop on the beach that sold surfing gear and souvenirs.

On the other hand, one million pounds, although an obscene amount of money, couldn't guarantee the success of my business. It didn't even guarantee TI's full support. Other than whatever they'd be paid for having arranged for me to contract through them, they had no skin in the game. Maybe Daniel and the label thought reuniting King's Cross was a lost cause and wanted to hire me as their scapegoat for when everything went to hell.

I looked around Daniel's office, at the promo photos on his walls, at the view of the ocean. This would only work if he was all in as well.

"I have a counter-proposal for you." When I was certain I had his undivided attention, I said, "Let's split the bonus and go into business together."

Daniel's brows rose. "You want to be a partner at TI?"

"Yes. If this goes well, TI could expand, add a new corporate service. With your contacts and my expertise, we could build something really useful. Add in TI's experience with event planning and we'd be sought out by every major business for leadership retreats. Not to mention—"

Daniel grinned.

I blushed to the roots of my hair. "Sorry. I got a little carried away."

Rising from his seat, he chuckled and came to sit on his desk in front of me. "No, no. I like how you think. It's a great idea. I'm fairly certain I can convince my partners to yield five percent of their stakes, so if this worked out, you'd have fifteen percent of TI."

"Fifteen percent."

"Plus half the bonus."

This was my chance. The best opportunity I'd probably ever have, and so not what I'd anticipated when I'd received Daniel's call yesterday.

But could I do it?

Could I get involved with Dev and Rod again without destroying myself? And was I good enough to save King's Cross?

If I could keep myself emotionally closed off from them... That would take care of my first concern, but the second remained. How could I get them to resolve their differences when I couldn't even imagine what had shattered their friendship?

"Do you know what the problem between Rod and Dev even is?"

Daniel leaned back and picked up his notebook. Reading off of it, he said, "Their manager says the best they could figure is that something happened between them about three months ago. Around the time that you facilitated some activities for the band when they started working with Reeling Records. They took a week vacation and when they returned, things were pretty cool between them. They continued to work together, doing a few performances and hiring a new guitarist at the label's insistence, but things have only gotten worse. Apparently, two days ago, after a photo shoot in London, Rod snapped and tried to quit."

I didn't understand this. When I'd left them, they'd looked so in love. What had happened after I left, and how could I get them past it?

In the week we'd spent together, that kiss, that hug, was the only time I'd seen them be physical together. It had seemed so natural, so right. If any two people were meant to be together, it was Dev and Rod. So why weren't they?

If I could figure this out, I'd be able to resolve their issues. Was their sexual connection, that love that I'd seen between them, my way in? Was I to be the bridge again?

Could I be the bridge again? It would mean doing things the same way we had in the past.

My heart squeezed.

I met Daniel's gaze. "If I agree to this, you need to understand that my methods are going to be unorthodox and somewhat unprofessional. Maybe unethical too." I looked away. "I would never do this with any other clients, but I *know* these guys."

"Know them?" Daniel's jaw tightened. "In the biblical sense?"

"Yes. If you don't agree with what I'm going to do, we shouldn't even try this. I think I have an idea what the problem is, and if I'm right, anything another facilitator would do won't come close to working in this particular situation."

Daniel set the pad down on his gleaming desk. He inclined his head slightly. "Whatever you have to do, I'll support you. This could be a really big opportunity for TI, and if you fix the band, it will be good for them too."

I stood and shook his hand. "A win-win all around."

Especially for me, as long as my stupid heart didn't fall for the siren song of my two hot British rock stars all over again.

17

Chapter 2

ROD

The caravan of my King's Cross bandmates and roadies left the small town of Temae, home to the only public airport on the island of Moorea, and headed onto a narrow two-lane road that appeared to circle the island. I rested my head on the seat back and stared out the window at the breathtaking scenery.

Water diamonds glittered in the high sun for miles on the gently rolling waves of the South Pacific. The place was a goddamn tropical paradise, but I knew it would be a torturous stay. A repeat of the last three months.

So why had I agreed in the first place?

I was riding by myself, not eager to speak to anyone in the band or crew, much less that cocksplat Nigel, or any of the support staff from Total Indulgence. And that included Sky.

Yeah, I'd asked for her, insisted I wouldn't even do this damn thing without her.

Because she was my last hope. My last hope for connecting with Dev. The three of us had worked before, maybe we could work again.

But now that we were all here?

The whole thing felt like a damn mistake. A fool's errand. A flat-out waste of time.

Because there was no way to fix this, was there?

Not if Dev wouldn't bend.

My mobile rang and I ripped it out of my pocket. Anything to distract myself from the inevitable answer to my question. I picked up the call without even looking at the caller ID. "Hello?"

"Rod? It's Mum."

I smiled at the sound of her voice. "Miss me already, do you?"

"Now don't be getting an even bigger head than the one you already have." The humor in her tone settled me. Mum had always had that effect on me, all those times she'd comforted me when my arsehole of a father had lashed out at us with his mouth and his fists, when even though I'd been the oldest of my siblings, I'd still been too young and puny to defend them, myself, or Mum. The only good thing to come of all the troubled times both before and after the scumbag had left was the unshakeable bond between Mum and me.

"Everything all right then?" I asked.

She sighed into the phone. "You know I hate to bother you when you're working."

"You're never a bother, Mum," I said and meant it. Next to Dev, my mum and my siblings were my top priority. I'd drop everything in a heartbeat for them, and they knew it. I made sure they knew it. My dad had been a shithead, and we were all better off with him out of our lives. Still... his departure had left a hole. An empty spot where the man who'd fathered us should have been.

"You're a darling to say so, Rod."

"Come on, Mum," I coaxed her gently. "Spit it out."

"It's Jonah."

At fourteen, Jonah was my youngest sibling. Born less than a year before our old man took to the hills, he'd never known life with a father, even an abusive prick like ours had been. I'd always thought he'd be the golden one in the family. The one with no scars, but I'd been wrong.

"What's the lad got into now?"

"The school rang this morning. Jonah earned himself a suspension."

My hand tightened on the mobile. "A suspension. What for?"

"Punched a boy. Broke the lad's nose."

"What?" My brother was small for his age. It made him a wizard at football, but he tended to shy away from anything physical.

Tony must have heard the worry in my tone. Over the years, he'd got close to the Taylor clan. His eyes locked with mine in the rearview mirror. I shook my head. "Did he say why he did it?"

"Won't say a bleeding word about it, no matter how much I prod."

"You think I should talk to him?"

"Would you?"

"Of course. I'll ring him right now."

"Thank you, Rod. You're the best son a mother could have. I love you."

My cheeks heated. "I love you too, Mum. And don't worry. I'll take care of this."

"I know you will."

As soon as I ended the call, I dialed Jonah's number. He answered on the second ring. "Well, that didn't take long," he said, with maximum teenage attitude. "Mum didn't need to get you involved."

"I'm your big brother, aren't I?"

"So. You're not my dad."

I certainly wasn't, but I was the closest thing he had to one. I ignored his jibe. "What's going on, Jojo," I asked, using his childhood nickname.

"A boy was taking the piss out of me. Wouldn't shut his gob even after I asked him *politely*, so I shut it for him."

"What was he going on about?"

There was a pause, a sigh. What sounded suspiciously like a sniff. "Nothing." Jonah's voice cracked.

"Hey, come on now. You know you can tell me anything." My life, the "Hot Rod Circus," as Dev liked to call it, was an open book. I didn't hide anything about myself from my family, and I expected the same of them.

"He said some stuff about…"

A pregnant silence filled the line. And I filled in the blank. "About me."

"Yeah."

This had happened to some degree or other with my middle brother, Thomas, and our sister, Kaitlin, but I'd been younger then, less well known, and more importantly, I'd been there to handle it with them. Shit. Another fucking reason I shouldn't have come here. Jonah needed me.

"I'll come home."

"No!"

His sharp reaction took me aback. "No?"

"Sorry. Didn't mean it that way. You know I love hanging with you. I just meant that *I'll* handle it. I don't need my big brother swooping in and saving the day like some sodding superhero. I'm not totally helpless, you know?"

"I know."

"I'm getting to be almost as big as you, anyway."

I snorted. "You know what they say about weeds and water."

"Sod off."

I laughed. Tony took the Range Rover over a steep hill and I glanced out the window, catching a glimpse of Mount Tohivea in the center of the island. Jonah would love it here. "Tell me what the lad said."

"It's not important."

"It upset you enough to punch the prat, yeah?"

Jonah huffed. "Fine. He said you were nothing but a flaming faggot who couldn't write a good song to save your life. He said Dev Stone was the brains behind King's Cross, and you were just a pretty face."

"He said I was pretty?"

"*Rod.*"

I cracked up at his tone. "Listen, kiddo. We both know the truth. It doesn't matter what some fourteen-year-old twat thinks of me."

"It rankled."

"I know. But you can't go around getting into punch-up with every knobhead who tosses a nasty word in my direction."

"Okay," Jonah said in a small voice. He sounded like he was three years old again.

"Is there something else?"

"No."

Maybe I was looking at this wrong. Maybe Jonah wasn't protecting me, but rather himself. "Are you ashamed of me, then?" Just asking the question opened a wound in my chest. I didn't care about anyone's opinion of me, unless they were family. And Jonah's opinion mattered.

"Of course not!"

The knot in my stomach eased somewhat. "Not even a little?"

Jonah blew out a breath and I heard some rustling as though he'd flopped back onto his bed. "I'm not ashamed. I'm proud. It's just sometimes a little part of me wishes things could be otherwise. I love you, Rod. But having you for a big brother can be… difficult."

"What? Are you saying that having an out and proud pansexual brother who is also the sexy lead singer for the biggest band to hit the UK since The Beatles and whose face is in the tabloid rags on a weekly basis isn't as easy as falling down?" I joked.

Jonah chuckled. "Don't think much of yourself, do you?" Judging by his tone, he seemed to have relaxed.

"I'm a pain in the arse and I know it, Jonah. But just as you can fight your own battles, I can fight mine. I am who I am, and anyone who doesn't like it can fuck right off. What's important to me is you, Kaitlin, Thomas, and Mum." *And Dev.* My heart constricted at the thought of losing my best mate. "Next time that boy or anyone else says something about me, just say, yeah, he's all that and a bag of chips."

Jonah's laughter roared over the phone line. "Picked that expression up when you were in America last summer, did you?"

Fucking Damon. The Yank bastard was rubbing off on me. "Something like that. Anyway, you get my meaning? You're smart, Jonah, and school's important. Don't let some silly prat sideline your dreams. And

I'll do what I can to ease your troubles." I scratched my chin. How could I possibly do that though?

"Rod?"

"Yeah?"

"Don't change."

I frowned. "What do you mean?"

"I know I said it was hard to be your little brother, but I don't want you to change. Don't tone it down, don't do anything differently."

I sat in stunned silence. If I toned down my persona, it would help my family and my relationship with Dev. It was something I'd thought a lot about over the last few months without Dev. Even if I could do it though, I'm not sure I would. What I'd told Jonah was the truth: people could take me as I was or not at all. It was up to them.

"Thank you," I told him softly.

"You're welcome." I could hear the smile in his voice.

"We good now? You won't get into any more trouble? Because if I have to fly over there and tweak your ear myself, I will."

"We're good, Rod. Now go concentrate on writing some awesome songs for your album and tour. I can't wait to hear them."

"Is that right?" I knew Jonah loved King's Cross, but I wasn't above fishing for a compliment.

"You know I'm your biggest fan, you wanker."

"Little shit, is that any way to talk to your betters?"

"I don't talk that way to my betters."

"Oh ho! Someone's getting too big for his britches."

He laughed again. "Thanks for calling, Rod. Maybe knowing you were half a world away made me anxious."

"I'm only a ring away. Call me anytime. I can hop on a plane and be back in London in a matter of hours."

We ended the call with a promise to keep in touch every day while I was on Moorea. As Tony continued to drive around the island, my thoughts returned to Dev and Sky and the fortnight ahead of us. I feared I'd made one of the biggest errors of my life in giving into the pressure from Nigel and Sonic High Records. Having the three of us in close proximity was bound to stir emotions, bring back memories. Unearth regrets perhaps best left buried.

What the fuck had I been thinking?

The Range Rover heaved over another bump in the dirt road we'd turned onto and by the time Tony stopped the vehicle and announced, "We're here," my mood had soured.

This was going to be a long, awful stay. And I'd be leaving the band by the end of it. Because there was no filling the chasm that had opened up between me and Dev.

"About bloody time," I grumbled and opened the door. The tropical heat and humidity were a slap in the face after the air-conditioned comfort of the vehicle. I looked around at the supposed "resort" we'd been booked into. A bunch of thatched-roof bungalows flanking some larger buildings greeted me. "Rustic" was the word that came to mind.

Sky approached. "So, Rod, ready to get to work?"

Her lovely voice washed over me, and I flinched. Bloody fucking mistake.

I jammed my hands in my pockets. "Where's the fucking hotel? I can't live in some straw hovel. And what about our music? Is there even electricity?"

She crossed her arms. "There's electricity. And a rehearsal space. In fact, that's where we're all headed next."

The heat in her words made me feel like crap. I ran a hand through my hair. "Listen, Sky, I—"

She raised her hand. "Save it. Just get your gear and get going. We'll talk when you're ready to be civil." She turned on her heel and walked off, arms still crossed, back stiff.

Bloody hell. I trotted to catch up to her. "Sky—"

"No excuses, Rod. I don't want to hear them." She wouldn't even look at me.

Fantastic. We'd been here, what, two minutes? And I'd already pissed her off.

"You never returned our calls," I blurted. "Just took off like a thief in the night."

She stopped walking and glared at me. "We're not talking about this now."

"But we will later."

"I'm here to do a job."

"You're here because I asked for you, love."

Her cheeks reddened, and she took a visible breath, slowly expelling it. "I'm aware. We'll talk when I'm ready."

She walked away, her brown curls cascading down her back, her lovely arse perfectly filling out her trousers. I was half-hard just looking at her, memories crashing into me—Sky in my arms, moaning my name, the way she stretched like a cat after a great fuck. The way Dev looked at her like she'd hung the moon.

Had he even seen her yet? I shouldered my rucksack and looked around for him. Sure enough, he'd caught up to her at the door to a spacious whitewashed building, his face lit up like it was Christmas morning as he chatted with her.

Christ. Had I just played matchmaker for the two of them? My gut twisted. Yeah, well if I had, at least I'd be leaving him with something if we couldn't fix this.

Because I bloody well was not about to sit around and watch the two of them sail off into the sunset together.

I caught up to Mick, Damon, Jules, and Tommy as they were walking inside.

"Nice of you to join us," Damon said.

"Cheeky bastard." I smirked at him. I didn't like that he'd taken Dev's place in the band, but I couldn't hold it against the guy. He was all right. For a Yank.

"*Someone* has to keep you in line," Mick said.

"You lot can sod off now." I stepped inside the building and cool air washed over me. Thank the saints this place had air-conditioning. I might have to stay inside the rest of this bloody trip.

Our roadies were hauling in our gear and setting up for us, so we took chairs that someone had pulled into a semicircle.

Sky sat next to Dev, the two of them still chatting quietly. How could he talk to her so easily? How could she?

And how come I couldn't talk to either of them without starting bloody World War III?

Fuck. I needed a drink. And a shag. And a little something to make me forget my troubles.

Once we'd all taken our seats, Sky turned to us, her eyes meeting mine, hers still glacial.

"In case you don't remember, I'm Sky River. We met three months ago when Reeling Records hosted that team-building exercise."

Damon raised his hand. "I wasn't there for that."

She grinned. "You're Damon Mercury, right?"

"The one and only. You're a California girl, yeah?"

She nodded. "That obvious?"

He raised a hand in the "hang ten" gesture of surfers everywhere. "From LA myself."

"Berkeley," she said and tucked her hair behind her ear.

Christ. Was she going to flirt with him too?

That twist in my gut intensified. What if she ended up in bed with Dev and Damon? I hadn't thought this through, had I?

She reached into a big bag at her feet and pulled out a box of protein bars and handed it around. "So, let me tell you all how things are going to go while we're here." She held up a couple of the bars. "This is today's lunch. You can have as many as you like."

What the fuck? "I'm gonna die if this is all I get to eat."

"You're not going to die," Sky said. "You can have all you want."

"Some real food is what I want."

Damon took a bite out of a protein bar. "Hey, I lived off these damn things for years. You're all caviar and champagne. That's the problem with this band. You've gone soft. Lost your edge."

Heat rose up my neck. "Since when are *you* an expert on this band?"

He shrugged. "Just an observation."

"Well, you can keep your big gob shut."

"Rod," Dev said, his voice so soft I almost didn't hear it over the blood roaring in my ears.

I crossed my arms. Fine. *I'd* keep my big gob shut since no one wanted to talk to me anyway.

"Why protein bars?" Tommy asked.

Sky blessed him with a smile. "Think of this like *Survivor*. If you all work together, you earn rewards. Like real food. If you don't, you get these." She wiggled a bar in the air.

Jules raised a hand. "How do we get voted off the island? I'd like to be first."

Everybody laughed. Everybody but me.

"No one is getting voted off," Sky said, her eyes coming to rest on me again. "The only way you get to leave is as a team—either you all agree to keep the band together, or you all agree to dissolve it."

"You can't bloody keep me here," I said.

"For two weeks I can," she said, her voice soft. "You agreed to it."

I had, idiot that I was. "The label can sue me."

"They will," Dev said.

"I don't bloody care."

"I do," he said, his brown eyes holding mine. "You do too."

"Don't presume to speak for me."

He held his hands palm out. "It's true. Or else you wouldn't be here."

It was on my tongue to snap at him, but for once I didn't. *This is all on you, Dev.* I wanted to say it so badly I could taste it. But this wasn't the time for that. And we'd already had this discussion.

Well, it had been a bloody row, more like.

Sky broke in. "Each day you'll get some kind of challenge. If you successfully complete it, you get a reward."

"I'm not a child."

She raised a brow. "You're doing a good impression of one."

"Burn!" Damon shouted, then sniggered behind his hand, the little prat. And Tommy, Mick, and Jules didn't even bother to hide their amusement. Dev was the only one who didn't laugh.

"What's today's 'challenge' then?"

"Today after rehearsal, you get to build your own shelters. The ones who finish their huts within three hours get to stay in the bungalows tonight and have real food for dinner. The ones who don't complete the challenge will stay in whatever they've built or sleep on the beach, and they get more protein bars for dinner."

Was she having a laugh? "You think these stupid little exercises will do the trick? If I'd known this was your brilliant idea of how to fix things, I wouldn't have asked for you."

"Well, maybe you shouldn't have dragged me into it again, but here I am."

"Again?" I asked.

Her lips pursed. "You know what I mean."

"Man, I wish I had some popcorn," Damon said, leaning forward like he wanted a better view of the drama.

"Fuck this." I was out of my chair and out the door before anyone could stop me. I charged into the blistering sunshine and grabbed my sunglasses out of my pocket.

The scent of cigarettes tickled my nose, and I turned. Bloody Nigel. "Where are you off to?" he asked.

"She's fucking with us. I don't have to put up with it."

The ginger-haired jizztrumpet took a long drag on his cigarette. "For someone who put up a one-million-pound bonus for the facilitator—the one *you* insisted on—you certainly don't seem motivated to make things work."

"I'm here, aren't I? If you and the label aren't happy, you can fire me." I stepped closer. "You'd love that. I know you would."

"I wouldn't be sad to see the backside of you. Except that King's Cross will fall apart."

"Then it's going to bloody fall apart."

I stomped off, not sure where I was going until I spotted some of the roadies hanging out at another large building nearby. No doubt one of them had something that could get my mind off the dog's breakfast I'd made of my life.

DEV

I smashed the hammer down on my thumb and had to bite back a bloody blue storm, although "Fucking fuck!" did manage to slip out. I dropped the tool into the sand and wrapped my pulsating thumb with my opposite hand, hoping to keep the pain down. It didn't work. I turned my back to the lads so they couldn't see how frustrated I was with this whole situation.

"Sorry, mate," Tommy said, sounding abashed.

"Wish we could help you more, but if we don't head to the canteen right about now, that slave driver will deny us our prize," Mick said. Everything was about food with that one. It was a bloody wonder he didn't weigh fifteen stone.

"No, no. You should go." I closed my eyes and breathed deeply a few times to calm myself before turning back to them with a feigned smile. A bead of sweat dripped down the side of my face, ever so bloody slowly. The lower it got on my face, the harder it was to maintain my smile. I'm sure I looked like a constipated baby by now.

I wiped my face with the hem of my shirt, then dug the hammer out of the sand and climbed up onto the wooden ladders Sky had allowed us to use to nail in the last plank. I glanced over my shoulder. The lads were all still there watching me. "Go on, now. It's not your fault that wanker couldn't be arsed to even show up."

If I was to sleep in this shitbox, at least it would have a roof. After I finished nailing the last plank in place, I stepped off the ladder, picked up a large palm frond that would help the roof shed rain, and began affixing it to the structure.

"Not your fault either, is it?" Jules asked. The whole lot of them were still lingering around.

I shrugged. Rod had said he couldn't stand the sight of me, so in a way it was my fault, not that I wanted to share the details with the others.

"All right. Like, it's been hella nice slaving away with you guys, but I'm outtie." Damon clapped me on the back. "Don't let the bed bugs bite, oh wait." His face broke into a wide grin. "You don't have a bed."

The lads' laughter continued as they trudged over to the canteen and disappeared inside, leaving me alone on the beach with my half-finished hut where I'd be spending the night. Just me, the waves, and the giant sodding mosquitoes that would soon be making their appearance. I didn't even want to think about what else might be out here burrowed in the sand or in the leafy canopy.

I shuddered and went back to finishing the fucking hut. With a handful of nails in my pocket, along with some twine, I carefully climbed onto the ladder. After another hour of hard work, the hut, my home for the night, was finally finished.

I slumped down in the sand, fine and white like powdered sugar, and closed my eyes. I was fucking knackered. The decisions I'd made about my future weighed heavily on my mind. I'd barely slept more than a few hours at a time since my aborted capitulation to my parents' demands. I still intended to tell them I'd marry Kalini, but I was giving myself until after Aahna's wedding to tell them. To commit myself to a future I'd never wanted.

The gentle susurration of the waves rolling onto the beach carried a mournful melody that reminded me of a song I've been working on since before meeting Sky three months ago. The subsequent cold war with Rod had siphoned all my creativity and the notes had never come to me.

But as I lay in the cooling sand, with the world's most colorful sunset in front of me, ideas formed. I sprang to my feet and grabbed my acoustic guitar out of its case. The Taylor was the only one I used for songwriting. I sat on a rock and began picking out the tune, changing a note here and there until I was satisfied. Then I started to hum, and the humming turned into words.

You left, you think you've won
But I have to tell you
We're far from done

Yeah. I liked that. Rod and I had a lot of unfinished business. I let the feelings pour through me, the pain I was feeling, the frustration as well as the desire for a different future.

You walked away from all of this
But you and I, we're unfinished.

That could be the chorus, or at least part of it. Lyrics weren't really my thing. They were Rod's half of our duo. The duo that no longer existed.

Fuck. My chest tightened, burned. He'd been my best friend forever, the Morrissey to my Marr. We'd gone through every major event at each other's sides. How the bloody hell did I think I could get through life without him?

My fingers stopped playing and I let my head drop.

"Oh, that was beautiful," Sky said.

Startled, I jumped to my feet and searched the area, only then noticing how dark it was getting. Sky stepped closer, a nervous smile on her lips. She wore a pretty dress in a floral print, one of those long, floaty ones that had a slit up the side of one leg and narrow shoulder straps. It looked amazing on her.

She pointed to a bundle at her feet. "I brought you a sleeping bag, a pillow, a mosquito net, protein bars, and some water."

"Ah… that was very kind of you."

She ducked her head. "Not really. It was my challenge that put you in this situation in the first place."

I shook my head. "Rod did that. Not you." I rummaged through the things she'd brought and found the protein bars. I ripped open the packaging on one and devoured it.

Laughing, she handed me a bottle of water. "I guess you're hungry."

"Mmm-hmm," I muttered around a large bite. The song had kept my mind so occupied, I hadn't realized just how starved I'd been. I took the water she held out and emptied half the bottle in one swig.

When she moved to drag the sleeping bag and pillow into the hut, I set the bottle down and went to help her. "Let me."

"It's all right. Enjoy your food. It won't take me more than a minute to set this net up over your bedding."

By the time I finished the second bar, she crawled out of the hut, a pleased smile on her face. "At least the bugs won't get you now." She rose to her feet in front of me and ran a finger down my cheek. "Wouldn't want this gorgeous face marred by bites."

"Er…"

Brilliant, mate. Brilliant fucking response.

The woman rattled my brains. She always had done.

"Do you… um… want to make a fire? There's a cord of wood by the canteen."

"Oh sure," I said. Another brilliant response. I patted my pockets. "But I haven't any matches."

"Not a Boy Scout, huh?"

Heat hit my face.

"Hey, I'm just teasing." She plucked a pack of matches from her pocket. "We're all set."

I collected some wood from behind the canteen, and Sky used her Girl Guide skills to build us a fire. Then we rolled a log over from one of the resort's main fire pits. We'd barely spoken more than a couple words during this entire process and the silence between us was becoming uncomfortable, a void that grew and gaped.

My mind raced with thoughts of what to do, what to say. I'd spent a week with Sky and Rod in Palm Springs. I'd told her I loved her. But now I realized the truth: I barely knew Sky. What was her favorite color? Her favorite book? What kind of food did she like? What did she refuse to eat? I'd never thought to ask any of these questions, because the three of us had been too busy. Too busy fucking.

I was a right poor gentleman.

To fill the silence, I pulled my guitar out of its case and began plucking at the strings.

Sky cleared her throat. "That song you were singing when I showed up, was it…" Her cheeks turned bright red as she looked down at her hands. "Was it about me?"

Surprised, I could only stare at her. The words replayed in my mind. Yes, I could see how she might have reached that conclusion. I gave her a sad smile. "No, but it does apply, yeah?" I'd told this woman I loved her, and she'd disappeared by daybreak.

She flinched and her gaze flicked to my face before returning to her hands. "I'm sorry I left like that."

"Are you now?"

"Yes."

"So why didn't you return any of my calls or texts?"

She pressed her lips together, then took a deep breath. "It just all got too intense."

"You mean when I told you how I felt about you?"

A frown marred her forehead for a moment. Then she said, "You don't remember?"

Now it was my turn to frown. "Remember what exactly?"

Ignoring my question, she waved toward the guitar I had propped on my thigh. "The song, it's about Rod then? The unfinished business you have is with him?"

I nodded. "Yes. He tried to quit..." *Us.* "...the band."

"I see." She stared into the fire. The dancing light of the flames illuminated her beautiful face and reflected off her dark hair.

The truth was, I had unfinished business with her as well. Sky was the only woman I'd ever loved. The only woman I'd ever imagined in my life. I was certain that had she not run off, I'd have asked her to marry me by now.

And what about Rod?

I gritted my teeth and began strumming my guitar. My feelings for Rod were too confusing to contemplate right now, not when I had a beautiful woman sitting next to me.

"Rod's probably on the pull, but we can have a little fun of our own," I said with a wink. "Do you know this one?"

I launched into "You Shake Me," a quirky, upbeat song from our previous album that had hit the top of the charts in England and had received a lot of airtime in America. I remembered her telling me it was her favorite King's Cross song.

When I finished, she clapped her hands, her face beaming. "That was so good. If Rod does end up leaving the band, you could step up and be the lead singer."

Her suggestion left me gobsmacked. "Me? No way," I spluttered, almost choking on my own saliva.

"Why not? Your voice is really good."

The very thought had my palms sweating and my heart beating like a drum. I wasn't like Rod. I could never handle all the attention he got from the media, or from the fans who wanted his body while knowing little of his mind. He deserved so much better than that.

And yet he wants you.

Which was something I could never give him. Not that way. But I would love him as a friend until my dying breath.

A light hand touched my shoulder. "Hey, what's wrong?"

I smiled at Sky. "What could be the matter when I'm with you?" I set the guitar down and turned sideways on the log to face her. I touched her cheek. "I've missed you."

Her eyes shone brightly even though she tried to hide her smile. "I've missed you too."

I scooted a little closer, one knee touching her thigh, the other resting against her bottom. She bent her head and a dark curl fell across her cheek. I brushed it back, hooking it behind her ear. Then, I traced my finger along her jaw to her full lips. I remembered their softness against my own, the taste of her mouth when we'd kissed, and I wanted it again.

I nudged her chin up to look into her eyes. "May I kiss you?"

Her throat worked when she swallowed, and her voice shook a little when she finally spoke. One single word. "Please."

Taking my time, I leaned forward until my mouth hovered over hers. Her breath feathered my lips as we stared into each other's eyes. Would it be as I'd remembered it all those lonely nights I'd spent in hotel rooms or in my bedroom at my parents'?

Anticipation was killing me, but so was the fear of disappointment. Had I imagined the fire between us?

She licked her lips, the tip of her pink tongue making her mouth wet and glossy. A groan tore through me, and I moved the final inch I needed to taste her. Our mouths met in a gentle reunion. My hand slid into her hair to hold her head in place while I ran my tongue across her plump lower lip. She gasped, opened, and invited me inside.

I shifted my hips so my right leg was completely behind her and she sat between my spread thighs. I wanted to feel her warmth, to feel all of her against all of me, even if we were both fully clothed.

My hand slipped beneath the skirt of her long dress, bunching it up at her waist. I touched her back, the skin so hot and smooth. I broke the kiss and sucked in a deep breath. "You feel so good."

Eyes slightly dazed, she twisted her body around to face me and threw both her legs over mine, straddling my thighs. "You feel really good too," she whispered, even though we were alone. She wrapped her arms around my shoulders and pressed her lips to mine. The kiss and the sensation of her firm breasts nudging my chest had made me hard. I cupped her ass and tugged her closer, close enough for her to feel the bulge in my shorts. Close enough for her to know how much I wanted her.

She moaned into the kiss and rocked her hips. The pressure of her pelvis pushing against my cock was divine, but I was a greedy bastard, and I wanted more.

I brought my hands to her sides and slid them up along her torso, using my thumbs to feel her tits. Her needy sounds threw fuel on the fire inside my belly. The small flame grew into an inferno. I was a man, and I loved women. I could be happy without Rod. I could be happy with Sky. "Sky, sweets, I want you."

"I want you too, Dev. But if we do this, there are no strings, and no exclusivity."

I wanted her so much, her words were like a meaningless mix of consonants and vowels. Her hand zeroed in on the waistband of my shorts, unbuttoning them, then pulling the zipper down. I lifted my hips to help her shove them down to my thighs. And when she reached under my boxers, releasing my cock and balls, I felt dizzy from the freedom of it.

Fuck Rod and his partying. He could have all the roadies he could handle. I was the one with Sky in my arms. And she was worth infinitely more than a one-night stand. I had no illusions about the future. I would still offer for Kalini after Aahna's wedding, if we got along. But for now, I could enjoy my time on the island with Sky. One last hurrah to my rock star life. A last hurrah for Dev Stone before he once again became Devkinandan Prakesh.

I rooted around my wallet until I found the johnnie I kept stashed there. I held it up proudly.

Sky grinned. "Maybe you are a Boy Scout after all."

Taking the condom from my hand, she quickly opened the packet and slid it over me. I hissed, the feel of her delicate hands on my aching cock almost sending me over the edge. I cleared my throat, and circled her waist. "Come here, sweets."

I reached between her legs and pushed aside the small scrap of cotton I found there, then I rubbed my cock along her wet pussy. My chest squeezed. It had been so long, too long, since I'd held her like this. Since I'd felt her shiver in my arms. I pressed my thumb to her clit and circled it gently, using her soft moans and small breathless sounds to guide me.

Her fingers dug into my shoulders as she rolled her hips. Fuck, I could come like this. So easily. But I wanted to be inside her. I glanced down between us, and seeing the light of the fire reflect on my cock, I deemed it and her wet enough to proceed. Still, it wouldn't hurt to check.

"Ready, sweets?" I asked.

"God, yes. Fuck me, Dev. I want you inside me."

You had to love Americans and their directness. Now that I'd been given the green light, I held the base of my cock with one hand and guided it to her entrance. Then, she lowered her weight and I sank into her, in one long mind-blowing thrust. We both groaned out our pleasure.

"Shit, that feels bloody amazing."

She was hot and tight, and everything I'd been missing.

"Oh God." Sky buried her face in my neck, her arms locked behind my head. I moved my hands under her dress, rubbing up and down her back, along her spine, around to mold her tits under her brassiere. They felt perfect in my hands, round and firm.

I wanted to kiss her, to look into her eyes, but she continued to grip my neck, and when her hips began to pump up and down, I forgot everything except the need to empty my aching bollocks.

Had anything ever felt so fucking heavenly? How could I have let her go after Palm Springs? How could I ever let her go when this stay in Tahiti was over?

I thrust up into her, holding her tightly, whispering sweet nothings into her ear as I got closer and closer to coming.

When her muscles tightened around my cock, and she made that sound in her throat, that low moan I remembered so well, I let myself go. Arching my back, I snapped my hips and a shudder racked my entire body as I emptied into her, wishing that not even a thin bit of latex separated us.

But even as I reveled in the joy of once again having Sky in my arms, my eyes searched out the shadows behind her, looking for something, looking for someone… looking for *him*.

ROD

A soft hand shook my shoulder. "Rod, it's almost half ten. Aren't you supposed to be at rehearsal?" Sharon asked.

Sharon? Why was I in her bed? Memories of the prior night came roaring back. She'd had some Ecstasy, and we'd spent the night drinking and dancing at a do the crew were having. We'd gone back to her room at some point. She was a cute little thing, certainly knew her stuff about our gear, but if we'd exchanged a dozen words before this, I couldn't remember.

And now I'd fucked her. And I barely remembered it.

She hovered over me, an expectant look on her face. I needed to set the record straight, right now. "Listen, love, I hope I treated you right—"

"You did," she purred, her fingers caressing my cheek.

"But—"

Her lips pressed together and she closed her eyes. "Yeah. You can stop there. I get it."

Bloody hell. And I thought Nigel was a wanker. "I'm a bastard."

She shrugged. "It's not like I didn't know better." Her eyes met mine. "And you didn't promise me anything."

"I'm an arse."

"An arse who'd better get his cute arse in the shower."

It was on the tip of my tongue to ask her to join me—her tits looked great in the early morning light—but best not encourage her.

I dragged myself through a shower, checked my phone for messages (one from Jonah about his return to school tomorrow, which I quickly answered), and headed to the rehearsal space half an hour late.

A box of protein bars sat by the front door, and I helped myself to one. At least it had something resembling chocolate as a coating. The insides could've been sawdust for all I knew.

Someone had set up a caffeine station for us—coffee, tea, and even chai for Dev. He bloody loved it when they did that. No doubt Nigel was behind it. He'd taken Dev's side in all this, and if he couldn't keep me happy, he'd bloody well suck Dev's cock, wouldn't he?

I poured myself a chai—it was homemade, milky, slightly sweet, with the lovely bite of cumin. It reminded me of spending rainy afternoons at Dev's home, his mum bringing us steaming mugs of the stuff.

I dared a look at Dev, strumming an acoustic guitar like it was a lover, his eyes half closed in concentration, his black hair falling into his eyes.

Why couldn't we go back to those days, when we'd been thick as thieves, never a cross word between us?

Why couldn't I just shut off my damn feelings and look at him like a brother?

Why did I have to go and fall in love and ruin everything?

Someone started to slow clap and I looked over. Bloody Mick and Damon. I bowed low in their direction. "*Now* we can get to work," Damon said.

Dev looked up, his eyes locking with mine. "So, what did you think of the music I sent you? Have you any lyrics yet?"

Heat flooded my face. He'd sent me a CD two weeks ago in the post—since we weren't talking—and asked me to give it a listen. I'd known what he was doing, trying to draw me in. Music had always bridged the gap for us.

But music didn't work anymore.

"Haven't heard it yet," I admitted.

He grumbled under his breath, then nodded. "Okay, then. We'll play it for you."

They started into a tune—quite lovely really—then Dev leaned into the mic and sang a few phrases—something about me leaving and thinking I'd won, that I'd turned my back on him—and the chai curdled in my stomach.

34

He was taking digs at me musically now?

He stopped singing and looked at me, his eyes holding both a challenge and a softness that undid me. "Well, mate, sounds like you don't need me."

"That's not what I meant. Just that I'd had an idea for a possible chorus."

"Sounds like a polite way to tell me to bugger off."

"Rod—"

"No matter, mate. I told you I didn't want to be here. And now I really don't."

"We're still under contract for the album and the tour. You can't quit."

"You know why that bothers you? Because you can't replace me like you did yourself. *I'm* the fucking face of this band."

Dev stiffened. "It made sense for me to step back and let Damon take the lead. We need to sharpen our sound."

"You're capable of that yourself, and you *know* it."

"Capable maybe. But it comes more naturally to Damon."

"That's a bloody excuse. We both know the truth."

"It's the right thing for the band."

"But it's not King's Cross anymore, is it?"

"It'll *always* be King's Cross, as long as it's you and me." His voice was soft, and the words sliced me through and through.

As long as it's you and me.

He meant one thing by those words, and I meant another, wanted another, craved another with every beat of my heart.

And it wasn't going to happen.

"I'm done." The words left my mouth without thought.

Sky's voice cut through the air. "Done? You haven't even started yet. Can't you at least try?"

"You want *me* to try when he already has one foot out the door?"

She brandished the box of protein bars. "I guess this is what you're all having for lunch, then."

"Rod, come on, mate," Jules groaned. "I can't face another one of those things."

Jules could fuck off for all I cared. Then Tommy piped up. "So, we all have to suffer just because Rod wants to play diva?"

"That's how this works," Sky said. "There's a challenge this afternoon. Everyone who shows up and participates can have real food for dinner."

I held her eyes. "I'm still not a bloody child. I'll decide what I do and what I eat. And if I want to leave the band, you can't stop me."

"Maybe I can't," she said. "That doesn't mean I won't try."

Try all you want, love. Doesn't mean I have to.

I caught Dev's gaze, the hurt in it making me wince. But if he wouldn't even admit what he was doing, if he wouldn't fight for our sound, for our band, for *us*, why should I?

I shoved on my sunglasses and headed outside.

Thirteen more days of this torture, and then I could say goodbye and good riddance to Tahiti, to Dev, to King's Cross, and to Sky.

I bloody well was done, and they just needed to accept it.

SKY

In contrast to the shitastic day I'd had, the sun setting over Moorea in a glorious display of pinks, oranges, and grays that lit up the surrounding French Polynesian Islands, was incredible to watch as I made my way across the resort to the canteen. Since the guys, except for Rod, had participated in my daily challenge, a blindfolded dart contest where I'd had to substitute for Rod, I allowed them all to have a real dinner. They were already seated at a table, full plates and half empty beer mugs in front of them. The guys were, evidently, sick of protein bars and water.

There was a free seat next to Dev. I hesitated for only a moment before slipping into it. I really hoped he'd understood me when I'd told him last night that I didn't want any entanglements. The words had been so hard to say… I wasn't sure I could say them to him again.

He turned to me with a smile. "Let me get you some supper. What do you fancy?"

"Oh, that's okay. I'll get it."

"No, no please. How about I just get you the same as me?"

He'd barely left the table when Mick, who was sitting across from me, leveled me with a glare. "With all due respect, Sky, this team-building stuff is shite. Today only proved that we're worse off than we were before."

"Well," I began, adjusting my blouse and uncrossing, then re-crossing my legs, "you aren't completely wrong. But, the argument Dev and Rod had this morning was a long time coming. It was a healthy first step."

Mick frowned. "Healthy? I'd say it was as far from healthy as you can get."

"It was more than they've said to each other in weeks," Jules said, sending me a weak smile.

"Thing is"—Damon scratched the dark stubble on his cheek—"how can things get better if Rod refuses to participate? After that fight, I doubt we'll be seeing him at rehearsal again anytime soon."

They were right, of course. My strategy for getting Rod in line wasn't working. Team building could only work when people were engaged, when the entire team participated. No matter how much Dev and the other guys wanted this exercise to be successful, it wouldn't be if Rod didn't commit to at least trying, to showing up.

Dev returned and silence descended upon the table. He set a beer and a plate in front of me. "The food here is a lot tastier than protein bars," he said, grinning.

"Thanks, Dev."

"My pleasure." He winked and heat pooled in my belly. Damn, maybe last night had been a mistake. During the day, Dev had kept things professional between us, but now that work was over, did he expect us to be a couple, for me to invite him to my bungalow and have sex with him again? Goosebumps broke out on my arms and my nipples stiffened. I'd certainly enjoy another night with him, one where clothing wouldn't prevent me from worshiping every inch of his gorgeous body and lovely brown skin.

My mouth went dry as I watched him settle into his seat. I picked up my beer and took several long soothing sips. I could sleep with him again, I knew he'd want to, but could *I* do so without giving him my heart? Last night, when he'd filled me so deliciously and held me so lovingly, I'd had to bury my face in his neck to keep from telling him the truth about my feelings for him. With each thrust, they'd bubbled up, closer and closer to the surface.

How stupid had I been to agree to this project in the first place? I wasn't made of stone. I hadn't managed to resist Dev even for one day.

"So, what were you talking about?" Dev asked, digging into his lamb shank.

Tommy, who'd finished his fish and rice, tossed his napkin onto his plate with a snort. "We're hoping Sky has some great ideas for how to handle Rod, because so far this effort has been for naught."

"Hey," Damon nudged him in the ribs. "At least you're getting a great vacation out of it, right?"

"Holiday."

"What?"

"This is a holiday."

"No, it's not, is it?" he asked, looking around the table. "You have Thanksgiving early like the Canadians?"

Jules burst into laughter. "Yanks are brilliant."

Damon continued to look confused and eventually I took pity on him. "Brits call vacations holidays."

He frowned. "So what do they call holidays?"

"Holidays," I said.

"Bank holidays, actually," Mick added.

"What the fuck does a bank have to do with anything?"

I shrugged. "Nothing really."

As though I'd just shattered his understanding of the world, Damon shook his head, and mumbling something that sounded like "fucking Brits" under his breath, he grabbed his mug and went off to get a refill.

"Well," Mick said, "as enjoyable as that was, I'm off to get some shut eye. Not that sleeping on that inch-thick roll you've allowed us is comfortable." He shot me a final glare before leaving the table.

Dev leaned closer to me. "Don't pay him any mind, Sky. Lad's all growl and no bite."

"Maybe. Doesn't mean he's wrong though." My way *wasn't* working. Two days had already passed, and I'd gotten exactly nowhere with Rod.

If this was going to work, I'd have to start doing things differently. I couldn't keep punishing the guys, for one. None of this was their fault. I had to get Rod to listen to me. To fall in line with the program. But how? What could I offer—

I froze as the thought hit me. I could give Rod something, something he desperately wanted.

My eyes shifted over to Dev, and I looked into his keen brown eyes, eyes I dreamed about along with piercing blue ones. "Any idea where Rod might be?"

Dev snorted. "Same place he was last night, I reckon."

Last night? What had Dev said? Something about the roadies and resort staff. That was it then. I had to find Rod and make things right. Anyway I could.

"Thanks for dinner, guys. See you at rehearsal in the morning."

"Whatever," Tommy said. "It won't make a jot of difference if Rod skives off again."

"He'll be there," I said with far more conviction than I felt.

I left the canteen and headed across the resort to the low buildings that housed the Total Indulgence staff and the King's Cross crew. There were about ten double rooms, and if Rod was in one of them, I was going to find him.

The search was short-lived. As soon as I approached the buildings, I heard loud music spilling out the sliding glass doors of a second-floor room in the left corner of the building. I entered, found the stairwell, and climbed up to the second floor. The closer I got, the louder the music got, until I could no longer hear myself think.

Groups of people clustered in the dimly lit hallway, drinks in hand. I recognized Vanessa, the pretty black social media intern who'd flown in with Daniel, and I approached her. "Hey, Vanessa. Have you seen Rod? I have to talk to him about tomorrow's rehearsal."

"Oh sure." She pointed to the open door. "He's in there."

"Thank you."

As I passed by her, she latched onto my arm. "Sky…" Her cheeks reddened and she looked away.

My senses went on alert. "What is it?"

She sighed. "There's a reason so many of us are out here."

I frowned.

"He's… they're…"

When I continued to frown, she shrugged. "Whatevs. You'll understand soon enough."

I looked at her for a moment and chewed on my lip. Whatever she been trying to tell me, it hardly mattered. I had to talk to Rod. Tonight.

I marched into the room determined to get my way. After all *I* was in charge here, wasn't I?

I froze.

Music blared from a boombox, and candles lit the room. The scene before me was something out of a sixties porn flick. Women and men were sprawled around the room, some on the beds, some on the couches, some on the floor. All were in various stages of nakedness. A layer of smoke made the dim lighting even hazier. And judging by the smell, it wasn't from cigarettes.

Holy shit.

I walked further into the room. And then I saw him. Rod rested in an armchair. His legs were spread wide as a long-haired brunette gave him an enthusiastic blow job. A swarthy man, who seemed to be a local, sat on the arm of the chair playing tonsil hockey with Rod.

I stood rooted to the spot as memories of our week together overlaid what I was seeing. The people Rod was with, they could be me and Dev, except that Dev had never kissed Rod like that, not that I'd seen anyway. Could that be the problem between them, that Rod was out and proud, and Dev was not?

One way to find out was to ask Rod. I wanted to breathe deeply, but I resisted. Too much of the smoke, and I'd be high as a kite.

Instead, I straightened my back, squared my shoulders, and walked up to Rod. I shook his shoulder. "Rod." When he didn't react, I shook it harder, digging my nails in. "Rod!"

He stopped kissing the man and slowly rolled his head toward me. His usually sharp blue eyes were hooded and dazed.

Great.

"Rod, we need to talk."

"What—?" The brunette, who I'd forgotten, started bobbing up and down on Rod's cock again. "Yeah, fuck, Sharon. Like that." Rod gripped her hair and groaned loudly.

I clenched my teeth, steeling myself against the memories that low sound elicited. "Rod!"

"I'm a little busy at the moment, Sky."

"I can see that. Get un-busy."

"All it will take is a minute. I'm almost there. Don't stop, doll."

The islander ran a hand through Rod's hair and resumed kissing him.

My patience hit its limits. I steamrolled through the room and ripped the cord of the boombox out of the wall. The music cut off, leaving only the sounds of sex.

Multiple people's sex.

Jesus.

"Everyone out. Go back to your rooms."

"You can't stop us, bitch," someone shouted. "Who the hell do you think you are?"

"I'm the bitch in charge of this shindig. And if I hear of anyone"—I turned in a circle, ensuring my glare reached everyone in the room— "*anyone* giving Rod Taylor booze or drugs while we're on the island, that person will be fired. I don't care if you work for TI, for King's Cross, or for the resort, you will be out of a job. Is that clear?"

Hearing a lot of grumbling, but no arguments, I returned to Rod. The brunette was still latched onto his cock. I put my foot on her shoulder and shoved. Hard.

Rod grunted, bent over, and covered his crotch with both hands before leveling me with a look that could kill. "That bloody hurt, you daft cow."

Ignoring him, I looked at both his partners. "Out, both of you."

Sharon stood, and wiping her mouth, she winked at Rod. "Catch you later, babe."

"No," I said, stepping between them. "If you want to keep your job, you'll stay away from him." I turned to the local man. "Same goes for you."

The local man held his hands up as he backed away. "I no want problem."

I nodded and he scampered out of the room.

Rod remained in his chair, his cock still hard, and still exposed. I grimaced. "Put that shit away."

"You used to like it," he said, his voice a sensual purr that stirred my arousal.

I gritted my teeth and lied right through them. "Well, I don't anymore."

"I doubt that."

I pinched the bridge of my nose. I had to control myself, or this would quickly devolve into yet another useless argument. But I couldn't talk to him here with the air redolent of pot fumes and Rod's hard dick hanging out.

Tempting me. Goddammit.

"Let's go."

"Where?"

"My bungalow."

"Now that's more like it."

I was about to clarify, but when he wobbled to his feet and tucked himself back into his jeans, I shut my mouth. I crossed the room and waited by the door as he picked his way around furniture, discarded bottles, and clothing. The closer he got to me, the slower he walked.

"Come on," I said in an attempt to encourage him.

He crossed his arms, and I could see suspicion dawning in his eyes. Shit.

He cocked his head to the side. "What are we going to do in your room?"

"We have to talk."

His shoulders stiffened, and his lip curled into a smirk. "When I wanted to talk to you, you brushed me aside saying you weren't ready. Now, Her Royal Highness has decided the time is right, so she interrupts a perfectly good jobby, and I'm supposed to trot along behind her like the Queen's most loyal subject? Bugger that. I've nothing to say to the likes of you."

"Rod." I ground my teeth so hard I probably cracked a molar.

"What?" He threw out a hand, stumbled, and almost face-planted. "Will you threaten to fire me too? Please do."

"Of course not. I just want to talk to you."

"Why the hell should I?"

I stuck my hands on my hips. I hadn't wanted to go there, but I was going to. "You're coming with me, and we're going to talk, you son of a bitch, because you fucking owe me."

Chapter 3

ROD

My still-damp, half-hard cock rubbed against my boxers as I followed Sky to her bungalow. I'd told Sharon we didn't have anything, and then I'd gone and stuck my dick in her mouth again, and my tongue in the mouth of some guy with the same golden-brown skin and black hair as Dev.

How pathetic was I?

Sky opened up her room, not bothering to see if I was following. I stepped in behind her and closed the door, shutting out the sound of crickets, frogs, and more insects than I wanted to think about.

You owe me. Her words still rang in my ears.

She walked over to the minibar and pulled out a couple Cokes. She tossed me one. "Maybe this will help sober you up."

"What if I don't want to be sober?"

"Whatever," she said and cracked hers open.

I carefully bled the pressure off mine, the can chilling my fingers, condensation already forming. "So, what do I owe you for?"

She froze mid-swallow, her eyes flashing. "Don't play stupid."

"I'm not."

"Fine." She took another swallow, her beautiful throat working, then she smacked the can down on the table beside her. "You can't get Dev on your own. I'm just a tool to you. That's *all* I've ever been." Her voice

42

thickened as she spoke, and her eyes welled with tears.

Fuck. "That's not true. I've always liked you, Sky."

"No. You liked the situation, because you got to have Dev in your bed."

My cheeks started to burn. "It started that way, yes. But things changed. Our week together is the longest relationship I've had with anyone."

"Except Dev."

"Except him." I walked toward her, getting so close I could see the dark rings around the irises of her whiskey-colored eyes. God, she was gorgeous.

"Are you sure you aren't gay?" she asked.

What the fuck? I took her hand and pressed it to my rapidly hardening prick. "That answer your question?"

She went to pull her hand away, but I held it there and lowered my lips to her ear. "You might think I don't see you, Sky, but I do. How much you care. How hard you work. How fucking hot you are. How ballsy. You run your own business. You don't take my shit. How generous you are in bed. How adventurous. And how bloody fucking smart. I see you, Sky. Even though Dev practically blinds me, I still see you."

She flexed her fingers against my crotch, the caress so soft I almost didn't register it. She wiped at her eyes and took a deep breath. "I know what you still want. What you need. And that's Dev."

"I want you too."

She held my gaze, her own turning to steel. "You think you deserve me?"

I shook my head. "Never said that."

"Just so we're clear, you don't " I wasn't even insulted; she was right. I didn't deserve her. Her fingers whispered against my crotch again. "I'll help you get Dev, but you have to make an effort to keep the band together."

"And what do you get out of it?"

"I get to keep my job."

Interesting. She didn't mention the million-pound bonus.

"If I tell you to do something"—her fingers stroked me again—"you do it. And you show up to rehearsals, challenges, everything. No more drinking yourself into oblivion."

The authority in her voice hung in the air, resonating inside me, and I felt something shifting. Yeah, I still wanted Dev, but I wanted Sky too.

"Seal the deal with a snog?" I asked, my gaze falling to her lovely full lips.

"I've slept with Dev, here on the island. Does that bother you?" she asked.

It did actually. But I played it cool. "I'm a bit jealous. But only because I wasn't there." I slid a hand around her waist, trying to draw her closer.

She placed a hand on my chest. "This is just sex. No strings. Not exclusive."

I grinned. We'd see about that—at least the "no strings" part. "Whatever you want, Sky."

"Do you really want to quit the band?" She almost whispered the words.

"No. But I can't go on this way."

She nodded. "Dev is miserable too."

"Not that he'll admit it."

"I'll do whatever it takes to work things out." She swallowed and looked away. "I'll be the bridge between you."

You'll be more than a bridge, love. You'll see. I tugged her to me, my mouth just inches from hers, her breath hitching when my cock pressed into her belly. "So how about that snog?"

"That is the most ridiculous word," she whispered, but she tilted her mouth up to mine, both her hands snaking around my neck.

With a groan, I took her mouth, not wasting another second. She melted against me, her lips parting, her tongue dancing out to meet mine, and I was harder than I'd been in months.

Because it was her. Because maybe this crazy plan could work. Because maybe, just maybe, we could all be happy.

And maybe I wouldn't have to leave King's Cross.

I kissed down her neck, licking and nipping at that spot below her ear that I knew drove her wild. She shivered in my arms, her breathing speeding up, her fingers clutching my skull. "Oh, Rod," she sighed into my ear.

"Get naked for me, love," I said, my fingers going to the hem of her blouse.

She let go of me and whipped the shirt off, her lovely tits still covered in too much fabric. Bloody brassieres. If I were king, I'd outlaw them.

She grinned at me, obviously seeing where I was focused, and reached up to undo the front clasp. She shrugged out of the offending material and I couldn't resist taking a taste of those rosy nipples. I licked the freckle on her left breast. "Ah, Beatrice, I've missed you."

Sky giggled, her amusement making me grin too, a warmth filling my chest. This felt so good, being with her again. Right. Like a hole had been filled. A hole I'd overlooked in my misery over Dev.

"You aren't naked enough, woman," I growled against her tits. She moaned when I sucked hard on her nipple and tugged it with my teeth.

She shoved down her shorts, and the scent of her arousal made my cock twitch. "Get on the bed."

She turned to comply, then gave me a saucy wink. "You going to fuck me fully dressed?"

No bloody way. I wanted us skin to skin. I stripped as fast as my shaking hands would allow, my heart pounding as she bent over the bed, spreading her legs in invitation, her glistening pussy beckoning to me. I grabbed a condom from my pocket and brought it with me over to the bed.

I shoved her hair out of the way, nipping the nape of her neck, enjoying her shiver when I kissed down her spine, ending on my knees between her legs. "Sit down on the edge, love."

Turning, she perched on the edge of the mattress, her legs open, no shyness in her. That was one of the things I admired about her. She knew what she wanted, and she wasn't afraid to show it.

I kissed the inside of her thigh, just above the knee, and a tremor went through her. Sliding my hand along her other thigh, I paused just an inch from her slick pussy. She rolled her hips, and I grinned against the silken softness of her leg. "So impatient."

"I could die before you get to it."

I looked up at her, then blew a stream of air over the finely manicured hair between her legs. "Is that so?"

"Bastard." She started to bring a hand down to touch yourself, but I grabbed her wrist and shook my head. "No, love. Let me."

She held my gaze, something in her eyes, something I couldn't read. Then she nodded and dropped her hand to the side.

I leaned forward and parted those delicate pink lips, revealing the glistening pearl of her clit. I swept my tongue from her entrance to that pearl, circling it, her fingers thrusting into my hair as she gasped.

I sucked hard on her clit, and it swelled under my tongue, her hips bucking, and I placed a hand on her left thigh to hold her in place.

God, she tasted good, so wet and ready for me. Memories of our time with Dev filled my mind, and a fierce ache filled my chest. Could we have that again? Could we all really be together?

I licked my fingers, thoroughly wetting them, before working two of them inside her. She moaned when I slid them in and out, her hips rocking in time with my exploration of her.

When I sucked her clit into my mouth again, circling my tongue around it, she came hard. Shuddering, she swore softly and held on to my shoulders, her fingers digging into me.

She fell back on the bed, panting, and I stood, rolling the condom on. When I nudged her entrance with my cock, she shook her head. "Just a sec."

I stepped back, palming myself while she panted. Then she rolled herself over, presenting me with her lovely bum.

"You want in the back, love?"

She shook her head. "Just from behind."

She wasn't looking at me, and I knew what she was doing. Shutting me out, pretending I wasn't there.

I recognized the signs because I was a master of fucking without feelings entering into it.

But I wasn't going to let that happen here.

I turned her around. "I want to know who I'm fucking." I held her gaze. "Who I'm with."

A shadow flickered across her face. "I didn't think you cared." The words were so low I had to strain to hear them, and my chest tightened.

I cupped her jaw and tilted her face up to me. "I never meant to hurt you."

"You weren't even thinking about me."

I lowered my lips almost to hers. "I should have been." I kissed her softly. "And I'm thinking of you now."

Tears welled in her eyes, and she softly struck me on the shoulder. "You don't fight fair," she murmured.

"Never said I did." I pushed her down onto the mattress and kissed her neck again, pulling her right leg up to wrap around my hip. I rubbed my aching cock against her, and she gasped again. "Still with me, love?"

She nodded. "You're a bastard, you know."

"I know." I thrust inside her, making us both groan.

I knew it. But that wasn't going to stop me.

I probably wasn't going to change.

But I was going to try.

DEV

I slammed a hand down on my mobile in a vain attempt to shut off the alarm. That had to be the world's most annoying ringtone. Why was the off button so bloody tiny? And why did my head feel so big? My eyes drifted to the reason for my sleepless night, Rod's still empty foam camping mat, which lay a mere yard away from mine. Hopefully, he was, at least, sleeping somewhere more comfortable. I sat up and pressed my palms to my throbbing temples.

Had Rod spent the night on the pull with the crew and TI staff again? Was he even now waking up in someone else's bed, sleep-warm and somewhat befuddled the way he always was when he awoke early?

Why the fuck do you care, Dev?

I didn't care. And maybe if I repeated it often enough, I'd actually begin to believe the lie. Sky had gone to fetch Rod after dinner. They'd both disappeared after, and that was something I desperately did not want to care about.

Only, I couldn't lie to myself about her.

I'd promised Sky there'd be no strings or expectations, that our relationship would be nothing more than a fling. After all, my destiny was to marry an Indian woman, maybe even Kalini. The truth, however, what lay in my heart, was something quite different. Making love to Sky two nights ago had revived all my feelings for her, effectively erasing the three months we'd been apart.

Pain lanced through my skull, nearly blinding me. I groaned and forced myself off the mat.

Paracetamol. A couple tablets would cure me of the misery in my head, if not the one in my heart.

I rifled through my shaving kit and swallowed the tablets with several sips of water from one of the bottles Sky had provided us. With any luck, we'd soon win our beds back via some challenge or other. My gaze returned to Rod's unslept-on mat, and I blew out a long sigh. I'd never win a challenge if Sky hadn't succeeded in getting Rod on board last night, and given that he wasn't here, I doubted she had. The tablets settled on my empty stomach with a burn. Better get some brekkie before rehearsal. I scrubbed at my stubble, then checked my watch. Food or shave? There was no contest.

I stepped into some cut-off jean shorts, my flip-flops, and threw on a white T-shirt, then walked across the resort to the canteen.

The guys, except for Rod, were already seated, eating and chatting with the roadies. I filled a large Styrofoam cup with strong chai and piled a plate high with fresh fruit, egg, and toast, then headed straight over to the rehearsal space. I was in no mood for a chin-wag.

The cool air inside the building was a welcome salve. My shirt was already stuck to my back. I had to wonder how I would have survived living in India like my parents and grandparents had and how many of my cousins still did. I set my plate on a stool and went to retrieve my Taylor. I worked on a few bars of "Unfinished" that were still giving me some pains while I ate and waited for the others to arrive.

Time flew and before I knew it, Damon entered with Tommy, Jules, and Mick in tow. "Rod not with you?" I asked.

"No, mate," Mick said. "We were hoping he was already here."

I shrugged. "Skiving again. Whatever." We still had an album to write. "Let's get on with it."

We set up and then I played the music I'd been working on for "Unfinished."

"That's good," Jules said, his eyes lighting up. "But maybe this bit in the chorus might be better?" He fingered his bass guitar to show me the few chords he thought needed adjustment. His cheeks reddened and he looked away, like he couldn't meet my eyes.

It made my chest tighten. Rod and I had done a shit job of building the band if the lads were afraid to voice their opinions.

"That's brilliant, Jules," I said, and it was. "I've been trying to figure that section out all morning."

Jules's face reddened even more, but his posture relaxed.

"Let's play it from the top," I said.

Mick started us off with the drums and Jules added in the bass. I then locked in with them, playing rhythm guitar. Tommy and Damon brought in the melody with the keyboard and lead guitar.

"That was great!" Damon whooped when we finished.

"Yes," I said, quite satisfied with how it had turned out. "Unfortunately, we still don't have much in the way of lyrics."

"Rod always writes them?" Damon asked.

"I sometimes write a line or two," as I'd done for this song, lyrics that Rod had definitely not appreciated. "But generally, I write the music and he writes the lyrics."

Damon frowned and looked at Tommy, Jules, and Mick. "What about you guys? You never participate in that part of things?"

"Oh, sure. We help out," Tommy said. "Like Jules just did."

"Huh."

I stared at Damon for a moment, considering, then cleared my throat. "I've heard you write songs."

"Hell yeah, I do. Been songwriting since first grade."

He really was the perfect replacement for me, and to be honest I wasn't certain how I felt about that.

"Maybe, I could play something for you sometime?" Damon asked, his voice and manner unusually hesitant.

I shoved aside my own misgivings and smiled at him. "I'd like that."

"Yeah?"

"Yes."

"Well, it won't be today," Rod said, startling me.

I'd had no idea he'd arrived. I checked my watch. "You're late. Again."

"Better late than not at all," he said, striding up to the mic. His eyes were clear, his hair damp, and his stance straight and confident. "I listened to the music you sent me, Dev. And I've some lyrics for you."

"You do?" I asked, surprised and envious at once. The man had been lying about for the past two days and simply waltzes into rehearsal with completed lyrics when I'd been racking my brain and my efforts had been for naught. "For which song?"

"The second one on your CD." He flashed me a mischief-filled grin. "I call it 'Just Friends.'" His gaze swung over to the band. "Hit it, mates."

When the music started up, he began to hum. The sound was low and sultry, and did odd things to my belly. No, it had to be indigestion from the tablets I'd taken for my headache. It was definitely not Rod's voice having this effect on me.

So many years
You've been by my side
So many tears
I've tried and tried.

Rod sang softly, heartbreakingly. My pulse raced. This song was going to be a hit for King's Cross. I could feel it in my bones, and excitement zinged throughout my entire body.

Rod took the mic off the stand, cradling it between his palms. He bent forward and belted out the next verse.

You claim we're "just friends"
A bigger lie there's never been
'Cause you and I were born to sin.

He turned to face me. His expression softened and he extended his arm toward me.

"Take my hand, jump on in."

A fire started in my chest and invaded my neck, my face, my entirety. My fingers froze on the guitar strings, causing a loud screech to echo through the amplifier.

A bigger lie there's never been 'cause you and I were born to sin.

Rod's words banged around in my head, making it throb worse than the headache had done. My chest heaved as I tried to get air into my lungs. My hands shook and thumped against the guitar. "How dare you!" I shouted. "How fucking dare you?"

Rod held his hands out at his sides and arched a brow. "It's the truth, innit?"

"No, it fucking isn't."

Rod sighed. The sound seemed incredibly loud as it was picked up by his mic. "Stop lying to yourself."

The lads shuffled uncomfortably, which only made me more pissed off at Rod for airing our dirty laundry in front of everyone. I gritted my teeth. "What, pray tell, am I lying about now?"

Rod grinned, but I knew him better than anyone else, certainly well enough to recognize the mask of bravado he'd slipped on. "You want me, mate. And you always have."

Seething, I worked my guitar strap over my head and deposited the

Les Paul none too gently in its stand. When I was done, I rounded on Rod and poked his chest with my index finger. Hard.

"At this point, *mate*, I don't even like you. We aren't 'just friends.' In fact, we aren't anything at all."

The silence that accompanied my escape from rehearsal was the loudest sound I'd ever heard.

SKY

A cool breeze washed over me as Dev and I crested the hill on the way to today's challenge: the guys had to cross a very high wooden suspension bridge across a river. Every team that completed the challenge got a TV added to their bungalow. The guys were all dying to catch up on their beloved soccer, or "footie" as they called it, so they'd practically stampeded out of the resort.

And Rod had shown up, just as he'd shown up to the rehearsal earlier. Of course, he'd managed to needle Dev enough to provoke him into storming out. But at least Rod had written a song. A damn good one too, from what I'd heard. Nigel had even given me a thumbs-up before Dev's departure.

Oh well. One step forward, two steps back. At least we were moving.

Well, they were. If the two of them weren't together by the end of the trip, it wouldn't be because I hadn't busted my ass.

Rod was up ahead, talking and laughing with Damon and Mick, Jules and Tommy occasionally pitching in a comment or two.

And Dev was as silent as his namesake stone at my side.

"Penny for your thoughts," I said.

"They're not worth even that much."

"A half-penny then?"

He grinned. "This isn't Dickens."

"No, it's not. It's the twenty-first century."

He stopped walking and looked at me. "So you're saying what? That I should just be the person Rod wants me to be? Someone like him?"

"If you mean bisexual, would that be so terrible?"

A pained look rippled over his face. "I can't do that."

"Because you aren't, or because you think you aren't supposed to be?"

He turned away without a word and set off again. I watched him for a moment, then quick-stepped to reach his side. "Dev—"

"Leave it, Sky."

"I can't. Just what do you expect the outcome of all this to be?" When he didn't say anything, I asked, "What do you want?"

"I want things to go back to the way they used to be. Rod and me, just mates."

There was an uncertain note to his voice, like even he didn't believe what he was saying.

I'd heard him tell Rod he loved him. I'd seen him in Rod's arms, his face nestled in Rod's neck. How could he deny that?

"Things will never go back to that point. You can't expect him to just forget everything."

"To forget what? The three of us?"

Heat burned through me. He could pretend all he wanted, but I knew what I'd seen. "No, I mean the two of you."

"What?"

"Why do you think I left Palm Springs?"

He stopped again and put his hands on his hips. "That is a damn good question, yeah? I told you I loved you, and you ghosted me the very next morning."

"I left both of you. Because I didn't want to be the third wheel. You didn't need me."

"You're not making sense."

"I saw you. The two of you, in each other's arms, heard you tell Rod you loved him. He was so happy to hear it."

He shook his head. "You have it all wrong, sweets. I was telling *you* I loved *you*. I was asleep. I didn't know you'd left the bed."

Could that be the truth? Maybe that was part of it, but I'd seen the longing in his eyes when he looked at Rod, and I'd seen the pain on Dev's face when he'd heard Rod's lyrics this morning, the truth of them striking him like blows.

He loved Rod, but he wouldn't admit it. What was he so afraid of?

"You can't expect Rod to forget that, to make all the sacrifices to make you happy."

Dev spun on his heel and stalked away from me, stomping over the roots, twigs, and dead leaves that lined the mountain trail. He shoved the low-hanging branches of a breadfruit tree out of his way. "What about *my* sacrifices?"

"What do you mean?"

"My family barely talk to me because of the band. Because I've refused every marriage match they've brought me. I've let them down. If the band wasn't successful, I'd really be in the shit with them. At least I'm able to help put on the wedding they want for Aahna."

"They really don't approve?"

"They've never felt that Rod was a suitable friend. Too wild. Too extreme."

"Too pansexual?"

He nodded. "They think he's a bad influence. That he's the reason I haven't settled down with a nice girl and a respectable job."

"Are they wrong?" I kept my voice soft.

"I can't be like Rod."

Was he trying to explain or to convince himself? "They might not like the idea, but surely they'll get over it."

He laughed, the sound sharp and bitter, and waved a large flying bug out of his face. "You don't understand. I *can't* be gay. Or bisexual. My family would be mortified."

"Gay marriage is legal in the UK."

"And homosexual activity is still a crime in India."

"But you don't live in India."

"Might as well, for all the difference it makes to my family."

"I didn't think it was that big a deal."

He smiled, his white teeth flashing. "You grew up in one of the most liberal parts of the world. My parents didn't, and most of our neighbors didn't either. It's just not done in our culture."

"I think it says a lot that you haven't done what your parents wanted in a lot of respects."

"They can tolerate a lot. Forgive it, even. But not that."

"Maybe you need to think about what would make you happy. Don't your parents want you to be happy?"

"They would tell you yes, that's what they want."

"Then if they love you—"

"That's not how this works. They know what's acceptable and what's not. They know what people will say—not just to them, but to me. And they know I couldn't possibly be happy when so much of the world still hates what Rod is."

He still wouldn't admit it, couldn't say the words. Just how hard could I push? "Okay then. Maybe you don't have to be like Rod, out and proud and loud. But can you meet him halfway? At least get your friendship back?"

"Rod doesn't do things by halves."

"But what if he could?"

"You mean the two of us, sneaking around like we had some dirty little secret?"

I shrugged. "Maybe. If that's all you'll allow yourself. It might be enough."

He snorted. "For Rod? Have you even met him?"

"You might be surprised at what he's willing to do."

"Compromise hasn't been a big part of his life."

"Just think about it, will you?"

He took a deep breath, then slowly let it out. "I'll think about it. But don't expect anything to change."

I touched his arm. "Something will have to change if you want to save King's Cross."

Dev placed a hand over mine. "I'll do what's necessary to save the band."

I started to smile, but something about his tone rang an alarm bell in my mind.

He didn't sound like a man determined to save the thing he loved.

He sounded like a man mourning something he'd lost.

Chapter 4

ROD

I stared in horror at the yawning abyss and the rickety suspension bridge made of warped wooden planks and fraying rope strung across it. "Are you bleeding mad, woman?" I said, backing up until my spine pressed against a large banyan tree.

"Come on, Roddy boy," Damon crowed. "Don't tell me you're afraid of a few sticks and some string."

"That right there is the problem, you sodding Yank arsemonger."

"Ooh, he's breaking out the insults, folks. Roddy boy must be really a-sceered."

Sky laughed and shoved his shoulder. "Knock it off, Damon."

"What? I'm just having a little fun."

She narrowed her eyes at him. "I'll go across first. That way everyone will know the bridge is safe."

"Why doesn't Damon cross first?" I suggested. I was only too happy to see him go. "That way if the rope doesn't hold, only Damon will plunge to his death."

Damon rolled his eyes. "Love you too, dude."

"No, no. I'll—"

Damon ignored whatever Sky was about to say and stepped onto the bridge. It rocked under his weight. He turned to face us and began walking backward.

"Oh fuck," Jules said. The tint of his skin turned green.

"Damon, be careful," Dev called out.

Of course Dev didn't want the git to die. Damon was his way out of the band. I shot Dev a glare, but he wasn't looking at me, hadn't done so since rehearsal this morning. Hindsight being 20/20 and all, perhaps blindsiding him in front of the band, Sky, and Nigel hadn't been the most intelligent thing to do.

I'd hoped he'd have been shocked into admitting his feelings. He'd been shocked all right, and maybe he had been truthful. Maybe it really was over.

My gut quivering, I quickly looked away from him.

Damon gripped the ropes on either side and began shifting his weight. The bridge swayed several feet to the left and right. "Oh, oh!" he mock-cried. "I'm so scared. Someone come save me!"

"Stop fooling around, Damon." Sky's voice held humor and a note of anxiety.

The creaking of the ropes made the hair on the back of my neck stand on end. Damon stopped swinging the bridge. "Okay, okay. I'll be good."

He grinned at us and continued to walk backward until he reached the middle of the bridge. Then, he gripped the guide ropes and flipped arse over teakettle. I'm not too manly to admit I closed my eyes and screamed. Jules joined me.

The others laughed. *Laughed.*

"What kind of bloody idiot does something like that?" I asked.

"A fucking Yank," Mick said, as he wiped the tears off his cheeks.

Tommy was bent in two, laughing his fool head off, hanging onto Jules's shoulder. My gaze locked with Jules's, and I saw my apprehension reflected in his eyes.

Fuck. I looked away. Anywhere but at the prat doing tricks on the flimsy suspension bridge. Finally, Damon stepped onto terra firma and the vise around my chest relaxed. I could finally draw breath again. Not that I gave a shit about the bleeding arsehole anyway.

"I'm next," Mick volunteered. He crossed the bridge like a proper Brit. Stiff upper lip and all. No fuss. All business. "Good man," I said once he'd joined Damon on the other side.

"Who's next?" Sky asked.

Jules swallowed. "I'll... I'll go." I could see his bottom lip quiver, and I knew exactly how he felt. Better him than me though.

"You sure?" Sky asked. I wanted to lunge across the rocky dirt separating us to slap a hand over her mouth. Jules needed to be next, because it put the deed off a little bit longer for me. Yes, I was just as much of a bleeding arsehole as Damon. I glanced down into the yawning jowls of Hell and shuddered. Could anyone blame me for trying to hold onto life for a moment more?

Jules clamped his lips together and nodded in response to Sky's question. I felt an urge to kiss him but restrained myself. In all honesty, it wasn't too difficult as my feet seemed to have grown roots and my arms were now wrapped around the tree trunk.

The poor fucker approached the bridge cautiously, testing the first wood plank with his toe.

"Take a step, dude. It won't bite," Damon called out, oh-so-unhelpfully.

"Ignore him, mate," Tommy said. "You can do this."

Jules looked at him over his shoulder, his eyes imploring. "Tell my wife I love her."

"You'll tell her yourself," Dev encouraged him.

"Don't worry, dude," Damon said. "We'll bring gifts to your kids every Christmas."

"Damon!" Sky scolded even as she pressed a hand to her mouth. Her red face and the shaking of her shoulders gave her away though. How could she be so blithe about our upcoming demise?

Halfway across the bridge, Jules stopped and looked back our way. "Tommy, you'll marry my wife and raise my little ones, right?"

Tommy smirked. "Get on with you now."

"Promise me!"

"Fine." Tommy grinned. "I promise to take great care of your lovely wife."

"And the babes."

"And the babes."

I wanted to laugh. I really did, but I was too busy trying not to puke. Christ, in a few minutes that would be me out there, shitting my pants.

"Good. Good." Jules took another step.

"Almost there, mate," Mick said.

"Whatever you do, dude," Damon said, deepening his voice like the narrator of a bad horror film, "don't look down!"

Mick shoved Damon and shot him an admonishing glance, one I totally agreed with. Damon was being a prick. My stomach churned, my lunch threatening to make an encore. I certainly didn't want to admit that he was getting to me. But, fuck, he *was*.

"Mate, the Arsenal match begins at half three," Mick told Damon sternly. "If I'm not in front of the telly with a pint in hand when the match starts, I will wring your fucking neck." And he had the size and strength to do it too.

Damon's gob snapped shut and he raised his hands in surrender. He actually looked pretty doing that. And for the first time since this sodding nightmare had begun, I drew in a deep breath, one that filled my lungs and expanded my stomach.

"Eyes on me, mate," Mick said, and moments later, Jules stepped off the bridge.

"I knew you could do it." Damon clapped Jules on the back.

Jules pulled away from Damon, his usually jovial face a mask of anger. "Sod off, you bloody Yank."

"Oh... such bigotry."

I smirked. Damon was an arse, but I did love arses.

Sky asked, "Who wants to go next?"

"Not fucking me." The words slipped out. She sent me a look that would have had me on my knees had we been alone. Hell, I might drop onto them anyway. Put off the inevitable.

"Me," Tommy said, then proceeded to race across the bridge as though it were nothing more than a strip of grass. He and Jules high-fived each other, laughing with the enthusiasm of survivors. It had to be the adrenaline. The knowledge that they'd stared death in the face and lived.

I was green with envy and the urge to chunder. I bet Sky would want me then. She'd think I'm a right god with sick all over myself.

"Rod, why don't you go next?" Sky asked. Only she, Dev, and I remained on this side of the chasm.

"No." I shook my head. "I prefer to go last."

Dev looked at me for the first time since we'd come up here and scoffed.

I narrowed my eyes. "What?" If the tosser was laughing at me, I'd—

"If we cross first, you're going to turn tail and head back."

I had to snort, because he wasn't wrong. The idea had crossed my mind.

He stepped closer. "I want that telly, Rod, and if I have to carry you across this sodding bridge, I will."

His gorgeous brown eyes sparked, and he was beautiful. Fucking beautiful. My mouth went dry as I imagined him over me, his eyes sparking for a much different reason. "F-fine."

Sky gave me a sideways hug. "You can do this, Rod." Her sweet tone unmanned me.

"Of course." My voice was small. Too fucking small.

Jesus. This tiny woman had bigger bollocks than I did. I peeled my fingers from their clutch on the tree trunk. I straightened my spine, trying to inject the semblance of bravery into it.

I was Hot Rod Taylor. Lead singer and founding member of King's Cross, the hottest upcoming band in the UK and America. I could fucking do this.

I wasn't a child. I wasn't scared of anything. Christ, I'd faced much worse than a dark valley in my life, even one whose shadows reached out to me like a monster's claws.

Swallowing down my fears, I placed one foot on the first wooden plank. It moved beneath me, and my hands flew to the ropes on either side.

I could do this. I was brave. Hadn't my entire life proved it?

I inched my hands forward and stepped fully onto the bridge. I took a few more steps, then and only then, letting out the breath that was trapped in my chest. A drop of sweat trickled down the side of my face. Without thinking, I let go of the rope and wiped it off.

The bridge swayed and, knocked off balance, I fell to my knees.

"Rod!"

I didn't know who'd shouted my name, but I prayed it wasn't God calling me to heaven.

Below me, a river rushed over the jagged rocks. The sound suddenly seemed incredibly loud. And far. So far below me. Boulders looked like pebbles.

Jesus. If I fell, I'd be smashed on the rocks. Pulverized into an unrecognizable pulp of blood and bone. My stomach lurched and bile flooded my throat. Fucking hell. I swallowed reflexively.

"Grab the other rope," Sky called.

Grab what? I was already holding the rope, wasn't I? I looked up to see that while I had a death grip on the right-hand rope, my left hand was scrabbling at the wooden planks.

But grabbing the rope meant letting go of the wood.

I tried. I really did. My hand refused to move. It ignored my brain's desperate commands. I was paralyzed. And worse, my vision was getting fuzzy. How could this be happening?

Get off the bridge. Stand up and walk off.

I tried to encourage myself. Cajole myself. Then order myself. But I couldn't manage it.

The bridge moved under my knees and terror filled me. My vision went from fuzzy to white. I was going to die. In Tahiti. In fucking paradise. Only I could make such a cock-up of my life.

"Can one die of fear?"

I thought I'd said the words out loud, but there'd been no sound. I had no breath.

Maybe I was already dead.

My gaze dropped to the river below. Maybe I was down there. My body on the rocks, broken and bloody.

Something touched my shoulder. I gave a silent, breathless scream.

A soft voice whispered in my ear, "Rod. It's me. It's okay."

Oh God. Dev.

"Am I…" A bare squeak emerged. I cleared my throat. "Am I dead?"

"Not unless I am too." Dev's warm breath brushed my neck.

"Are you?" If we were dead, would we know it? If we were alive, would he be on this bridge with me? "I must be dead."

The hand, Dev's hand, stroked my back. "You're not dead. Do you trust me, Rod?"

"With my life."

"Then trust me to get you across the bridge?"

I started to nod, but when the bridge moved beneath me, I reconsidered any unnecessary movement. "Okay."

He covered my back with his body, completely surrounding me, then placed his hand next to mine on the wood plank. "Put your hand atop mine," he instructed.

Not daring to even breathe, I slid my hand horizontally until I touched his, then slid it over his fingers.

"Nice work, mate," he said. "I'm going to lift my arm. Keep holding my hand."

"I might never let it go." I tried to joke, although I heard the truth in my words. Had he? I didn't care anymore. If my life was to end today, at least it would end with Dev holding me.

Dev remained silent and raised our hands to the rope. He gripped it with my hand on top of his. "Now, try to stand."

My stomach roiled at the mere thought. "I don't know if I can."

"You can. I'm right here, Rod. You're safe. I won't let anything bad happen to you."

"You have though, haven't you?"

"What do you mean?"

"I'm already dead." My breath hitched.

His arm came around my body and held me against his chest. "You aren't dead, Rod. We're both here. Feel me. We're alive."

I closed my eyes, memorizing his heat. He hadn't understood my meaning, but at least he'd given me something to hold onto. "Okay, I'll stand. Just don't let go."

"I won't."

With a death grip on the two ropes and with Dev's reassuring arm across my torso, I forced my legs to obey, forced the frozen muscles in my thighs to unclench. Dev helped me and soon I was upright. Shaking, but vertical.

"Brilliant," Dev whispered. Once again, his warm breath washed over the back of my neck, and my emotions went into a tailspin. I was scared out of my wits and turned on all at once. My brain was a bloody scary place.

"Slide your hand forward," Dev ordered.

I did as he asked.

"Now your right foot."

We continued this way, with Dev's strong body molded to my back, his groin to my ass, his arms and legs against mine, until both my feet were once again on solid land. His arms squeezed my waist, and I could've sworn I felt his lips against my neck, but perhaps that had simply been wishful thinking.

He separated himself from me, and I knew then that he was taking my heart with him.

And I also knew that I'd have stayed in the middle of that damned bridge for the rest of my life, be that a minute or a century, if it had meant having Dev there with me.

DEV

Another day, another failed challenge, but at least this time we'd both given it our all. After yesterday's bridge challenge, something had changed between Rod and me, and I was glad of it. We were becoming a team again.

Rod whipped off his soaking wet T-shirt and dropped it on my head as I shut the door to our bungalow behind us. "Prat," I said, laughing as I pulled it off my hair. We'd both been pathetic at the standing paddle board challenge. We'd spent more time in the water than we'd spent out of it.

Everyone else was off with Sky, enjoying a boat ride and a fancy meal. At least she'd taken pity on us and allowed us to order room service instead of having protein bars for dinner.

Rod eyed his sinewy arms, which were starting to darken a bit after the sunburn from yesterday's hike and bridge challenge. He was looking much healthier than he had when we'd first arrived. He looked... sexy.

But then he always did. That was his thing. The bloke practically oozed it, his sleek body so graceful and sinuous when he performed.

Had I ever been that comfortable in my own skin?

That confidence, that swagger, Rod had—it'd always attracted me. It had been the thing that had sparked our friendship. The way he'd fearlessly defended me in the schoolyard, when I'd been the smallest chap in class, the little brown boy no one had wanted to befriend.

Except Rod.

Rod hadn't given a toss what anyone thought.

So why did I care so damn much?

He plucked the room service menu off the low table the TV sat on. "What's your fancy?"

We settled on the "sampler feast," a hodgepodge of seafood, meat, and vegetable appetizers. And of course we ordered some beer.

The order placed, Rod hung up the phone and shucked his swim trunks, not caring that he was bare underneath. I tried not to look, but Sky's words and Rod's lyrics kept going 'round and 'round in my brain. *I saw you... heard you tell Rod you loved him... You said we're "just friends," a bigger lie there's never been...*

That week with Sky, I'd seen Rod starkers dozens of times. But Sky had always been with us. Except for the morning when she'd left. When I'd woken up in Rod's arms, our bodies pressed together, his hard cock touching mine, the few moments I'd let myself lie there before I pulled away, before we had the fight that had driven us apart...

Rod smirked at me and wagged his hips, his cock flapping back and forth, slapping his thighs. "Like what you see?"

I grinned and shook my head, peeling my own wet shirt off and flinging it at him. "Not everyone wants you, you bloody tosser."

"That so?" he asked, then strolled out of the room to the shower like he knew full well my eyes were glued to his creamy white arse.

My cock stirred. Fuck, fuck, fuck. I was just... confused. Seeing him in the nude again was reminding me of that week we'd spent with Sky, that's all.

I sat cross-legged on the floor and grabbed my guitar, picking out the notes to "Unfinished." I had the music now, but the lyrics had eluded me. I started to hum, and then then words began flowing:

There are things I want
There are things I have
There are things I can't
There are things I crave
And then...
There's you...

I launched into the chorus:

You left, you think you won
But I have to tell you
We're far from done
You walked away from all of this
But you and I, we're unfinished

My fingers found the notes, but my chest was aching, the words that slipped out a hoarse whisper:

You're in my heart, in every beat
You are the life I long to keep
But life's not fair, it's never been
And you and I, we'll never win

Rod stepped around the corner, a towel in hand, still gloriously naked, and my fingers stilled on the strings. How much had he heard? I'd completely tuned out the sound of the shower. When had it shut off?

Rod dried his hair, his voice half-muffled when he spoke. "Interesting choice."

My face was on fire. "Yeah, well…"

"It's a great song, mate. A hit, no doubt." He started drying his chest and arms, his eyes meeting mine. "And with your voice, that rawness…"

I closed my eyes. He'd heard it all, hadn't he? "I won't be singing it."

"Why not?"

I opened my lids and met his gaze. "That's your territory, not mine."

"We never said we had to stay in boxes. You should sing it."

He dried his legs and midsection, utterly at ease. Or was he teasing me? "Having a laugh, are you?" I asked.

He shook his head. "I'm not taking the piss. I mean it."

"I'm not you. I can't be out on stage singing."

"Why not?" He wrapped the towel around his waist, then sat on his bed mat.

"I'd make a fool of myself."

He leaned forward, resting his forearms on his knees. "You'd drive a saint to drink, Devkinandan. You're a bloody rock star."

I plucked at the strings of the guitar. "It's not the same."

A knock came at the door and Rod answered, letting in the guy with our food, which he placed on the table in front of the sofa.

I tipped the guy and he left. Rod grabbed the remote and flipped on the telly, scanning the satellite channels until he found a game of footie. He settled on the couch and patted the seat beside him, then cracked the top off a bottle of beer.

When I didn't move, he tipped the bottle at me. "Am I going to be drinking alone?"

Fuck. *You can do this. You can sit next to him and have a meal and a laugh and a beer. And it doesn't matter that he's practically naked. Nothing's going to happen.*

I rose, then remembered my wet shorts. "Give me a sec."

I jumped in the shower and rinsed the salt off my skin, then toweled off quickly. I'd left my clothes in my rucksack in the other room. Wrapping the towel around my waist, I went out to get them.

Rod whistled long and low when I appeared. I couldn't help laughing.

"Wanker," I said.

"That's what the girls will be doing when you sing."

"I'm not singing it," I said, turning my back to him as I dressed.

He whistled again at my bare arse, and my cheeks went up in flames. "Fuck, Rod."

"Haven't seen that view in a while. I can appreciate it, can't I?"

"I'd appreciate less enthusiasm."

He snorted, choking on his beer as I turned around. He sputtered for a second, then smiled. "You're sexier than you know, Devkinandan."

I loved the sound of my name rolling off his tongue. He said it teasingly, tauntingly, his voice low and laced with innuendo.

Taking the seat beside him on the couch, I was all too aware of the six inches or so between us. I could touch his bare thigh if I wanted, so easily…

I twisted the cap off my beer and took a long swig. Shite, shite, shite. Mustn't let my mind wander like that.

Nothing was going to happen between us. Nothing.

I already knew how everything was going to play out.

I'd leave Rod with a hit album and a new guitarist. King's Cross would live on without me.

That was the way it had to be.

Right?

Rod picked up a cold chunk of lobster and popped it in his mouth, moaning at the taste. "Bloody delicious," he said. "Have some."

I took a bite. It was heavenly. A million times better than bloody protein bars.

We were silent for a bit, digging in to the food, our eyes glued to the screen where Chelsea faced Man U. Chelsea was our team, and we both cheered when they scored a goal. We slapped palms and clinked the necks of our beers together.

"Dev?" Rod said, his voice soft.

"Yeah?" I glanced at him. His eyes were on the screen, all casual, but there was a tension in his body that hadn't been there a moment ago.

"Would you be willing to try it again?"

My heart started racing. "Try what?"

"You, and Sky, and me. The three of us."

My mouth went dry. Could I risk it? Could I let myself do it again, enjoy the idea again, the three of us in each other's pockets? Heat rolled through me as memories did the same.

"I need to think about it."

Rod said nothing for a while, then he nodded. "Okay, mate."

We finished the game, then he asked what I wanted to watch. I shrugged. "Whatever you want."

He grinned, and I knew from the glint in his eyes that I'd made a mistake. "Porn it is, then."

I had to laugh at the glee on his face. "Cheeky monkey."

"You know you love me," he said, his voice light.

"Not that way, mate."

He glanced at me and took a swig from his second beer. "We'll see, mate. We'll see."

Rod flipped the channel to a porn video in progress. Some bloke was giving it hard to a brunette with long hair and huge tits. She was attractive, but Sky was a million times sexier than this bird.

I heard Rod's towel rustling and looked over. Sure enough, he had his cock out, lazily stroking it. My pulse quickened, my eyes riveted to what he was doing.

We'd jerked off together a lot when we were teens, but it had been ages since we'd last done this.

And never with Rod's challenge still hanging in the air. *We'll see.*

My cock hardened in an instant, and Rod looked over at me, smirking when he saw where I was looking, then chuckling when his eyes dropped to the bulge in my boxer briefs.

"I could help you with that," he said, his eyelids half-mast, his voice husky and low.

"I can take care of it myself."

"Will you now?"

The girl on screen started moaning, and even though I knew it was fake, the sound still made my cock thump.

I could feel Rod's eyes on me, the heat of his gaze, as I pushed my shorts down, freeing my cock. I palmed myself, my face blazing, my heart thudding, my mouth a desert.

I looked over at Rod, not meeting his eyes, but seeking out the place where he was touching himself, my eyes going to that long, thick cock he had trapped in his fist. The head was a deep red, almost purple, and he squeezed himself hard, a low groan leaving his mouth and shooting right to my cock.

"I could be touching you right now," Rod murmured. "Or Sky could be. If that's what you'd prefer."

An idea flitted through my head—Sky and Rod taking turns sucking my cock—and though I'd barely touched myself, I was teetering on the brink of coming. My fist started pumping.

Rod chuckled, the sound low and dirty. "What's going through your head, Devkinandan?"

"It's private," I growled between clenched teeth, my hand moving faster, my body tight as a guitar string.

"You're bloody gorgeous," Rod whispered. "Always are, right before you come."

I looked at him, his eyes mere slits as he focused on me, his hand pumping quickly, his chest heaving like a bellows, the tendons in his neck and arms standing out, his abs clenching, and then he came with a grunt, cum shooting out in ropes onto his hands, his chest, and the sight finished me, my cock pulsing hard, making its own mess as I groaned out my bliss.

Fuck. I hadn't come that hard in months. Except for Sky.

I slumped back against the couch, panting, my whole body boneless and loose, like I'd just had the fuck of my life, instead of a wank sitting next to my best mate.

Shite, shite, shite.

Rod mopped up with his towel, then rose, heading to the shower again. "Want to join me?" he asked, pausing in the doorway.

My fingers tightened on the fabric of the sofa. I did want to, wanted to see where this could go... but I couldn't. I shook my head, unable to meet his eyes.

"Your loss," he said, his tone casual, but he was right.

It was my loss, and I was all the poorer for it, my cum cooling on my belly.

I could be under the water with Rod, could be touching him, kissing him, feeling all that smooth skin.

But that way lay madness.

The ache in my chest intensified. I rose and washed off at the sink while Rod soaped himself in the shower, our eyes meeting in the mirror, my cheeks hot with shame.

I was a coward.

A bloody coward.

And I didn't deserve Rod.

Or Sky.

SKY

I slid under the refreshingly cool water of the swimming pool and dipped my head back as I surfaced.

Dinner with the band had been wonderful, as had the boat tour. Tahiti had to be one of the most beautiful locales on Earth. Each island seemed a world unto itself, the topology of one completely different from the others. Whereas Marlon Brando's island was sand and water, miles and miles of flat terrain, Moorea was all trees and mountains.

I swam a few laps, enjoying the stretch and the sensation of the water sliding over my heated skin. The sun had just set and a couple small pool lights lit up the water in some areas while leaving others in shadows. I felt cocooned by it as I slipped into one of the darker sections of the pool. A gorgeous arrangement of rocks and fragrant *tiare tahiti*, a local variety of gardenia, followed the edge of the pool. I leaned against the wall and, hooking my arms over the ledge so my feet could float up, let myself breathe. Just breathe. In the dark woods behind me, night creatures hooted and insects buzzed. Their song soothed me. Helped ease my worries, of which there were many.

The dinner and boat ride had been fun, and talking with the band about their careers and their thoughts on the future of King's Cross had been illuminating. I hadn't realized to what extent Dev and Rod led the group, while the others basically played what they were told. Damon seemed to be the most irritated by it. Maybe it was an American thing, this notion that everyone had to have an equal say. King's Cross was definitely more of a dictatorship than a democracy.

I heard a noise. As I tried to figure out what it was, I sank farther into the shadows created by the arrangement of plants and flowers. I couldn't clearly see anything beyond the lights of the swimming pool.

Footsteps. Someone was coming.

A shape emerged. Formed into the body of man.

There was the sound of a zipper being lowered. Shorts and a shirt were flung aside.

A splash when the man dove into the water.

Who was it?

I felt a little miffed that my quiet time alone had been invaded. Ridiculous really. The pool was for everyone's use. If I'd wanted privacy so badly, I should've stuck to the dipping pool on the deck of my bungalow.

My foot brushed against something. I screamed, kicked, and pulled myself out of the water and onto the ledge.

A head burst out of the water. It was Dev.

"Oh, fuck." I pressed a hand to my chest, where my heart was beating a quick step. "You scared the crap out of me, Dev."

Dev's laughter continued, the smug shit. I kicked my feet rapidly, bringing up a ton of water, right into his handsome face.

He sputtered and coughed and raised his hands in surrender. "Okay, all right. Stop!" He wiped the water off his face with his hands and grinned. "Forgive me?" he asked without even a modicum of regret in his voice.

"No, I'm not going to forgive you," I said, pouting playfully.

The pool was no deeper than five feet, even in the deep end, which allowed Dev to easily walk up to me. His palms landed on my knees and pushed my legs apart. He stepped in between them and his finger grazed along the low waistband of my black and white bikini bottoms.

"You look edible in this itty bitty cozzy."

My lips curved into what I hoped was a sultry smile. "You hungry, big boy?"

"Starved," he said in a strained voice. Dev stuck a finger into each side of the waistband of my bikini bottoms and tugged. "Lift up."

I hesitated. We were in a public place even if it was dark and secluded. Dev kissed my neck. "Don't worry, sweets. No one will see us."

He couldn't possibly know that. I wasn't shy about my body. Growing up the way I had ruled that out. But I was on the job here. Dev sucked on my earlobe and chills raced up my back. A wave of yearning crashed over me. I wanted Dev again. All those months alone, thinking about him. About Rod. And now I had him. I wasn't going to waste this chance.

I raised my hips and brought my knees together as he stepped back and tugged the bottoms off my legs. He tossed them onto the deck of the pool, but they slid into the water. Dev pushed my legs apart again, but this time, he pressed his lips to my pussy and then I couldn't think about anything else.

I moaned with pleasure. "That feels so good." My hands flew to his head and my fingers dug into his thick hair, holding on. Holding him.

He drew back and nibbled my sensitive flesh, before soothing it with a simple swipe of his tongue. Desire anchored itself in my belly. My breasts ached with the need to be touched, and my pussy throbbed with the need to be filled.

I hadn't had sex in months before coming to this island, and now I couldn't get enough. "Oh God," I cried when Dev sucked on my clit, his tongue doing a particularly wicked swirly thing. I was having sex with two men, only one of whom knew about the other, all in the name of work. Did that make me a whore? I was using my body, after all.

Only I didn't feel like one. I couldn't say I felt good about what I was doing. Guilt was definitely weighing on my conscience. But each time one of them touched me, kissed me, sank his cock into me—it didn't feel dirty. It didn't feel wrong.

It felt like destiny.

Like the life I was supposed to be living.

Like the life I'd almost had.

If only I hadn't run away.

A finger eased into me, and I immediately clenched around it. Dev pumped his hand a few times, then slid a second finger in, pressing against my inner walls. When he spun his fingers around and rubbed my G-spot, I saw stars. My hips bucked and I was fucking his face, squeezing his head between my thighs. The bristles of his beard chafing me just right.

He flicked his tongue quickly against my clit, and I curved myself around his head. My orgasm hit me like a runaway freight car. "Dev. Ohhh." I moaned.

He held me as I continued to rock my hips through the aftershocks, his amazing fingers playing me like a guitar.

When the sensations eased, I relaxed my death grip on his head, and let my arms and legs fall.

"Jesus." I exhaled heavily. "You're really fucking good with your fingers."

He chuckled softly, flexing them. The moonlight reflected off the wetness of my juices. "It's the dexterity exercises."

"Whatever it is, don't give it up."

He slid his fingers into his mouth, the same two that had been inside me, and moaned. "I love the taste of your cunt."

I must've made a sound, because he looked up, his brow furrowed. "What is it?"

I grimaced. "That word."

"What word?"

"The C word."

"C word?" His expression cleared. "Oh, you mean cunt? What of it?"

I rolled my eyes. "It's not a nice word in America."

"We aren't in America, are we, sweets?" He grinned and traced a finger down my slit. "And this is a very nice cunt."

"Jesus," I muttered and tried to close my legs, suddenly feeling very exposed.

He held my knees and refused to let me hide from his view. "Dev."

He slid his torso between them, keeping my legs spread with the breadth of his chest. His arms circled my waist. "Come here," he whispered, lifting me off the ledge and into the pool.

I shivered as the water enveloped me. It felt warm on my skin, which had chilled in the cooling night air.

He brushed some hair off my face. His eyes were intense. Hot. He kissed me softly, and I tasted a hint of myself on his lips.

"You're beautiful, Sky. Every inch of you." He paused and searched my face with his gaze. "I wish…" His words trailed off. He looked away, and the longing in his voice reminded me of what was at issue here, and it wasn't my heart.

"Things seem better with you and Rod," I said.

"They are." He looked up. "And it's because of you. I must say, I'm impressed."

"Impressed?"

"We've made so much progress already, and we've only been on the island a few days. Whatever you said to Rod seems to have been the catalyst."

And there it was again, that needling guilt. I couldn't tell Dev about the bonus or the partnership deal I'd made with TI. Or the promise I'd made to Rod to give him and Dev my body, to be the bridge between them.

I believed in what I was doing.

I believed that Dev and Rod belonged together.

Just as I wanted to believe I could do this for them without losing my heart to either one.

I cleared my throat of all the mixed emotions clogging it. "You guys are really the ones doing the work. You and Rod. I'm just nudging things along." I focused on his neck instead of on his face. It was far safer territory. Except for that bead of water slowly sliding down its long length, and I was suddenly consumed with the need to lick it.

"Rod... Rod mentioned something today," Dev said softly.

"Yeah?" I tried to focus on what he was saying, but the drop rolled onto his collarbone and followed its path to the notch at the base of his throat. A notch I knew he loved to have licked.

"He asked if I'd like to try it again."

Something about his tone caught my attention. "It?" I asked.

"A threesome. With him and... with him and you."

That definitely caught my attention. Rod sure hadn't wasted any time. "What do you think of that idea?"

My question was answered by silence. I raised my gaze to his face. His eyes were closed. "Dev? You seemed to enjoy it before."

Dev opened his eyes and fixed them on mine. He pressed his lips together, then said, "What if I get jealous?"

"Of who?"

"Rod, of course."

Dev might not know I was sleeping with Rod now, but he certainly knew I had slept with him before, and Dev had never seemed even remotely bothered by it during our week in Palm Springs. In fact, he used to love watching Rod fuck me. "Are you sure about that?"

"Yeah." He cocked his head to the side. "If you had to choose, which one of us would it be?"

His question made me squirm. I enjoyed both of these men in very different ways. Dev was calm and dependable. He was the intellectual, the reflective one. We could talk about almost anything for hours. Rod, on the other hand, was exciting and unpredictable. He could be a dick one minute and incredibly thoughtful and romantic the next.

"I could never choose." The truth was: I wouldn't want one without the other. They belonged together, and I wouldn't be the selfish bitch who drove them apart by picking one over the other.

Dev snorted.

"I'm serious. I want both of you." I took a deep breath and hoped he didn't get upset with my suggestion. "What if... what if Rod promised not to touch you? Or initiate anything between the two of you?"

"What do you mean?"

"Well, if you were to say, initiate something, then and only then, would Rod be free to respond."

"I'll... I'll think about it." The look on Dev's face, a mix of hope and fear, of wanting and despair, reflected so perfectly what was in my heart that I wanted to cry.

Dev might want my body, but he was in love with Rod. He just wasn't ready to admit it yet. Just as I wasn't ready to admit that at the end of this trip, I'd be alone again.

Dev's arms tightened around me and I felt the hardness of his cock at my belly. I arched a brow. "In the meantime, think about this." I grabbed his cock and tugged him into the shallow end, where I proceeded to make us both forget about Rod. At least for a little while.

Chapter 5

ROD

"What the fuck is an averrhoa carambola?" I read from the instructions Sky had given us for the scavenger hunt. The teams that found all the items would be treated to a Tahitian feast tonight. She'd split us up into two groups, and Dev and I had been stuck with that plonker Damon.

"It's a species of tree in the family *oxalidaceae*," Damon said, a question more than a fact as he read off his mobile.

"Not helping, Yank." I crossed my arms. "Sky has to be taking the piss," I said. We'd been traipsing about the island for half the day and had barely managed to locate and photograph ten of the items on her list of fifteen.

"The carambola is a tropical fruit…" Dev said.

"A fruit? We're looking for a pissing fruit on a tropical island. Brilliant. You sorry lot aren't telling me anything."

"…also known as the star fruit," Dev finished with a smirk.

Finally. "I'm sure as shit not climbing a sodding tree to take a photo of a fucking fruit," I said, shuddering at the memory of the rickety suspension bridge. In a sick twist, my cock twitched because as scared as I'd been, I'd cross that bridge again if it meant having Dev pressed against my back and ass.

"Never fear, dude." Damon slapped his hand on my shoulder. "I'll brave the heights. Nothing is keeping me from winning this challenge. I can almost smell the roasting pork now." He sniffed the air dramatically.

Dev laughed. "You're a right nutter. Come on then, let's find you a carambola tree to climb."

After fifteen minutes of trekking, Dev stopped and pointed ahead.

"What is it?" I asked.

"A carambola tree."

I looked, stepped forward, then squinted. "Where?"

"There. Follow my finger."

The tree, its branches heavily laden with orange fruit, stood about a quarter mile ahead, straight up a steep bit of the mountain.

"That looks…" I swallowed. *Way too fucking tall.*

"Amazing!" Damon said, pushing past us. Like a sodding monkey, the lad raced up the rocky hillside.

"Well now." Dev watched him, arms crossed. He turned to me. "Shall we?"

"Christ." I shook my head. "That daft woman is out to kill me."

Dev smirked. "Is she?"

"Yes. And maybe you're in on it. A ploy to get me out of the band."

Dev's smile disappeared. "I don't want that, Rod. You have to know that."

I punched his shoulder. "Just pulling your leg, mate."

"And breaking my arm, you arse."

I gripped the back of his neck and tugged him along. "Come on. Let's make sure the Yank bastard doesn't fall to his death." I tapped my lip and shot Dev an evil look. "Although…"

"Stop it, you knobhead. Murder is a felony. Besides, the Yank is growing on me."

"Yes, like mold."

He laughed. "Or a particularly tenacious fungus."

The good-natured ribbing with Dev felt so familiar, it was hard to believe we'd been fighting so much the last three months. I could almost think that the worst was behind us. That we were friends again.

Except, did I want that?

Did I want to come full circle and be back in the same spot we'd been in before Palm Springs?

Was some of Dev better than none of Dev? I didn't know. But he hadn't freaked out when I brought up the idea of a threesome with Sky, and he'd most definitely got off on it in the past.

Dev's face as he'd shot his load, his eyes on my spent cock covered in jizz, had become my favorite memory. My cock started to harden as it always did when I thought of Dev in the throes of orgasm, and I tripped on a root, going arse over tit. I landed on my stomach, the breath knocked out of me.

There was a scuffling sound, and then Dev was next to me. "Rod, are you all right? Shit, shit."

He gently rolled me over. His hands touched my arms, my chest, and my world was filled with his gorgeous anxious face. His skin had darkened in the Tahitian sun and his beard had grown in, setting off his perfect white teeth.

"I'm fine. Help me up, mate?"

"Yes, if you're certain."

"Just shook up a bit."

We clasped hands and he tugged me to my feet. He plucked a leaf from my hair and then swatted my back and ass to rid it of dirt and flora. I didn't hide my grin. "Thank you, Dad."

"Sod off, you muppet." He laughed, then released me, and for that I was sorry.

We climbed the rest of the way without further incident, if you discount the fact that at least fifty percent of my body's water content had been imbibed by my shirt. When we reached Damon by the tree, he was stretched out on a rock, eyes closed. I kicked his foot. "Having a bit of a kip, are we?"

"You guys took so hella long to get up here, I figured I might as well."

"Fuck off."

Damon got up and held his hand out to Dev. "Camera?"

Dev handed him the disposable digital camera Sky had given each team. Damon slid it into the front of his shorts and proceeded to climb up the tree.

My heart jumped into my throat. The higher he went, the worse I felt.

"Probably shouldn't watch," Dev said quietly.

I sat down on the rock and closed my eyes to concentrate on taking deep breaths until there was a thud. For a moment, I thought the idiot might have fallen, but then Damon said, "What's next?"

I opened my eyes to see him try to hand Dev the camera back. Dev's face scrunched up and he backed away. "You had it in your pants, mate."

"Underwear."

"Pants."

"Whatever." Damon shrugged.

Dev looked at the list to see what was next. Before he could speak, I groaned. "Can we take a break? It's hot as fuck"—I tossed my rucksack onto the ground and swatted at a mosquito on my arm—"insects are crawling up my arse, and I've yet to catch my breath."

I pulled my shirt off and hooked it into my back pocket before grabbing a bottle of water from my sack and emptying it on my head and chest. "Oh fuck. That feels good."

Damon's eyes zeroed in on my wet chest. He licked his lips and stepped up to me. "Dude, I'm feeling really thirsty all of a sudden." He bent forward and swirled his tongue around my nipple, then moved to the other.

Dev watched, his expression stoic. Caught up with the irresistible urge to push him, to make him fucking react, I cupped Damon's face in my hands and planted a big wet kiss on his mouth. Damon's dark eyes twinkled as he opened his lips and licked my tongue like we were in a porno.

My gaze flew to Dev, who was definitely no longer calm. His face darkened and his eyes narrowed to slits.

Damon grinned at me as he made a show of wiping his mouth. "Now I understand the constant lineup of people wanting to crawl at your feet."

Dev muttered something under his breath, something that sounded coarse and angry. Damon's kiss had got my dick stirring, but it was the pure fury on Dev's face that really cranked my shaft.

"I'll leave you two lovebirds to it then, yeah?"

"Oh, come on, Dev," Damon called after him.

I laid a hand on Damon's shoulder. "Leave it."

Damon's face twisted with worry. "He knows we were just kidding around, right?"

I got a sick pleasure seeing Damon so utterly unsettled. I squeezed his shoulder. "That was a really hot snog."

"What?"

I let my hand fall off his shoulder and trail down his generous bicep. The lad definitely worked out. "What if it weren't a joke?"

Damon blushed, took a step back. "I saw Dev's face. I'm not going to be the Yoko in this situation." He lowered his chin and looked up at me. "That Sky's job, right?"

"What about Sky?" It took everything in me not to bristle. I picked up my kit and started walking down the hill.

Damon kept pace. "Well, we all know she's sleeping with both of you. I was hoping to get some of that action too."

Dropping my rucksack, I rounded on him, ready to get in his face. "Keep your fucking prick away from her."

Damon laughed, and I wanted to punch him in his stupid handsome face. "Just yanking your chain, dude. I know she's off-limits."

"Bloody fucking right."

"I've got my eye on someone else anyway."

I think I knew who he meant. "That pretty little black bird from TI?"

"That's the one." Damon grinned. He looked so cocky, the arrogant little shit. So certain he was going to get the girl. I hadn't known the bloke for long, but I'd seen the way she'd been eyeing him, so he was probably right. He would get her if he wanted her.

I just wished I were as self-assured in my desire to get Dev. My little attempt to stir his jealousy might have worked all too well.

DEV

"Wake up, you lazy sod!" Rod bellowed in my ear and gave me a hearty shake.

I blinked up at his wicked grin as he started stripping off his clothes and dropping them on the floor of our bungalow. Strutting around starkers, as usual.

"What time is it?" I asked, looking for my phone. Judging by the low slant to the sun coming through the windows, it must be early evening.

"We have half an hour to get ready for the Tahitian feast," Rod said, tossing his boxer trunks at my face.

I batted them away and sat up. "I didn't think we could go." Since I'd stalked off before we'd finished the scavenger hunt, I'd figured we'd be having protein bars and a sulk for dinner tonight while everyone else went out.

"The Yank and I finished it," Rod said as he rooted through his luggage, looking for a clean shirt. "He's really not that bad, once you get used to him."

Rod, singing *Damon's* praises? My gut clenched. I knew it. I fucking *knew* it.

Rod hadn't come back to our room and he certainly hadn't chased after me, and I'd wondered if he'd gone off and fucked the bastard.

All afternoon I hadn't been able to stop thinking about the two of them, my mind spinning sick fantasies that had tormented me and turned me on at the same time. Rod kissing Damon. Damon sucking Rod's cock. The two of them fucking Sky…

I kept hoping Rod would turn up, but he hadn't. I must have drifted off at some point. After I'd tossed off for the hundredth time… after those fantasies had started blending with my memories. Rod, and Sky, and me.

I could have that again, maybe. If Rod hadn't already moved on to Damon.

"He must be pretty good at sucking your cock," I finally said, my eyes glued to Rod's arse. The arse I wanted to touch. But couldn't. Wouldn't.

Rod turned to me, a colorful flower print shirt in his hands, a smirk on his lips. "You sound… jealous, Devkinandan."

"Should I be?" Did I even want to know?

He narrowed his eyes at me, his gaze dropping down to my crotch, to the bulge that had grown there. "Would you be if I said yes?"

Was he just going to play games with me? I turned my head. "Bugger off."

He said nothing, apparently going back to rifling through his things, judging by the rustling of cloth, the clanking of his jewelry. "You want to know if I slept with him, is that it?" he finally said.

"No, I don't."

He scoffed. "You're gagging to know."

I looked up at him. He was still turned away from me, holding up two pairs of board shorts, apparently trying to decide which to wear. "Where have you been?" I asked.

"Not with Damon."

Relief washed through me. A relief I *didn't* want to feel.

"I bet he does suck cock really well though." Rod's voice was low, teasing, and he cast a sly glance at me over his shoulder. "Maybe we should find out?"

He let the question dangle, his eyes locked on mine, and I shook my head. "For fuck's sake, Rod, just... *don't*."

"Have a little fun, Devkinandan."

I closed my eyes. How did he always make my name sound like an invitation to crawl into his bed?

"Let me guess," he said. "Spent all afternoon wondering whether I'd been testing that out? Thinking about trying it yourself?" I kept my eyes shut, not wanting to give him the satisfaction, but heat crawled up my neck and into my face. "How many times did you toss off, Devkinandan?"

There it was again. That insinuating lilt he added to my name. That lilt that said I'd enjoy it, that he'd make it worth my while, that he'd make it my everything...

He chuckled, and I heard him head toward the shower. "Better get moving, old chap."

I waited until the water turned on, then I shoved my hand into my shorts and wrapped my fingers around my rigid cock, pretending they were Rod's lips, his mouth I was thrusting into... then Sky's mouth, then Rod's again... then Sky's... then Damon's...

In seconds I came with a grunt, utterly disgusted with myself, and lay back on the bed. I was fucked, wasn't I?

So many things I wanted. So many things I craved. So many things I couldn't have.

But maybe I could have some of those things.

Rod and Sky had both indicated their interest in the three of us sharing a bed again. We'd been happy then, so happy.

Could it work again? Would it be the solution we needed to fix things between Rod and me, to keep us together?

To keep Sky in my life?

Maybe I owed it to all of us to give it a try.

Feeling better than I had all day, I mopped up my cum with my shirt, then started tearing through my clothes. I was suddenly hungry, and not just for the feast that awaited us.

Less than an hour later, we piled out of the vehicles in front of the Moorea Tiki Village Theater. It was just past dusk, darkness settling over the village.

We were greeted with welcome drinks—something tropical, fruity, and strong—then led to a large open arena by a handsome bare-chested man dressed in a sarong and a necklace made of wooden beads and animal tusks. His dark brown skin glowed under the theatrical lighting. He introduced himself as Ponui and introduced several of the dancers, a mix of men and women. The gorgeous, long-haired women wore coconut bras—not traditional garb, they pointed out, but a nod to modern sensibilities—and long flowing grass skirts or sarongs with flower leis and crowns.

Everyone was well-tanned and toned, and with a pang, I realized that this was the first time I'd been so completely surrounded by people as dark as me, other than my own family.

We were shown around the village and taken through an exhibit showing photographs of the island and its people over the decades, then taken back to the arena, but not before stopping at the earth oven, which they called an *umu*, where tonight's feast was cooking. We'd be eating slow-roasted pork, chicken, roasted breadfruit, and taro root, among other items. It all smelled heavenly.

Ponui brought out some coconuts. "Who would like to learn how to open one of these?" He looked at the lot of us, his eyes settling on Sky. "You, my lovely?"

Sky flushed, her cheeks pinking up prettily, and stepped forward. She was wearing a long, multicolored sarong over her bikini, her dark hair gone wavy, and I thought I'd never seen a more gorgeous creature in my life.

Rod nudged my shoulder. "You might want to reel your tongue back into your mouth, mate." He grinned as he said it, the firelight gleaming in his eyes, highlighting his cheekbones, the bump of his Adam's apple, the veins cording his bare arms.

Correction: I'd never seen a more gorgeous creature than Sky or Rod.

Ponui demonstrated how to open the coconut with Sky's assistance, his eyes glued to her just like mine were, and an insane jealousy gripped me when he made her laugh. He placed a crown made of flowers on her head to thank her for participating. Between the flower crown, the lei, and her sarong, she looked like a Tahitian princess.

When Sky returned to her seat, Rod gripped her around the waist and insisted she sit between us. "Where you belong, love," he said, his eyes flicking from her to me, the heat in them clear.

A thrill ran through me. I wanted it, the two of them, again. I wanted it so badly my skin prickled all over with awareness at how close they both were, how I could reach out and touch them, how easy it would be to just let go...

But then what? How else would this end, but in heartbreak?

When the dancers and singers started weaving a mythical tale about a long-ago princess, one of the women pulled Sky into the dance, teaching her some moves. Sky looked great shimmying her hips in a tight circle, and one of the male dancers came up behind her, not quite touching, but doing some kind of lascivious move that made Sky burst into laughter and earned hoots and cheers from the lot of us in the audience.

Rod, of course, jumped in, doing his own thing, his hips moving to a slinky rhythm only he heard, one that dried my mouth and earned him a wolf whistle from Damon, the prat. Vanessa took a few snaps with her phone, and I thought Daniel would break something trying to snatch it from her before she posted anything to Instagram.

"You're no fun," she complained as Daniel grabbed her phone and deleted Instagram from it.

"You know the rules," he said. "No posts until the very end of the trip. The last thing we need is the paparazzi descending on this place."

Just the thought made me shudder. It had been so nice, being on our own, not worrying about fans or the press or anything.

Well, other than the fate of the band.

Sky and Rod started dancing together, the two of them looking hot, both sporting light tans and grins that weren't at all forced. In fact, they seemed downright flirtatious, Rod playfully trying to pull down her sarong. She grabbed his hand and pushed it away, but didn't let it go, and he tugged her close.

Rod's eyes slid to mine, and then he beckoned me forward and handed Sky off to me. He yanked Damon and Vanessa into the dance, planting a kiss on Vanessa's lips, then one on Damon's. The two of them burst out laughing, but they didn't jump away.

And then Rod gave me a pointed look, a look that blazed with heat. A look that said *See what you're missing?*

My stomach did a funny flip. I could have that. *We* could have that.

If only I could get over myself.

Sky cleared her throat. "That's our Rod. Always stirring the pot." I focused my attention on her, not caring that we weren't doing the dance correctly, or at all. I had questions I needed to ask.

"You and Rod seem to be rather cozy," I said in her ear. "Did something happen between you?"

She stiffened in my arms and looked into my eyes. "Yes."

My heart started pounding. "What, exactly?" I couldn't keep the bite out of my voice.

She stopped dancing. "I never said we were exclusive."

"Which means?"

"I'm as close to Rod as I am to you."

"You're fucking him too? I got the impression you weren't happy to see him when we first arrived here."

"That's true. But we... reconnected. And I understand him better now."

"You understand *what*? Rod wants to quit the band."

Her voice cut into me. "*Does* he? Or does he want something else?"

I knew what she meant. Clearly, she and Rod had talked as well as fucked. "I can't give him what he wants."

She laced her fingers around my neck, her hips started to sway, and my hands found their way back to her waist. "Maybe you can give him something close to that." She paused, but when I didn't respond, she continued. "Why else did you ask me about the threesome when we were in the pool?" Her hips bumped against mine, her perfume rising around us. "Obviously the idea appeals to you in some way."

I shrugged. She was right of course, but also wrong. I'd enjoyed our time together, but I'd hated how it had ended.

With her gone, and Rod and I both bleeding like we'd been gutted.

Though Rod's wounds were mostly my fault. I'd held him in my arms that final morning, I'd let him hold me too, and I'd teetered on the brink of saying yes, of just giving in to what he so desperately wanted.

What I... wanted.

But there was no use starting something I could never finish.

"Dev," Sky said, her voice soft yet insistent. "I've seen the two of you together. The way he looks at you, the way you look at him. The way you held him the other day on the bridge."

"I can't be with him like that. I've told you about my family."

"They're not here. This is a safe place to explore things."

My throat tightened, my voice deepening when I spoke. "I don't want to lead Rod on. I don't want to hurt him any more than I already have."

"But aren't you both hurting right now?"

I looked at Rod, at him watching the two of us, the expression on his face a mixture of hope and wariness, the same things swirling in my belly, in my chest.

What if I just let go? At least for now? Explored this, or some version of it?

My family was thousands of miles away. No one had to know. And maybe… maybe if I got this out of my system, I could settle down with a nice Indian girl and a steady job and be the good Indian boy I was supposed to be.

I looked at Sky, saw the same hope and cautious excitement in her gaze, and I nodded. "Okay, but Rod has to follow some rules."

"He doesn't touch you unless you touch him. He didn't initiate anything; you have to."

I closed my eyes, a wave of excitement rushing through me. "I hope I don't regret this."

She placed her lips beside my ear, her breath brushing my overheated skin. "You aren't alone, Dev."

SKY

The whole trip back to the resort, I sat between Dev and Rod, practically vibrating with excitement. And more than a little nerves.

Can I actually do this again? Make love to them, be with them, then walk away when it's all over?

Rod reached out and took my hand, his fingers straightening mine out where they were clenching my sarong. Then his lips were at my ear. "You don't have to do this, love."

"I want to," I whispered back. And I did. I wanted to, very much.

I was just scared out of my wits, that was all.

Dev put a hand on my left knee, his warm palm searing through the thin cloth. "Okay?" he asked.

I nodded, gave him a smile. "I am."

He squeezed my knee, his long fingers brushing my inner thigh as he moved his hand higher. I glanced at Tony, the driver/bodyguard behind the wheel, looking to see if he was eyeing us through the rearview mirror, but he seemed oblivious.

Or maybe he was just used to sexual shenanigans happening around these two.

Rod kissed my neck, his tongue darting out, teasing my skin, and I wanted to moan, it felt so good. Instead, I pressed my lips together and shifted in my seat, the leather cool beneath my legs, which seemed to part of their own accord. I wanted their hands on me, their mouths on me; I wanted to be overwhelmed by them again.

Desire pooled low in my belly, and when Dev pushed my sarong up to my hips, his hand touching the crotch of my bikini, I didn't try to stop him. His fingers grazed the thin cloth covering me, tracing the plump lips of my sex, and I shivered.

He kissed my neck, his short beard tickling my skin. He inhaled, then let his breath wash over my neck. "I've missed this," he murmured.

"Me too, love," Rod said, shifting in his seat to cup my right breast, his fingers brushing over my already hard nipple.

I looked up at the rearview mirror again, and this time I caught Tony looking, our eyes locking in the mirror. I should have been embarrassed, should have slapped their hands away and straightened up, but I didn't. Instead, I hooked a leg over Dev's, and let my head fall back on Rod's shoulder.

Rod chuckled against my skin, his soft beard tickling me like Dev's. They both looked a bit scruffy and rough, dangerous and intent, in the low light of the vehicle.

Dev eased a finger underneath the edge of my bikini, the touch soft, teasing, and I felt myself go slick and ready. Rod pinched my nipple and captured my mouth at the same time, muffling my moan, absorbing the shudder that moved through me.

I glanced up at the rearview mirror, and again Tony's eyes met mine, then slid away.

I was out of control, and I knew it, and I absolutely did not care. Rod and Dev were intoxicating; I could resist them no more than addicts could resist their drug of choice.

Dev and Rod were *my* drug of choice. They were the reason I hadn't been with anyone else since I'd left them.

Because I might have left them physically, but emotionally…

Emotionally, I was trapped. Still theirs. I shouldn't be doing this, should be running the other way, but dammit. I wanted this.

I wanted this pleasure, this euphoria, however long it would last. Even though I knew it was temporary. For right now, for the next week or so, I could pretend it was forever.

The vehicle slowed, turning off the main highway and onto the dirt road to the resort. Dev smoothed my sarong back into place and kissed my cheek.

Rod growled in my ear. "Just when things were getting interesting."

I laughed. Keeping my voice low, I said, "What? Thought you were going to fuck me in the backseat?"

"I would have. You didn't seem to mind the audience."

A blush stole over my cheeks this time. It was one thing to just react, but to admit it… "I didn't mind."

"Didn't mind? I bet you're more than ready for me. For us."

The Range Rover bumped over a few ruts in the road, then came to a stop, sparing me from answering.

We climbed out of the vehicle, my skin already overheated despite the air-conditioning in the Range Rover. The humid air slid over me, the low hum of insects and night creatures surrounding us as we walked to my bungalow. Geckos darted across the stones that lined the path and shimmied up the tiki torches that attracted moths and other flying insects.

I let us inside my bungalow, barely getting the door closed before the guys were on me again, Dev untying my sarong and pulling it off, leaving me in a turquoise bikini that looked great next to my tan.

Rod's eyes lit up. "Cor, love, you look a fucking treat."

They both started touching me again, then Dev paused and stepped back. He looked at Rod. "We're clear on the rules?"

Rod raised his hands in the air as if he'd been caught red-handed. "No touching—you anyway." He turned to me. "I plan to be all over you, love."

Dev joined in. "Me too."

I grinned at them. "Just like Palm Springs."

"Except we're in Tahiti, love," Rod said. "So, the same, but different."

Dev was looking at Rod, something in his gaze changing at Rod's statement. *The same, but different…* Was Dev actually thinking of letting things go where Rod wanted them to?

And if he did, what did that mean for me?

Stop it, Sky. You're here to do a job, that's all. And you're doing it.

Rod peeled off his shirt, his muscles flexing beautifully as he did so. His sunburn from the day of the bridge challenge had mellowed into a nice tan that looked great against the leather bands around his wrists and the silver St. Jude necklace shining in the dim lighting of the bungalow.

The patron saint of lost causes… Was this one of them?

Dev removed his shirt as well, and my eyes bounced between them, unsure where to look, each one a visual feast. Dev so dark and Rod so fair in comparison.

Rod shed his board shorts, revealing a not-surprising lack of underwear. He was already hard, and I noticed my eyes weren't the only ones drawn to the erection he so proudly palmed.

Dev seemed to freeze for a moment, then he stepped out of his Bermuda shorts, dropping his black boxer briefs along with them. He too was hard, and I wanted to touch them both.

Rod gestured to me. "Catch up, love."

I grinned. I'd stood there like a lummox just staring while they'd stripped, too mesmerized by them and the idea of what we were about to do to get with the program and get naked.

I took my time finding the ties to my bikini top, pretending it was giving me trouble, and Dev laughed, coming over to me. He kissed my shoulder. "Need a hand?"

"Or four?" Rod said, appearing on my other side.

Before I knew it, they had my suit top and bottom untied and on the floor.

They both went for my neck, Dev on my left and Rod on my right, their hands roaming over me, Dev caressing my breasts, Rod my ass, then my pussy, his fingers going where I wanted them to.

Encountering the moisture between my legs, Rod chuckled. "You *are* ready, love, just like I thought."

I moaned my agreement as his fingers circled my clit, lightly playing over it, his touch sending a thrill through me.

Dev latched onto my breast, his tongue swirling over my nipple, and when he added suction, I groaned and clutched his thick hair.

I'd almost forgotten how intense being with them was, just this side of too much, too fast.

Dev's hand joined Rod's between my legs, his fingers massaging my mound, Rod's fingers parting me. "Let's get you horizontal, love," Rod said.

We stumbled over to the bed, none of us wanting to let go of each other. They pushed me down onto my back, Dev's mouth closing over mine, Rod parting my legs and diving in. I gasped at the touch of Rod's tongue, and Dev raised his head. "Oi, mate, save me some."

They exchanged a grin, then Rod said to Dev, "How about you lead this dance?"

A glint came into Dev's eyes. "It's my show?"

Rod nodded and looked at me. "Sky?"

I smiled. "Whatever you want."

Dev tapped a long finger on his lips. "You can warm her up for me."

Rod grinned. "Can do." He descended between my legs, his tongue going to work on me while Dev went back to my breasts, sucking on one nipple while pinching the other. Then Dev moved up over me, his lips finding mine in a searing kiss, his tongue invading my mouth. I wrapped my arms around his neck. A surge of emotions swamped me when he brushed the hair out of my face and gently traced my eyebrows.

"You okay, Sky?"

"More than okay." I gasped as Rod added his fingers to the mix, stroking my G-spot expertly while he sucked my clit. He intensified the suction, the pressure of his strokes, and soon I was moaning his name, the pleasure coiling inside me, building and building until my hips bucked, and I wailed out my climax, Dev holding me tight.

"Ready for more?" Dev asked.

I nodded, panting.

I was ready; I was so ready.

But was my heart?

Chapter 6

DEV

I motioned for Rod to crawl up onto the bed on Sky's other side. Normally I'd have wanted to take her first, but some part of me wanted to watch. I'd loved seeing her come apart under Rod's tongue.

Now I wanted to watch him come. He looked at me expectantly. "What's next, Devkinandan?"

"I want you to fuck her." The words came out low and raw, betraying my excitement.

Rod saluted me. "Aye aye, captain." He moved over Sky, kissing her urgently, stroking her cheeks. "Ready, love?"

She nodded and gestured to the nightstand. "There are some condoms in the drawer."

I grabbed a couple and handed one to Rod, who quickly rolled it over his thick cock. I had the insane urge to touch him again like I had earlier in the day, like I had the day we'd wanked off together, but I kept my hands fisted at my sides. There were limits to what I would allow myself. There had to be limits. Right?

Rod lifted Sky's leg, curving it around his waist as he entered her. She moaned, the sound going straight to my own cock, which throbbed to be inside her as well.

What would it feel like, if we could both be inside her lovely cunt at the same time? His cock sliding against mine, my cock sliding against his, the three of us joined in a way we'd never been before...

Rod's hips and ass rose and fell as he thrust into her, the sight driving me mad, and a different idea came to me. "When you're ready to come, do it on her belly." I looked at Sky. "I want us to mark you."

Her eyes widened, sparking with desire. "Dirty boy," she whispered, her fingers twining in my hair as she pulled me in for a kiss. Would she go for my other idea if I asked about it sometime? My mouth met hers, her tongue slicking over mine when I pushed it between her parted lips. She tasted so sweet, like pineapple and mangoes.

Rod groaned in my ear and a shiver ran down my spine. My lips were only inches from his. All it would take would be tilting my face, turning to him...

I looked at him out of the corner of my eye, saw the heat in his gaze, felt how easy it could be...

Then I released Sky and lay back, grabbing my straining cock and rolling the condom over it. He was close; I could see it on his face, and I didn't want to let Sky catch her breath between us.

Suddenly Rod pulled out and whipped off the condom, spurting onto her belly. The sight of him coming on her, his chest heaving, his hand gripping his cock, his eyes meeting mine, had me close to the edge myself.

He glanced down, saw the state I was in, and moved out of the way, lying down on his side next to Sky, only inches away.

I moved between her legs and thrust into her hard, both of us groaning at the contact, the sheer bliss of being joined.

She was so tight, so wet, and I was where Rod had just been, my cock filling the place his had filled, stroking Sky where he had stroked her...

That fantasy slipped into my mind again. The two of us inside her sweet pussy at the same time...

A shudder rolled down my spine, and I stared into his eyes, his own locked on mine as he lay back, stretching like a lion, his skin glowing, his demeanor that of a man who'd conquered a mountain.

But whether that mountain was me or Sky, I couldn't say. Though I suspected that it had something to do with me.

I tore my gaze from him and looked down at Sky, my beautiful Tahitian princess, and my heart leapt. She reached up and cupped my cheek, her eyes speaking volumes.

She wasn't upset by the intensity of my focus on Rod. Instead, she seemed energized by it as her hips writhed beneath mine, as she moaned my name and clutched Rod's shoulder.

He leaned over and suckled one of her gorgeous tits, and a red flush spread over her chest and neck, and then she cried out, convulsing beneath me, and I knew I couldn't hold on a second longer.

I pulled out, tore off the condom, and came so hard I almost saw stars, my cum mixing with Rod's on her skin.

She was well and truly marked by us, and as she lay there panting, looking up at me, I knew I couldn't let her walk away again.

Nor could I deny my fascination with Rod, as dangerous as it was.

But could I act on it?

And if I did, could I stuff the genie back in the bottle when it was time to leave Tahiti?

ROD

My feet never touched the ground as I walked with Dev and Sky to the canteen for brekkie. Last night with the two of them had been bloody incredible, even if Dev had not laid a single finger on me. He hadn't had to. His eyes had done it for him. The way he'd practically ordered me to fuck Sky, then put his cock where mine had just been, and kept his gaze on me all the while.

And then that idea of his to shoot our loads on her, our cum mixing on her belly.

Our Dev was a bit of a kinky fucker after all.

My mouth watered at the memory.

Dev touched my arm and I almost jumped out of my skin. It took me a moment to remember where we were and what we were doing here. Dev angled his head toward the overflowing buffet. "Let's help ourselves to some grub, yeah?"

"Right," I said, my voice hoarse.

Sky looked at me curiously, but didn't say anything. Then again, maybe she knew.

I spotted the lads and headed over to their table after stacking a plate high with eggs, bacon, beans, and toast. All that sex had left me good and starved.

I sat next to Dev, Sky on his other side. I couldn't keep the grin off my face. Fucking soppy is what I was. Imagine that, me, Hot Rod Taylor, a soppy sod.

Damon kicked my foot under the table. I frowned at him. The stupid tosser just grinned. "Don't you three look cozy this morning."

I kicked him back. I didn't need him to make things uncomfortable. Dev was as skittish as a deer, and I didn't want him scared off.

Vanessa sat beside me. She kept shooting glances at Damon. An idea struck me. Leaning into her side, I swiped a thumb along her cheekbone.

"You look knackered, love. Come here. Let me brighten you up."

I tugged her onto my lap and nuzzled her neck. Beside me, Dev huffed. I smiled and winked at him, pleased when he relaxed and smiled back. Just a small curve of his mouth, but it made my day.

Vanessa ducked her head and stole a guilty glance at Damon. So the dirty Yank had managed to bag the girl after all.

I patted the seat Vanessa had vacated and inclined my head to Damon. He got the message and like a young pup, scampered around the end of the table.

"Now, how about that kiss, love?"

Her cheeks flushed, her gaze darting between Damon and me. Laughing, I pressed my lips to one of her pretty brown cheeks, while Damon did the same on her other side.

She giggled. "Oh my God. I'm in a King's Cross sandwich!"

With the speed of a rabbit on crack, she whipped a mobile out of some secret female hiding spot and snapped a series of photos in quick succession.

"Vanessa!" Daniel's voice boomed out over the canteen as he charged over from the next table and snatched the mobile out of her slender fingers.

"Hey!" she cried, a frown marking her otherwise smooth forehead.

"I warned you, Vanessa."

Sky pushed up from her chair and, arms akimbo on her hips, leaned over Vanessa. The poor girl trembled. "This better not be going on Instagram," Sky scolded her.

Daniel navigated her mobile and even I recognized the Instagram icon. "Dammit," he barked. "I deleted that app last night!"

Vanessa shrugged and Sky glared at her

"I'll take care of it," Daniel said, his face like thunder as his eyes drilled into the girl.

"Geez, guys. Calm down," Damon said. He took Vanessa's hand in his.

"I can't live without my phone," she said, directing her complaint at Damon and me, no doubt hoping to garner our support. There was no way I was taking her side over Sky's though. I knew who was buttering my toast.

Vanessa abandoned her quest for our support and directed her argument to Sky and Daniel. "How am I supposed to do my job without it? I'm the damn social media specialist!"

Daniel looked to the ceiling and there was only silence for a few seconds as though he were counting to calm himself.

"That," he said, "is for after. No one can know the band is here right now."

Vanessa huffed and shifted on my thighs. "What am I supposed to be doing in the meantime, huh?"

Daniel's face was stern. "Helping Sky. We talked about this already."

Vanessa's eyes shifted to take in Dev and me. She smirked. "I think Sky's helping herself just fine."

In a magnificent display of synchronicity, Sky and Dev both blushed. Sky looked away, and Dev practically buried his nose in his plate of beans.

Laughing, I lifted the girl off my lap. "Come on, lads. Let's go. We have music to make!"

Like a sheepdog, I herded them all into our rehearsal space. Energy from last night hummed through my body. I itched to move, to let the music fill me, to let it heal my soul.

I stepped up to the microphone. "What do you want to start with, mates?"

"Let's work on, 'Aching for You,'" Damon said. "I'm trying to work out the chorus."

"Righto," I said.

Mick and Jules laid down the beat. Tommy and Dev joined in, giving it depth. Heart. Then Damon began playing the melody.

One bar, two. I started to sing the first verse. It was slow and sexy, building up to the chorus. I clutched the mic between my palms and dug in to hit the chorus's high notes with just enough power.

Damon stopped playing. "Shit. I can't seem to get that chord right. Something about it just seems..."

"Off," Dev finished for him. He went over to the guitar stands to the left of the room, set down his Les Paul and picked up the Telecaster.

Tommy whistled. "Dev's going to play his Fender. It's been ages, mate."

Dev shook his head. "Just helping the lad out a bit."

My pulse quickened nonetheless.

Mick started up the drums a couple bars before the chorus and the others joined in. I began to sing, but kept my eyes on Damon and Dev. They stood next to each other. When the chorus started, Damon stopped playing and focused his attention on Dev's fingers as they flew over the frets up and down the neck of the guitar. It was a thing of beauty to watch him play. And once again, I was torn between being fucking turned on and fucking pissed off. *This* was what Dev was meant to do. He was a master at lead guitar. Not that Damon wasn't a fantastic guitarist, but Dev was... well, Dev was Dev. The chorus ended and Dev's fingers stilled. The music died down.

"That's it, dude!" Damon's face glowed. "Maybe we could add a little riff at the end?"

Dev nodded. "Show me."

The lads started playing in the same spot as before. Dev and Damon played up to the chorus together while I sang. Then we all stopped and let Damon continue.

He swung his hips into it, his fingers racing up and down the strings. It was a fantastic riff, and when he ended it, the proud look on his face said it all. He arched a brow at Dev. "What do you think of that, dude?"

"Good. It was good."

Damon frowned. The lads all snickered. We knew what Dev was doing; he'd issued a challenge.

"You think you can do better?" Damon asked, swaggering up to Dev.

"Ho ho!" Mick said.

"It's on!" Tommy crowed.

"Let's see." Dev took a step back and played a few notes. His expression relaxed, his eyes closing as he got lost in the music, his fingers dancing along the fretboard. They were slightly curved, in exactly the same position as when he wanked off.

Heat raced up my chest and to my face as I watched him. My shorts grew tight. I wanted this man. Had always wanted him. Had come so fucking close to having him once, only to lose him. But not this time.

Because this time, I had help. I glanced over at Sky, who stood by the outer wall. Her eyes shone as she watched Dev play, as entranced by him and his performance as I was.

When he stopped playing, the room was silent, everyone in awe.

"Brilliant, Dev," I said, my voice choked. "Bloody brilliant."

Damon clapped him on the shoulder. "It absolutely was, dude." He shook his head and grinned. "Am I going to have to watch my back? You looking to take your spot at lead guitar back?"

Dev shook his head and went to set the guitar back on its stand. He picked up the Les Paul. "I'm good with rhythm guitar."

"You're good with anything, mate," I said, truly meaning it. Few people had the dedication to their art that Dev had, and it destroyed me to see him throwing it all away.

We decided to take a quick break before getting back to work.

I sidled up to Vanessa and spoke out of the side of my mouth like an old movie gangster. "So, doll. Can you arrange a night for me and Sky at one of those treehouse resorts I saw yesterday?"

"For you and Sky?" She chuckled.

"Yeah."

She rolled her beautiful brown eyes. "Oh, come on. It's for the three of you, isn't it?"

"I will neither confirm nor deny those allegations."

She rested her hand on my arm with a serious look. "You can trust me."

Could I? My gaze went to Dev and Sky, having a chat in the corner near the refreshments. It seemed I didn't have a choice. "No Instagram, yeah?"

She crossed a finger over a generous tit. "I promise."

"Then yes, it's for the three of us. No one can know."

"I'll arrange it for tonight, and I won't tell a soul."

As rehearsal started back up and I saw Vanessa leave to make arrangements for a treehouse room, I had to wonder if I was doing the right thing, or whether this would all turn into a giant cock-up.

I'd put a tenner on the latter.

ROD

I unlocked the door to the treehouse bungalow Vanessa had reserved for me, and the sheer delight in Sky's eyes proved I'd made the right decision.

I'd owe the girl an autographed selfie for her to post on Instagram. She'd really come through for me.

We stepped into the posh wonder, thick white carpeting, a giant king-sized bed, black furniture, and enormous windows with a wide view of the island. The treehouse was quite literally built in a tree on a hillside, so we had the rugged coast at our feet.

"Wow," Sky said, turning in circles as she took it all in. "This is fantastic."

Dev stood by the door, shifting nervously from foot to foot.

"Come on in, mate." I walked over to an alcove that featured a full wet bar with a granite counter, bar stools, and a stocked fridge. On glass shelves behind the counter were several top-shelf bottles of booze. I flipped over an etched glass tumbler and filled it with ice. "Fancy a drink?"

He closed the door and came to lean an elbow on the bar. "Give me a Stella, yeah?"

I grinned. "At your service. Sky? Some wine?" I chose a bottle of chilled white from the selection in the wine refrigerator and held it up for her inspection.

"Sure. Thanks."

I hoped the alcohol would do its job and loosen them up. Right now, they were both wound tighter than my nan's bun.

After serving the drinks, I picked up the remote that sat on the counter and pressed the button with a musical note on it. Some pop crap blared out the hidden speakers. I cringed and stabbed at the forward button.

When the pleasant beat of an R&B song filled the room, I adjusted the volume and set the remote down. I took Sky's glass from her and put it on the counter. "Care for a dance?"

She winked. "How romantic."

I laughed. "I've been called worse."

Dev snorted.

I spun Sky into a turn. Her body pressed against mine, and heat flared everywhere we touched. I lowered my hand to the curve of her spine and smirked when her eyes went round, giving me no doubt she'd felt my cock pressing into her belly.

I slipped the spaghetti strap of her dress off her shoulder to kiss the soft skin beneath. She moaned and moved into me. I licked a path over her shoulder and upper neck, nibbled on her earlobe, then sucked it into my mouth.

We continued to sway to the music. My gaze landed on Dev, whose hungry eyes tracked our every move. I let my gaze roam over his body, settle on the tent in his trousers. He'd dressed up tonight, our Dev. Having foregone the shorts, he looked quite fit in dark trousers and a smart white button-down. It was a far cry from his usual rock star garb, but I wanted to eat him up just the same. I motioned to him with my fingers.

Dev set his empty glass down and moved in behind Sky. He molded his pelvis to her ass, his hands on her hips, and joined our rhythm.

"Now everything is perfect." With a smile on her face, Sky raised an arm and draped it around his neck. She moaned when Dev lowered his mouth to the other side of her neck.

We danced that way, with Sky between us, both of us lavishing her neck and shoulders with kisses and nibbles. The scent of her perfume and Dev's shampoo enveloped me and made my legs a fucking custard. I wanted to kiss her, to kiss him, to fuck her, to fuck him. It was torture to continue swaying side to side when what I most wanted was to thrust back and forth.

Unable to stand it a moment longer, I slid my finger under the other strap of her dress, nudging Dev out of the way so it could slip down her arm. He quickly caught on and helped it along, pushing down on both straps, baring her tits. A feast for my eyes. High and firm, they were glorious and fit snug in my palms.

I caught them both up, massaging as she moaned. Dev moved his hands to her stomach, and further up to tweak her nipples. I ceded the ground to him and dropped my hands to her hips. I watched them, mesmerized by the tableau before me. I couldn't believe how much it excited me to see Dev pleasure Sky, to see him take pleasure from her. I'd shared lovers before and didn't tend toward jealousy, but even so, I'd never experienced anything quite like what I felt when I was with Dev and Sky. Their joy was mine. Their hunger was mine. Their pleasure was mine.

Every moan, whimper, and sigh fed my soul.

When Sky's nipples were hard peaks, Dev scooped her tits up in his hands and held them out for me. My cock pulsed and throbbed, both at the offer and the fact it was him making it. Sky clung to Dev's neck with both arms while I closed my lips over one firm bud. Dev pinched the other between his fingers.

I curled my tongue around that sweet nub. Sky squirmed, straddled my thigh, and ground against it. My knee touched Dev's leg, and I froze. He looked up. Eyed me over Sky's shoulder, but didn't move away.

Relieved, I returned my attention to the goddess in front of me. I switched tits and continued my assault. Dev lowered his hands, finding the fabric between us, and pulled her dress down over her hips. I moved my legs and the dress floated to the floor around our feet.

She stood there, naked except for a pair of lacy black knickers and black high heels.

She was a fucking vision.

A strangled groan came from Dev. His eyes glued to her ass, he rubbed his hands up and down her sides.

"Oh God," Sky whispered. Her eyes were closed, her face flushed. She released Dev's neck, and as her legs were trembling, I led her to the bed.

"Have a seat, love."

Once she was sitting on the mattress, I kicked off my shoes, shed my shirt, and shucked my jeans, then my boxers. Completely naked, I stood between her parted thighs. Dev climbed up and sat behind her, in only his briefs, his long bare legs alongside hers. I quivered seeing my cock so close to Dev's mouth.

Good girl that she was, Sky took me in hand. I moaned. "Like that, do you?" she asked, a sassy lilt to her voice.

I looked at her, at Dev right behind her, his face next to hers. Both of them with dilated pupils and reddened cheekbones. I fucking wanted them both, but since there was only one I had the right to touch, I laid my hand on Sky's cheek and pushed my thumb into her mouth. When she sucked on it, I smiled. "What I'd like even more is to feed you my cock."

Sky purred like a sex kitten and opened her mouth.

I replaced my thumb with my cock. Her plump lips closed around my cockhead as it rested on the flat of her tongue. She kept her eyes locked with mine and pressed the tip of her tongue into my slit, moaning at the taste, making me groan in return.

"You are such a dirty girl," I managed to ground out.

She released me and laughed. "You wouldn't want me any other way."

"Ain't that the truth." She opened for me again and I rocked my hips, pushing my cock into that hot mouth, that mouth that opened wide so I could sink to the back of it. She gagged, but held me firmly in place with her arms around my hips. Her eyes watered. Still she kept me there. Finally, her throat relaxed, and I slid in a little farther.

My eyes rolled back. The fluttery sensation of her throat pulsing around my cock was hot and addictive. I was going to fucking come if she didn't stop.

"Fuck, Sky," I said on a groan that seemed torn from the depths of my soul.

I pushed gently on her shoulders until she let me go. "Give Dev a try?" I said to afford myself a bit of a break. If I came now, I'd be out of the action for a while, and I didn't want that.

Dev stared at my cock. It was hard and wet and red and only inches away from him. What was he thinking? Did he find it attractive or repulsive?

He raised his head. That burning brown gaze rooted me in place. Dev wanted me. I knew it sure as I knew my own fucking name.

Don't touch him!

The reminder came not a moment too soon. I dropped my raised hand onto Sky's shoulder. She looked up at me in sympathy. Fuck.

We had an arrangement, Sky and I. She would help me get Dev so that she could keep her job, and although she hadn't mentioned the bonus she'd be getting, the one I was paying for even if she didn't know that, it had to also be weighing on her. Having come from nothing myself, I knew how far one million pounds could go.

When Dev lowered his lips back to Sky's shoulder, I nodded to her, an infinitesimally small incline of my chin. She'd told me to follow her lead, and since my way hadn't worked for shit, I'd be at her command like a well-trained dog.

I needed this to work, more than I needed air to breathe.

Smiling like a jezebel, Sky laid a hand on Dev's cheek. "There's something I'd like to try if you boys are game."

Dev raised his head, and the desire in his deep brown eyes sucked me in, kicked me in the bollocks. Christ, I wanted him. "What do you have in mind?" he asked softly.

Her lips curved even more, and her voice turned sultry. "It's something I wanted to try in Palm Springs. I guess we never got around to it."

Because you ran off.

The response flashed in my head like a tacky neon sign, and a spark of anger flared in my stomach. Its appearance shocked me. Why was I angry about that? I hadn't been at the time. Or maybe I've been too let down by Dev's reaction and his subsequent denial of our intimate moment together to even let myself feel anything about Sky's abrupt departure.

I could feel it now though, if I were being honest. It had hurt. And yes, there was anger. But was it because I'd lost Dev after coming so close to finally having him, or was it something more?

I watched Sky and Dev intently as she lured him into her web. I had an idea of what she was planning, and I was all in.

Dev licked his puffy lips. They glistened tantalizingly. His gaze flicked to mine, then back to hers. "Tell us."

"I, um…" Her cheeks pinked up. She really was quite a beauty, especially like this: nude, her tender skin reflecting the soft lights, aroused, her nipples hard as diamonds, and her pussy wet and eager.

"Go on, love," I said quietly.

She nodded. Inhaled. "Okay, I want to take you both… at the same time."

"Front and back?" I asked. "Or—"

"Front and back. Yes."

Her pallor at the possibility of "or" made me laugh.

Her bottom lip pushed out into a pout and she crossed her arms beneath her tits, which pushed them up deliciously. "Well, if you aren't interested—"

"Oh, I'm interested all right." I stroked her long dark hair, then shifted my gaze to Dev. "Dev?" The heat hadn't left his eyes, but it was now mixed with something else—intrigue? Excitement? Trepidation? I honestly wasn't certain what it was.

Surprising me completely, he flattened his tongue on top of Sky's shoulder and licked a broad path up to her ear. "I'm very interested as well," he whispered loudly enough for me to hear.

Sky shivered. I knew exactly how she felt.

"We should talk about… um… positions," she said.

I raised a brow at Dev. "You choose, mate." He'd seemed to enjoy running the show last time. And I wanted him to be utterly comfortable with what we were going to do, because there would be a lot of contact involved.

Our gazes connected and held. I couldn't have looked away from all that smoldering passion even if my life had depended upon it. And in a way it did.

Dev smirked. He raised his heels onto the mattress, slipped his briefs off his legs, and scooted himself back into the middle of the bed. He gripped his long cock and gave a couple of languorous pulls. Christ. Seeing Dev like this was going to make me come. He closed his eyes and moaned softly before reaching for a condom packet on the dresser. Vanessa had really thought of everything.

Sky and I were riveted to the action taking place in the center of the bed. My cock ached, it was so hard, and I could hear Sky's rapid breaths. There was a catch in her throat when Dev held his hand out to her. "Come on, sweets. Climb on."

To say that I was shocked by his choice would be a gross understatement. Arranged like this, the man lying on the bed was in a submissive position. I'd never have imagined Dev making himself vulnerable to me in this way. Even though I'd often dreamed of it.

I assisted Sky onto the bed. My mouth watering, I watched her straddle

Dev's hips. He fondled her tits while she palmed his cock and held it straight up. And then she took him into her wet pussy, into her hot body. I listened to her gasps as she sank down onto his lap. I listened to his groans as he filled her to the brim.

I listened to myself moan at the beauty of their joining. How I wanted to be a part of it. Of them.

On cue, as though they'd both agreed on it, Sky and Dev turned their flushed faces and bright eyes toward me.

"You coming, mate?" Dev asked.

Yes, I was coming. Christ. I stepped around the bed to get a condom, squeezing the base of my cock to stave off the orgasm that was already making my balls tingle. I took calming breath after calming breath, rolled the condom on, and picked up the lube. Despite this being a little more than a business task for Sky, I did want her to enjoy herself. We'd never even talked about whether or not she'd ever had anal sex. I really was a self-centered bastard. Biting back a snort, I knelt on the bed and crawled up between Dev's legs. I ran my hand up Sky's tense back, along her spine, and back down and over her hip, trying to calm her. She had a fine arse, round and firm. And I wanted in.

I applied some pressure to the middle of her back. "Lie down for me, love."

Dev smiled at her and slid his hands up her sides to her shoulders. "Give us a kiss," he said. His husky voice went straight to my cock. At this rate, I'd have the johnnie filled with pre-cum before I even entered her tight arse.

Sky lowered her chest onto Dev's, and they snogged. It was a little tentative at first, no doubt due to nerves, but soon they seemed ravenous. They moaned and there was quite clearly tongue involved.

Dev's magic relaxed her, but it had the opposite effect on me. I glanced down at the view in front of me. Sky's perfect arse, the pale cheeks and pink hole, and Dev's hairy thighs, his heavy balls cushioning Sky's pussy. He stroked her hips and flashed me his cock.

His hole was only a few inches lower, hidden from my view between his cheeks. I felt faint at the notion that my cock was a few mere inches from Dev's hole. From nirvana. I started to shake. A few beads of sweat rolled down the sides of my face. I wanted to be inside him, but not like this. Never without his permission.

There was someone else who had given me permission. Someone else whose arse awaited my cock to fill it.

I squirted some lube on my hand and gently spread it around that pink bud. At my first touch, Sky jolted, but then she settled down. She moaned and pushed against my finger. Dev stopped moving. He held Sky close to him and murmured in her ear. His eyes were on me.

Burning into me.

I squeezed a little more lube and pushed it into Sky's hole, following it with my finger up to the knuckle. She tensed and a soft groan escaped her tightly compressed lips. Dev stroked her back lovingly. "That's it, sweets. Take Rod's fingers. That's a good girl."

She let out a shuddery breath. Her muscles relaxed, and my finger slid in all the way. The suction was intense, and I couldn't wait to have all that heat and tightness gripping my cock.

I added a second finger, gently thrusting them into her. I could feel Dev's hardness inside her. God. My head spun. This was as close as I'd ever come to touching Dev's cock. Only a thin membrane separated him from my fingers.

Sky moaned. Her back arched like a cat's. "More," she said. Her raspy voice ran over me like a rough tongue.

I pulled my fingers out of her. Her ass chased them. "Soon, love," I soothed her. I pressed three fingers inside and she tensed with a hiss. It was tight. So bloody tight. And Dev's cock was so bloody hard. I turned my hand slowly and pressed the pads of my fingers against her inner walls as I pumped into her.

Dev groaned and thrust his hips. Sky shuddered. The ripple started deep inside and rolled throughout her body, leaving her covered in gooseflesh.

It was time.

I removed my fingers, wiped them on the bed sheets, and crawled closer. My hands on Sky's hips, I asked, "Ready?"

"Yes!" They both answered in unison. I'd have laughed, but I was too far gone.

Delirious with lust, I brought the crown of my cock to her sweetly glistening hole and pushed it inside, slowly and steadily.

"Oh Jesus. There's so much pressure." Sky groaned.

Once the entire crown was inside her, I stopped moving and rubbed her back. "That's it, love, let your body soften. It will feel good soon."

Dev cupped her face in his hands and raised her head up. He looked into her eyes. "But if it doesn't, you tell us. We'll stop straight away. Okay?"

Her head bobbed. "Okay."

A few moments later, she arched her back. "Oh!"

Yeah, that was what I'd been waiting for. The burning sensation and the pressure must be shifting into something else. She rounded her back, her face buried against Dev's neck. Then she arched it again and pushed back. I let her have control as she impaled herself on my cock, only lending her the steadying support of my hands on her waist.

When I was all the way in, she glared at me over her shoulder. "Move, damn you."

I smacked a beckoning arse cheek. "Demanding wench."

Her moan sizzled through me. Fuck, I wanted to come, but I wanted this more. Thinking of England, I pulled out almost all the way, then slammed back in. I wasn't sure who groaned the loudest. They probably heard us all the way back at the Hideaway Resort.

Dev's hands rubbed down Sky's back. He opened his bent legs wider and pushed down on her arse. When he pulled back, I pushed in. Each time one of us moved, I could feel Dev, his hot cock along the entire length of mine. I could also feel Sky. Her heat surrounded me, her tightness gripped me, and her excited moans seared themselves into my memory.

I could never repay her for this experience, the utter joy she was giving me. Holding on to Sky's waist, I thrust into her, moving slow and steady, unrelenting. Her lithe body quaked under my hands. She writhed and wriggled her ass, her moans mingling with Dev's groans and my strangled gasps. His hips pumped into her, small strokes in counterpoint to mine.

This was heaven.

This was hell.

This was everything.

DEV

Sky screamed and her body shook in my arms, the waves of her release cascading over her. Her tight little cunt gripped me like a fist, pushing me to the edge. It was all I could do not to topple over along with her. I kept my gaze on her face, on the slight whisker-burn on her chin, on her gaping mouth, her closed lids with the lashes brushing her prettily flushed cheeks. She was stunning.

She opened her eyes, brown pools of ecstasy. Aftershocks continued to pulse through her body. Her grip on my shoulders tightened, her hips bucked forward and back a final time, and then she stilled.

I smiled.

"Shut up," she murmured, collapsing onto my chest.

I brushed several long curls off her cheeks so I could see her expression, that post-orgasmic haze that I'd have set to paper had I the talent to do it.

This was the look I'd kept in my heart all those months she'd been gone. I loved seeing her so relaxed and sated. I'd have loved to see that expression on her face every day.

My gaze shifted to Rod looking so beautiful, a Greek god kneeling before a bountiful feast. The skin on his cheeks was tight, flushed. His pupils blown, his blue eyes hazy with unfulfilled lust. Like me, he was still hard, buried inside Sky's tight little body. My gaze snagged his and I felt him tremble, felt him throb deep inside her, where we almost touched.

My cock jumped at the knowledge of Rod so close. Every time he moved, even the smallest amount, I felt it. It was so close to the fantasy I'd had last night.

I was a bundle of emotions. Being with Sky again was even better than it had been in Palm Springs, but being with her at the same time as Rod, well... there was something indescribable about it. Something decadent, like eating a cream-smothered pastry. But like the chocolate-iced chocolate cake Rod loved so much, would it get old quickly? Was this threesome adventure something Rod would tire of before Sky and I did? He'd always moved from partner to partner, rarely staying with the same person—or people—for more than a night.

I stretched my legs a little, bringing them in. My foot touched Rod's. He stilled, eyes blazing.

I might not be able to have him. Fuck, I knew I couldn't, but maybe tonight, here in this safe place with Rod and Sky, I could have a taste of chocolate-iced chocolate cake.

I rocked my hips, eager to chase my release now that Sky had had hers, eager to help Rod chase his as well.

Sky moaned, and it was not the pleasure-filled kind.

"Ow." She moaned again.

I froze, as did Rod.

"Sweets?" I said, smoothing down her hair with my hand. "What's wrong? Did we hurt you?"

She pushed herself up with her arms and blew out a breath. "It's just that, um..." She cast her eyes downward, suddenly shy. That bit of vulnerability shredded my heart.

"It's okay," I said, kissing the tip of her nose.

Rod pulled out slowly, and Sky seemed to relax. She lifted her hips off me and tumbled onto the bed next to me.

"I'm sorry, guys. I'm just so... yeah. I can't keep going. I came and now..."

"You aren't feeling it anymore?" I suggested.

She nodded.

Rod asked me for a tissue, then pulled off his condom before lowering himself to hover above her. He kissed her gently. "No worries, love. A lot of girls find double penetration too awkward or painful after they've orgasmed. We'll know for next time." He winked at her.

She giggled. Her hand snuck between their bodies, and when it closed around Rod's cock, he hissed and closed his eyes.

"I can still help you guys out," she said, her eyes going to me. She raised her brows in a questioning manner. She repeated this action insistently several times.

What exactly was she asking me? My gaze drifted back down their bodies to where she fisted Rod's cock, slowly stroking him. His hips moved languidly, his eyes closed. He was so beautiful like this. I wanted to touch him. Really touch him, without anything between us.

Rod made a sound, a small gasp. A groan.

I looked at Sky. She raised her brows again.

This might be my only opportunity. I had to try. I cleared my throat. "Rod…" It seemed to take hours for him to turn his head in my direction, to open his eyes, but when he did, I was trapped by the intense focus he turned on me. Was it just the need to come or was it something more?

I knew Rod wanted me. He'd said it often enough. But to see it, so clearly, so unequivocally, made up my mind for me.

I was going to have a taste of that bloody chocolate-iced chocolate cake.

"Allow me?" I asked. Heat immediately seared my face, but I forged on. I studiously kept my gaze on his, refusing to let it rove lower.

Rod's eyes widened, and he made a choked sound. "You want to—?"

"Yes, if I may?"

Rod pushed himself up into a sitting position. He swallowed, and if I wasn't mistaken, he seemed a bit nervous suddenly. "How… how do you want me?"

I patted the bed. "Lie down."

Rod practically threw himself into the small space between me and Sky. He lay on his side facing me. I couldn't meet his eyes. Instead, I slowly let myself look at his body, get my fill of his shoulders, the hair on his chest and arms that was both lighter in color and amount than mine, if I didn't shave my chest. He had just the right amount of chest hair to leave it natural, not like the Austin Powers rug I had. Okay, it wasn't that bad, but it was more than I liked.

I followed the trail of light brown hair over his abdomen, more defined than you'd expect from someone who partied as much as Rod did. Few people knew he spent hours each day in the gym lifting weights or running on the treadmill. He had to, or he wouldn't be able to perform the way he did onstage.

My gaze slid over his nooks and crannies, bumping along the V-shaped line of his obliques, and down his treasure trail to the nest of dark curls that circled his erection. His cock stood hard and proud.

On instinct, I reached for it. Touched the tip with the pad of my index finger. Rod sucked in a breath. He tracked my every move, but said not a word. A bead of pre-cum pooled in his slit. It called to me. I dragged my finger into it and smeared the slick liquid over the smooth crown. His flesh felt like mine, but it was lighter in color. Redder.

The reality of the situation hit me then; I was touching Rod's cock.

Taking a deep breath, I curled my fingers around his shaft. Did he enjoy a tight hold or a light one? Though I'd watched him jerk off that day in our bungalow, and before when we were teens, I'd been too shy, too caught up in the illicit nature of the moment to give his technique the attention it deserved. How did he like to be touched? As well as I knew Rod, I didn't know that.

I ran my fingers over the head of his cock to slick them with pre-cum, then I returned to his shaft and stroked him. My movements were tentative at first. I let myself savor the moment. The silky-smooth feel of his skin, tight at the head, veiny toward the root, the sensation of his pubic hair tickling my pinky finger and the side of my palm. Most of all, I memorized the length, the girth, and the heat of him.

My movements accelerated. I tightened my grip. Rod moaned, and my gaze shot to his face. Was I doing it right, or was I hurting him?

His lids appeared half closed but only because his gaze was locked on my hand, tightly curled around his cock.

"Faster," he murmured, and the hoarseness of his voice, the rawness of his need, almost had me coming. Pre-cum dribbled onto my thigh.

I was enjoying this.

Why it felt like a revelation I had no idea. I'd tried so damn hard to never allow myself to think about men, about loving a man, about Rod, but one couldn't escape one's dreams, the idle fantasies I'd been having more and more since this trip had started. Since that week we'd spent together in Palm Springs.

The scent of his sweat, clean and manly, mixed with the scent of sex in the air was an aphrodisiac more powerful than anything that could be manufactured in a lab.

Rod was a drug, and right now he was mine.

I held his essence in my palm, and I wanted to see it spill. I jerked him faster, tightened my grasp, and flicked my thumb over his darkening crown every few strokes. Rod's moans became louder, more frequent. His eyes rose to my face and held my gaze. They looked like the ocean, like sapphires, dark jewels in an alabaster face. But they weren't cool like stones.

They were hot. So hot I feared I'd be left a mess of blisters. Rod thrust his hips, began fucking my fist. I imagined, for a moment, that he was fucking me. I knew that's what he was imagining too. I could see it on his face. His jaw dropped open. His eyes rolled back and closed, and then warmth spilled onto my hand.

I watched as ribbons of cum, white and creamy, shot toward my stomach.

I gasped as it landed on my abdomen, a few drops rolling down to be lost in my pubic hair. I stared at it amazed, confused, elated, and lost. Rod's cum was on my skin, in my hair. What should I do?

Hearing Rod's throaty chuckle, I shivered. He smiled, a crooked smile that made me want to lick his lips, suck them into my mouth, and sink my teeth into them. He looked down at my stomach, at his mess on me. "May I?" he asked, echoing my earlier words.

Fully expecting he was offering to fetch a flannel from the toilet, I almost had a heart attack when he slid farther down the bed and licked a dollop of cum off my stomach. I made a strangled sound somewhere between a gasp and a moan.

Sky scooted over into the space Rod had vacated and curled her arms around my head. "Let Rod take care of you, Dev." She smiled. "You want him to, don't you?"

Of course, I did. The thought of Rod's mouth around my cock was so sinful, so honest, so much what I wanted that I'd never fully let myself imagine it. But those dreams, those bloody fantasies that had been rolling through my head...

I looked down my body to Rod, who lay alongside my legs, his head held rigid above my groin, poised for action. His gaze was hungry. Ravenous despite the fact he'd just come.

I wanted this.

And maybe I could do it for us both.

I nodded. Rod's face split into an enormous grin.

The retort I'd intended to speak aloud got stuck in my throat when his flat tongue licked up the underside of my cock like it was an ice lolly on a blistering summer day. He smacked his lips together. "Mmm... I always knew you'd taste like sin."

Before I could catch my breath, he opened his mouth wide and swallowed me whole.

"Oh fuck," I whispered hoarsely. There was no air left in my lungs, no rational thought left in my head.

My world was my cock.

And Rod's mouth.

Rod's mouth on my cock.

That was all that mattered. He lifted his head, looked up at me, then lowered it again, going lower still, taking more of me each time. His lips were around the root of me, his throat pulsing around my crown.

"Bloody hell!" I shouted as his throat fluttered brilliantly. I'd never had a blow job like this before. It was magical. Priceless. Rod was the king of cocksuckers. "You're fucking ace at this..."

I'd wanted to call him "mate" like I always did, but somehow it seemed wrong. Rod wasn't a mate like Mick or Tommy or Jules or Damon.

I closed my eyes. No, he was so much more than that. I *wanted* him to be more. It just wasn't possible.

We did have right now though. And if this was to be my only time experiencing the incredible reality of having Rod's mouth on me, I was going to give it my full attention so I could replay every exquisite detail in my mind for years to come. These moments would have to suffice me for a lifetime.

I began to roll my hips. Rod stilled. I felt his lips smile around my shaft. His tongue licked around my crown, and I almost came.

Sucking in a breath, I grabbed onto Rod's head, let my fingers dig into his hair, into his scalp. He blinked at me.

"Thank you," I murmured before I let loose.

I fucked his mouth, driving my cock into it as though if I could get in deep enough, I could remain there, in some kind of limbo where Rod and I would always be together.

I slammed my hips harder. My cock hit the back of his throat, making him gag. His eyes watered, but he didn't pull back, so I kept going. His hand cradled my balls, gently rolling them between his fingers, in sharp contrast to what I was doing to his mouth.

I slowed down, pulled back a bit. Let him breathe. I filled my own lungs, then he took me in again. This time, I kept the pace slower. Kept the frenzy-bordering-on-panic at bay. He was making me feel too much, more than I could handle. It wasn't his fault I was weak. He wasn't the one I needed to punish. I relaxed my grip on his hair, but I didn't release it. I enjoyed it too much, and if the flare in Rod's eyes each time I gave an involuntary tug on it was any indication, he enjoyed it too.

All too soon, the pressure in my cock and the tingling in my balls erupted, and so did I. My body convulsed as I shot my cum into Rod's hot, greedy mouth. He swallowed, his eyes going soft, and his deep moan vibrated through my groin.

When I was calm again, he licked my prick until it lay flaccid along my thigh.

"That was fucking brilliant," I said, because I had to say something and because it had been fucking brilliant.

"Yeah?" he asked as he levered himself up onto his knees. He seemed unsure of himself, as though he'd shed his confidence like a cloak.

I smiled. I could feel my walls building back up. But still I smiled. "Yeah."

He dropped down onto the other side of Sky, spooning her. He whispered something in her ear. She smiled and wrapped her arm over his. They looked so beautiful together, but then again, Sky always looked bloody gorgeous.

I rolled over onto my side facing her. A few curls had fallen onto her forehead, and I brushed them aside with my thumb, cradling her jaw in my palm. She leaned into it, smiling sleepily. She'd made this happen for me. Rod was talking to me again, because Sky had made it happen. I owed her so much. I loved her for that, and for so much more.

In Palm Springs, I'd told her I loved her, and I'd meant it. I still meant it. And even though she might not believe me, I had to tell her again. Rod and I weren't a possibility, but Sky and I could be.

I moved closer to her and pressed my lips to hers in a tender kiss. I hoped she could feel everything I was trying to say with it, the thanks, the hope, the adoration. After several long minutes of lazy snogging, I released her lips. "I love you, Sky."

Her eyes rounded in surprise.

I chuckled. "I know you didn't believe me when I told you before, but it was true then, and it's true now."

She looked at me warily, a hint of tension in her shoulders. "Dev—"

"Shh," I said, placing a finger on her lips. "I just wanted you to know." I looked at Rod over her shoulder. His eyes were closed. The bastard was knackered.

I smiled and settled my hand on her hip. "Sleep, sweets."

When she continued to stare at me wide-eyed, I began to hum. Some words came to me then. Words that had never been more true. Words that were meant for both people sharing the bed with me tonight. I sang them softly.

You own my life,
You are my heart.

Chapter 7

DEV

Stoked from the incredible night with Sky and Rod, I strode into the rehearsal space ready to see King's Cross make magic. Damon, Tommy, Mick, and Jules were there, noodling around with their instruments.

But Rod wasn't here. And he hadn't been in our room either when I'd gone there to shower and change.

He'd left me and Sky in the treetop bungalow, just after dawn, and I'd thought nothing of it. Just Rod being Rod, or maybe it was just him wanting some space, a little break.

Rod had never been known for his punctuality, but he was usually on time when it came to the music, especially when things were going well between us. They were certainly going well now, right?

So why did I feel so on edge?

He'd gone quiet last night after we'd made love to Sky. After I'd touched him. After he'd taken me in his mouth... My heart started pounding again, just thinking of it, and my cock woke up. The whole night, the three of us, the sensation of both our cocks inside Sky at the same time... A shudder ran through me.

Fuck. I wanted to do it again. All of it. I didn't know how much further I could go with Rod, but maybe what we'd done was enough to make us both happy... And enough to keep me from feeling like I'd betrayed my family.

I picked up my Taylor and started working on a chord progression for a song I had in mind. Damon walked over, studying my fingering.

"Damn, you're amazing," he said.

I blushed. "I'm no Hendrix. Or Clapton."

Damon scoffed. "You're a lot better than ninety percent of the guitarists out there."

I kept my eyes on the strings. "Thanks, but I still think you're being generous."

Sky walked in, followed by Daniel. But Rod wasn't with them. I glanced at the clock on the wall. Fuck. He was at least thirty minutes late. I took out my phone, sent him a text. "Where r u?"

I waited, but no response came. My stomach tightened. Something was wrong; I could feel it.

Sky came over to me. I let my eyes travel up her long tanned legs to the hem of her sundress. It was a pale pink with large blue flowers on it, and it suited her so perfectly I wanted to remember this moment forever.

"Where's Rod?" she asked.

I shrugged. "I've texted him, but he's not responded."

She pursed her lips. "Where did he go this morning?"

Again I shrugged.

Daniel came over. He didn't look happy. "Is Rod ill?"

"Don't think so."

"Then where is he?" Daniel asked.

"That's the twenty-five-thousand-dollar question," Sky said and crossed her arms.

Daniel gave her a meaningful look, one that said he was sick of our shit.

I didn't blame him. I was sick of it too. I thought we'd fixed things, or at least had started to. And then off Rod went again, for no reason I could discern.

"I'll find him," Sky said.

"After you and I talk," Daniel muttered, and part of me bristled at his tone. This wasn't Sky's fault. Rod and I needed to work out our issues ourselves.

Or rather, I needed to work out my issues. And I had a critical decision to make.

Did I stay and fight for the band I loved, or did I walk away?

The two of them left, and I tried to focus on the song again. But all I heard in my head was *coward, coward, coward.*

It wasn't just the band I had to decide to fight for.

One thing at a time, right? If Rod and I couldn't work things out, I at least had to leave him a working band.

Taylor in hand, I walked over to the others. "Rod's not feeling well, so we're on our own today."

"You can sing then," Damon said.

I huffed. "Not on your life."

"Why not? You could be the front man," Damon said. "You've got the voice and the looks for it."

"It can't be anyone but Rod."

"Why not?"

I looked over at Tommy, Jules, and Mick. "Explain to Damon why Rod is the face of the band."

Tommy spoke up. "Because he sings the best."

"Yes. But that's not all it is."

"What else, then?" Mick asked.

For fuck's sake. Were they blind? "The way he looks. The way he moves. He's hot. Fuckable."

Tommy snorted. "He is?"

Heat raced up my neck. "Surely you all know this." I racked my brain for a comparison. "What about Chris Hemsworth? I think we can all agree that he's fuckable."

Damon waggled his eyebrows. "Well, for Chris, maybe I'd bend over."

"See?" I said, looking at Tommy. He looked blank. Jules and Mick were more of the same. "Seriously? You don't see it?" Three heads shook in unison.

I looked to Damon, and he gave me a thorough up and down. "You know, *you* look pretty fuckable to me."

The heat spread from my neck over my face. "No one wants to see a band with an Indian front man. Besides, my parents would lose their shit if I had any more visibility."

Damon's brow wrinkled. "Are you kidding me? They aren't proud of you?"

Mick enlightened him. "He was supposed to be Dr. Prakesh."

Damon whistled. "No shit."

"I dropped out of med school."

"Still… you had to bust your ass to get in."

True, but that was irrelevant. "It doesn't matter that I tried to do what they wanted. The point is, I failed to do it in the end."

"Failed? Don't they know how hard it is for a band to make it to the top of the charts? Don't they get how famous you are?"

I smiled, but it was bitter. "Oh, they're well aware. They still think I'm an embarrassment."

Damon stared at me open-mouthed, then finally snapped his jaw shut. "Well, if you won't take the mic, I guess I will."

I nodded. "Thank you."

He started to say something, then clammed up, which I didn't think he was capable of. But apparently even Damon had his limits.

"What?" I asked.

He glanced at me, then away. "I have some songs I've written. If you want to hear them."

For a second, anger flared in me, then I tamped it down. I wanted to say that Rod and I wrote the songs, that we didn't need his help.

But if I left, Rod was going to need a new writing partner.

A weight settled in my stomach, like I'd swallowed a stone.

If I left…

Fuck. I didn't want to.

But if I had to—

I cleared my throat, pasted on a smile. "Let's hear them, mate."

A grin broke out on Damon's face. "Okay. This one is called 'Bleeding.'" He launched into a midtempo song that was soon speeding along, his voice rough as he sang about the person who'd shredded his heart.

Was that how Rod would feel if I left?

But if we couldn't repair things, what other choice did I have?

Damon was good at what he did. He was even a decent singer. I was sure Rod could file the rough edges off the lyrics and with some tweaks, we could make the song work for the album.

We.

The word slapped me in the face.

Rod and I had been a team forever. The month before we'd come to Tahiti had felt barren to me without Rod in it.

Was I really considering a lifetime of that? A lifetime of not talking to my best mate? Of not seeing him every day?

Of never sharing the stage again, never writing a song together again, never sharing that high when we knew we'd written a hit?

Fuck.

If he couldn't accept what I had to offer, that was it for us.

The only bright spot in all this was Sky. I could see myself with her forever, see our little golden-skinned kids racing around…

The stone in my gut grew heavier. Mum and Dad would have a fit if I didn't marry a nice Indian girl of their choosing.

But how could I marry anyone but Sky?

They'd just have to accept it. Sky would be my price for giving up the band, giving up my music.

Giving up Rod.

Damon brought the song to a close and gave me an expectant look. "What do you think?"

I'd barely heard the last third of it. "We can work with it." I tried to put more enthusiasm into my voice. "Nice work."

I gave him a smile I absolutely did not feel and glanced at the clock.

Rod was never this late for a session he intended to make. And my phone hadn't vibrated with an incoming text.

Something was definitely wrong.

How many times were we going to fly apart before we finally split for good?

SKY

Like a naughty schoolgirl following the principal to his office, I slinked behind Daniel to the suite where he'd set up his temporary residence. On the top floor of the building housing the rest of the TI staff, the King's Cross roadies, and Nigel, Daniel's suite was larger and swankier than the bungalows where the band and I were staying. Hell, with two rooms, a large dining room/living room combo, and a small kitchen, it was bigger than my apartment back in Berkeley.

Daniel led me to the second room, which had been turned into an office for him. He sat in the leather chair and folded his hands on the chrome and glass desk. His eyes burned into me as I took a seat across from him.

I crossed my legs and adjusted the skirt of my sundress while I waited for him to get to the point, although I already knew what was on his mind. Rod. The gorgeous rock star was on my mind too.

Daniel leaned back in the chair, its leather creaking loudly in the quiet room. "What's going on, Sky? Why wasn't Rod at rehearsal this morning?"

"I don't know," I said in all honesty. After last night, I'd expected him to be on cloud nine, but when Dev and I had woken up this morning, he was already gone. He'd arranged for a car to bring us back to the Hideaway Resort, but I hadn't been able to find him. I didn't even know if he had come back himself.

Daniel's jaw jumped visibly. "You told me yesterday that things were fixed, or at least getting there."

"And I thought that was the case, right up until he didn't show for rehearsal. We had a long... um... talk last night." My face heated. "Rod and Dev seemed to be getting along." I raised my hands, then dropped them into my lap. "I don't know what went wrong."

"A talk, huh?"

I closed my eyes. This was why I preferred to work alone. I didn't like answering to anyone. I rubbed my temple. This was only temporary though. A necessary evil. If all went well, Daniel would become my partner, as would Javier and Arianna. Opening my eyes, I glared at him. It was time I showed Daniel that I was no pushover. He wouldn't make me feel guilty about what I'd done, at least not without shouldering some of the responsibility as well. "You know it wasn't."

"I don't know any such thing." He returned my glare. "As CEO of Total Indulgence Tours, I *can't* know any such thing." He pushed his chair back with his foot, turning it a bit to the left, then to the right. He rubbed his jaw and looked up at the ceiling. "I shouldn't have agreed to this."

"Then why did you?" I snapped.

"You told me you had a personal relationship with Rod and Dev. That you could fix this. Rod asked for you specifically, after all."

Fighting the blush that threatened to engulf my entire body, I continued. "I don't know what happened. They were fine last night. All I know is that I want this partnership, and I'm going to make it happen."

Daniel abandoned his laid-back pose and leaned his elbows on the desk, his fingers pressed to his mouth. "Are you sleeping with Rod or Dev?"

I looked down at my lap and picked at an imaginary piece of lint on my dress. "Both," I whispered.

"Fuck, Sky." Daniel exploded out of his chair and paced the narrow width in front of the window. He raked a hand through his hair. "Maybe Rod didn't show up today because he's pissed, jealous that you slept with Dev."

"It's—it's not like that," I stammered.

"What then? Is he mad because you're playing them against each other?"

I looked at a spot over his shoulder. "No."

Daniel stopped in his pacing and looked at me. His bewildered expression almost made me smile. Almost. "They *know* you're sleeping with both of them... and they're okay with it?"

I swallowed, my mouth suddenly dry. "Yes." Okay, Dev hadn't been happy about it at first, but last night he'd obviously been very okay with it.

Daniel's eyes didn't leave my face for the longest time, then he blew out a breath and dropped back into his chair. The leather complained loudly. "You're all together. A threesome."

"Yes."

"Jesus. Is there something in the TI water bottles?" he muttered while scrubbing his face with both hands.

"What does that mean?"

"Nothing." He waved it off. "Look, Sky. I didn't think you were going to sleep with them. If I'd known—"

I cut him off. "You knew. I told you I'd do whatever needed doing."

"I thought you were going to flirt with them, cajole them into it. I never thought you'd use your body as a—"

"Bridge?"

"—bargaining chip. But it seems like you have other thoughts on the matter."

"No." I shook my head so violently my hair swung into my face. I swiped at my cheek with the palm of my hand to brush it back. "This is business."

Daniel's face darkened, and his jaw tightened. "I'm not a fucking pimp. If you're going to be this mercenary about it, I'm not sure we should be in business together."

My stomach dropped. "What?"

"I've offered you fifteen percent of TI. My partners and I have a lot riding on this deal. The reputation of our business. Shit." He rested his head on the back of the chair. "This company has been our lives for years. I've known you for what? A minute? I can't let you destroy what we've worked so hard to achieve."

My stomach churned with anger and hurt... with defeat. Hadn't I known from the start that this was stupid? That it was wrong to use sex to get what I wanted?

What was I trying to accomplish? Had I really slept with Rod and Dev for that fifteen percent of TI? If that were truly the case, then Daniel was right. I had no place at TI.

But were the partnership at TI and the bonus the real reasons I'd taken the job, or was it that I couldn't give up the chance to see Rod and Dev again? That I couldn't give up the chance to talk to them again? Kiss them again? Feel them inside me again?

My eyes filled with tears. I wrapped my arms around my waist and slumped over my crossed legs. "I have feelings for them. I always have." A sob escaped my throat.

"And now you're in love with them," Daniel said softly.

I wiped at my wet cheeks and sat up straight. "But I *can't* be."

"Why not?" Daniel eyed me curiously. "If they both want you, and you want them..."

"They want each other." The truth of my words stabbed me in the heart. I wanted to throw myself onto the floor, sink into the plush carpeting, and disappear forever. Anything to end this pain.

"Ah... I didn't know Dev was bisexual." Sympathy softened Daniel's expression. "Where does that leave you in all of this?"

"Dev has a hard time accepting that aspect of his sexuality. As for me"—I shrugged—"I'm the bridge between them. That's all I've ever been."

Daniel picked up a box of tissues and handed it to me. Giving him a watery smile, I plucked a few from the box and blew my nose.

When I was done, Daniel smiled gently. "I think you're right—and you're wrong. I've seen how they look at you. Have you tried telling them how you feel? Do they know about our agreement? The partnership and bonus?"

"I can't tell them yet." I grabbed another tissue and dabbed at my eyes. "I'll tell them when they're solid. When I know they'll have each other."

Daniel walked around to the front of his desk and leaned against the edge. "I think…" He waited until I looked up. Then he tilted his head forward a little and narrowed his eyes. "You need to come clean with them, now."

He was the judge; his words were the gavel. My sentence was clear.

I swallowed and nodded. I would tell them. As soon as I could, and I would bear the brunt of my punishment.

Even if it meant I would never see them again.

SKY

I pulled myself together and went looking for Rod. He wasn't in his bungalow, he wasn't in the canteen, he wasn't in the pool. I finally found him nursing a beer amid the hut that Dev had built, the one that Rod had never worked on. He looked up at my approach and gave me a weak smile.

I sat down on the log next to him. "You didn't come to rehearsal."

He took a swig of his beer and nodded, but didn't say a word.

"Why not?"

He kept his eyes fixed on his bare feet burrowing into the soft white sand. "It's always one step forward, twenty steps back with him."

I touched his arm. "What do you mean?"

"Come on, Sky. You're not thickheaded."

I reviewed the night in my head, the way they'd touched, the way I'd felt during and after, the things we'd said…

And then it struck me.

Dev had told me he loved me.

But he hadn't said the same to Rod.

I took Rod's free hand in both of mine. "It's what Dev said to me, isn't it?"

He tipped the beer in my direction. "Give the girl a prize."

"But that doesn't mean he doesn't love you."

It didn't mean Dev loved me either. It had been nice to hear, but I didn't see how it was possible, not really.

Dev loved Rod; a fool could see it.

Dev didn't even know me.

Rod blew out a breath, his head hanging between his shoulders. "He won't let himself love me. He won't. Nothing's changed."

"Rod, he's trying. He just needs to go slow."

Rod shook his head. "Fact is, I'm not sure I deserve it. Not sure I'm capable of it myself."

"Why do you say that?"

"You're my longest relationship, Sky. Aside from whatever it is I have with Dev. And look how I fucked things up between you and me."

"It's not your fault—"

He shook his head. "Oh, it is. You were right. I used you to try to get Dev. I was an arsehole. I didn't care what you wanted, what he wanted. All I cared about was myself."

"You *do* care about him."

"Do I?" He pinned me with his blue eyes. "Shouldn't I just leave him be? Shouldn't I just swallow this down and be a big boy and go on with my life?" He drained the beer and placed the bottle between his feet. "If I cared about Dev, shouldn't I let him live his life the way *he* wants it?"

"But he does want you."

"Not enough."

I rubbed Rod's hand, and he looked up at me, his eyes a bit glassy, his nose reddening. He blinked furiously and looked away. When he spoke, his voice was hoarse. "And you—Jesus, Sky, I've been a right shit to you."

I touched his cheek, wishing I could take away his pain. Then I smiled. "You have, but I forgive you." I did my best impression of Rod. "You gobshite."

He laughed and took my hands in his. "I am a gobshite. And I wish I could start over with you."

"Maybe you can," I said, an idea forming. "What if we went on a date?"

He raised an eyebrow. "A date?"

"Yeah. You and me. Spend the day together."

He smiled. "What's your fancy for this date?"

I gestured to the reception area of the resort. "They've got scooters we can rent. We can go over to the Lagoonarium and feed the fish."

"And ditch Tony and everyone else?"

I nodded. The last thing we needed was the others around. And we didn't need Tony if we disguised Rod a bit.

Minutes later, we had our scooter and Rod's disguise: a pair of reflective aviator sunglasses and a ballcap we'd bought off one of the workers at the canteen.

Rod took the wheel of the scooter and I climbed aboard behind him, putting my arms around him. The sundress rode up my thighs, so I tried to tuck it under me. He cupped one of my bare knees, then looked back at me. "Ready for our date?" he asked.

I kissed his cheek. "Let's see what this scooter can do."

We sped along the coast, a warm wind whipping in our hair as Rod expertly guided us to our destination. It was nice being this close to him, touching him, but not in a sexual way. It was weird to realize we'd rarely touched outside of the bedroom.

And we'd never spent time together that wasn't about Dev in some way.

We pulled up to the jumping off point for the Lagoonarium and got off the scooter. We'd be met by Lagoonarium staff who'd ferry us from Moorea out to the tiny island of Motu Ahi just off the coast.

While we waited for someone to greet us, Rod stepped in behind me and pulled me close, putting his arms around my waist. He whispered in my ear. "I'm sorry, Sky. I truly am. I started us off on the wrong foot. And that wasn't fair to you."

A lump rose in my throat. "It's okay."

"No, it's not."

Tears blurred my vision, and I was glad he couldn't see my face. The tears really weren't about him anyway. At least, not entirely. The wreckage of my past reared its head. I'd never received an apology from Blue or Sunshine. They'd made it clear that *I* was the one who had to grow up and learn not to be so possessive, like I was a toddler who couldn't share my toys.

Instead of a woman who'd discovered my best friend and my fiancée fucking behind my back.

The image of the two of them in *my* bed, the bed I'd shared with no one but Blue, made me shudder and a sob lodge in my throat.

Christ, that was eight years ago. You'd think I'd be over it by now. But I wasn't, and this business with Rod and Dev was pouring salt in that wound.

Rod turned me in his arms and took off his sunglasses. Then he clasped me to his chest, cupping my neck in his palm. "Ah, love, you're breaking my heart." His own voice sounded raw. "I don't know how to fix this." He closed his arms tightly around me. "All I know is that I want to."

I pulled in a breath and relaxed against him. He smelled good, like sunshine and sea air, and something spicy that was all his own.

I wiped at my eyes and looked up at him. "It means a lot that you care."

He smoothed the hair out of my face where the wind was whipping it around. "I have a confession to make."

"I'm all ears."

"I know about the bonus."

A chill slid down my spine. "What bonus?"

He smirked. "The million-pound bonus I put up to make sure you took the job."

I stepped back. "What? I thought that was from the label. It was from *you?*"

He nodded. "I wasn't sure why you'd left Palm Springs, but when you didn't answer our calls, I figured you must be upset about something." He looked away for a second. "And I wondered if you'd figured out my agenda."

I stared at him until he looked at me again. He held my eyes. "I needed you to help us, Sky. That's why I put up the bonus. But it's a bit more than that, if I'm to be honest."

Anger flared in my stomach, and I crossed my arms. "Please do."

"I missed you. You're the only person, the only one besides Dev, I want to spend time with."

I scoffed. "Come on, Rod. It's not like there hasn't been a steady stream of people in your bed and in your life."

"In my bed, sure." He caressed my cheeks with his thumbs. "But that's not what I mean. I mean spend time with. Talk to. Hang out." He gestured around us. "Go on a date with. God knows I don't know how to date someone. I've never had to. It's pretty much been 'Fancy a shag?' on my part, and then off we go."

He bent down, his lips inches from mine. "I *want* to know you, Sky. Really know you."

I thought he was going in for a kiss, and I stiffened, not sure I wanted to let him off that easily, but still craving the touch all the same.

But he stepped back and slipped on his sunglasses again, and I realized that a couple vehicles had pulled up and people were piling out. It was close to feeding time, the best time to see the fish at the Lagoonarium.

A small boat motored up to the dock and a staff member waved to us. Rod took my hand. "We'd better get moving."

I followed him, my mind racing, my feet stumbling along.

I want to know you, Sky. Really know you.

No one had ever said those words to me before. Not even Dev.

And Rod was the last person I'd expected to hear them from.

We boarded the small boat and headed to Motu Ahi and the Lagoonarium. I'd had the place in mind as a possible reward for a challenge, but it felt like a good thing for today, if only to get Rod out of his head.

To get *me* out of my head.

Rod was still wearing the ball cap and sunglasses, but we'd need to ditch his disguise for snorkel gear. Hopefully no one would recognize him while we were getting ready to enter the water. I'd taken to wearing my bikini under my clothes, and Rod was in a pair of board shorts with an unbuttoned long-sleeved shirt over a tank top, so once we'd reached Motu Ahi and the staff had handed out our snorkel gear, it took us only a few seconds to get ready.

Fortunately, the families around us were so excited about getting to feed the fish that no one took much notice of Rod and me.

We were just a couple, like everybody else.

Except we weren't.

And yet, Rod put a steadying hand on my lower back and offered me his arm as needed as we stepped over rocks and waded out to the reef, treating me like I was precious.

The water was clear and warm, and fish darted around us, some striped like zebras, others covered in dots, and large gray and white stingrays swooped through the water. Even a turtle or two approached.

We were encouraged to participate in the feeding, getting handfuls of chopped-up fish and holding them out.

Some fish tugged at what I was holding, some nibbled. And then a ray sucked the fish out of my hand, the sensation so peculiar I giggled.

Rod was watching me, his eyes meeting mine. "This was the perfect thing to do today."

Warmth filled my chest. "I'm glad you're enjoying it."

"I'm glad you are too."

Another ray whooshed up to me, and I trailed my fingers over its flesh before holding out another chunk of fish.

Small sharks with black-tipped fins cruised past, and black moray eels oozed out of crevices, their jaws working as they snatched at the fish we were offering. We'd been told not to be frightened, but I let go of the fish I'd been holding when an eel came too close.

Rod put his arm around my waist and nuzzled my ear. "This is the most fun I've had in a long time."

We snorkeled for a bit, admiring the brightly colored fish, the diversity of the coral and sea anemones, the lumbering pace of the turtles and the sleek gliding of the rays as they seemed to fly through the water. A few of the Lagoonarium staff demonstrated how to "ride" the largest rays by grabbing onto them and letting them tow you along.

Rod tried it first, and I watched him glide past me, a big grin on his face. Then I tried it.

The ray tugged me through the water, its fins rippling as it glided over the sea floor. Its flesh was firm under my palms, and it seemed unbothered by my presence as it moved along. A fish with bright orange fins darted past my face, startling me, and I lost my grip, scrambling to find my footing among the rocks and trying not to step on the corals. Rod was there in seconds, offering me his arm and helping me stand upright. We rose out of the water, and I swept the hair out of my face, a laugh bursting out of me.

"How about we head back to Moorea and get something to eat?" he suggested.

"Great idea."

Once we were reunited with the scooter, we zipped up the coast and found an open-air thatched-roof restaurant that had a cluster of vehicles outside.

We stepped out of the blistering sun into the shade of the roof, Rod getting us two beers before we'd even sat down. After we'd ordered our meals, we settled back with our beers. Neither one of us spoke, but the silence was comfortable, not tense.

It felt good to be away from the others, away from the pressure to fix things between Rod and Dev, away from the pressure to secure my future with TI.

"Question time," Rod said. "Where and when were you happiest?"

"Ever? Or most recently?"

He shrugged. "Whichever. Or both."

"When I was a kid, I remember how happy I was when my cat, Tiger, had her kittens. Holding those mewling little fluff balls… They were so precious."

"You love moggies, eh?"

I smiled. "Moggies?"

"Yeah. Cats."

"You Brits and your silly expressions."

He puffed out his chest. "Moggie is not an absurd word in the slightest, madame," he said, his accent going all plummy and "posh," as he liked to put it.

"And don't get me started on how ridiculous 'snog' is."

He smirked at me. "Oh, I'd like to. Snog you, that is. And then shag you silly."

I couldn't help giggling, even though he looked dead sexy as he leaned over the table. His light brown hair had dried into tousled spikes, and he'd rolled the sleeves of his shirt up to his elbows, exposing the cords of muscles and veins that popped out along his tanned forearms.

"Have you ever been in love?" he asked, his voice soft and low.

I picked at the label of my beer bottle. That was a story I didn't want to tell. Not now. Maybe not ever. "Pass."

He raised a brow, but didn't press. "Your turn to ask me something."

Searching for a topic as far from love as I could get, I looked at the assortment of rings on his fingers. I bet they each had a story behind them. "Tell me about your rings."

He pointed to the wide black and silver one with Celtic knots that he wore on his right thumb. "Got this on my first trip to Ireland. And this one"—he indicated a thick silver signet ring with a roaring lion in its center—"this one should be obvious."

I thought for a second, then shook my head. "I don't have a clue."

He gave me a teasing scowl. "Did you forget why the band is named King's Cross?"

"It's because Platform 9 ¾ is at King's Cross station, right?"

He waved the ring at me. "And what's on the House Gryffindor crest?"

I covered my face. "A lion."

He laughed at my embarrassment. "*And* I bought it because I'm a Leo."

I rolled my eyes. "Couldn't have guessed that, Mr. Loves The Spotlight."

With a grin, he lifted his left hand, showing me the ring on his index finger. It was black with gold musical notes etched into its surface. "I bought this one when King's Cross hit it big. Those are the notes to the opening bar of 'Summer Fun,' the first song Dev and I wrote together." Then he tapped a slim gold band on his pinky with three inset diamonds on it, the center one set in a square of silver, the other two flanking it in shield-like silver settings. "This is my nan's wedding band. She told me to give it to someone special someday."

His eyes met mine, the intensity in them searing me. The question was out of my mouth before I could reconsider. "Have *you* ever been in love?" I held my breath, waiting for him to object, but he just held my gaze.

"I'm not sure I can love anyone," he finally said.

"You're just afraid of rejection."

He didn't answer.

I leaned forward. "What about Dev?"

He shrugged. "I suppose I've loved him since we were kids."

"Why haven't you ever told him?"

"He knows. Besides it's not like I'm the most lovable person on the planet."

"So, Dev is easy to love, and you're not?"

He nodded and took a swallow of his beer.

"Your family loves you."

"My mum does, sure. My old man certainly didn't."

"Why do you say that?"

His eyes slid away from mine, and he played with the bottle of beer, making a series of linked rings on the wooden tabletop with the condensation rolling down the glass. "He was a drunken sod. Used to bash us all but good. I fought him sometimes when he'd light into Mum. He took off when I was thirteen. Said I was a fucking brat, a pain in the arse. Too wild. Too much trouble."

"I'm sure that was just an excuse."

Rod snorted. "I *am* trouble, love. Always have been. Always will be. And while trouble is fun for a while, no one wants it long-term. Dev certainly doesn't."

"You don't give yourself enough credit. If Dev didn't like trouble, why has he bucked his family again and again, to be with you?"

He shook his head, and we were interrupted by the waitress bringing our meals. I waited until she left, then reached for his hand.

"Look at me," I said. When he did, I squeezed his fingers. "You don't realize how wonderful you are, Rod. Truly. So talented, so much fun. Yes, a giant pain in the ass at times. But you're worth it." I squeezed his hand again. "And Dev sees that too."

Rod withdrew his hand from mine and dug into his fish and chips, avoiding my gaze. "Not wonderful enough."

"You are to me," I said, my pulse quickening.

He looked at me then, a smile breaking across his face. "Am I now?"

I nodded, and this time he reached for my hand. "I hope you know I'm going to snog and shag you silly before the day is through."

My heart fluttered in my chest and I had to break his gaze.

I was falling even deeper, even harder than I already had. My stupid, stupid heart was going to be my downfall. Again.

Chapter 8

ROD

I meant what I'd said to Sky. I did intend to snog and shag her silly.

But something had changed. I didn't want to just have sex with her. I wanted to make her happy. I wanted to sweep away that pain I'd seen on her face. Pain I'd caused.

We left the restaurant and cruised along the coast until I found a secluded inlet with a lovely beach. I pulled off the road and looked around. No one else was in sight. Perfect.

Sky stepped off the scooter, and I missed the feeling of her body nestled against mine. Her long curly hair was windblown, a messy tangle that made her look like she'd just rolled out of bed. She smiled at me and crossed her arms. "What are you staring at?"

"You." I stepped close to her, putting my hands on her slim shoulders. A light dusting of freckles across her nose and cheeks made me smile. I traced a finger along her cheekbone. "You're a lovely lass, Sky."

Her brown eyes held mine. "And you, Rod Taylor, are dangerous."

I cupped her cheeks and pressed a kiss to her full lips. "Falling for me, are you?"

She slid her arms around my neck, and I dove in for another kiss. Her tongue met mine, her luscious tits pressing into my chest, her nipples pebbling against the thin material of her sundress. I reached down and grabbed her

119

bum, pulling her tightly against my crotch, and she whimpered, relaxing into me.

Then she broke the kiss. "I am falling for you," she whispered, not looking at me. "And it scares me."

"Ah, love..." I turned her face so she was looking at me. "The feeling is mutual. And it scares me too."

I could tell her it was because she'd pulled a runner once. But that wasn't it.

I was scared of *me*. What if I wasn't cut out for this? What if I was just as broken and fucked up as Dev thought I was?

As I knew I was?

I'd spent my whole adult life avoiding entanglements. Avoiding feelings. Avoiding what was real.

But Dev had sneaked under my radar. Sky too.

Was I man enough to make this work?

"What are you thinking?" she asked.

"Wondering if I'm good enough for you, love."

She brushed the hair off my forehead and smiled. "If you're asking the question, you probably are."

"I don't want to hurt you again."

"Then don't."

I smiled. "You make it sound so easy."

"It kind of is. Just don't be a selfish shit."

This time I laughed. "I may need some reminding."

She stepped away from me, but took hold of my hand and tugged me toward a stand of palm trees. "Don't worry. I'm not Dev. *I'll* call you on it."

I followed her into the trees. "I'll hold you to that."

She found a spot where some palm fronds had fallen onto the sand, making a nest. She shed her dress and sandals, revealing that turquoise bikini that I loved on her. "Let's take a swim," she said. I ditched my shirt and shoes and followed her to the ocean's edge.

It was like stepping into a tepid bath, waves lapping around my ankles. The water was so clear I could see the white, sandy bottom, the fish darting about. Sky and I waded out until we were waist deep, then she leaned back until she was floating, her dark hair fanning out around her.

Christ, she was beautiful. She deserved to be loved, to be cherished.

To be held close and never let go.

I understood why Dev had told her he loved her. I understood completely.

I let myself float beside her, and when our hands touched, I entwined my fingers with hers.

We drifted like that for I don't know how long, the water lapping gently against us, the sky so clear and blue above, seabirds occasionally flying overhead, their cries carried off in the breeze.

Was *this* love? This feeling of contentment, of peace?

Of finally being home after so many years of being alone?

After a time, Sky let go of my hand and started swimming for shore, her strokes long and confident. She was definitely a better swimmer than I was.

Just as she was probably a better person than I was.

But I wanted—for the first time in my life—to be a better man.

For her. For Dev.

I followed her onto the shore and up the sand, back to the place where we'd left our clothes. We were surrounded by trees and various plants, sheltered from any prying eyes from the road.

Her gaze locked on mine, and she untied her top and shed her bikini bottoms. She stood before me gloriously naked, her skin lightly bronzed, her dark hair hanging in thick, wet ropes down her back. She reached up and squeezed some water from it. Then she laid her suit out to dry on the branches of a nearby bush.

Realizing I was staring like a schoolboy with his first naked girl, I removed my shorts and laid them out to dry like she'd done. I let my eyes roam over her, eating her up like she was a feast.

"Fancy that shag, love?"

She tossed her hair over her shoulder and shook it out. "Thought you'd never ask."

I backed her up against a palm tree and went in for a kiss, my hard cock pressing into her belly. She kissed me for a few minutes, both of us breathing hard, then she sank to her knees and took hold of my cock. "Grab onto the trunk," she said.

I leaned forward slightly, my eyes glued on her, my hands grasping the tree. She licked the middle finger of her right hand, then brought it down to her pussy, her finger touching her where I wanted to. She shivered slightly and my cock jumped. She was showing me something new, a side of her I hadn't seen before.

Then she leaned forward and took my cock into her mouth. She licked around the tip, moaning against my slick flesh while her finger worked between her legs. I could hear how wet she was, could see a flush rising to her face and chest.

"Come for me," I said, and she raised her eyes to mine, our gazes locking, her pink lips stretched around my cock. She took me in deep, her tight fist sliding along my shaft the way I liked it, her other hand moving faster between her legs. Then she closed her eyes and moaned, her body shaking as she came.

When she opened her eyes again and looked up at me, she added suction, her cheeks hollowing out as she bobbed up and down my cock, and I thought I'd died and gone to heaven. I thrust the fingers of one hand into her wet hair, caressing her skull, reaching down to cradle her nape. I tried to hold myself back from thrusting into her wet heat, but she was making it damn difficult.

Finally I had to stop her before it was all over, and I withdrew from her mouth reluctantly. There was a palm tree not far from us that was bent over, growing almost horizontally, and I thought it would be perfect for what I had in mind.

"Have any condoms, love?"

She nodded at her handbag. I went over and picked it up. "There's a small zippered compartment," she said.

I found it and retrieved a condom, then suited up. I patted the trunk of the bent-over palm. "Hop up here."

She grinned at me and rose, perching herself on the trunk. It gave a bit beneath her weight, but it supported her the way I'd hoped it would. I kissed down her neck. "You are bloody brilliant, Sky. I don't think I've ever said that, and I wanted you to know."

She cupped my cheeks in her palms, her eyes filling with tears. "Who *are* you?" she asked. "And what happened to Rod 'I don't give a toss' Taylor?"

"You happened." I kissed down her chest, sucking on first one nipple, then the other, her slim fingers cradling my neck, her little whimpers making my cock jump. Dropping to my knees, I spread her legs wide, inhaling the spicy scent of her arousal. Finding her swollen clit, I teased it with my tongue, making her squirm and cry out, until I had to hold her still with my hands on her hips. I loved the sound of her heavy breathing, my cock aching to be inside her.

"Rod, please," she panted. "I want more."

She didn't have to ask twice; I wanted inside her just as much. I rose up, and she wrapped her legs around my waist. Supporting her with one hand, I teased her entrance, coating my cockhead thoroughly in her juices, and she chased me with her hips. "Ready, love?"

"More than," she panted.

I thrust inside her, both of us groaning. She felt so fucking good, hot and tight, her body a live wire quivering around me.

I pulled out slowly, then pressed back in, keeping the pace slower than I needed, wanting to make this last, these precious minutes away from everyone else. The two of us joined in a way that no one else could understand.

I wanted to make love to her; I wanted her to feel how I felt, to know that she wasn't just another notch on my bedpost.

And to know that the only way I was ever letting her go was if she asked.

She moaned in my arms, her legs crossed behind my back squeezing me closer to her. "Please," she moaned. "Harder."

"As my lady wishes." I slammed into her, making us both gasp and the tree trunk sway beneath her. Then I did it again, my cock craving to be deeper, to own her, to make her forget everyone else but me.

And Dev.

Thoughts of all three of us together flooded my mind, and my throat ached. I wanted him here, I wanted him to be a part of this, a part of us, but who knew if he could ever let himself go?

Swallowing hard, I pistoned into Sky, my hands cupping her bum, forcing her legs wider, allowing me in just a fraction more. "I'm not ever letting you go," I said in her ear. "You hear me?"

"I do."

"You believe it?"

"I do." She looked into my eyes, her cheeks flushed, her eyes bright.

I wanted to say it, to tell her how I felt, the words catching in my throat. But I wanted to be sure before I made her that kind of promise. I braced my thighs against the trunk of the tree and fucked her hard, the tree shaking beneath my assault, her breath gusting in my ear, her cries of "Oh, Rod," driving me mercilessly into her until she shuddered and cried out.

I slammed into her several more times, then came so hard my legs shook, and I collapsed against the trunk, barely keeping us both from falling over it.

I kissed the hollow at the base of her neck. "My brown-eyed girl," I crooned to her, and she laughed, the sound easing my heart.

Maybe I hadn't been able to say it with words, but I think she heard me anyway. She kissed my cheek. "You could really wreck a girl, Rod Taylor."

"But I won't," I said. And I meant it.

Now I just had to hold myself to that.

Even though my heart still cried for Dev, part of me felt more at peace. I had Sky. And if I couldn't have them both, she would be enough.

Enough to keep me from flying apart.

As if she was reading my mind, Sky placed a palm flat against my chest and looked up at me. "Dev's come a long way, Rod. Just be patient. Don't push."

I nodded. "I know. I just..." I scrubbed a hand through my damp hair. "I just want it all." I took her hands in mine and held them pressed to my chest. "I'm a greedy fucker."

A corner of her mouth curved up. "Don't ever change."

I raised one of her hands to my mouth and pressed my lips to her palm.

"Too late, love. I already have."

Her smile faded and she held my gaze. "You mean that?"

"I do."

She nodded and flashed me a smile, then she hopped off the trunk and started to dress, her back turned to me, her eyes avoiding mine.

A tendril of unease curled up around my heart.

She'd pulled away again.

What had I done?

DEV

"Mum, I can't return to London today. You know this." I pressed the mobile closer to my ear and looked around my bungalow for somewhere to sit. Hurricane Rod had managed to throw his clothes everywhere. I scooped a pair of his board shorts off my bed and leaned back against the headboard.

I already had a headache from Rod's incessant smirking during this morning's rehearsal, and my mother's haranguing was most certainly not helping.

"I do not understand why you needed to go to Tahiti, of all places. Your sister's wedding begins in only a week. Tell me, Devkinandan, how will it look if Aahna's oldest brother is not on hand for the celebrations?"

I had to wonder whether Kalini would be so dramatic for our wedding, if marrying her was to be my fate. I wasn't certain I would survive it if such were the case. "I only have six days left here."

There was a sharp pain in my belly. Despite the ups and downs with Sky and Rod, my days on Moorea had been some of the happiest in my life. And knowing the announcement I was going to be making at the end of Aahna's wedding, they were also the most bittersweet. Because in less than a week, I would be committing myself to the future my family had always dreamed of for me. A future I'd never wanted.

But by acquiescing, I was fulfilling my duty to my parents, to my family, and to my community, every one of whom would be disgusted by what I'd done with Rod and Sky, but most especially by what Rod and I had done to each other.

Oh, I wasn't stupid. Gay men, bisexual men, existed in the Indian community. However, it was never spoken of, never seen, and never accepted.

When these men reached a marrying age, they firmly closed the closet door and dedicated themselves to living for their families. Their needs, their desires, were meaningless. Duty to family and devotion to living a pure life were all that mattered. Their sacrifice made them better.

At least, that was the theory.

Sure, many Indian couples were happy. But many others lived with unhappy marriages, dissatisfied spouses, addictions, and depression. We might live in England, but as a community, we believed ourselves better than the English. We had higher morals, better values. We strove to be altruistic, and through self-realization and self-knowledge, we sought to attain *moksha*, freedom from *saṃsāra*, the cycle of death and rebirth.

These were certainly very respectable goals to have. The problem? Far too many of us thought we were only better than others if that meant we had a bigger house, more expensive cars, or wore fancier clothing. Standing. Appearances. Those were our guides. It was all a crock of shite.

"Devkinandan? Are you there?"

Bollocks. I'd got so lost in my head, I'd missed what my mother had said. "I'm sorry, Mum. You were saying?"

Her heavy sigh filled the line. "Am I so unworthy of my eldest son's attention?"

"No, Mum. It's my fault. Please, I'm listening now. I promise."

Of course, Rod would pick the moment of my embarrassing groveling to saunter into our shared bungalow. By the rolling of his eyes, it was clear he'd heard. My face heated, and I turned my back to him.

"As I was saying," my mother began, "your cousin Arjun and his family would like to attend the wedding."

Not knowing why I should care, I played my part and asked, "Who is cousin Arjun again?" I thought I had a good handle on all my aunts and uncles as well as their children.

"Arjun is my great uncle Ishaan's grandson."

"So not my cousin."

"He is family," she said, her tone brooking no argument.

A second cousin once removed, but whatever. "How many people are we talking about?"

"His wife, her parents, their five children, and his wife's little sister."

"So, ten." Ten people I'd never met in my life. "Will they stay at the house?"

My mother laughed uproariously at that. I held the phone away from my ear until it subsided. "Dear sweet Devkinandan, the house is already full to the rafters. Cousin Arjun and his family will stay at a hotel."

I rapidly calculated last-minute airfare for ten people, hotel accommodations, and meals for a week. The amount was staggeringly ridiculous. Why hadn't good cousin Arjun decided on this trip earlier?

At least the airfare would have been cheaper. "That's going to cost at least thirty thousand pounds."

Rod made a choking sound, reminding me of his presence. I turned to look at him. His lips were wrapped around the neck of a water bottle, reminding me how they'd been wrapped around my cock not even forty-eight hours earlier. My dick began to swell. The experience had been incredible, far better than anything I could have imagined.

But it had been wrong.

Guilt swamped me, and my dick went limp. I slumped back onto the pillows. With my eyes closed, I said, "Use the American Express Platinum card on my dresser. It has a fifty-thousand-pound limit. That should cover it." As well as any other unexpected family that surfaced with a burning desire to see someone they'd never met get married.

"Thank you, Devkinandan. You are a good son." Her tone had brightened now that she'd won.

"I try."

"I know. I also know we will be the proudest of parents when it is you standing before the community beside your beautiful young bride. I dream of the day I hold your son in my arms."

Words failed to me. I knew the words I was supposed to say, but as I watched Rod munch on a candy bar from the mini fridge, the words refused to leave my mouth. I couldn't surrender to my mother's will in front of Rod, the man who'd been by my side since we'd been but boys. Rod would never subjugate himself to another's will the way I was about to do. He'd never understand why I had to.

"Sleep well, Mum," I said.

"Sleep well, my darling."

I ended the call and put my mobile on the nightstand. Now that beds and furniture had been restored to the bungalow, it was rather nice, and I was determined to make full use of it. As was Rod, apparently.

He perched against a table by the window, his eyes drilling into me.

"They're fucking bleeding you dry, Dev. What's the tally for the wedding now? Hundred and fifty K? Two hundred K?"

I threw my legs over the side of the bed and shrugged. "It's only money. I've more than enough."

Rod pushed off the table. The sensual movement reminded me of a panther on the prowl, and my mouth went dry. Letting him suck me had been a mistake. Touching his hot cock, so sodding hard, had been an even worse one.

I couldn't look at him without reliving the joy I'd felt in those moments, without remembering the pleasure in those sexy blue eyes, without feeling and smelling his cum on my fingers. Without wishing I had tasted it. Without wishing for more of him, more of Sky, more of us.

Rod stepped closer. I shoved my shaking hands between my thighs to hide their trembling. "It's not just money, mate," he said with a frown. "They're using you."

"No." I shook my head. He didn't understand that wasn't our way. The money I earned belonged to my family. "That's not how it is with family. You send money to your mother too."

Rod waved my words off. "That's different. *She* never asks for it. I'm giving it to her, and she uses it to raise my younger brothers and sister, not to impress the bloody neighbors."

I sighed. "Rod, please, leave it. It's a cultural thing that you wouldn't understand."

He scoffed. "Fine. Tell yourself that." He flopped down onto his bed, grabbed the remote, and turned on the telly.

"What are you doing?" I asked in a near panic. I'd been pissed off at Rod for staying away all night, but now the reality of having him stretched out only a few feet away from me was too much to bear.

"Having a lie down before today's challenge." He shot me a sidelong glance. "What do you care?"

His cocky attitude combined with my general arousal reawakened my anger. "You aren't spending the day with your girlfriend again?"

The words were barely out of my mouth before I wished I could shove them back in my great gob.

"*My* girlfriend?" Rod's brow arched.

I wanted to wipe the smirk off his bloody handsome face. I jutted my chin out instead. Yes, I was acting like a five-year-old. Yes, I knew I was in the wrong here. But I didn't care.

I wanted to fight with him.

Rod narrowed his eyes. "Sky slept with you when we first got here, then she slept with me. And then with both of us. And then with me again. None of us set any rules. So what are you so upset about?"

"I'm not upset," I said mulishly.

Rod sat up and turned to mimic my position. We sat face to face on the edges of our beds, our knees only a few feet apart. He stared at me for several long moments. I felt his penetrating gaze sink into my body, and my cock jumped again. Bloody hell.

I watched him back, and realized I'd matched the pace of his breathing. The knowledge quickened my pulse.

His full lips curled into a smile. "You're jealous."

"Yes, you sodding prat!" I exploded. "Of *course*, I'm bloody jealous. I tell Sky that I love her, and then she runs off with you. For the entire fucking day. And night. How the hell else should I feel?"

"So, this is just about her?" Rod's voice was soft in contrast to his hard-edged features. "What am I in all of this? Christ." He rose and stepped around the end of his bed, his fingers digging into the mass of his light brown hair, hair I now knew was as soft as spun silk. "This isn't a bloody fucking episode of *The Bachelor*, you miserable twat."

I hung my head. I hadn't meant to hurt Rod, yet I clearly had, and I was about to hurt him even worse. "I love her," I whispered.

Rod spun around. His glare hit me like a laser beam, searing my chest raw. "Why did you start touching me then, eh? You seemed to enjoy it, not to mention having your dick in my mouth. You didn't have any complaints then, did you?"

"Rod," I choked.

"Your words say one thing, Dev, but your actions say another."

I could admit that I'd been playing with fire, that I'd been curious, that I'd wanted, just for a moment, to give in to the heat between us. But I refused to admit that it had been on me. "I didn't ask you to do that."

Rod stepped over to me. He braced his hands on the bed by my hips, his mouth inches from mine, his breath warm on my lips.

He snarled. "You sure as hell didn't push me away. And you touched me first."

Before I could blink, his hot palm was on the swelling between my legs, his fingers circling my rigid cock. "You're hard," he said, his voice suddenly low and hoarse. His nostrils flared. He wasn't unaffected.

I sat frozen, my eyes on his, every nerve in my body on alert. I couldn't move, couldn't think. I could only feel.

Feel his hand on me. The squeeze of his fingers. The ache in my cock. The pre-cum spurting from my slit, wetting my shorts.

"Don't tell me you didn't want everything that happened. Don't tell me you didn't want more."

His palm pressed down on my cock, the pressure delicious. I could give in to him now. Give in to the desire, to the energy between us. I'd been denying it for so long, and I was so damn tired. Rod was right. I'd wanted every minute of what had transpired that night. Every sigh. Every grunt. Every breathless moan. I'd wanted the heft of him in my palm, the tightness of his throat around my cock.

But I'd also wanted things that hadn't happened: his lips on mine, the taste of him in my mouth, my cock deep inside his arse.

My brain short-circuited on that last image. "I do want more," I said, my voice strained, choked.

His expression softened and, oh God, I wanted him so much my chest ached and my cock throbbed. But if I succumbed to my desires, I stood to lose everything, especially him.

Using every bit of willpower remaining in my dwindling supply, I pressed my palms against his chest, and pushed him away. He stumbled back, his jaw dropping open.

I stood and slowly let my hands fall. "But I can't, Rod. I *can't* want you."

And once again, I left the man who consumed me, body and soul.

SKY

Bubbling with excitement, I approached the makeshift podium where the King's Cross roadies had assembled a mic and a speaker so everyone could hear me.

Today was a big day for me and the band. A day, I hoped, that would help bring Dev and Rod closer together, maybe all the way together. If this worked, then I'd do as I had promised Daniel, and I would tell Dev and Rod about my arrangement with TI and tell Dev about the bonus. They'd be pissed, and they'd likely hate me for what I'd done, but at least they would be together, and King's Cross would go on. I couldn't live with myself if I lost them *and* they lost each other.

A love that lasting had to win.

I stepped up to the podium and tapped the mic to make sure it was turned on. There was a thump and a squeal of feedback. Half of those gathered around, TI staff, King's Cross's crew, some resort staff, and, of course, the band, covered their ears and laughed.

When the sound guy adjusted some knobs on the soundboard and gave me a thumbs-up, I started. "Welcome everyone, to the last event of our mini Olympics. The guys have been great sports so far. Well, some more so than others." I glanced toward Dev and Rod, who'd been teamed together but had barely spoken a word to each other all day. Dev, in particular, practically vibrated with tension. Rod's constant mocking had done little to help.

"The standings after the six-legged crab race, the electric eel swim, the monkey swing, the slip and slide, and the seashell scramble are: Damon and Mick with three points."

Loud hooting and wolf whistles interrupted me.

"Tommy and Jules with two points."

"You got it, lads," someone shouted.

"And Rod and Dev with zero points," I finished. This announcement was met with a round of cheers and jeers, which Rod took in stride with his usual arrogant style. Dev, on the other hand, looked murderous. His dark scowl landed on some of the louder men, silencing them immediately.

"For our last event, I've instructed our athletes to wear jeans." I turned to the crowd and winked. "And the tighter the better."

The ladies, and some of the men, clapped. Rod held his arms out and made a slow circle. He'd definitely taken my advice to heart. There was a loud whistle. My eyes scanned the crowd until I found its source. Sharon, of course.

Too bad, lady. He's mine.

The thought came quicker than I could stop it, and a lump formed in my throat. Rod wasn't really mine, and after I told him and Dev the truth about my reasons for being here, he probably never would be.

Not to be outdone by Rod, Damon turned his back to the crowd and started twerking. Mick cupped his hands to his mouth and began to beatbox, the others egging Damon on. I laughed. It was impossible not to. We'd only been together eleven days, but each and every one of these men would forever have a place in my heart.

"Okay, okay, guys," I said to get their attention back. Damon bowed, and everyone clapped. "Thank you for the impromptu demonstration, Damon," I joked. "Who wants to know why they're wearing such scandalously tight jeans?"

The crowd shouted.

I smiled. My eyes went to the guys. "Before I answer, I'm going to ask you to remove your shirts."

That was a bit of grumbling from some of the men, but soon their T-shirts were in a pile in the sand.

"Thank you. Our next event will consist of two rounds of…" I paused, letting the anticipation mount. Then I picked up two bottles of olive oil and held them up. "Turkish oil wrestling!"

Damon, Rod, and Tommy cracked up. Mick, Jules, and Dev looked uncomfortable. I might even have heard a "fuck" and a "bloody hell." Our audience, on the other hand, was ecstatic.

"I will need a few volunteers to oil the men up."

I handed the bottles to Vanessa. She winked. "You're my hero, Sky."

I smiled wickedly. "You're welcome."

While the men were being oiled up, I explained how things would proceed. "The goal of Turkish oil wrestling is to exert control over your opponent by getting a firm hold of their pants… um… jeans, thus preventing them from moving. Regular wrestling moves are allowed, but let's not hurt anyone, okay? This is supposed to be fun."

I waited for the now slicked-up men to nod. "The first round will be Dev against Jules, Damon against Tommy, and Rod against Mick. The names of the winners will be put in a bag, and I'll pick two. Those two will wrestle for the championship. If you win the first round you get one point. If you win the second round, you get three points. Any questions?"

Jules raised his hand. "What's the prize for this again?"

"The first and second place teams will spend the night at the Marlon Brando Island resort."

Cheers and hoots rose from the audience, and I could see the band members doing quick calculations. Dev and Rod still had a chance, if they each won their matches and one of them won the second round.

Rod nudged Dev with his shoulder. "We can do this, mate."

Dev scowled at him and stepped away.

The hurt in Rod's eyes dug into my heart like claws. I wanted this for him so badly. After the day we'd spent together, I had a new understanding of the man. I only wished Dev could see him the way I did. I swallowed against the tightness in my throat. "Men, please take your places."

The opponents squared off in half-crouched positions. I allowed a pregnant pause before proclaiming, "Begin!" I started the timer on my phone. I'd let them go until one of them won, or I'd call a draw after ten minutes.

I stepped down from the podium to stand beside Vanessa and the other TI staff. Daniel crossed his arms. "I hope you know what you're doing."

"Me too," I said.

Vanessa squeezed my arm. "This is amazing, girl."

Another woman I recognized but didn't know the name of high-fived me. "Fucking awesome idea."

I blushed and returned my attention to the men wrestling on the beach in sunny Moorea. Wow. It *had* been a fucking brilliant idea. Rod's muscles gleamed and rippled with each move he made. He looked good. Really good. A lot healthier than when he'd first arrived, despite some peeling skin on his shoulders.

Tommy's outraged shout rent the air. "You aren't supposed to grab my bollocks."

"I'm not?" Damon said, his voice and face dancing with humor. "I thought that was the point."

"Oh God," I said, laughing.

Not far away, Dev grunted as he heaved Jules into the sand. It stuck to their skin. I winced. Man, that had to be uncomfortable. In the videos I'd watched, the wrestling had always taken place on grass. Now I understood why.

Dev grabbed the back of Jules's jeans and twisted until he had a handful of denim. Jules squealed like a pig to the amusement of everyone watching. "Let me go, you bloody tosser. My wife wants another kid. If you castrate me before I can get the job done, she'll bloody murder you."

Even Dev cracked a smile at that. "Hold still, then, you stonking whinger." He threw a leg over Jules's, and that was it.

I blew the whistle and declared Dev the winner. This spurred the others on, and soon all three matches were over.

I returned to the podium. "Whew!" I said, wiping my brow. "Was that hot or what?"

"Yes!" everyone shouted.

"Dev, Damon, and Rod have won their matches, so the standings are now Damon and Mick with four points, Tommy and Jules with two points, and Dev and Rod also with two points."

Jules and Tommy were out of the running for first place, but could still tie for second if Rod and Dev lost. On the other hand, if Dev or Rod won this match, they would win the challenge. If Damon won, he and Mick would win the challenge. The audience was antsy with excitement. Dev seemed a little more centered, less jumpy, but every time he looked at Rod, a scowl formed between his brows.

I made a show of putting three pieces of paper with each of the men's names into a bag I'd brought along. "I'm going to pick two names for the final match."

There was a fifty-eight percent chance I'd pick both Dev's and Rod's names. But if I picked Damon's, would I lie? I hadn't decided yet. Either way, Damon and Mick would still go to the resort. But I'd potentially be punishing Tommy and Jules.

Vanessa extended the bag toward me. I held my breath and stuck my hand inside, praying for luck to be on my side. I read the first name. "Dev."

Time for the second name. I had a fifty percent chance of picking Rod's name. *Please, please, please,* I begged the universe.

I pulled out a second piece of paper and slowly unfolded it. Rod. Thank God. My breath came out in a rush, and I smiled. "Rod. Dev and Rod, you will face off for the final round. Please assume the position."

Dev threw down the bottle of water he'd been drinking. His face darkened, and he glared at me. I widened my eyes in surprise. He no doubt thought I'd arranged this, all to get him and Rod together. He wasn't entirely wrong, and the guilty pangs in my stomach attested to that.

He closed his eyes, then looked away and faced off with Rod, whose bright blue ones twinkled. I couldn't tell if it was amusement at Dev's discomfort or mischief.

"Are you ready?" I asked the crowd.

"Yes!"

"All right, then. Begin!" I started the timer on my phone and stepped off the podium to join the others.

Daniel nudged my shoulder. "Convenient."

I handed him the papers still clutched in my fist. "Fate."

Dev moved first, grabbing the back of Rod's neck and pulling him forward so their foreheads touched. Rod managed to get a hand on Dev's neck as well. They circled each other, both breathing hard. My stomach tumbled with tension. This match looked far too serious.

At the same time, they both looked gorgeous in their ferocity. The two men were slender, their muscles sleek, their skin glowing from the sun, Rod's a light tan and Dev's a rich brown. I wanted to glide my hands over their chests, their backs, their sides. I wanted to explore every oiled ridge and valley.

Dev shot a hand out and wrapped his fingers around Rod's ankle. He tugged hard, and Rod fell into the sand on his side. Dev fell on top of him. I gasped. It was so hot. Rod obviously agreed. His eyes widened as he held Dev's stare.

Dev snarled and closed his fist around Rod's denim. Rod twisted his hips sharply, forcing Dev to let go. Then in a move worthy of our little Olympics, he flipped Dev onto his back and straddled him.

With a roar, Dev hooked a leg over Rod's throat and pushed, throwing Rod off him. Everyone around me groaned as Rod landed hard in the sand. Was wrestling something Brits learned in school? Rod and Dev seemed to have more than a casual understanding of the sport.

Rod quickly got to his feet, and they circled each other again. In a flash, Rod lunged forward, his arms wrapping around Dev's waist, and tripped him. Dev tumbled to the ground and twisted to his side, trying to get his feet under him. But Rod gave him no chance, once again tackling him. His chest pressed against Dev's side. He shot the crowd a wicked look.

My stomach clenched. I knew exactly what Rod was going to do. I could barely watch, even though I really wanted to. Because honestly, seeing two oil-slicked men rolling around, their chests gliding against each other's, their legs intertwining, wow… It made my heart thunder and heat pool between my legs. The pure strength, the total masculinity. It was the ultimate aphrodisiac.

At least to me.

So, mesmerized, I held my breath as Rod reached around Dev and plunged his hand down the back of Dev's tight jeans.

Dev stiffened, his body going as rigid as a plate. If looks were lasers, Rod would be a dead man right now. Defying gravity, Dev pulled his arm back and bolted upright, punching Rod in the nose.

"Oh!" I covered my mouth with my hands, stunned to see the blood pouring down Rod's face.

Rod froze, a beautiful bloodied statue.

Dev growled and knocked Rod's hand from his pants. "Why the fuck did you do that?"

The words seemed to rouse Rod from his stupor. He struggled to his feet and spit a gob of blood into the sand. He wiped his mouth with the back of his hand. "It was just a joke, mate. Calm your tits."

"Calm my—" Dev sputtered. If his eyes got any bigger, they'd pop out. He swung his fist again. This time Rod ducked it easily.

"No! Stop," I cried, running toward them.

That seemed to get everyone moving. Mick grabbed Rod, and Damon grabbed Dev, pulling them apart. "Break it up," Damon said.

Dev struggled out of his hold. "Let me go." He held his hands up. "I'm done here."

He sent me an icy look before loping across the beach and disappearing into the woods.

Rod shook his bowed head, looking more defeated than I'd ever seen him. "It was just a joke."

I was certain that to Rod it had been, but to Dev? It had been a slap in the face. A public admission that his relationship with Rod went far beyond mere friendship. The sad thing was that had he laughed it off, no one would have been any the wiser.

Beside me, Daniel grunted. He pinned me with his scowl. "You need to fucking fix this."

My shoulders slumped and my belly did a slow roll. This entire situation had gone to shit, and far too many people would be affected by the outcome if I couldn't fix things between Dev and Rod. For the first time in a long time, I had other people to consider, and for the first time ever, I really understood the burden Dev carried.

Did Rod? Could he? For everyone's sakes, I certainly hoped he could dig deep, find the bonds that had created their friendship and held it together for almost two decades. I'd wanted to be the bridge between them, I'd wanted to be the one to save them, because if their love endured because of me, if they stayed together, then in some small way, I'd feel as though I still had them.

And that mattered more to me than my business, than any potential partnership with TI, than any amount of money. Their happiness mattered more to me than my own heart.

They mattered more to me than anything.

And it was time I showed it.

I went to Rod and wrapped my arms around his shoulders. His body trembled against mine. He buried his face in my neck. "I'm a sodding idiot, Sky. I didn't know—" His voice broke. "I didn't expect—"

"I know." I rubbed his back. "I know you didn't mean to hurt him."

"I can't do this again." His arms tightened around me. "Fuck. We were so close, Sky. I thought..." His rough voice cut off.

"You weren't wrong, Rod. He is coming around. But this is really hard for him. It goes against everything he's been taught, everything he believes about himself."

"You're right." He wiped his tear-filled eyes discreetly since everyone was still milling around us. When he looked up, my breath hitched in my throat. He looked so broken. If I hadn't known how deeply he loved Dev before, I knew it now. It reaffirmed my goal.

"You have to go to him, Rod. Talk this through."

Rod scoffed. "Talking is what always gets me into trouble."

I offered him a soft smile. "You can do this."

"What do I say?" His voice and eyes implored me. "Please, Sky. Tell me what to say. Tell me how to make things right again. I've been trying... God." He looked up at the crystal blue Sky and closed his eyes, shutting out all the beauty. "I've been trying for so bloody long, Sky. I've wanted him forever, since I first realized I was attracted to men." He gave me a half-smile. "We were just boys at the time. You don't know how confused I was, what with wanting to get in his pants and also wanting to get under Annabelle Watson's skirt."

I laughed at that, squeezing his waist. "Good to know some things never change."

His expression collapsed, and his eyes glistened with returning tears. "Some things do."

"No, Rod." I cupped his face in my hands and kissed him lightly. It was tender and affectionate. I wanted him to know I was there for him. "Just tell him what's in your heart. Dev loves you. A blind person could see it. But he's also scared. Talk to him. Let him know how you see the future. Let him know you understand his fears. Share yours with him. Be his *friend* again."

He let out a huge breath, one that seemed to uncoil all the tension in his body. A slow smile curved his luscious mouth, and he was beautiful to me. Wicked grin and wrecked eyes. This was Rod at his most elemental. "Thank you, Sky."

"Always," I said, wishing it were possible, yet knowing it wasn't.

Chapter 9

ROD

My nose was still throbbing from that punch, but my eyes had stopped burning by the time I found Dev. Of course, the fucker had to be sitting on the edge of a cliff, his legs dangling over the edge. How could he not worry about the ground giving way?

My fingers tightened around the necks of the beers I was carrying, the bottles slick with condensation.

Dev didn't turn at my approach, but his shoulders stiffened.

"I brought some Stellas," I said, standing as close to the precipice as I dared, my pulse racing, my breathing going shallow. I could blame my nerves on the fucking chasm of death before me, but my biggest worry was Dev. Had I pushed him too far?

"Don't want any."

"Mate, we need to talk."

He still wouldn't look at me. "What is there to say?"

Fuck. I edged closer, forcing myself to sit beside him. I crossed my legs under me. No fucking way was I going to dangle my legs over the edge the way he was.

I offered him a Stella and kept my eyes from looking down. Instead I focused on the horizon, slowly allowing my gaze to drift downward a bit to take in the valley below.

It really was gorgeous here. So different from England.

Just as Dev was so different from me. Though he'd grown up in the same country as me, he hadn't grown up in the same culture, had he? No matter how the two of us felt about each other, I was asking a lot of him. A fuck of a lot.

"I'm sorry, mate. I truly am. I didn't think."

Dev took a swig of his beer. "I'm sorry I hit you."

"You really surprised me with that punch." I looked at him out of the corner of my eye. He still wouldn't look at me. "You were obviously enjoying yourself. I could feel how hard you were."

"I won't deny that I was, but… feeling you like that, being that close. Knowing that everyone was around us… And then your hand in my pants… How could they not know about us?"

"Is that so terrible? Everybody knows about me, and the world hasn't ended. Damon obviously doesn't give a fuck. He'd probably join us if we asked—"

"For fuck's sake, Rod!"

"—and the other guys don't give a fuck either. You're the only one who's worried about it."

"And you know why." He turned to me then, his eyes blazing. "My family absolutely will *not* accept us together." He took a gulp of his beer. "They'll barely accept Sky."

A spark of anger flared in me. "She's not yours, mate. She's ours."

He looked at me. "Yeah, she's ours. But I thought maybe if I married her…" He let his voice trail off.

"You thought what?"

"Maybe they'd leave me alone."

"Your family isn't here. Everyone else is a friend or under an NDA. You can do what you want here. What you *really* want, for once in your life."

Dev was silent for so long I thought he wasn't going to respond. And then he did. "You push and push and push, and you always get your way. Not this time."

Fire poured into my gut, into my blood. "Why the fuck do you think I'm always pushing? How many times did we swear to be best mates and make music until we die? I bloody *love* you, and it's killing me. You *know* this, and it doesn't even bother you."

"You love me?" The git had the nerve to smirk. "I'm not even sure you're capable of it. You go through bed partners like toilet paper. Rock star to the max, right? I'm not going to throw away my whole life for one night. Or a dirty weekend. Or whatever you're going to allow me before you get bloody bored."

I stared at him, rubbing at the ache in my chest. Was that what he really thought, or was he just scared? "I told Sky this wouldn't work."

"What wouldn't work?"

"You're in denial, mate. You're lying to yourself. Ruining our whole relationship because you're a bloody coward."

Dev pitched his beer over the cliff and dove at me, tackling me hard. I fell onto my back, my right arm dangling over the edge, and I bucked wildly beneath him, rolling us to my left. Then he rolled us over again and pinned my arms to the ground. He was breathing fast, his eyes hard as diamonds. "How am I a coward?"

"You stepped back from lead guitar. You won't even consider singing in my place. You're letting Sonic High and those Yank bastards at Reeling dictate *our* sound. This is *your* band, *your* music, and you're basically erasing yourself from it." I rolled us over again, and this time I had Dev pinned. "You're training your own replacement so you can kowtow to your bleeding parents. *I'm* not the one who wants out. *You* are!"

Dev stared up at me, his eyes misting over, his voice breaking when he spoke. "I don't. King's Cross is the only thing keeping me sane. I stand up to my parents every day. If I didn't, I'd be married and in med school right now."

"You have your own money. You're paying for your sister's wedding. You bought the house your family is living in. So why are you letting *them* dictate to *you*? You keep choosing your family over yourself."

Dev growled. "I'm not choosing them over myself. I'm choosing *you* over *them*. That's the problem! From the day I first introduced you to them, they've wanted me to stop seeing you." He took a deep breath, his chest heaving against mine. "Every decision I've made in my life has been to keep myself near you. With you."

His luminous brown eyes held mine, a lifetime of anguish written all over his handsome face.

I wanted to believe what he was saying. I really did.

But I couldn't live with half-measures, half-truths, any longer. I needed him to make a choice. I needed him to put us both out of our misery.

DEV

I stared up at Rod, willing him to understand, willing him to believe me. Willing him to accept what I could offer. Hoping he'd stop pushing for more.

I could be his friend. I could share Sky with him.

But the rest?

"Stop lying to yourself, Devkinandan," Rod said, his voice soft, devastating. "Every decision you've made has been about the band. You love music, and that has *nothing* to do with me."

His eyes glittered with tears, with hurt. And something inside me broke.

What was I doing to him? To myself?

To us?

"It has *everything* to do with you. That's why I'm in the band. So I can be with you. I love you so fucking much." The rest caught in my throat, and I coughed. "I do *all* of this so I can spend a few hours with you a day. I've chosen *you* every fucking step of the way."

Rod's face screwed up, his skin flushing deep red. "You haven't!"

I threw him off me, quickly rolling on top of him. He tried to strike me in the face with his elbow, and I smashed his arm down, my fingers digging into his wrist. I grabbed his other wrist, forcing it flat to the grass.

He writhed like an eel beneath me, but I'd spent more hours than him in the gym, especially lately, and I used that to my advantage, bearing down on him, forcing him to give up fighting.

We were both panting, his wiry body quivering beneath mine. My cock was hard, so bloody hard, my crotch smashed to his. Rod let out a sound that was half lust, half frustration, a sound I understood all too well.

It might as well have come from my own heart.

"You're killing me," he whispered. He shifted beneath me, his hard cock sliding against mine, the touch heaven and hell all at once.

I wanted him. I loved him. I couldn't deny it.

And just once in my life, just once, I wanted to let go.

I wanted him to know how I felt. To know I shared his misery.

To know I shared his love.

I slid my crotch against his, both of us moaning. He stared up at me, his eyes glassy with tears, and I couldn't stop myself any longer.

I lowered myself on top of him, brought my lips to his, and he opened to me, his tongue meeting mine in a caress that made my whole body shudder.

I ground our hips together, our tongues clashing with each other, and then I let go of his wrists, brought my hands to his cheeks, and snogged him for all I was worth.

Rod wound a hand into my hair, the other going to my low back and pressing us together, the slide of our cocks intensifying. He threw a leg over my arse, the added pressure making me move faster.

I loved him. I did.

I've been in love with Rod Taylor most of my life.

As wrong as it was.

No matter what my family thought, being with Rod felt right. Holding him in my arms, grinding against him.

Loving him in the way I'd always wanted to.

He arched beneath me with a guttural cry, his body stiffening as he came, and I sped up the pace, imagining that I was fucking him. Electricity shot from my balls through my cock, making me shiver as I came so hard I thought I'd pass out.

I lay atop him, panting, my body slick with sweat, my cum cooling in my jeans, my heart pounding.

Rod stroked my beard, his eyes wary. "You'd better not deny this, Devkinandan. Or you're dead to me."

I shook my head and kissed him, feathering my lips over his, tasting the beer he'd been drinking, inhaling the scent of his sweat, the scent of our combined arousal, our sex. "I can't deny it. I won't," I whispered.

He caressed my hair, hugged me close. "I won't be kept in the closet, Dev," he said.

I nuzzled his neck, my mind whirling. "I can't be you though."

"I'm not asking you to be."

I pulled back and looked at him. "So... what? You want to be boyfriends and get married?"

He studied me for a second. "I wasn't thinking about just us two."

"You mean Sky. How is the three of us any better? We already have the Hot Rod Circus as it is."

He smiled. "She makes us better, and you know it. I want you both in my life."

"I do too." But how would all this work?

Rod shook his head and sighed. "We're going to need her, you know."

I grinned at him. "I know." I touched his cheek. "I love her."

"I know you do," he said. "She's much easier to love than me."

I shook my head. "That's not what's been holding me back."

He cupped the base of my skull. "It's okay. When you said you weren't sure I was capable of loving someone—"

"I was angry. I didn't mean it."

He stared at me. "You *did* mean it. And with good reason. I've wondered the same thing about myself."

My pulse quickened. What was he saying?

"I've kept everyone at arm's length my whole life. I've been a bloody coward, Dev. Too afraid to let anyone know me. Too afraid they wouldn't like what they learn." He broke our eye contact, and I placed my fingers under his chin and made him look at me again.

"I know you, Rod Taylor. Warts and all. And I'm good with all of it."

He grinned at me, then glanced to our left at the edge of the cliff inches away, his face going a bit pale. "For the sake of my heart, can we head back to our room before we plunge to our deaths?"

I roared with laughter, then kissed him once more before letting him go. He scrambled away from the edge and eyed it warily. I put a hand on his shoulder. "I'll always have your back, mate."

He placed a hand over mine, and I kissed the nape of his neck.

I had no idea how any of this was going to work, but I knew one thing: I wouldn't be happy without Rod in my life.

I had to figure out some kind of solution.

And I had to hope my family would forgive me.

ROD

I woke up to the most delicious sensation of wet heat engulfing my morning wood. A tight throat squeezed me, then the flat of a rough tongue slid up from root to crown before firm lips closed around the head of my cock. I shivered and thought I might have died and gone to heaven when the tip of said tongue poked into my slit.

"Fuck."

Awake now, I cracked open an eyelid. A dark head bobbed in my lap. Not such a rare sight honestly. What was rare—as in never before in a million years—was Dev's gorgeous face looking up at me. His dark eyes twinkling with an endearing mix of hope and humor.

"W-what the hell are you doing?" I stammered.

Dev released my cock with a loud pop. He grinned. It was shaky and a little vulnerable, and I fell a little deeper in love with the man, if such a thing were even possible.

"If you don't know, I must be doing it wrong."

His fist remained clasped around my shaft. He moved it up, then back down in a torturous stroke.

I wet my lips. "Just surprised." He stroked me again, pulling a groan from me. "You're doing it splendidly."

Dev grinned and took me into his mouth again, his lips chasing his hand up and down my cock. It was absolute bliss. Still...

I weaved my fingers through Dev's hair. It was coarser than mine, thicker, and I loved feeling it slip over my skin. I bent my knees so I could touch the sides of his head with my legs, feel all that hair against my thighs. The sensation was intense, and I arched my back. I was so fucking close already.

"Dev. Dev, you don't have to do this."

He released me. Smiled. "I know." And then my dick was back inside all that heat, that wet tightness. Christ. I had to look away from him before I lost my load. I didn't want this to end yet.

Dev's fingers closed around my sac. His gorgeous face stared up at me, his soft eyes holding mine, his red lips stretched thin around my straining cock.

It was all too much. I gripped his hair in an attempt to signal what was coming, that *I* was coming.

But he wasn't having any of it. He doubled down, sinking farther on my cock, farther than any blow job virgin had a right to be able to handle. He squeezed my sac, fingered my balls, gave a little tug and—

I went off like a fucking firecracker. Forcing myself to hold his gaze, I snapped my hips and fucked his mouth a few times. He gagged but held on, valiant knight that he was, gripping my thigh with his free hand. I shouted and colors exploded in my eyes as my bollocks emptied into Dev's sinful mouth, in burst after stunning burst.

His throat worked as he swallowed my load. A few drops of the whitish liquid slipped out of the corner of his mouth, trailed into his dark beard. If I hadn't already orgasmed, that would have done the job. Nevertheless, my cock did pulse again letting out another squirt of cum. "You are so fucking hot."

How had I survived so long without him?

I stroked Dev's head and encouraged him to crawl up beside me. I kissed him, deeply. Licked away the traces of my cum in his beard. Tasted myself on him, in his mouth.

Dev chuckled, the sound a touch uncomfortable. "You're bloody dirty, yeah?"

"Yeah." I grinned, then playfully slapped the arse that had got me into so much difficulty the previous day.

He laid his head on my shoulder, his lips against my neck, and sighed. "I never thought I'd ever be like this with you."

I trailed my fingers up and down his muscled arm. "Is it how you hoped it would be?"

"Better."

We snuggled together and I'd almost fallen asleep, when a movement in the sliding glass door caught my eye. A flash of light golden skin, dark brown curls.

Sky.

She held her hands to the sides of her head and peered through the glass, a smile breaking across her pretty mouth when she spotted us.

I grinned and motioned for her to come in, to join us. A three-way shag would be a perfect start to a brilliant day.

But instead of hurrying inside as I'd expected, she pointed to her watch. What was so important that she couldn't spend a few minutes with us? A thread of fear trembled in my belly, but I immediately tamped it down. Dev and I had cleared the air. We had a chance, and I wouldn't be the one to cock it up again. I beckoned to Sky again. She signaled ten minutes, then disappeared.

What the fuck? Why hadn't she come in? She'd seemed entirely too businesslike for so early in the day, especially when Dev was in my arms. I knew she enjoyed watching us together. Just as I enjoyed watching her with Dev.

I realized then how much I truly wanted her too. As much as I wanted Dev. It was all within reach. I could sense my happiness, our happiness, all three of us, that ephemeral something within inches of my fingertips. I desperately wanted it for myself and for them, but it would take a lot of convincing. Dev still had his family concerns, and Sky, did she still think this was all about the deal with me?

That sodding deal. The guilt of what I'd done lay heavy on my conscience. Did it weigh on hers too? Or was this all truly about her job? About the money? Christ, I hoped not.

I nudged Dev's shoulder. I decided to be honest with him, and while some truths were more difficult than others to share, this one I wouldn't be hiding. "Sky was here."

He raised his head and gave me a lazy look. "When?"

"Just now."

Dev sat up. His expression was confused. "Where did she go? Didn't she want to join us?"

I raised my shoulder. "I waved her in. But she just pointed to her watch and signaled ten minutes, then took off."

"Did she seem upset?"

"Not particularly." I gave Dev a light kiss. "I'm sure it was nothing. She probably just wanted to give us some time together."

Dev stood and reached for a pair of clean boxer briefs in his dresser. I snorted. "My, aren't you eager this morning."

He stepped into his briefs, then his shorts. His lips curved at the corner. "I wouldn't want her to get lonely without us."

"Is that right?"

Damn, this man was perfect. If he'd allow himself to be a part of this, we could have something really beautiful together. I hopped out of bed and began dressing. Dev snorted. "I haven't seen you move so fast since that fat-arsed footballer chased you across the yard in middle school."

"Christ." That was not one of my fonder memories. Although… "I seem to remember you running right alongside me."

"Bloody right. No one beats on my friends."

"Except you," I said with humor. Dev punching me yesterday had been so unexpected.

"Fuck." Dev rested his hands on his hips and dropped his chin to his chest. He shook his head, then looked up at me, his eyes shiny with tears. He took two big strides and stopped right in front of me. His hand went to my jaw and his thumb lightly stroked my still-tender nose. "I'm so bloody sorry for hitting you." His voice cracked. "That's not who I am."

"I know, and I forgive you."

"It won't ever happen again."

"I know." I pulled him in for a hug. When the feel of his smooth chest against mine started to get a rise out of me, I gave him a final kiss. "We better get going. We have an album to write, haven't we?"

Dev smiled, at ease for the first time in a long while. This was the Dev I'd first fallen for. I hoped that I could hold onto him. But to do that, I needed Sky. Together, the three of us were a perfect fit. No other combination was viable. I knew that now. I understood it.

Would she?

Or had the sodding deal I'd made with her in a moment of despair fucked things up between us for good?

Her refusal to join us did not bode well.

Not at all.

Chapter 10

SKY

After seeing Rod and Dev in bed together, my heart was a bruised, broken mess. I was thrilled for them though. Fixing their relationship was the whole reason I'd accepted Daniel's offer in the first place. They deserved each other, deserved to be together, deserved to be happy.

It was what I'd wanted for them since Palm Springs. So why wasn't I happy about it? Why did I feel so let down, so alone? I should be ecstatic. The guys were together, and King's Cross was no longer on the verge of breaking up. Sonic High and Reeling would be happy, everyone would keep their jobs, TI would get 500,000 pounds, and I'd get 500,000 pounds in addition to fifteen percent of TI.

I should be floating on air. Jumping for joy. Instead, tears burned the back of my throat.

The band walked into the rehearsal space, a boisterous group, talking and joking, razzing each other. Dev and Rod followed. Rod's arm was slung around Dev's shoulders. It looked friendly, but I knew better. They were all smiles, happy and relaxed.

Despite my heavy heart, my insides warmed. It was good to see them like this. The others must've agreed, because there was a lightness in the air and an energy that had been missing since we'd first arrived on the island. The band seemed united around its two principal members.

Daniel walked in accompanied by Nigel and Vanessa. Daniel looked at

Rod and Dev, and the stiffness left his shoulders. He broke away from the others and came over to me. "Mission accomplished?" he asked in a low, hopeful voice.

"Mission accomplished," I affirmed. I smiled despite my desire to cry. Now I could tell Rod and Dev about the TI deal. Rod, of course, already knew about the bonus; that was something else we'd have to come clean about to Dev. I'd take all the blame.

Daniel beamed. He patted my shoulder. "Great work. Now to get through the final three days."

I nodded, my stomach twisting into a knot so tight a scream stung my throat.

As soon as he wandered off to relay the good news to Nigel, Rod and Dev came over to me. Dev's smile almost knocked me on my ass.

Rod tilted his chin up. "Why didn't you join us earlier?"

"I didn't want to interrupt. You looked very cozy." I shot them a teasing wink I wasn't feeling. At all. "Guess you worked it out?"

Rod shot a glance at Dev and smirked. "More like fucked it out."

Dev elbowed Rod in the ribs. His face went red, but he did nothing to hide his soft gaze when he looked at Rod.

"Congratulations," I said, forcing a jovial tone. "We can all go home now."

Dev surprised me by taking my hand. "Not so fast."

"Oh?"

Rod held my stare. "We've been talking."

"You had time for that, did you?" I chuckled. A tiny bit of envy colored the sound. I'd have loved to be in that bed with them this morning, to share in their newly admitted love for each other.

"A minute or two," Rod said with a wink, and Dev's blush deepened. The man was so sweet. How could a rock star be so easily embarrassed? Based on the stories I'd heard from the roadies through Vanessa, the two of them hadn't held anything back when it came to having sex with fans and crewmembers. Yet here Dev was, blushing like a schoolboy at veiled references to his nocturnal activities with Rod.

Dev squeezed my fingers lightly. His serious expression was filled with concern. It made my pulse race. "I think we need to talk, the three of us. Tonight," he said.

I tamped down my anxiety. I knew what he wanted to discuss. I knew how this would end. But I really wanted to hold onto my dream until the end of this trip.

Three more days. God, please give me these three days.

I cleared my throat, plastered on a smile. "Okay, we'll talk." Dev opened his mouth. I arched a brow. "*If* you win today's challenge."

Rod's brow furrowed so deeply a V appeared on his forehead. "What is it?"

"You'll find out soon enough," I said. I motioned for them to follow me over to the others.

When we reached the rest of the band, I stood silently and waited for them to notice me. When the talking died down, I clasped my hands and brought them under my chin. "Today will be a little different than our usual routine. You have one last challenge."

Amid groaning and whining from the guys, I pressed on. "It's come to my attention that some of you don't feel like full-fledged band members. And honestly, from what I've observed, I understand that feeling completely."

Rod rolled his eyes. "What's this now?"

Dev, on the other hand, looked guilty as hell. He'd spent more time with the band than Rod had, and Damon wasn't as shy as the others about voicing his opinions.

"So, the challenge, your final challenge, is to write a song as a *group*." I emphasized that last part. "Everyone must participate, and everyone will share equally in the songwriting credits."

When Rod opened his mouth, I held up my hand. "It's already been cleared with Nigel and the label."

His jaw shut, although he continued to watch me with narrowed eyes.

"You will have until three this afternoon to complete this task. If you manage to do it, tomorrow will be a free day with a big bonfire party in the evening to celebrate my birthday, and you're all invited."

The guys cheered.

Rod and Dev looked surprised. "It's your birthday?" Dev asked.

I nodded. "If you don't succeed, Daniel, Vanessa, and I will go to Papeete and party." I looked at all of them. "And this song you write, along with the others you've put together already, will need to be finalized today because…" I paused dramatically. Six sets of eyes tracked me expectantly.

"Because you have a gig in Papeete in three days. We're going to close out this trip with one hell of a bang!"

"Fucking A!" Damon shouted. He jumped around, hugging and high-fiving the other band members. Only Dev and Rod didn't seem as elated as the others.

"Something wrong, boys?" I asked.

"Three days to write and fine-tune songs and prepare for a show? I don't believe that's possible," Dev said.

"It's not possible, Sky." Rod turned to Nigel. "What the fuck were you thinking, mate? Dev and I are going to have to work like dogs while those tossers are sunning their white arses on the beach."

"You and Dev?" I asked. Had they not heard a word I'd said?

Rod indicated the other four men. "They don't have to win a free day. They get one by default."

I gathered my hair into my hands at the base of my neck and shook it off my damp skin. Someone needed to turn up the air-conditioning in here. It was hot, humid, and I was getting a little upset with Rod and Dev's attitude. Out of the corner of my eye, I saw Damon coming toward us. His normally bright expression was screwed into a grimace, his eyes throwing darts at Rod and Dev.

"You see," Damon said when he reached me. "That's the sort of shit Jules, and Mick and Tommy have been putting up with for years." He shook Mick's hand off his shoulder. "If having a stiff upper lip means shutting your mouth while others walk all over you, then fuck that. I'm American. I'm loud, and I'm fucking proud."

Jules and Tommy had crossed their arms, the two of them eyeing the floor with sudden interest. Mick scratched his chin and shrugged, his gaze bouncing from Damon, to Rod, to Dev, and then me. I expected him to say something, but he just looked at me, as if taking my measure.

"Damon's right," I said. Damon nodded and his stiff shoulders relaxed a bit. I focused my attention on Rod and Dev. "My instructions were clear. King's Cross will be writing this song, and I hope others, as a group. Not just the two of you." Rod still looked baffled.

I sighed. "Look, if you truly want King's Cross to not only survive, but to thrive, you need to work as a team. Each of you"—I looked from one to the other—"has different skills and different talents. Put all your best skills and talents together, pool your assets, so to speak, and you won't only be a good band, you'll be a great one."

"It's not that simple," Rod said. He still looked like he wanted to argue.

"You trust me, Rod?"

He hesitated for a moment, a second really, then nodded.

I swallowed. "Good. I've been doing this for long enough to have proof positive. You all have different experiences, different influences. Use them to enrich your music, to evolve your sound, and perhaps, reach a broader audience."

I took his hand. I knew he had the most to lose from this. I hoped he could also see how much he stood to gain. "Give it a try, please?"

He tugged on my arm, pulling me flush against his body. I squeaked in surprise, which made him grin. "For you, I'd do anything." He gave me a big, sloppy, and very work-inappropriate kiss. Then, he swung me out of his arms with a swat on my ass. "Now, let us get to work. I have a busy evening planned."

"Okay then." I wiggled my fingers. "Ta-ta for now." I left the rehearsal space with more spring in my step than I'd had walking in.

Until I remembered my promise to Daniel. I couldn't put off telling Rod and Dev why I'd taken this job, why I'd done what I'd done. I just hoped they wouldn't hate me because of it.

ROD

Sky and her bloody challenges. One day to write a song together. It was hard enough sometimes when it was just me and Dev. And now we had four other opinions to consider?

Did she think hits were written by committee?

They came from the gut. The heart. Writing a song wasn't some free-for-all where everyone pitched in a bit.

And on top of throwing four others into the mix, Dev and I were rusty as a songwriting team. We hadn't done a damn thing together—well, nothing new—in months.

Because writing a song together, throwing ideas out there, took trust.

He and I had that now again. Finally. But what about the others? I looked them over, Sky's words sinking in. About how they felt like second-class citizens.

My eyes landed on Damon. The handsome fucker stared back at me, his arms crossed like mine.

He'd probably been hoping I'd walk away from the band and let him step into my place.

He could sod off. King's Cross was my bloody band.

Mine and Dev's.

Damon lifted his chin. "I can take the lead, get us started. I have some ideas."

"Oh really? You think you write songs?" I asked, not bothering to disguise my disbelief. "Give us a taste, then."

The Yank wasn't stupid; I'd give him that. He knew a challenge when he heard it. He grabbed his guitar and launched into something hard and fast.

Something I bloody hated. It wasn't our sound. And the lyrics were mostly shit. I let him finish though. He did have some good moves at the mic, and the riff wasn't terrible.

It just wasn't us.

He finished and looked at me. "Well?"

I shrugged. "It needs more personality. Everything you were singing? It was bollocks. Rubbish you didn't mean." I tapped my chest. "*This* is where hit songs come from."

Dev stepped forward and cleared his throat. "I like the melody. I think we can work with that. Let's slow it down, lighten the sound, and then let it get a bit harder for the chorus."

He grabbed his Telecaster and started playing. It was more or less the same song, but in Dev's hands, it was transformed from something generic to something with heart.

To give the Yank some credit, he was nodding his head and grinning. When Dev finished, he clapped. "Fuck, dude, I said it before. You are *much* better at this than you give yourself credit for."

Dev shrugged, but I could see he was chuffed.

An idea came to me. "Can you both play lead?"

"At the same time?" Damon asked.

Dev nodded. "We could. We could write two lead bits that intertwine."

"Let's hear it," I said.

Damon and Dev noodled around for a bit, starting and stopping, Tommy, Mick, and Jules joining in, Dev gently directing the show, coaxing the song together.

I stood there, watching, absorbing the beat, the rise and fall of the melody, seeing the joy on Dev's face, the charge he was getting out of writing a new song, the ideas coming fast and furious from Damon and the others as they improvised.

Maybe this could work. Maybe King's Cross needed to change.

I'd been so focused on Dev and me, I hadn't even realized where else we were weak. Why Sonic High and Reeling thought we needed to freshen things up.

This new song was still King's Cross. But better.

And we had Sky to thank for it. The girl who'd turned everything upside down. She'd walked in the door, stolen my heart and Dev's, and brought us together.

The girl who still wasn't quite ours. And then I knew what this song was about.

I stepped up to the mic and started to sing:

You're just a waif of a girl
But you shook my whole damn world
Though you're not "just" anything
Oh no, you're everything

I looked over at Dev and he smiled. When we hit the chorus, I sang:

You said "no strings"
And I hoped you were lying

I didn't have the rest yet, but Dev picked up where I left off:

You said "no strings"
I said "yes" but inside I was dying

"Bloody brilliant!" I said into the mic. I started the next verse:

The day you came into my life
You brought along a ray of light
But ever since you up and left
It's only been eternal night

We worked out the rest of the lyrics, Dev getting the idea for the third verse. "Something about owning my heart, I think," he said.

"Yeah." I ran with it, then changed up the last refrain of the chorus, Dev realizing where I was going, joining in on the final lines:

Oh I knew I was lying
Oh I knew I was dying

We finished with a fist bump, and I wanted to kiss him. I almost did, but I pulled back at the last second. I wasn't sure if Dev was ready to be public with the guys.

But yeah, Damon wasn't dumb. He looked from Dev to me and repeated the chorus, shaking his head. "I fucking *knew* it!" he said.

"Knew what?" I asked.

Mick, Tommy, Jules appeared to all be all ears.

"The three of you," Damon said. "Hot damn!"

I met Dev's gaze and he smiled, but I'd take his cue. When he didn't confirm anything, I just raised an eyebrow at Damon. "Think what you will. Dude."

"Dude, come on!"

I winked at him.

We'd "come out" when all three of us were ready, and not a second sooner.

SKY

For a pre-birthday surprise, Rod and Dev booked us a night at a five-star resort that featured private overwater luxury bungalows.

Tony drove us to the resort. The ride over had been a little tense as I worried about what I'd say to them and what they might want to say to me. When we arrived, the sight of the sun setting over the lagoon took my breath away. We stood on the deck of our bungalow with our arms around each other's waists, me between my two strong men.

My.

The thought stalled in my brain. They weren't mine to keep, were they? I was operating on borrowed time. As though sensing my discomfort, Dev bumped my hip with his. "Fancy a swim?"

"Now?"

"Why not?" he asked, then looked at Rod. "Yeah?"

Rod grinned. "Righto, mate." He whipped off his shirt so quickly, I laughed.

"I don't have a suit."

Rod shoved his jeans down his long legs, leaving him in only a pair of mouthwatering black trunks. He winked. "Neither do I, love."

"Come on, Sky." Dev took off his shirt. "It's dark. No one will see."

Rod shot his hand out and rubbed it over Dev's well-defined abs. "Can't say I care one way or the other."

Dev chuckled and shoved his hand away. "There'll be none of that."

"Ha! You won't be able to keep your hands off me." He slid his hands down his own chest. My eyes followed his movements, down to the growing bulge in his trunks. I could see the ridge of his cock through the thin material. I wanted it. Shit. Maybe Rod was right. Maybe I wouldn't be able to keep my hands off him.

Dev unzipped his jeans and wiggled out of them. Rod's grin widened when he saw Dev's arousal. Rod was definitely right. Neither one of us would be able to keep our hands to ourselves.

Both men closed in on me. Dev smirked. "You're falling behind, sweets."

"Yes..." God, I couldn't think, much less be coherent, when he looked at me like that. With a hunger and intensity that said he wanted me. Now.

I turned around. "Could you—?" I indicated the zipper down my back.

"Straight away." He stepped behind me and lowered the zipper. Slowly. I felt something warm brush my skin. A kiss. With every inch he exposed, Dev kissed my spine. All the way down my back. By the time he reached the bottom, I was breathing hard and panting. Rod slipped the straps off my shoulders and the dress dropped to the floor, leaving me standing between them in only my sandals, panties, and bra.

"You're bloody gorgeous." Rod's voice lowered to that husky tone I loved so much. His eyes trailed over my body, taking in every curve, every valley, before he looked over my shoulder. "Our girl's a beauty, yeah, Dev?"

Our girl.

Oh God. My legs shook. Dev's arm caught me about the waist and he kissed me below my ear. "That she is, mate, a right beauty."

My entire body blazed with heat everywhere Dev touched mine with his skin and everywhere Rod touched me with his eyes. I wanted them both. Not just for now, but forever.

"I love you, Sky." Dev's whispered words were like a dousing of water, eliminating all the heat I'd been feeling. I struggled out of his hold. "You don't love me, Dev."

"I do."

"No, you don't. You might think you do, but you can't."

I kicked off my shoes and dove into the crystal-clear water. I had to get away from them, just for a few minutes. Just long enough to get my thoughts in order.

But Dev had other plans. He dove in after me, Rod right behind him. He surfaced in front of me and wiped the water from his face. It was stern with more than a touch of hurt in his eyes. "Explain to me why I can't love you."

Since I couldn't touch the bottom, I had to tread water. "You don't know me, Dev. Neither do you, Rod."

"Then tell us, sweets. Tell us what you think we need to know. Tell us what you think negates how I feel about you."

I rolled my eyes. "Including the weekend in Palm Springs, you've spent a total of what? Twenty days with me? You *can't* love me. Heck, you don't even know where I'm from, do you?"

He blinked, glanced at Rod. "From America, eh?"

Rod snorted. "I think she means for us to be a bit more specific than that, mate."

"Berkeley," Dev said suddenly.

Rod held up his hand for a high-five as though they'd just answered a question on a game show. "How did you know that?" Rod asked.

"I remember her telling Damon the first day we were here."

"Righto. I missed that day, didn't I?"

"Oh, for fuck's sake," I groaned. "Fine. What did I study? How did I grow up?"

Rod pressed his palms to my cheeks. His eyes burned into mine, and when he asked, "Who hurt you so badly?" his voice was so gentle I choked on a sob.

"Yes, exactly. You don't know anything about me." I dove under the water and swam a few yards away before coming up for air. I floated on my back and looked up at the tropical evening sky, where a few vestiges of color still remained.

The water around me burbled, and then Rod and Dev were there. I straightened and treaded water to keep my head above the surface.

"I told you about my family, Sky," Dev said.

"And I told you about my dad," Rod added. "Whatever happened to you, you can tell us."

"It's really nothing," I said, backpedaling. I really didn't want to dredge up all those old feelings.

"Nothing isn't what's keeping you at a distance," Dev said.

"I'm not—" I began.

"Yes, you are, love. You go through the motions, but you never let yourself go. You're always in your head, always in control. Your heart is shrouded behind a steel curtain." Rod pulled me into his arms. "I want in behind the curtain."

Dev swam up beside Rod and held my neck. "As do I. Let us in."

My eyes welled, and a tear rolled over my lashes to mix with the water of the lagoon. I didn't deserve their kindness, not after what I'd done, but they did deserve my honesty. And even if I couldn't be completely truthful yet, I could give them this.

"Okay." I nodded. "I'll tell you. Let's go back to the bungalow first."

"Last one there is a rotten egg," Rod said, dropping me like a hot potato.

I sank below the surface, laughing and sputtering in surprise. "Oh, you are such an ass!" I shouted at his retreating back as he swam toward our bungalow.

He paused for a second and threw over his shoulder, "Now, now, love. Name-calling is very unbecoming of a lady."

Dev shook his head, but his mouth was quirked into a grin, making it clear how much Rod amused him, and how happy he was to have his friend back. Dev and I swam back at a much more sedate pace, and when we reached the deck of our bungalow, Dev climbed up, then held his hand out to me. I took it, and he hauled me out of the water.

We found Rod lazing in the hot tub. He'd opened a bottle of white wine. It and three glasses sat on a table near the tub. "Hop in, love. Your teeth are chattering."

He was right. They were. I stepped into the water and groaned in delight as the heat enveloped me. Dev got in and sat beside me, with Rod on my other side. He kissed my temple, "Go on. Tell us."

Now that my story had so much lead up, I was sure they'd be let down. It wasn't a story of strife and hard times.

"All right, but you're going to be disappointed."

"I doubt that," Rod said. He handed me a glass of wine and one to Dev before taking the third for himself. "To the truth setting us free."

"Ha." I said.

"Cheers," Dev said.

We drank. I set my glass on the edge of the tub and stared off into the night. "So, I grew up in a fairly unconventional way. My parents raised me in a cohousing environment." When they gave me identical blank looks, I said, "Think of it as a commune."

"Ah," Dev said. "That explains the name."

"Sort of. When my parents joined this community, they changed their names and picked River as their last name. My mother's name is Moon."

"That fits," Rod said. "Moon River. Nice tune."

"And my father is Jerry."

Rod frowned. "That doesn't."

"No?" I said. "Think about it."

"Gerry Butler?" he asked.

I laughed. "No. Jerry with a J. Grateful Dead?"

Rod shrugged. "I've never much listened to American music from the '70s."

"Jerry Garcia," Dev said. "The man was a genius with the guitar."

Rod threw a hand in the air. "Fine. You win that round, mate."

Grinning, I shook my head and got back to my story. "Anyway, living in the community when I was a kid was amazing. My parents have a souvenir shop/surf shop on the beach, so I spent almost every day at the shore, scavenging for material for my dad's art projects with my friends."

"Your father is an artist?" Dev asked.

"Well,"—I raised a shoulder and dropped it—"he likes to think so." I chuckled. "He makes these huge sculptures out of junk—literal junk. Things that people forget on the beach."

"And he sells the sculptures?" Rod asked, looking skeptical

"Surprisingly, yes."

"Americans," he said, rolling his eyes. That one word expressed so much, I had to laugh.

"My two best friends were Blue and Sunshine."

"Of *course* they were," Rod snorted.

"Oh, do let her continue," Dev said, giving Rod the side-eye.

"Fine." Rod made a zipping motion over his lips. "I'll keep mum."

Now it was Dev's turn to roll his eyes.

"Blue, Sunshine, and I did everything together, and when I turned seventeen, Blue became my boyfriend."

"Oh, Blue is a boy?" Dev asked, his expression one of utter perplexity.

"Yes." I patted his hand. "Blue and I dated for a couple years. Everything was great the first year. But then I went to college. I still lived at home because I went to UCLA Berkeley, but let's just say if going to college hadn't been bad enough, my choice of major was."

"He didn't approve?" Rod asked.

"Not just him."

Dev frowned. "Your parents were disappointed that you went to uni? I'm confused."

Given what I knew of Dev's history, I understood. I flattened my lips. "Wanting a higher education was not seen as something benefiting the community. Sunshine even told me I was a snob, that I wanted to prove to everyone that I was better than they were, but that wasn't it at all."

"What did you study?" Rod asked.

"Business administration."

He nodded.

"At the end of my freshman year, Blue proposed, and I accepted. I was so happy. I thought he was the love of my life."

"You were engaged? At seventeen?" Dev's eyes were round and disbelieving.

"Well, I was eighteen by then."

"You aren't married now, so I'm assuming things didn't work out?" Rod asked with surprising gentleness.

"What I didn't know when I accepted his proposal was that he expected me to quit school. I obviously refused. Blue was particularly upset about my being away at school and having to study so much. He wanted us to spend our days on the beach or working in the shop my parents ran for the community." I looked at Rod, then at Dev. "But I wanted more, you know?"

Dev put his arm around my shoulders, a silent show of support.

I took a deep breath and forced the next words out of my mouth. "One day, I came home and Blue and Sunshine were having sex in the room I shared with Blue."

Dev's eyes went round. "You shared a room with your boyfriend in your parents' home, and you were only eighteen?"

"Well, it isn't exactly their home. It's the community's home, but yes. It was expected."

"What did you do?" Rod asked.

"Just what you think. I yelled and screamed."

"And them?"

"They invited me to join them."

Rod snorted and Dev looked pole-axed. "To join them? Well I never!"

"I'd have done the same," Rod said.

"Truly, mate?" Dev asked. "If you found Sky in bed with, say, Mick, you would ask to join them?"

Rod's face hardened, his lips pressed together.

"Right," Dev said.

"Well, to be fair," I said, "I'm kind of the oddball in that community. When I found out about my parents' open marriage, I didn't know how to feel. I just knew it wasn't for me. I'd shared all of this with Blue and

Sunshine. Hell, I'd shared everything with them over the years, but I wasn't going to share Blue. They didn't understand how I felt. They told me I needed to grow up." Tears wet my cheeks. "I left that night and never went back."

Rod scooted over, closer to me. Our shoulders and thighs touched. "I'm sorry they betrayed your trust, love."

I leaned my head on his shoulder. His heat and comforting touch soothed me. "That means a lot."

Dev laid his hand on my thigh. "What bothered you most—that they slept together, or that they didn't include you?"

I looked at him sharply. "How can you ask me that?"

"Isn't it obvious?"

I glanced at Rod, who seemed equally lost. "No."

Dev used his hand to indicate the three of us. "I'm not sure what you call what we're doing, but there are three of us, not two, and it doesn't seem to bother you."

His hand returned to my thigh. A flash of annoyance had me stiffening. But that wasn't right. I relaxed and forced myself to think about his question. "Living in a poly-type situation can be difficult. There can be unexpected jealousies, disappointments, not to mention having to be concerned about multiple people and protecting everyone's feelings. It's really a juggling act." I looked up at Rod, then back at Dev. "We've already had a taste of that."

"I understand. But you didn't answer my question," Dev said. "What were you really upset about?"

I nibbled on the nail of my thumb as I tried to put into words exactly what I'd felt seeing Blue and Sunshine in bed together. "I guess... I can't really say I had objections to being in a threesome... although I'm not really into women. I suppose Sunshine and I could have shared Blue." What I'd said was the truth, but it wasn't the crux of the problem, was it? My throat closed. I blew out a breath and pressed my hunched shoulders down. "We'd always done everything together, and... and... they'd left me out of that part of their relationship. I mean, yes, Blue and I had been sleeping together without Sunshine, but she did know about it. Hell, everyone knew about it. What they did behind my back... not telling me... I just couldn't live with it."

Dev nodded. "So, you didn't want to be in a threesome with Sunshine, or you didn't want an open relationship? Actually"—he bit his lip, an innocent gesture that made him look years younger—"I'm not exactly clear on the difference."

"Well, I'm open to a threesome, obviously, but not a free-for-all. An open relationship is one where each partner is free to have other partners. Typically, there is no obligation for the partner to know about the others.

However, that's totally dependent on each couple's agreement. Most people in the community are only open to sharing their partners with others in the community. We all lived and worked together, so generally everyone knew about everyone else's partners."

I shuddered, remembering how awkward I'd felt the first time I realized how many of the men and women at the dinner table had slept with my parents.

"It does seem a healthy way to live," Rod said.

Dev glared at him. "Does it now?"

"Theoretically." Rod grinned. "Don't worry, poppet," he leaned over me to level a smacking kiss on Dev's mouth. "I only have eyes for the two of you."

"Poppet?!" Dev choked.

Rod laughed. "Darling, doll, dove, pet, honeysop?"

"Please stop." Dev groaned and dropped his head onto my shoulder. "What are we going to do with him?"

Rod pulled me into his lap and scooted us both over next to Dev. He reached over Dev's lap and fisted his cock, then dropped his other hand between my legs. "I can think of a few things."

The low growl in his voice had me forgetting about my parents, about Blue and Sunshine, about all the fears and questions racing around my mind. I'd have time to think about them tomorrow. Or never.

For now, all I wanted was to enjoy my two men in Tahiti while I still had them.

Chapter 11

DEV

Although I wanted to get to the sex that Rod had initiated in the hot tub, I wanted to make sure we didn't forget the other part of our girl's birthday gift. I put my hand over Rod's on my shaft and squeezed to halt his movements. I looked at him, meeting his eyes and said, "Hold up, mate. Did you forget?"

He gave me a blank look. Rod had a one-track mind when it came to sex, and once he was in that zone, it was nearly impossible to shake him out of it. But I didn't want to spoil our surprise for Sky. While we weren't quite ready to debut "No Strings" for her, we had something else we wanted to sing instead. I started humming it, then Rod caught on and began crooning Van Morrison's "Brown-Eyed Girl" in her ear.

I joined in on the chorus, but of course we changed "my" to "our."

Sky was our brown-eyed girl. The girl who'd stolen our hearts.

The girl we wanted with us forever.

Tears rose in Sky's eyes and she wiped at them. I leaned forward to kiss them away as Rod finished singing.

"You okay, love?" he asked.

"I'm just overwhelmed."

"I think we all are," I said, leaning in and kissing her. I pulled her off Rod and onto my lap, cuddling her close, Rod kissing the nape of her neck, then pressing kisses all along her throat. He stopped and looked at me, our mouths only inches apart, then I leaned forward and snogged him.

Sky sucked in a breath, and I turned to her and kissed her again, then Rod gripped her chin and took her mouth, the sight stirring something in me.

The three of us together—it just felt right. Like everything I needed. But how much longer could I have it?

She shifted in my lap, her pussy brushing against my stiffening cock, and I wanted inside her. She reached between us, gripping me in her fist.

"What do you boys say we take this to the bed?" she asked.

"No argument here," Rod said. He rose and offered her a hand out of the hot tub. She stepped out, then reached for me.

"Hurry up, slowpoke," she teased.

I piled out behind them, and we quickly dried off with the fluffy white towels the resort had stacked next to the tub.

They were both so fucking gorgeous—Sky with her brown skin, her high, full tits calling to me, Rod with his well-muscled narrow-hipped perfection, his long, thick cock jutting upward, begging to be touched, to be sucked.

He took Sky's hand and ushered her to the bed, throwing me a teasing wink over his shoulder. "Play your cards right, Devkinandan, and you can have us both."

My cock twitched at the idea. Having them both… Feverish images filled my mind, and I knew what I wanted, and how.

"Get on your back," I said to Rod.

He raised a brow at me. "Want to be in charge again?"

"Yeah. That a problem?"

He shook his head and looked at Sky. "Love?"

She smiled and shook her head. "Where do you want me?" she asked, looking me up and down, her eyes landing on my rock-hard cock. I palmed it, and heat flared in her gaze.

"I want you on top of Rod, sixty-nine style."

Rod lay back on the canopy bed, looking tanned against the white drapery of the canopy and the sheets. Sky crawled up next to him on all fours, flashing me her glistening pussy.

"Leave room for me behind you, Sky," I said, the words low and raspy, betraying my excitement.

She and Rod scooted down the bed, and she straddled his face. "Like this?" she asked.

She looked so sexy, her open legs just inches above Rod's mouth. He was already caressing her arse, trying to urge her down to his lips.

"Perfect. Now lean forward and take Rod in your mouth," I said, reaching for the condoms lying on the nightstand. I started rolling one on while watching them. She took his cock in hand, licking all around the head like it was an ice-cream cone, and I thought about joining her. But he'd be getting a different sort of attention from me later.

Instead, she was going to get loved by both of us.

She'd sunk down and let Rod suck on that sweet little cunt, and the sight of her grinding down on his face, the way he ate her, revved me up more than I thought possible.

He added a couple fingers to the mix and she moaned, grinding on him harder. Our beautiful Sky wanted to be fucked, I could tell. I climbed up on the mattress behind her and pressed down on her back, making her spread wider for Rod. "Arch a bit, sweets," I said.

She did, and Rod chased her pussy with his tongue. I lined myself up, then slid inside her, making us both groan. I fucked her gently, enjoying the way she moaned for me around Rod's cock.

I felt a hand on my balls, then a tongue. Rod of course. He was good at improvising, but I wanted Sky to feel us both pleasuring her. I'd have my moment with Rod later.

"Focus on Sky, mate," I said. "You'll get your turn."

"So bossy," he said, a smile in his voice.

I knew when he went back to her clit because she sucked in a breath and let out a moan. "That feels so…" She seemed a loss, then said, "Fucking awesome."

"You like it, both of us at the same time this way?" I asked, leaning over to whisper it in her ear.

"I do. I love it," she said, reaching back and hooking a hand around my neck, pulling me in for a kiss.

She'd risen up and let go of Rod, but he apparently didn't mind. He lapped at her harder, the sound of him working her, the hitch in her breath making me want to fuck her harder. I pressed her forward again, then upped the pace as she took Rod in her mouth again.

She pressed back against me, and Rod held her hips tight, not letting her move much. I placed my hands over his, squeezing his fingers, and we focused on her, making her shudder and cry out around Rod's cock.

Her pussy clenched around me, and she convulsed, almost making me tip over the edge myself. I pulled out quickly, not wanting this to be over. I wasn't done. Far from it.

It was Rod's turn to be the focus.

I picked up the tube of lube and got off the mattress. I walked down to the end, where Rod's legs dangled off the edge.

"Put your feet up on the mattress, mate," I said.

He did as I asked, peering at me around Sky's hips. "Are you—" he started to ask.

I held up the lube. "I am."

His eyes lit up. "Be gentle."

I smacked his flank. "Be gentle?"

He laughed. "You know me too well, Dev."

Well, actually, I didn't know this side of him very well. But I could guess, based on the stories he'd told me.

I squirted some lube on my fingers, noting how Sky's eyes tracked my movements even as she resumed blowing Rod. She must've done something particularly nice because his fingers tightened on her hips, and he groaned. "Fuck, love. Slow down a bit until Dev joins the party, or I'm going to be done in."

She grinned around him and backed off, watching me start fingering Rod's hole. I circled it, teasing him, and he shifted his hips restlessly, trying to chase me. I finally pressed one finger inside, and he sighed, impaling himself on it.

My cock was eager to get inside him, to finally feel what that would be like, to love Rod the way I'd wanted to for so long. But I didn't want to hurt him.

I added a second finger. He was so damn tight, but he eventually relaxed a bit, and I pushed my fingers in deeper, then withdrew them, then again, waiting for him to press back against them. When he did, I knew he was ready.

I withdrew my fingers and guided my cock to his hole with a shaking hand. I looked at Sky.

"Let's blow his mind," I said to her. She nodded and sank down farther on his cock as I pushed inside him.

So fucking tight.

He groaned and stiffened, and I didn't dare move until he relaxed again.

"Okay?" I asked.

"You're fucking big, you know?" he said.

I grinned. "Am I too much for you?"

"Give me a second, you wanker."

"I'll give you more than that," I teased, wiggling my hips a bit.

He laughed and then pressed against me. "Give me all you have," he said.

I met Sky's eyes. "Shall we?" I asked.

She licked Rod from root to tip and winked at me. "Let's."

Sky descended on him, her pretty lips stretching around his shaft, the sight almost as mind-blowing as being inside my best friend for the first time.

Rod felt fucking amazing. I gripped his hips, holding him in place as I fucked him, my body taking over, knowing what it wanted, my cock driving so deep inside him he'd feel me for days.

Sky's head bobbed up and down and Rod let go of her, his hands gripping the sheets as he thrust up into her mouth, a strangled moan coming out of him. "Fuck yeah," he growled.

We worked him between us, and he twisted in my grip. I firmed my hold on him, pressing into him, listening to his breathing, the way he was starting to shudder, his back arching, and I knew he was going over. I snapped my hips harder, faster, and came hard myself, Sky's gorgeous throat working as she swallowed Rod's release.

God, I loved them. I loved them both.

I pulled out and cleaned up in the bathroom. When I came back, they were snuggled together on the bed, and Rod patted the mattress beside him when he saw me.

I lay down next to him, taking him in my arms and leaning over to kiss Sky.

"Fuck, mate," Rod said, snuggling into my arms. "That was incredible. I thought I'd had my mind blown before, but that was something else."

I grinned and kissed his cheek. "Well, now I know what to get you for Christmas." I stroked his well-trimmed beard. "I love you."

He smiled at me. "Love you too." Then he looked at Sky. "We have you, our lovely brown-eyed girl, to thank for all of this."

She smiled at us and shrugged. "All in a day's work."

We laughed and nestled together. After a moment she asked, "So, how did the songwriting go?"

"It was fucking brilliant," Rod said. "We have you to thank for that too. We'll have some great songs to play for the gig."

"I'm glad," she said, playing with the sparse hair on Rod's chest.

Then why didn't she seem glad?

"Sweets?" I asked. "Something wrong?"

She shook her head. "Just tired out. You two take a lot out of a girl." She smiled at me, and it almost looked real.

I reached over for her hand and squeezed it. "I love you, Sky."

She nodded. "I suppose you do."

"But?" Rod asked.

She shrugged. "Don't mind me. It's been hell of a night."

"You're not getting off that easy, love."

She sighed. "I need a little time to digest all of this, okay?"

Rod touched her cheek. "We're not Blue and Sunshine. Or Rainbow. Or whatever the fuck their names were."

"I know," she whispered. "Just give me a chance to catch up, okay?"

I hoped that was all it was, just her needing to adjust. To accept that she was ours, and we were hers.

SKY

Night was falling as I made my way through the grounds of the Hideaway Resort. My birthday bonfire was already burning on the beach; I could see it flickering through the trees. Vanessa and Daniel had taken over the birthday planning, and that was a good thing.

I hardly felt like celebrating. Sure, Rod and Dev had worked things out. They even seemed to want me with them. But was what they felt truly real? Was it more than just lust mixed with gratitude?

And would it be strong enough to allow them to forgive me?

I hadn't wanted to ruin last night by telling them, but I'd chickened out for the last time. I had to come clean with them about the partnership with TI. And Dev still had no clue about the bonus.

Daniel was right; I had been unethical, using my body to fix this situation, to bring Rod and Dev together. Mixing business with pleasure... and losing my head and my heart in the process.

How could Dev and Rod ever trust me again after that? How could they trust that my feelings for them were genuine? Was that why I didn't trust theirs? Because I wasn't sure myself why I'd done all this, what part the money and the partnership had played in getting me here, what part my own heart had played?

I did love them; I knew that. But would I have come here if the bonus hadn't been dangling in front of me? If Daniel had said no to the partnership idea?

Or were those the convenient excuses I'd used to get myself to go, to risk my battered heart once again?

I was almost to the beach, my heart in my throat, hoping they'd understand what I'd done better than I did. Knowing they might not. But the words had to be said.

I couldn't let myself love them unless they knew the truth. Unless they forgave what I'd done.

Two familiar voices called out my name behind me, and I whirled around, not quite believing my eyes as I made out the dim figures coming my way. "Mom? Dad? What are you doing here?" I asked as they hurried toward me, arms outstretched, Vanessa behind them, grinning from ear to ear.

I wrapped my arms around Mom, and Dad put his arms around us both, enveloping us in a bear hug. I hadn't seen them in weeks, and tears rose to my eyes.

Mom kissed my cheek. "Happy birthday, honey."

Dad kissed me on the other side. "Surprise!"

I wiped my eyes and started laughing. God, it was great to see them. "I still don't understand?"

They gestured to Vanessa, who was snapping pics of our reunion. She waved at me. "It was Daniel's idea. He wanted to do something nice for you."

I guess at least Daniel had forgiven me. Hopefully Rod and Dev would too—whenever I had a chance to tell them.

Dad looked at Vanessa. "Tell me there's food coming." He rubbed his round belly. "I'm starving!"

Mom elbowed him. "Jerry, you ate on the plane."

"You know how I get when I travel. I get nervous. And then I eat."

I couldn't stop myself from smiling. Their hair might be getting grayer, but my parents would never change. And I loved that about him. They were who they were, and they didn't care what anyone else thought.

And though I knew they loved me, they wouldn't love what I done. But they'd forgive me.

That I knew with every fiber of my being. Their love was constant, unwavering.

But was Rod and Dev's love for me that way?

I wanted to spill my guts the moment I saw them, but now was not the time or the place, especially with my parents newly arrived. My confession was unfortunately going to have to wait a little longer.

I walked arm in arm with my parents to the bonfire, the voices of the band and the crew getting louder as we approached.

When we stepped into the firelight, a cheer went up, and Daniel cupped his hands to his mouth and yelled, "Happy twenty-seventh, Sky!" which just increased the hooting and hollering as people held up bottles of beer and glasses of fancy mixed drinks in an impromptu toast.

Rod and Dev stepped forward. "These are your parents?" Dev asked. "Moon and Jerry?"

"Yes," I said, ushering them forward. "Mom, Dad, meet Rod Taylor and Dev Stone of King's Cross." They all shook hands and exchanged hugs since my parents had never met a person they didn't want to hug.

Ever the quick study, Mom glanced between the three of us and said, "So... you two are looking at my daughter like she's your favorite thing in the world."

Rod glanced at Dev, who nodded. "She *is* our favorite thing in the world."

Mom turned an impressed grin on me. "Are they good to you?"

My cheeks blazed, and Vanessa snickered. I gave her a mock glare before answering. "They are."

"They'd better be," Dad said, giving them an assessing look. "Sky is very special."

"We know," Dev said. He and Rod both leaned in and kissed me on my cheeks. "Don't you forget it," Dev whispered.

Would he still feel that way once he knew the truth?

Dev brushed a strand of hair from my face. "Sky, what's wrong?"

I shook my head and plastered on a smile. "Nothing. Just realizing I'm one year closer to thirty."

Dad laughed. "You're still a baby."

"With age comes wisdom," Mom said.

Dad sniffed the air. "I smelled something delicious." He looked at Vanessa. "Where's the food?"

She laughed and ushered him over to the earth oven that had been dug into the sand. "Roast pork and chicken coming up!"

Dad dug into the bowls of fruit and veggies laid out on a buffet table, and Mom put her arm around my waist. She shooed Rod and Dev away. "We need a moment," she said.

They walked off, grinning at each other.

"Mom, that was rude."

"I just want a minute." She gazed at me, her pale blue eyes serious. "After what happened, I'm a bit surprised to see you with them."

"I'm surprised too."

She squeezed my hand. "Blue and Sunshine… they should have been upfront with you. That's the only way this kind of relationship works."

A lump crowded my throat. "I know."

"Are the two of them"—she nodded in Rod and Dev's direction—"together with each other too?"

"Yes. They've been friends since they were kids, but this part of their relationship is new."

"Ah." She gave me a long look. "You know you're getting into? The need for honesty, openness?"

My cheeks started burning again. "I know." God, did I know.

"Okay then, honey, I wish you all the best." She wrapped her arms around me and chuckled. "Two men. I'm so proud of the strong woman I raised!"

I couldn't stop myself from laughing. "I'm not sure 'strong' is the right word. 'Greedy' is probably more like it."

She squeezed me harder. "A woman—a goddess—really does need more than one man to fulfill her needs. Your father knows this."

I rolled my eyes. "Mom!"

She patted my back and let me go. "For a woman with two men, you sure are shy sometimes."

"I really don't want to know any more about your sex life than I already do."

"There's nothing wrong with being a sexual person, Sky."

I crossed my arms and smiled at her. "And there's nothing wrong with having boundaries, either."

Daniel broke in. "Having fun?" he asked, his eyes darting between us.

"Thank you," I said, my voice getting a little thick, and I gave him a quick hug. "I didn't know I needed them here."

"Happy birthday," he whispered before releasing me.

Rod came over and slung an arm around my shoulders. "Trying to nick our girl, eh?" he asked Daniel.

Daniel laughed. "She's all yours." He walked off and Dev joined us, slipping an arm around my waist and kissing my neck. I did my best to swallow down my nerves. I'd tell them after the party. And I'd pray they'd understand. In the meantime, I couldn't let all of Daniel and Vanessa's hard work go to waste.

The booze flowed freely, the food was superb, and it wasn't long before someone grabbed a couple guitars. Soon Dev and Damon and Rod were treating us to acoustic versions of King's Cross's hits, Mick, Tommy, and Jules improvising with sticks and palm fronds and cracking us all up.

The hours flew by, but eventually it was just Mom and Dad, Daniel, and Damon and Vanessa sitting around the fire with me and my guys, Dev and Rod cuddling me from either side.

I'd calmed down. I could do this. I could tell them, and it would be okay. The love in their eyes was so strong, so clear. I would tell them as soon as we got back to my bungalow.

Dad leaned over Mom to talk to Daniel. "So, you're really going to take our Sky away and make her a partner in Total Indulgence?"

Ice slid down my spine. *Oh no. No, no, no!* I looked frantically at Rod and Dev. *I* should be telling them.

Daniel glanced at me and nodded. "She earned it, just like she earned her half of the bonus. If it wasn't for her, King's Cross wouldn't be together."

Dev's eyes bored into mine. "What bonus?" His voice was sharp as broken glass.

"What partnership?" Rod asked.

My stomach wanted to turn inside out. Fuck. This was not how this was supposed to go. "I can explain," I said, the words coming out in a croak.

I looked at Mom, and she put a hand to her mouth, her eyes so full of pity I could've died.

Dad looked between us and said, "What? I thought everybody knew."

"No. *We* didn't," Dev said.

"Well, I *did* know about the bonus," Rod said. "Since I put it up."

"What fucking bonus?" Dev asked.

"A million pounds," Rod said. "I wanted to be sure she'd come."

"So, this is what?" Dev asked. "A *job* to you? 'All in a day's work,' isn't that what you said?" He directed those words at me, and I wanted to crawl into a hole.

Dev would never understand. And the looks Rod was giving were a bit dark as well. I should have at least told him already. He'd understand better than Dev.

After all, Rod had hired me, more or less. And he'd agree to use me to get what he wanted.

And now he had it.

"I fucking told you I *loved* you," Dev said, his face darkening, his tone harsher than I'd ever heard it. "Didn't that mean anything to you?" He smacked Rod on the arm. "Tell her. Tell her how you feel."

Rod started to open his mouth, but I didn't want to hear it. He hadn't told me he loved me for a reason.

He hadn't told me, and I knew why.

I cut off anything Rod was going to say. "Rod let me know me a long time ago where I stand."

"That's not fair, love. A lot has changed since then."

Dev looked between us. "What are you two talking about?"

I rose. "I did this for the two of you. There isn't room for me here."

"Bollocks," Dev spat. "There was plenty of room for you last night."

I looked at Rod. "I think you and Dev need to have a talk so he'll understand."

"So, this really was about the money?" Rod asked.

I crossed my arms and shook my head, my heart breaking. I couldn't even answer, and before I knew where I was going, I was running back to my bungalow, tears streaming down my cheeks.

I'd ruined everything. But better to know now than to learn later.

Right?

ROD

A giant hole opened up in my chest, and the longer I watched Sky merge into the shifting shadows on the other side of the bonfire, the larger it grew. Beside me, waves of hurt and anger rolled off Dev, nearly swamping me with their weight. With my own guilt.

What a bloody cock-up.

I closed my eyes and pinched the bridge of my nose. Dev shifted. I looked at him.

"I'm going to—" He vaguely indicated our bungalow with his thumb. What wasn't vague was the clenching of his jaw and the way his eyes avoided mine. "Dev…" I began.

He kept his face turned away from me, but at least he hadn't walked away. I stepped in front of him, crowded him so our chests touched and my face was in his neck. Dev stiffened. I took courage from the fact that he didn't move. "Please, Dev. I'll tell you everything. Just, please, don't give up on me," I whispered.

His shoulders slumped, and when I felt Dev's hands on my waist, fear gripped me and I held my breath. Would he pull me in or shove me away?

When Dev's arms slid around me, one hand at the small of my back, the other hand at my nape, the air in my lungs came out in such a rush, I felt dizzy.

He trembled against me. "It's too late, Rod," he said.

My heart tripped. "No, Dev, no."

He tightened his arms around me. "I can't ever give you up now."

It took a moment for his words to sink in, but when they did, I clutched his arms and stared into his beautiful wrecked eyes. "You sodding plonker! I just about had a heart attack."

Then I pulled him against me, my arms locking behind his head, and I kissed him in front of anyone and everyone who might be looking. It was sweet and possessive, and rough and tender, and desperate. I'd experienced a virtual roller coaster in the past ten minutes, and my heart was pounding out of my chest.

Dev moaned, arching his neck to deepen the kiss. He pressed into me, and his hard cock rubbed against mine. I shuddered under his assault, and my head spun. Not only was he letting me touch him like this in public, but he was touching me back, kissing me back.

I released his mouth, my hand cupping his cheek, and pulled back to look at him, to see the passion that tightened his jaw and softened his eyes. His pupils were blown so wide they looked almost black, and he was lost in a haze of lust, a sloppy grin on his face.

"Hi," I said, laughing softly.

He tilted his head, his eyes on mine. Then he blinked a few times and looked around us. His eyes widened as though seeing everyone for the first time, just now realizing we weren't alone.

When his gaze returned to my face, he nuzzled my palm and smiled. Christ, I'd missed him smiling at me like that. It made my insides quiver and my legs shake. No one had ever had that effect on me. No one except Dev.

"Take a walk with me?" I asked. There were things I needed to tell him. Things he needed to hear.

Dev waggled his eyebrows. "Is this your way of asking me back to our room, Hot Rod?"

I grinned and bumped my groin against his. "No denying I want that.

But we should talk first."

His smile fell and the playful light in his eyes dimmed. "You're right. I have some things to say too."

Dev's stride matched mine as we left the party and followed a path that took us to the other side of the resort where we wandered through the botanical garden. It was illuminated by small solar-powered lights that cast a romantic glow onto the indigenous plants.

"It's beautiful here," Dev said in a hushed, almost reverent voice.

"The garden or the island?"

He shrugged. "Both? If magic exists at all, it exists here."

I stopped walking and tugged on his arm. "I don't want the magic between us to end tonight, or once we head back to London."

"Does it even still exist without Sky?" He pushed his hands into the pockets of his shorts and started to walk again.

And there it was: the big elephant in the middle of paradise.

I hurried to catch up and fell in beside him. "So... about Sky. I suppose I have a few things to explain."

"You do."

Butterflies fluttered in my stomach. "I hurt her."

Dev turned his head sharply and frowned.

"Not physically," I clarified. "Although I'm not certain that makes it any better." I exhaled loudly. "In Palm Springs, I invited her to join us, not so much because I wanted her, although I did, but because I thought she could help me get closer to you."

"How so?"

I raked a hand through my hair. "I've always wanted you, Dev, since I discovered what a cock is for anyway." I chuckled dryly. "But you knew that. I've never tried to hide it."

Dev's frown deepened. "So, you orchestrated our week together in Palm Springs to get me in bed?"

"It worked, didn't it?"

"Yes, but—"

"But I hurt Sky, and I almost lost you entirely."

We continued to stroll in silence for a few minutes. I cleared my throat. "The thing is, I might have started out using her, but by the end of that week, I realized I liked who I was when we were all together."

Dev playfully jabbed his elbow in my ribs. "I liked who you were too."

My eyes swung to his face. "Not at the end."

Dev's cheeks reddened and he looked away. "If we're being honest, I... I lied to you that last morning in Palm Springs." He paused and kicked at the gravel that made up the path. "I knew it was you I was hugging."

"So, you…" My jaw dropped.

He touched my chin with his finger. "I've known I was in love with you for a long time."

"I'm…" There were no words to explain the rush of emotion filling my body in that moment. I felt light enough to float in the air like a balloon.

"Gobsmacked?"

Now there was a word. I nodded. But I couldn't let us get side-tracked. "Anyway. That's why I insisted that Sky be brought here. I offered a million-pound bonus through the label to ensure it. And I told them if they couldn't make it happen, I was walking. I couldn't stand it anymore. I had to do something. I'm not proud of my actions." I remembered Sky's face when she'd said I told her exactly where she stood with me. I groaned. "I never intended to hurt her again, but I did. I used her to get to you, again. I made a deal with her, here on the island. I'd cooperate, as long as she helped me get you into bed." This time Dev's mouth dropped open. "I wanted us to get to that place again, to how we'd been in Palm Springs. And somehow along the way, I…" I shook my head. There were only two people in the world I felt so strongly about, and I'd hurt them both. Horribly.

I searched his expression, trying to gauge his reaction. Was Dev angry? Jealous? Over the course of our nearly two decades as best mates, I'd learn to read Dev fairly well, but the man had quite the poker face when he so chose, and this was one of those times. I firmed up my spine and my courage.

The moment stretched between us, my words hanging in the warm night air

He crossed his arms. "You bleeding wanker! It's no wonder she doesn't believe anything we say. You've made such a fucking hash of everything! At this point, I'm not even sure I believe you love me."

"I do, Dev. I love you with my whole heart."

"And manipulating me, playing sodding games, that's love to you?"

"No, I—"

"Fuck you."

He paced away and I followed him. "Dev—"

"You think I should just forgive this? That I should trust you?"

"I've changed, mate. I have. I know it was wrong. All of it. But I didn't know what else to do. You were so bloody stubborn."

He looked at me for several seconds, then he nodded. "That's true." Then he looked away. "How could you use her like that though?"

"I was at a loss. It was either make the deal, or walk away entirely."

He closed his eyes. "You could have let *me* walk away."

I put my hands on his biceps. "Music is your life, Dev. It's what you were born to do. I couldn't let you give that up." He paused. "I couldn't give you up without a fight."

"But you could give up Sky. That was the deal you made, right?"

"That's what I thought at first. But I got to know her during this trip. I got to spend time with her, build a relationship with her. And that's when things changed."

"Changed how?"

I took a deep breath. It was time to say the words I'd hesitated over for so long. The words that were in and of themselves a promise. "I fell in love with her." A grin I couldn't control curved my lips. "I can't fucking believe it, never thought this would happen, but I love her."

Dev cuffed me on the back of the head. "I thought so, you bleeding idiot! I've never seen you so happy with anyone, the way you are with her."

"The way I am with both of you. I fell for us, Dev. I love the three of us together."

Dev put his hand on my hip and a slight smile curved his lips. "So do I, Rod. The two of you are what I've always wanted."

"We are?"

Who was this man standing before me, confessing to a long-held desire for a triad? "You never let on."

Dev snorted. "How could I? If I'd given you an inch, you'd have insisted on the whole foot."

I shot Dev a sexy grin. "You are quite hung, mate, but a foot? No need to exaggerate."

Dev punched my shoulder. "Sod off."

I took his hand and marveled at the sensation of having his palm against mine. Aside from Sky, I'd never done this before, held hands with anyone. Somehow, it felt more intimate than kissing.

"Whatever happens with Sky, we're not going back to how we were before, yeah? I know you don't want to be out. At least not yet. We'll take it one day at a time." I swallowed and pushed down the fear rising in my throat. "I-I can't lose you again, Dev."

"You won't lose me. I can't be that man anymore. I need to be me, not who my family wants me to be."

"I wish the two could be one and the same."

Dev lowered his gaze and bit his bottom lip. "I do too."

I slid my hand behind his head. He looked up and I held his gaze. "I also don't want to lose Sky."

"Then we're on the same page."

"For once." I winked.

Dev barked out a laugh. "Oh, I can think of a few other instances when that's happened."

The sparkle in his eyes, the playful tone in his voice, lit me up like a fireworks display. I gripped his hair and pulled his head back to kiss that long perfect neck. "I want you so fucking much."

He moaned, his back arching into me. "Here?"

"You kinky bastard," I said and smacked his firm ass. "I was thinking of our bungalow."

"Yeah? What do you have in mind?"

"Race you there? Winner decides."

"Righto."

As soon as his acceptance was out, I dropped my hands from his sexy body and took off running toward our bungalow. Unfortunately, Dev was much more fit than I, and it wasn't long before he caught up to and even surpassed me.

By the time I reached the bungalow, the door was already open. Dev's shirt lay on the floor. Like Hansel and Gretel, I follow the trail of crumbs, in this case Dev's clothing, and found him naked in the shower.

My pulse quickened at the sight of him underneath the spray, all that wet brown skin begging to be licked. I quickly shed my jeans, boxers, and shirt. I opened the shower door. "Care for some company?"

Dev smirked. "What took you so long, old man?"

"Old man? Bugger off, you wanker. I've naught but a month on you."

"Must be all that hard living then, the sex, drugs, and rock 'n' roll."

"Again, I repeat, bugger off."

Dev reached down and wrapped his hand around his long, mouthwatering cock. When he began to stroke it lazily, I groaned. I wanted it in my mouth, I wanted Dev's taste on my tongue

I fell to my knees and pressed Dev against the shower wall, my hands on his thighs. He hit it with a sigh I barely heard as my mouth engulfed his crown. I licked all around it, savoring the drops of pre-cum leaking from the tip. I loved the weight of him in my mouth, the stretch of my lips around the flared head of his cock.

Dev moaned and his fingers raked my shoulders. I shivered. How would those nails feel on my arse? He pushed on my shoulders. Ignoring him, I relaxed my jaw and took him in deeper, to the root.

Dev shook, and he shouted, "Rod. Wait."

I looked up then and slowly released him. "What's the matter?"

"I want to… to show you how much you mean to me." The nervous quaver in his voice and the multitude of possibilities he'd implied went straight to my cock. It pulsed against my abdomen.

"How?" I asked.

"I want to know what it feels like to give myself to you."

He looked vulnerable and adorable and so fucking sexy as his eyes met mine. I shot to my feet and touched his cheek. "Are you certain? You don't have to, you know."

Dev licked his lips. "I want to feel you inside me."

"Oh fuck."

I smacked my palm on the tap to turn the water off and practically dragged Dev to my bed. He laughed when I rather forcefully helped him onto the mattress, making him bounce a few times.

"Eager?"

"You've no idea how many times I've imagined this." It was hundreds of times, maybe thousands. My hands shook as they retrieved a condom and lube from the drawer in the nightstand.

"Did you wank off when you did?" Dev asked, his tone pure aroused male.

"Christ, Dev. If you talk dirty to me, I'll come before I can get inside you." Already my cock was leaking and my bollocks tingled.

"Oh, come now, I've heard the tales about your stamina. Or were they simply urban legends?"

"Nothing but a load of poppycock, at least where you're concerned."

"Am I so special then?" Dev teased.

I knelt between his spread thighs and pushed his legs up and over, so his knees were at his shoulders, which left his pretty hole perfectly exposed. I growled as want claimed me. "You know you are."

Before he could respond, I swept my tongue along the crease between his arse cheeks. Dev's reaction was immediate. He shouted and laid his hands on top of mine where they held his legs up. "Oh fuck, Rod!"

I circled my tongue around the puckered muscle, then speared it inside. Dev's head came forward, then slammed back against the pillows.

"Dirty enough for you?" I asked between forays.

"Bloody hell, Rod. If I'd known what you could do with that mouth..."

I thrust my tongue back inside his ass. Dev gasped. His eyes closed. Oh, this was fun. "What would you have done?"

He opened his eyes, met mine. "I-I'd not have wasted so much time."

"Fuck." Dev had no idea how completely he owned me. How completely I was his. And to have him give himself to me like this, well, it meant everything.

I reached for the lube and squirted some on my finger. I pressed it into his hole while I continued to lick around it. I wanted him to be as ready as possible for me. I added a second, and paused when Dev hissed. "Okay, mate?"

"Yeah," Dev said breathlessly. "Give me a second." I held still, except for my tongue, which I used to lap at his bollocks. I took one into my mouth. "Oh! Fuck. Oh, that feels..."

I laughed and the vibration made him moan. Pre-cum leaked from his tip. It was my sign. I thrust my finger in and out of his ass, changed the angle and tapped his prostate.

Boom!

Dev yelled and kicked up his legs. "Now. Rod, Fuck me now."

Christ, the look on his face—a look *I'd* put there—would be my undoing. My hands shook as I rolled on the condom and smoothed some lube onto it. I held his legs behind his knees and pulled him up onto my thighs, positioning his hole perfectly. I released one of his legs and pushed my cock down so the head was at his entrance. "Ready?"

He bit his bottom lip in a shy gesture that melted my heart and nodded.

"I'll make this good for you," I promised.

A smile tugged at the corner of his mouth. "You already have."

I tilted my hips and leaned into him a bit. My cock pushed against his loosened muscle. It stretched and the flared head of my cock slipped in.

Dev groaned. I looked up to see how he was doing. "Breathe," I said, holding still.

I watched, sweat forming on my brow from the effort of not thrusting into all that tight, delicious heat. I thought my skull might explode from the pressure. The sweet seductive torture.

When Dev's hips lifted involuntarily, I gave him what he sought and pressed in another inch. His cheeks flushed and his eyes met mine. "How is it?" I asked.

"Unimaginable."

I grinned. "Hold on." I was about to tilt his world. Slowly, inexorably, I pushed until I was fully seated inside him.

"Oh fuck."

I widened my thighs and leaned over him. I took his mouth with mine, kissing him deeply, exploring and tasting every corner. Dev moaned. He gripped my ass cheeks, ground against me, and raked his nails up my back. I shivered and raised up onto my hands. I hovered above him, and began to move in deep, steady, strokes. I kissed him again. His hands roamed my body, touching everywhere they could. Emotions overwhelmed me, and my eyes filled with tears. I was inside Devkinandan, my best friend. The love of my life. In my arms, I held everything I'd always wanted. My heart was his. "I love you," I whispered.

"I love you too, John."

"Oi mate, who the fuck is John?"

Dev laughed. "No, *jaan*." He spelled it for me. "It means 'my life.'"

Warmth filled my chest. "You're my life too."

All our secrets were out in the open. We'd been laid bare. I felt shredded, flayed open. Raw and elemental.

I shifted my hips, pounding into Dev, making sure to hit his prostate with each thrust. Through it all, I held his stare. Saw the lust, the love, the wonder in his sweet face. Reaching between us, I fisted his cock and gave it several strong pulls.

"Rod. I'm going to... Oh fuck!" Dev arched, and his eyes rolled back. His cock swelled in my hand and then hot spunk coated my fingers.

I pressed my weight onto him, gave two more thrusts and joined him in ecstasy.

Once I return to consciousness, I rolled off Dev and tucked him into my side. "How do you feel?"

I wasn't sure what to expect, but it sure as shit wasn't the glow of happiness I saw on his face. I chuckled. "You look like you enjoyed that."

"I might have done."

I kissed his nose. "Wanker."

"I might have done that too."

"I fucking missed you. Missed this. Us."

He ran his fingers lightly over my chest. It felt good. Better than good. It felt right.

"I know you meant the teasing and joking," he said, his tone suddenly serious. "Losing that was one of the things I was most afraid of."

I trapped his fingers and brought them to my lips. "You were always my best mate, even when we weren't talking. There's never been anyone else..." My words trailed off, because what I'd been about to say wasn't exactly true anymore, was it?

"Except Sky?"

I nodded. "I want her with us." I pressed his hand to my chest. "I know I can be happy with just you and me." I looked at him. "You *are* enough for me. But if I'm honest, I think we can all be happier together: you, me, and Sky."

"So that means there's only one thing left to do."

We grinned at each other. "Win her back!" We spoke in tandem and high-fived each other.

Just like old times, only better.

Chapter 12

ROD

Tahiti had left its mark on me. On all of us. And I wanted a way to commemorate it. Sky had saved King's Cross. Not only that, but she'd made us a better band. A stronger, more dynamic one.

King's Cross wasn't just Dev and me anymore. It was all of us, even sodding Nigel. And I wanted to make sure everyone knew it.

Vanessa helped make the arrangements, and it wasn't long before the tattoo artists arrived at the resort. Three of them, ready to brand us all with a slightly changed-up version of our band logo.

We gathered on the beach, beside the remnants of last night's birthday bonfire for Sky. Dev and I had gone looking for her this morning, but apparently, she'd decided to take her parents on a little sightseeing jaunt around the island. No doubt she was avoiding us, but she couldn't do that forever.

We wouldn't let her.

Dev and I had already stripped off our shirts and taken seats in the first two chairs sitting in the shade. My stomach flipped; I wasn't entirely sure Dev would like the design.

I wasn't even sure he really wanted to do this. His family wasn't exactly big on tattoos. In fact, I remember his mum moaning about the first one I'd got, and threatening Dev with bloody murder if he ever got one.

I looked over at him as the others started filing over to us, all of them, including Nigel, looking a bit the worse for wear, even though it was well past noon.

I probably would have felt the same if it weren't for what had happened between Dev and me last night.

He'd given himself to me.

All of him.

He'd sworn I'd never lose him.

My heart was so full it felt like I'd burst with happiness. But then my eyes fell to the ashes of last night's fire, and I remembered who wasn't there.

Sky.

My throat tightened. This really was all my fault. If I hadn't been such a selfish, fucking bastard, we could've been together and happy all this time.

And Sky wouldn't be hurting right now.

But I'd fix it. I had a plan. And she was never going to doubt how I felt or how Dev felt about her again.

This was our last day in Tahiti. Tonight was our gig in Papeete. And Sky was going to be ours, heart, body, and soul, starting tonight, if I had anything to say about it.

Damon scrubbed a hand over his jaw and yawned. "So… we here to ogle you two or what?" he asked.

I leaned forward and flexed for him. "While I'm sure that has its appeal," I said, kissing my bicep and making the guys groan, "that's not why you're here."

I gestured to Manua, the tattoo artist who'd worked with me. "I want us all to get these." Manua held up a drawing of the tattoo. It was a stylized cross with a crown, similar to our band logo, but Manua had added Tahitian touches to the design.

I looked from Damon, to Tommy, then Mick, then Jules, and lastly at Dev, a lump forming in my throat. "I know I've been a fucking prick these last few months, and I nearly tore the band apart, and I treated all of you like second-class citizens."

Then I looked at Nigel. "And I treated you like something I'd scraped off my shoe." He started to wave off what I was saying, but I held up a hand to stop him. "No, mate, I need to say this. I didn't want to listen to what you and Sonic High and Reeling were saying about our sound. I didn't want anything to change. And I didn't know how to fix things with Dev. Unfortunately, you bore the brunt of my frustration. And…" I paused, wanting to be sure he was really listening. "I'm sorry."

Nigel blinked at me for a second, then held his hand up to his ear. "Care to repeat that?"

Bleeding wanker. But I deserved it. "I'm sorry, Nigel. And I owe you everything, because you didn't let me walk away from the band. We wouldn't be here today if it weren't for you."

He gave me a crooked grin and nodded. "Please tell me this isn't a sign of the Apocalypse. Hot Rod Taylor apologizing. Wasn't sure it was even possible."

"I'm a changed man."

Damon made a buzzing noise like I'd blown a question on a quiz show, and I suppressed a grin. I wasn't done being a sentimental sap yet.

I coughed and paused for a second, forcing myself not to turn this into a joke like I always did. "I want you all to know that you are my brothers. And that King's Cross belongs to all us. We're a *band*. A tribe of six. Well, seven, including Nigel. And I want everyone to know it." My voice went a little hoarse.

No one said a word. They all just stared at me like I'd walked on stage naked or something.

Shit. Maybe things weren't as rosy as I'd thought. "Of course, if you don't want to—"

"I'm in," Dev said.

"Me too," Damon said.

"Me three," Tommy chimed in.

Jules and Mick looked at each other and started taking off their shirts. "We're in," they said in unison.

Nigel began unbuttoning his shirt. "This is the one and only tattoo I will ever get."

I blew out the breath I'd been holding, taking in their smiles as Damon settled into the chair beside mine, and Tommy, Mick, Jules, and Nigel sat down on the logs around the fire to wait their turns.

Damon leaned over to me, a grin on his face. "You aren't half the asshole you'd like everyone to believe." He tapped me on the sternum. "Might even be a heart in there after all."

"Sod off," I said, unable to keep from laughing.

He shook his head, laughing as well. "Now will someone *please* explain why you all seem to think that's an insult? Might as well be saying 'Turf off!'"

We all started howling with laughter. I clapped him on the shoulder. "You're a Yank bastard, through and through. But you're *our* Yank bastard."

That made him laugh harder, and it took us a while to settle down for our tattoos. The artists had just started transferring the designs to our skin when Damon said, "Okay. But seriously. Can someone explain?"

Tommy shook his head. "You're bloody hopeless!"

Damon shrugged. "I like to think I'm charming."

"You're… something, all right," I said, and then we were all laughing again.

It felt good, even as the tattoo needle bit into my skin. "We're going to slay that crowd tonight," I said.

And Dev and I were going to win back our girl.

SKY

Vanessa, Daniel, and Nigel had done a great job finding a location for King's Cross's surprise gig in Papeete. The bar was big enough to hold about two hundred people, but intimate enough that it felt cozy, like a special night between the band and its fans. They'd worked with a couple local radio stations and given away fifty tickets, selling out the rest in minutes.

A huge crowd was milling around outside, hoping to get in, but the extra security the label had brought in were firm about keeping them out. They'd just have to settle for the video clips that Vanessa was having recorded for YouTube and the live Facebook stream that Vanessa had been doing off and on throughout the evening. She was in her element, her face glowing as she showed Daniel how King's Cross's and TI's followers on Instagram and Twitter and Facebook were exploding.

"You're a social media genius," Daniel said to her and raised his drink. "To Vanessa!"

Daniel, Nigel, and I toasted her, my Tahitian mahana cocktail going down a little too easy. It was my third of the night so far, and it should be my last. But I couldn't stop hearing Dev say those words. *So, this is what? A job to you?*

And it wasn't like Rod had jumped to my defense, was it? And he certainly hadn't coughed up an "I love you" either when Dev had pushed Rod to tell me how he felt.

No. Rod had said nothing. Because he knew who I really was. And Dev didn't. Or hadn't.

But he knew now.

I'd managed to avoid seeing them all day, using my parents as an excuse. And really, they'd flown all this way. Might as well show them a great time while they were here. I could afford it now, right? I'd booked them in for a week at the Hideaway even though they'd protested. They were coming up on their thirtieth anniversary, so I'd told him it was my present, and they'd finally accepted. They'd been invited to the gig, but they were still dealing with jet lag and wanted a quiet night in, so we'd said our goodbyes and I'd left them in Moorea.

When I'd taken them to the Lagoonarium earlier in the day, it had been fun, and I'd loved seeing that the light on their faces when they were surrounded by the fish during feeding time.

But all I could think about was when I'd gone there with Rod. I thought we'd connected that day, that something had changed between us. But that had been wishful thinking.

He had room for only one person in his heart. And that was Dev.

Nigel gently elbowed me. "I'm proposing another toast." He held up his drink. "To Sky. For doing the impossible. Not only fixing King's Cross, but making them better."

Daniel and Vanessa raised their glasses to me and I raised mine, slipping back the dregs of my cocktail. Christ. I *should* be ecstatic right now. The band sounded fantastic as they tore into their old hits, the new arrangements Dev and Damon had come up with making the songs sound fresh and new, even while the fans chanted the lyrics they knew by heart. The two of the had been switching off on lead guitar, sometimes even playing together at the same time, the band's sound harder and somehow more emotional, more urgent, as a result.

Nigel leaned toward me. "You're bloody brilliant, Sky. If you ever want to leave TI, you can have a job at the label as..." He paused, thinking. "A band whisperer." He grinned lopsidedly. "I don't know how you got them all working together—mean, I *saw* what you did, but getting them to actually listen... especially Rod. Lord love him, he's absolute brilliance on stage, but..." He looked down at his empty pint. "He's a sodding prick most of the time, to be honest."

Daniel hooted with laughter. "Don't hold back, Nigel! Tell us how you really feel."

Nigel blushed furiously, to the roots of his red hair. "Maybe I need to lay off," he said, pushing his beer aside.

I gave him a weak smile. "It's true. But we love him anyway."

Nigel clasped my shoulder. "Not sure I'd go *that* far, but he did apologize to me today, so I'm starting to see his appeal. And I'm glad I don't have to try to replace him. Sonic High and Reeling are over the moon about the demos they've heard for the new album. They told me to tell you and Daniel"—he nodded in Daniel's direction—"that TI has Sonic High's and Reeling's business in full, including their next corporate retreats."

Daniel nudged me from the other side. "Welcome to TI, partner."

Yay me.

The band wrapped up "Just Friends," the music stopping for the first time since they'd started. Rod growled into the microphone, and the crowd roared its approval in response.

Rod practically glowed under the stage lights, the blond highlights in his brown hair standing out, his customary dark eyeliner leading him a sinister, predatory look. He'd already stripped off his shirt and leather jacket. His lean, ripped torso gleamed with sweat, his St. Jude's medallion and the rings on his fingers catching the light. He'd painted his fingernails black for the evening to match his jacket and pants.

Rod was every inch a rock star. No, a rock god, as he strutted across the stage in his skin-tight leather pants and put an arm around Dev, who looked sinfully delicious as well. Dev was in a pair of thigh-hugging distressed blue jeans and a form-fitting white tank top, but he'd shed his stylish black blazer, and his brown skin shone with a golden glow under the spotlights. He didn't need eyeliner like Rod. His thick eyelashes and chocolate brown eyes drew you in just as they were.

And though Dev didn't have Rod's predatory edge, he didn't need it. Dev just was—a virtuoso guitar player, someone so in tune with his instrument, so in love with the music, that he commanded your attention, caught and held it, without any theatrics.

Dev was a musical genius. When he was onstage in front of a crowd, he came alive in a way that was simply mesmerizing.

My eyes drank them both in, memorizing every detail, my heart filing this moment away. I loved them, I truly did, even though I couldn't have them.

I'd always known that, hadn't I? That had been why I'd run from them in Palm Springs, why I'd stayed away, even when they'd begged me to call, to text. Something.

And it was why I should have stayed away. Should have shielded my heart from this pain.

This hollow emptiness.

My only consolation as Rod hugged Dev tight was that at least I'd given them this—their band back and each other, as they'd always been meant to be.

And if the cost was my own happiness?

So be it. I'd pay that price. Because seeing them together and happy soothed the ache inside me, just a bit.

I closed my eyes, holding onto this feeling, tears starting to sting my lids. I loved them. I love them *so* much…

My throat was aching, a sob trying to burst from my chest.

Daniel had warned me. And I hadn't listened. If only I'd come clean sooner. Maybe then Dev would've understood… maybe then Rod would have trusted me. But it was too late now.

Rod spoke into the mic. "I know you've all been enjoying the old songs," he said, and the crowd whistled and cheered. "But now we have some new ones for you—first time anyone, anywhere, will be hearing them."

A roar went up, and I opened my eyes. Vanessa started a new Facebook live video. "OMG!" she shouted. "Here's some world-premiere music for you!"

His arm still slung around Dev's shoulders, Rod spoke again. "We have a very special song we'd like to play for someone who means everything to us."

He looked over the crowd in front of the stage, his eyes zeroing in on me. "This one's for you, Sky."

Vanessa squealed and hugged me, and I tried to smile, but my lips were trembling so hard I couldn't. All I could do was hold Rod's gaze as the opening notes of the song started.

My heart was pounding. He'd said I meant everything to them. Did that mean there was still a chance?

I wanted to hope, and yet I didn't dare. I sucked in a breath, my whole body quivering, and wished I was drunker. Calmer. Anything but the nervous wreck I was now.

Rod held my eyes and started to sing.

You're just a waif of a girl
But you shook my whole damn world
Though you're not "just" anything
Oh no, you're everything

His voice caressed the words so tenderly, so sweetly, his timbre dropping on "everything," and the ache in my throat intensified. Oh Rod…
The music shifted, moving into the chorus.

You said "no strings"
And I hoped you were lying
You said "no strings"
And I said yes, but inside I was dying

I swallowed hard. Was that really how Rod had felt?
He moved on to the next verse.

The day you came into my life,
You brought along a ray of light
But ever since you up and left
It's only been eternal night

He sang the chorus again and tears started streaming down my face. Why hadn't he ever said this to me?

You own my heart
You are my life
Won't you let me be part
Of your lovely light?

You said "no strings"
And I knew you were lying
You said "no strings"
I said yes but I knew I was dying

Oh I knew I was lying
Oh I knew I was dying

A sob wrenched out of me and I had to bury my face in my hands. Vanessa rubbed my back. "They *really* love you!" she shouted in my ear as the crowd went wild.

And that was before Rod and Dev jumped off the stage.

The crowd surged around them, but Rod still had the mic in hand, and he said, "Just give us a minute, lovelies, then we'll be right back with more. There's a girl out there who needs a proper snogging."

Cheers went up as he strode toward me, Dev on his heels, and I gasped for breath, trying to get my sobbing under control.

Rod caught me up in his arms, hugging me tight, then he took my face in his palms and kissed me, his lips gentle, yet searing, the touch lighting up every nerve ending in my body. Then Dev leaned in and kissed me as well, and a roar of surprise went up from the crowd.

Rod stroked my cheek. "I'm absolutely shite at talking about how I feel. But I hope the song told you what you need to know." He took my hand and pressed it to his gleaming chest, his skin slick under my palm, his heart pounding beneath my touch. "I love you, Sky. With every bloody fiber of my miserable being."

I started to laugh, couldn't help it, and Dev smiled. "Me too. We both wrote part of the lyrics." He stroked my cheek, and I trapped his hand with mine.

"Does that mean you forgive me?"

He smiled, his white teeth gleaming against his tan. "Rod told me what happened, filled in the missing bits, and I get it. There's nothing to forgive." He elbowed Rod. "Except me for this one's stupidity."

A chant of "More! More! More!" was rising in the crowd, and Rod swooped in to kiss my cheek. "Got to go, love."

Dev kissed my other cheek, and Vanessa whooped as she snapped a picture of us. "This will be perfect for Insta!"

I grabbed the phone. I had to be a running mascara raccoon-eyed disaster by now. "Absolutely not!"

Vanessa gave me a glare that wasn't entirely fake and then turned to Daniel. "She's been at TI for all of five minutes, and she's already bossing me around!"

Daniel laughed, and Rod and Dev loped back onstage. They started in on another song, and my heart finally settled into something like a normal rhythm again.

How lucky was I?

Luckier than I had any right to be.

And tonight I'd make that clear to them. I couldn't have everything I wanted, but that was okay. I was ready to make the sacrifice I should have already made.

Because Rod and Dev were worth more to me than all the bonuses, all the partnerships in the world.

SKY

With a warm hand on my lower back, Dev ushered me into the suite he was sharing with Rod at our hotel in Papeete. I shivered with excitement and trepidation when Rod closed the door behind us. Watching them perform, hearing the song they'd composed, knowing they'd written it about me, it was all so overwhelming. Earlier in the day, I'd thought for sure our adventure was over, that I'd lost them both. In that moment, I'd regretted accepting Daniel's deal and coming to Tahiti. Now the only part I regretted was the money and the partnership involved.

I cleared my throat and shifted awkwardly on my high heeled sandals that sank into the plush carpeting. "I have some things to say." I looked at them both. "Please?"

Dev's face lost some of its color. He indicated the cozy seating arrangement. "Let's sit."

I nodded and perched on the edge of the couch. The guys exchanged a look, and then Rod dropped down on one side of me and Dev on the other. Rod stretched his arm along the back of the couch behind me and crossed his legs at the ankles. His fingers toyed with my hair, and I shivered at the delicious sensation.

"What's going on, love?" he asked softly.

I reached for his hand. He smiled and gave it to me. When I turned to Dev, he offered me a reassuring smile and gripped the fingers of my other hand. I let out a big breath. "That song you wrote for me, well… It touched me deeply. The truth is, I've been in love with the both of you since Palm Springs."

"Why did you leave us then? Why did you never contact either of us?" Dev asked.

I kept my eyes focused on our joined hands in my lap. "Because I was scared. I saw how much Rod loved you even then, and when I heard you saying you loved him too, all I could think was that history was repeating itself."

"You're referring to Green and Rain, was it?" Dev asked.

I laughed. "Blue and Sunshine, but yes." He gently squeezed my fingers and tears welled in my eyes. "I was the third wheel with them, and that was the last thing I wanted to be with the two of you."

A tear slid down my cheek. Dev cupped my jaw and whisked it away with his thumb. "You were never a third wheel, Sky."

Rod leaned into my side and with his arm around my shoulders, tucked me against his chest, and kissed the side of my head. "I felt exactly the same way that first night we were all together here and Dev told you he loved you."

Dev made a sound in his throat and slid his free arm behind me to bring his hand to Rod's neck. "I'm so sorry for making you feel that way. It was never my intention. I wanted to say it to you both. I just... couldn't."

Rod smiled. "It's all behind us now." He kissed my head again. "It's a good thing our girl was so brave. She put us all back together again."

I scoffed at that. "Hardly. I really didn't want to take this job. I didn't think I could be around either one of you again without all the old feelings coming back." I raised their joined hands to my chest. "Leaving you in Palm Springs broke my heart."

Dev kissed the wetness on my cheeks. "Sweets."

"I knew that if I saw you again, I'd just end up brokenhearted."

"Why did you take the job then?" Rod asked.

"Honestly? I took it because I couldn't have lived with myself if I hadn't taken this opportunity to see each of you"—I turned my head to Rod, then to Dev—"one last time." I huffed out a laugh. "I guess you're my drug, and I needed one last fix before going cold turkey and living the rest of my life without you. But I couldn't admit to myself that that was the reason, so I convinced myself to do it for the money. The bonus and what it could do for my business, and it allowed me to forge an even better deal with Total Indulgence. In a screwed-up way, I justified the insanity of walking into a situation where I knew I'd walk out devastated."

"But you aren't walking out devastated, are you?" Dev asked, a smile in his voice.

I grinned. "No, I'm not. But I am going to tell Daniel that I don't want the bonus or the partnership at TI."

Rod sat forward sharply. "What's this?"

"You can't turn it down, Sky," Dev added.

"I have to. It just feels wrong to personally gain from this. I'll keep freelancing."

"Love, you have to do what's best for you, but I don't see how turning down this great opportunity is that."

My gaze shifted to Dev. He was the one to who'd been hurt the most by my and Rod's scheming shenanigans. "What do you truly think, Dev? Would you feel better if I turned it all down? I don't want to cheapen what we feel for each other. I don't want you to have any doubt why I'm with you."

Dev glanced at Rod, then touched a finger to my chin. "I understand what you're saying. But life is like that, isn't it? Some of my best songs were the result of, let's call them—unusual—circumstances." His eyes twinkled as he glanced over my head at Rod.

Rod snorted. "Are you talking about 'Watching You, Watching Me'? Now that was one hell of a bash, and a rather revealing one," he said with a smirk and a wink.

There was a story I'd like to hear someday. Dev's cheeks colored, but he continued to look into my eyes. "We made a ton of money off that tune. Anyway, you do what's right for you, but for my part, I take no offense to you profiting from this. In fact, it makes me happy, because this whole fucked-up mess brought you back into our lives. And for that I could never be sorry."

He took my mouth, his tongue gently licking my lips. When I sighed and opened for him, he continued his gentle exploration. He caressed every corner of my mouth before brushing his tongue against mine. We parted as gently as we'd come together. The tenderness of that kiss brought on a fresh wave of tears.

"I love you, Dev," I said.

He smiled. "I love you too."

"Hey now," Rod kissed the corner of my mouth. "I want in on this too."

His tongue swiped at my already wet lips. We both groaned, and when I opened my mouth, Rod and Dev both licked and kissed me at the same time. Their tongues entwined with mine and with each other's. My heart swelled at the perfection of the moment.

"I love you, Rod," I said.

"Love you too, Sky. Both of you, so fucking much."

I looped my arms behind their necks and pulled them in tight. "I never thought I'd have you both like this. You've made me the happiest woman in Tahiti."

"Only in Tahiti?" Dev teased.

"Okay, the world!"

"Now you're talking," Rod said. "But I do have a bone to pick with you, missy."

I arched a brow and focused on his groin. "A bone, huh?"

"Naughty poppet," he said with a mock glare.

"Okay, what's this bone about?" I wanted to finish up with the talking so I could be with my two men again, so we could be with each other.

Rod disengaged his hand from mine and gripped my waist, then hoisted me onto his lap so I straddled his legs and faced him. My dress was hiked up around my waist. "For the past two weeks, you've been issuing us challenges."

His gaze swung over to Dev. Dev nodded. "Right you are, Rod. I think it's well past time we issued a challenge of our own to Sky."

"A-a challenge?" I narrowed my eyes at him. "What kind of challenge?"

Rod's hands left my waist, skimmed over my hips, and cupped my ass cheeks. He squeezed them and pulled me roughly against his erection. "Your challenge, Ms. River, is to see exactly how much pleasure you can take."

Dev rose and stood behind me. A piece of silky material covered my eyes. "Guys?" I was more nervous than I cared to admit. They loved me, so even if they were miffed with me, they wouldn't hurt me, right?

"Do you trust us, Sky?" Dev whispered next to my ear.

Did I? I thought about everything we'd been through, all the lies and half-truths, the misunderstandings, and the confessions. Most of our issues had been due to my own lack of trust. And sure, given my history, I had cause, but if I wanted things to work between us, I had to put the past where it belonged.

I swallowed. "I do."

"Then let us love you." Rod's seductive voice had desire quivering in my belly.

A pair of hands cupped my breasts. Pinched my nipples. Another set of hands lifted my dress up and over my head. I shivered as the cool air hit my heated flesh. Warm hands returned to my breasts, yet more warm hands skimmed over my torso, my abdomen. I caught my breath as they skirted my pussy, and I rubbed my thighs. A long finger traced the edge of my panties. I shuddered with need.

The blindfold heightened all my senses, and already I was so close to coming. I arched my back, pressing into the hands that kneaded my breasts. I didn't know who they belonged to and I didn't care.

The hands on my thighs moved lightly over my skin, back up to my waist. I was lifted off of Rod's lap and onto my feet. A hard body—Dev's?—met my back. Hot breath brushed my neck, and teeth scraped my nape.

"Oh God." I trembled against him, pushing my ass into his groin. The warmth at my back disappeared. I stood alone. My ears perked for any sound. And I waited.

Fingers tucked into the sides of my panties and tugged them down my legs. I felt around and grasped a shoulder to steady myself before I stepped out of them. Whose shoulder was it? I tried to remember how Rod's had felt, how Dev's had felt. Dev's shoulders were slightly more developed than Rod's, although both men had similar builds. Before I could decide, the hands pushed on the inside of my knees, urging me to widen my stance.

Then I was alone again.

I heard the scraping sound of furniture being moved. A hand pressed against the middle of my back, forcing me to bend at the waist. I reached out in front of me, and my hands connected with the couch.

The hand at my back disappeared.

Cool air washed over me, but it did nothing to extinguish the fire building in my belly. Moisture flooded my exposed pussy, and I moaned wantonly.

Hands touched my breasts. Squeezed. Pinched. But the movements were uncoordinated, and I knew the hands belonged to different men. Somehow that made the situation even hotter.

Warmth touched my ribs on one side, then soft kisses were pressed along my spine as the owner worked his way down. When the kisses reached the base of my spine, and a swipe of tongue was added, I arched my back, squirming with pleasure.

The warmth left me. I cried out in protest.

Before I could form a coherent argument, heat—warm and wet—assaulted me in two places at once—my clit and my back entrance.

I screamed and my hips bucked.

Firm hands held my waist. Two more held my butt cheeks open.

I think, for a moment, I lost my mind. A tongue circled my hole while another lapped at my clit. Fingers were pushed into my mouth. I accepted them willingly and curled my tongue around them. Once they were wet, the fingers were retracted. I held my breath, wondering where they'd end up.

And then I knew. One entered my pussy, the other pressed into my ass.

A tongue licked around both fingers as they pushed in and out in an alternating pattern, much like Dev and Rod had used when they'd taken me together.

My pulse skyrocketed when a warm mouth closed over my clit, sucking gently. I moaned loudly. "Oh yes."

The fingers inside my body worked in tandem to press all my buttons.

"I'm so close," I said.

Instantly, all touch was gone for my body.

"No!"

A hand smacked my ass sharply, and I sucked in a breath, my pussy awash in heat. Somewhere to my right, Rod chuckled. "Easy, love. What kind of a challenge would it be if we let you come too soon?"

Damn. And here I'd thought the challenge would be to see how many times I could come.

Lips kissed the hot spot on my ass where I'd been smacked. Then a hand landed on the other cheek.

"Oh!"

It didn't tickle, but it didn't exactly hurt either. Instead, heat radiated out, enveloping my pussy. I could feel my juices dripping down my inner thighs.

An arm wrapped around my chest and tugged me upright. I inhaled deeply to see who was holding me. Dev and Rod usually had distinctive scents, not today though. Had they showered together, used the same soap and shampoo? The image of them wet, together, loving each other, tightened the coil of arousal in my belly.

A hand pressed on my shoulder, forcing me to my knees. Another hand, or the same one, clasped the back of my head and pulled me forward. The scent of musk tickled my nose, and then the head of someone's cock touched my lips. I opened my mouth and circled it with my tongue, lapping up the pre-cum. Was it Dev's or Rod's? I thought maybe Rod's. I raised my hands to touch and test my theory.

"Uh-uh-uh. No touching," Rod said.

Hands clasped my wrists behind my back and tied them together, perhaps with another tie. I'd never been into kinky games, but so far, this one had been very fun.

When whoever was done securing my hands slid a finger down my crease, I shuddered. My ass had never been an erogenous zone for me before meeting these two. How many other pleasure spots would they discover?

I moaned around the cock in my mouth at the thought.

The person behind me moved away, and then a second cock touched my lips. I released the first to welcome the second. I licked the crown and probed the slit, tasting the pre-cum gathered there. On my knees, with my hands at my back, I was at their mercy. But I had no fear.

I trusted them.

I leaned forward and took the cock deep into my mouth, sucked in my cheeks and withdrew. I move back to the first cock and repeated my actions. Two hands gripped my head, pushing me down, moving me to the other.

Above me, I heard moans, and—was that kissing? Picturing Rod and Dev in an embrace, their tongues dueling, left me dripping. I moaned around the cock in my mouth, and the hands on my head tightened.

The cock thrust into my mouth, harder, deeper. I wanted to touch myself, but I couldn't. Instead, I pressed my thighs together, and squirmed. One of my men groaned, a deep reverberating sound. The cock in my mouth swelled, and moments later, it pulled out and warm spunk landed on my chest.

Almost immediately, eager lips grazed me. A tongue lapped at my breasts, cleaning up the cum. Then a mouth latched onto a nipple and sucked deeply. Electricity sizzled from my breast to my clit. I moaned and pressed my thighs together more tightly.

Before I could make sense of what was happening, I was lifted up and impaled on a rigid cock. I threw my head back and cried out at the sudden invasion that filled me completely. Hands touched me everywhere. Stroked my skin, tugged my hair, squeezed my ass, circled my clit. A mouth closed over a nipple and another took mine in a searing, devastating kiss.

My mind was completely occupied by them, my world whittled down to this room, this moment, the three of us.

The cock inside me withdrew, then plunged in again. Hands rocked my hips, while the mouth on mine drew my tongue in.

"I-I can't—"

I couldn't take it anymore, I had to come. Now.

"You win. You win, please," I begged.

The finger on my clit circled faster, and the cock pounding into me thrust harder, and then I flew.

Behind the blindfold, colors exploded as I floated out of myself, out of my mind. I was freer than I'd ever been.

The powerful orgasm tore through me, rendering me a quivering mess. My muscles clenched around the cock so deep inside me. I heard a couple of muffled groans, and arms gripped me as my lover came inside me.

A hand stroked my hair while I panted, boneless against the chest in front of me.

The tie around my hands and the blindfold were removed.

I blinked at the sudden light. Looking over Rod's shoulder, I saw Dev sitting behind him, hugging him against his chest with one arm, his other arm extended toward me. He continued to stroke my hair. "You're so incredibly beautiful together."

My face flushed at Dev's tender expression. I smiled. "So are the two of you."

Rod looked down at where our bodies were still joined. "I'd say this is proper fucking beautiful too."

Dev groaned, and I laughed.

We continued to stare at each other as I—and I assumed they too—tried to make sense of what we were feeling.

"You know, this is probably the first time in my life I've done this," I said.

"Let go completely?" Rod asked.

"Trusted completely?" Dev asked at the same time.

I nodded. "Yes, and yes."

"We know," they said together.

"You do?"

Dev rested his hand on my arm, his calloused fingers pleasantly rough against my over-sensitized skin. "We talked about it yesterday. Whenever we were together, sexually, you always held back. And... er... by we, I mean with me or Rod or both of us."

"We wanted to find a way to get you there," Rod added.

"Well." I fanned my face. "It certainly worked."

Rod smirked. "That good, eh?"

I had to give credit where credit was due. "Yes, that good."

These two men had taken me to places in my heart and in my mind where I hadn't dared tread since Blue and Sunshine's betrayal. "There's just one problem." I looked up into both their stunning faces. My heart was so full of love and fear, I could barely breathe. I raised my hands, then let them fall in defeat. Sometimes I wished the realist in me could take a backseat and let me be a dreamer like my parents. "How can this—the three of us—possibly work?"

Chapter 13

DEV

My gaze darted between Sky and Rod as I tried to process what was happening. Sky's beautiful brown eyes filled with tears, and Rod's expression of elation melted off his face. Sky sniffed and with a wince, she climbed off Rod's lap. There was a throw blanket on the couch. She picked it up and wrapped it around herself, hiding her gorgeous tanned body from our eyes.

I was gutted. Simply gutted.

"What's going on, Sky? Why can't it work?" Rod asked, ripping the words from my mouth.

He rose and offered me his hand. I took it and he tugged me to my feet. I was more thankful than I could say for the comfort of his touch. He grimaced at his softening cock and the condom drooping off the end. "Give me a second. I'll be right back."

"Of course."

While he was gone, I could barely look at Sky. I knew her worries were about me. I stepped into my jeans. I'd started to do up the buttons when Rod returned. Wonderfully unashamed of his nakedness, he sprawled on the couch and patted the seat beside him. "Come on, love. Talk to us."

Sky sat down, her back stiff.

"Tell us why you think this won't work," he prodded.

My gut churned, and my mind fabricated reasons faster than a spider spun silk.

She eyed Rod, then me. "You said you wanted me to take the TI partnership, right?"

"Right," Rod said.

I nodded.

"And you're going on tour in four weeks, right?"

"Yes."

"For how long?"

"Six months," I said.

She gulped, and her eyes widened. "Wow. That's even longer than I thought."

"What does it matter?" Rod asked.

"You could come with us," I said.

She smiled at me sadly. "I'm not a groupie, Dev. Even without TI, I have a business to run. And if I become a partner at TI, I can't disappear for six months."

"So you join us when you can. And we'll come to you when we have a break in the schedule," I said.

"And what will we tell people?" she asked.

I frowned. "What do you mean?"

She stood and came over to me. Her hand stroked my cheek. "If I'm not someone's girlfriend and I'm not working for King's Cross, I have no business on the tour."

My stomach dropped and I felt like I might be ill. I knew what she was implying. It wasn't anything I hadn't considered before. Yet, I had hoped to put it off. Rod had even said he understood that I couldn't be out yet. Sky understood it too. Despite that, it was now abundantly clear that either way, there were consequences. The question was: which would be worse?

I held Sky's hand against my cheek. "I can't lose you, Sky."

"I can't lose you either. It hurt so bad the first time. Maybe though... this is the way it has to be, at least for now," Her words ended on a pained whisper.

Rod shoved himself off the couch. "This is fucking shite. I'm not letting either of you go." He slid an arm around Sky's waist and mine and pulled us against his sides.

"You won't lose me," Sky said. "Not unless you want to."

"Sky," Rod said, his voice heavy with exasperation. "I'll admit that before Palm Springs, the tension between Dev and me had been brewing. But you"—he paused to kiss her lips, and my cock gave a very decisive jump. Seeing them together never made me jealous or envious, well, at least not anymore. Now, it made me randy. It made me want them. Both of them.

When Rod pulled back, he smiled. "You opened my eyes to what the three of us could have together."

"Mine as well," I said.

Rod and Sky looked at me with equally surprised expressions.

Heat rushed to my face. "Yeah. Of course, I've thought about it ever since Palm Springs." A grin curved my lips. "Fantasized about it a million times. The three of us are sodding hot together. I just didn't want to admit it."

Rod raised his brows. "I thought I was the only one."

"I thought *I* was the only one," Sky said.

Rod chuckled. "So here we are."

"But how do we move forward?" she asked.

I pulled her into my side so the three of us formed a circle. "You've taught me a lot, both of you, about having courage and taking a chance."

Rod's hand squeezed my waist. "What are you saying, Dev?"

I licked my lips and took a few deep breaths. "I can't risk losing this. Losing us. You both mean too much to me." I looked between them and let our love for each other fill the empty voids in my heart, voids I knew were about to get even larger. "After Aahna's wedding, I'm going to tell my family."

"Tell them what exactly?" Rod asked.

Sky stroked my back.

"About my bisexuality, about us, about the three of us."

"Bleeding hell, Dev."

"How do you think they'll react?" Sky's soft voice and continued caresses indicated she had a good idea already.

"They won't be happy." I chuckled dryly at the understatement. "You're both invited to the ceremony, by the way. So if they kick me out, you can give me a lift."

"Oh, Dev." Sky's eyes welled. "Do you think it will really come to that?"

I snorted, but my throat was too clogged by fear to form words.

"I'm sorry, mate." Rod turned his head into my neck. His lips brushed my skin in a sweet kiss. My legs shook with emotion.

"We'll be there for you. And I don't know how we'll do this long-term, but we'll make it happen," Sky said.

Rod raised his head and winked. "Private jet, love. That's how."

Hope surged in my belly. "Yes. We'll fly to you, or you'll fly to us. And when we're not on tour, we can be based in Miami."

Sky smiled, and it was everything. "You'd do that for me? For us? Come out to your family—"

"—to everyone," I said. If we were doing this, I wasn't going to hide anymore.

"You sure?" Rod raised a brow. "You've seen how the media chews me up."

"Yeah. But after my family, the rest won't matter."

Sky kissed me. "You're amazing, Dev. I'm sure I'll be able to work away from the office a lot of the time."

"Some time together will be better than none," Rod said sagely.

"Oh hello," I teased. "We have a philosopher among us."

"Sod off, you prat. I'm just saying that Jules is married and has a family. He and his wife work it out. We can too."

I looked at Sky. "Yeah?"

"Yeah. Let's try."

"Good," Rod said. His hand dropped to squeeze my arse, and Sky's too, I was certain. "So let's start now."

I laughed. "How?"

"Let's fuck."

"Didn't we just do that?" Sky said in an amused tone that I was all too happy to hear. The previous conversation had made me tense as hell, and I was more than ready to follow Rod's suggestion.

"Dev will be tied up with his family for a week." Rod dropped to his knees and grabbed my cock. "And I need to get my fill of this incredible man before he goes."

My gaze met Sky's. She grinned. "Fuck on."

DEV

Whoever had decided that Indian weddings needed to be days long could kiss my brown arse.

I looked around the packed reception at the utterly gorgeous Gibson Hall, trying not to mentally tally up how much this was all costing me, then caught a glimpse of Aahna's glowing face and smiled.

Fuck it. It was just money. And if my parents had invited oh, maybe an extra hundred people without mentioning it, I could handle it. Aahna's happiness was what mattered.

She and Raj looked overjoyed, the two of them arm in arm, Aahna every inch the bejeweled princess in her red and gold sari, Raj a worthy prince beside her in his gold and red embroidered sherwani.

Someone tugged on my arm. Kalini, Raj's cousin, who his parents (and my parents) thought would be perfect for me. She was pre-med, top of her class, and I actually liked her. She'd been a lively and sympathetic companion these last seven days.

And she'd made it more than clear that she had no interest in marrying me. But she was happy to pretend for now, for the duration of the wedding festivities. Apparently, she had her eye on someone else. A white boy in her class. Someone her parents wouldn't approve of.

"Story of my life," I'd told her. Though that was minimizing things just a bit.

Kalini handed me a plate of chapatis. "You haven't eaten a thing all day," she said.

I took the plate, though I had no appetite. "Thanks."

She looked me in the eye and said, "Can I ask you something?"

"Anything."

"I saw the videos of King's Cross in Tahiti. It looked to me like..." She blushed prettily, then continued. "It looked to me like there was something between you and Rod and that girl, Sky." She met my gaze again. "Or did I read that wrong? Is it just him and her?"

My heart pounded wildly. Could I trust her with this? Then again, hadn't I come to this wedding with the intention of telling my family, my parents, the truth today?

This would be good practice for later. And if Kalini had a big mouth? Well, she'd save me the trouble of coming out on my own.

I nodded. "You read that right."

Her pretty mouth formed an O. "So, you and Sky and Rod?" When I nodded again, she laughed, putting her hand over her mouth, her eyes sparkling. "Lucky girl!"

"We're all lucky. Being together the way we are." I could see Kalini wanted to ask the question, so I saved her the bother. "Yes, we're *all* together."

She raised an eyebrow. "You like *both* men and women?"

Now I was the one who was blushing. "Yeah." Just one word, so hard to say, but so good to admit. "Yeah, I'm bi."

She elbowed me. "You are a dark horse, Devkinandan." Then she grew serious. "I take it your parents, and Raj's, don't know."

I shook my head. "I'm planning to tell them today." My palms started sweating at the thought, and I dried them on my sherwani. "I actually meant to do it already, before Sky and Rod got here. But..."

I didn't have to fill in the blanks for her. "You don't want to wreck your sister's wedding."

I nodded. "And I'm a little concerned about how Raj's parents will take it. Dad is all excited about going into business with the Guptas, and I don't want to mess that up by springing that on everyone in public."

She patted my hand. "I get it. You can tell them right after."

"That's what I was thinking."

She squeezed my arm, and a grin lit up her face. "If it's any consolation, you'll be helping me. After this, my parents won't be too appalled when I tell them my news."

I grinned at her. "He's a lucky man, Kalini. Truly."

She sobered. "I hope your family will take it well."

I swallowed hard, a stone forming in my stomach. "They won't. But I can't live a lie forever."

Her eyes misted. "None of us can. I've waited long enough to be honest with my family, and my news isn't nearly so... surprising."

She could've chosen a dozen other words that would be more accurate, but yeah, it was going to be a hell of a surprise.

I just hoped it wouldn't be the end of my relationship with my family.

ROD

The limo snaked through the streets of Bishopsgate toward Gibson Hall where the final reception to Dev's sister's wedding was being held. My stomach burned, and I hadn't been able to eat much of anything all day.

Except for Sky's pussy. I could eat her out anytime, even on my deathbed. My cock pulsed in my tuxedo trousers. I placed Sky's hand on my crotch, waiting to see if she'd take advantage of my dick's decision to wake up. She gave me a light squeeze and turned to me, an amused expression on her pretty face. "And here I thought you were worried."

"Contrary to popular opinion, I can walk and chew gum at the same time."

Sky smiled, then it slipped off her face. Her arm wrapped around her midsection. "Have you heard anything more?"

I pulled my mobile out and reread Dev's last message. *I'm fine. Can't wait to see you both.* "Nothing new."

"Call him?"

I dialed his number. After what seemed like forever, he picked up. "Dev?" I asked.

"Rod?"

"Dev?"

There was so much noise I could hardly make out what he was saying. "How are things?"

"What?" he asked. "I can't hear you."

"We're almost there."

"What? When are you coming?" he asked.

Clearly, he couldn't hear me. I sighed and ended the call. I shoved the mobile into my pocket. When I looked up, Sky was watching me. I shrugged. "I don't know why, but I'm worried."

She snuggled against me. "I'm worried too. You've known Dev's family a long time, right?"

"Since we were boys."

"What are they like?"

I rubbed my jaw. "That's hard to say. It's strange because, growing up, I always thought they liked me. But Dev told me last week that they think I was a bad influence on him."

Sky threaded her fingers through mine and held our hands on her lap. "My guess is they're looking for someone to blame for Dev not snapping into the life they have mapped out for him."

"And now they'll have even more reason to hate me." I dropped my head onto the leather seat back. I'd never much cared what other people thought of me. This hurt though, and I wasn't certain why. Perhaps, because for me, the Prakeshes had always represented stability, continuity, security. Things that had been lacking in my own life.

But if they didn't accept Dev for who he was, then they were the ones lacking. Dev was an amazing person and a devoted son, and if they couldn't see that, then they could fuck off.

Still, I didn't want to muck things up for him if he had managed to tell his parents and things had gone well. I was wearing a dark gray suit with a black waistcoat and a button-down shirt in a lighter shade of gray. My tie was a shiny slate. All in all, rather respectable for me, until you noticed the rhinestones running along the leg seams of my trousers and lining the lapels and cuffs of my jacket. I had skipped the eyeliner and nail varnish today though. "Do you think this outfit is over the top for an Indian wedding?"

Sky smiled. "You look amazing."

"Maybe I should have gone with something less flashy."

"But the fingerless black leather gloves and the heeled black and white boots make the suit." Sky winked and straightened my tie.

"Now you're just taking the piss," I grumbled.

She leaned into my side and kissed my cheek. "You're a rock star, Rod, and you'll look like one regardless of the clothes you wear."

I ran a finger along the edge of her jaw. "And you look every inch the successful, confident, and dead sexy woman you are."

Her smile lightened my mood, until my thoughts returned to Dev and the multitude of things that could have gone wrong with his coming out to his parents. If they'd hurt him in any way... My fists clenched. I pressed the call button on the console beside me.

Tony answered in his deep voice. "Yes?"

"Any news about Dev?"

"Should there be?"

"Text Hugh, ask him how things are going."

"Yes, sir."

Hugh was Dev's bodyguard. He'd know if Dev was in trouble.

A moment later, Tony said, "Hugh says everything's cool."

"Thanks, mate."

"No worries."

Sky peered through the darkened windows. "I think we're there."

"Thank fuck," I muttered, taking her hand in mine.

As soon as the limo pulled up in front, we scooted out and entered the reception hall. Dev had really pulled out all the stops. The rhythmic thump of Indian pop music filled the air, and mountains of food in warming pans filled the outer hallway. People milled about eating and talking. The doors to the main reception room opened, affording us a look inside. Multicolored lights bounced over a packed dance floor, where men and women danced with their arms in the air.

I tugged on Sky's hand, and we crossed the lobby. As we approached the open door, I spotted Dev dancing with a pretty Indian girl. His face glowed, probably from sweat, and a big grin split his face.

The sodding prat was having a grand fucking time while I've been losing my shit in the limo?

Sky scooted closer to me. "Is she one of Dev's sisters?"

"No, she fucking isn't. And don't they look cozy?"

Seeing Dev with Sky turned me on. Seeing Dev with this woman enraged me.

What. The. Fuck?

I took a step toward him, and that's when my arrival was noticed. Squeals and shouts of "Hot Rod!" peppered the air. Within moments, we were swarmed. "Shit," I grumbled as I tried to keep Sky by my side, but the throng was too thick and she stepped back.

Tony stood to my left, keeping a watchful eye over the young fans who were begging for my autograph and for selfies. The only way they'd leave me in peace was if I cooperated, so I smiled and became Hot Rod.

"Oh my God, it's Rod Taylor! I love King's Cross," a young woman, maybe eighteen, exclaimed.

"Thank you, darling," I said.

"Can I have a photo with you?"

"Of course, anything for a beauty like you." I winked and she, very predictably, squealed. Damon would have had a field day with this one. Not me though. The only woman I wanted was Sky. My eyes searched her out in the crowd, and my shoulders relaxed when I spotted her standing off to the side with Dev.

Dev sent me a big smile, and the knot in my gut unwound a bit.

Maybe things really were okay, and my worrying had all been for naught.

There was a shuffling in the crowd and then Patag, Dev's younger brother, stood in front of me.

"Hi Rod." His eyes were bright with excitement.

"Look at you all grown up and shit." I grabbed him around the neck and pulled him to me in a hug. "The girls must be falling all over themselves to get a piece of you."

He blushed and ducked his head. "Starting uni this autumn."

"Fucking brilliant, mate. Dev says you want to be a barrister? You'll be amazing." Patag was a sweet kid, like Jonah but without the hard shell.

His blush deepened. "Nah. Not as amazing as you lot. I watched the videos from your gig in Papeete. The new album is going to be a smash. I just know it." He held up his mobile. "Mind if we get a shot together?"

"Are you fucking kidding me?" I threw my arm around his shoulder and ruffled his hair. "You're Dev's brother. That makes you mine as well."

Patag beamed. He held up his mobile. "Cheers."

"Cheers," I said as he snapped a selfie.

When he stepped away. I squeezed his arm and looked straight into his eyes. "You ever need something, I'm just a ring away, aren't I?" I knew how difficult Dev's parents could be, and although Patag had Dev on his side, I wanted him to know he had me too.

"Thanks, mate." Patag nodded his head. "That means a lot."

A girl shouldered in front of him, and it was back to work for me.

By the time I finished up with the fans, Dev and Sky had moved into the lobby, where it was quieter. They were walking along the line of food warmers, and Dev was piling delicious looking food onto a plate for her. Sky smiled at him like he'd hung the moon.

Something fluttered in my belly, and I was once again hit by how much I loved these two. Of course, it didn't hurt that Dev looked exceptionally striking in his black sherwani with gold buttons, or that Sky was radiant in her classy red dress that was just tight enough and short enough to tantalize.

And was I tantalized. Very tantalized.

I walked over to them. With each step closer, my heart lifted. My future was these two wonderful people, and the future was now. I stopped in front of Dev and smiled. "Hi."

For the first time in my life, I was secure in the knowledge that we were solid. That we'd made it through the storm and had come out not only intact, but victorious.

I bent to kiss him.

Almost frantically, Dev pulled away.

The light in my chest extinguished, and I closed my eyes. *This can't be fucking happening again.*

Chapter 14

DEV

I recoiled from Rod's kiss, my eyes darting around to see who was watching, who had noticed the near-miss, my heart going twenty to the dozen.

I was a coward. A horrible, horrible coward, and I didn't deserve Rod or Sky. I didn't deserve Sky's soft hand on my arm or the sympathetic look on Kalini's face.

But I sure as hell deserved the scowl on Rod's.

What the fuck was I doing?

Hurting the man I loved. Rejecting him. Telling him once again that he wasn't enough. That he didn't *matter* enough.

Well, fuck that. I was done. I was done denying who I was.

And I was done denying what Rod meant to me.

Rod's eyes were shining bright, too bright, his body so stiff he could have been made of granite. He stepped back, his arm going to Sky's waist, and I couldn't stop myself.

I lunged for him like he was drowning.

But I was the one who was floundering. I was the one who couldn't breathe.

Until our lips met, until his mouth started moving against mine, until he wrapped his arms around me and let me kiss him for all I was worth.

My whole body felt like it was on fire, every inch of my skin burning, hundreds of eyes on us, the collective gasps and exclamations of what seemed like the entire Indian community almost overpowering the music that still blared from the speakers.

But none of that mattered. Only Rod did. Only Sky did.

I blindly reached out a hand for her, my mouth still joined to Rod's, and when her soft palm met mine, her fingers gently squeezing my own, my heart leapt. I broke the kiss and pulled her to us, Rod and I enveloping her in our arms, both of us kissing her too.

And then a hand on my shoulder wrenched me from that warm embrace. "What is the meaning of this, Devkinandan?" my father bellowed, his voice deeper and harsher than I'd ever heard it.

His face had flushed so dark I feared for his heart.

Mum raced to his side. I expected her to try to soothe him. But she turned to me, her own face similarly dark. "How could you shame us this way? With this… perversion?"

"I love them." They were the only words I could think of. The only words that mattered.

"These people are more important than your family?"

"They are my family too. They mean everything."

My father tapped his own chest. "You come here, you shame us, you ruin our name. Is this all a game to you?"

My throat tightened to the point where I was afraid I couldn't speak, and hot tears stung my eyes. I looked away, right into Aahna's shocked gaze. Raj had his arm around her, his stare hard as he looked at me.

I'd ruined my sister's wedding. "I'm sorry, Aahna," I said. "I didn't mean for any of this to happen "

Indira, Patag, and Geena had just reached us. "What's going on?" Geena asked. She looked at me, at Rod, at Sky. "I heard something… something that cannot be true."

"It *is* true," I said. "I'm in love with Sky… and Rod. The three of us are together."

Geena gasped and took Aahna's free hand. "You cannot mean that." But she was stepping away even as she said it.

Hands took mine from either side, one delicate and feminine, the other large and masculine. But it wasn't Sky and Rod who were flanking me. It was Indira and Patag. The lump in my throat came back. "We're with you," Indira whispered, and Patag squeezed my hand.

Raj's parents stepped out of the crowd, and his father spoke. "Our son cannot be part of a family that allows such deviance."

Aahna's mouth dropped open, horror on her features. To his credit, Raj pulled her closer and shook his head. I had to fix this. Now.

I looked at my father, my heart thundering in my chest, my knees weak. I'd always known it would come to this, hadn't I? "Do what you know has to be done, Dad."

His lips pressed into a thin line, and he shook his head. Was he going to take my side after all? A spark of hope lit in my chest.

He finally spoke. "You are no longer a son of ours." His voice grew hoarse. "You are no longer a Prakesh."

Gasps and exclamations filled the air around us. I looked at Mum, and her eyes dropped to the floor, her hand tightening on my father's arm, and he pulled her close.

Indira and Patag both leaned into me, silently giving me their support, support I desperately needed.

My stomach knotting so hard I thought I'd vomit, I turned my gaze to Aahna. Her eyes were blazing, Geena's too. "I'm so, so sorry, Aahna." She looked away, as if I didn't exist.

I forced myself to address Raj's parents. "All of the shame falls on me, not my sister. Not my parents." Then I turned my focus to Raj. "If my sister isn't the happiest bride ever, I will ruin you, and I will ruin your family's business." I drew myself up to my full height. "And we both know that as Dev Stone, I have the power to put action behind those words."

Raj nodded, and the Guptas had the good grace to stay silent.

I took one more look at my own parents, but they seemed frozen, and I knew the feeling.

It was time for me to leave. I squeezed Indira's and Patag's hands. "Thank you for standing by me."

"We'll walk you out," Indira said.

I released their hands. "You both still live at home, so no, you won't." Patag opened his mouth. "Dev—"

"I'll be okay." Sky and Rod stepped forward. Taking the hands of my two lovers, I forced my feet to start moving to the reception hall's front doors.

I was Dev Stone now. Devkinandan Prakesh was dead.

I didn't belong here anymore.

ROD

The mood in the limo when Tony and Hugh drove us back to my flat was somber to say the least. Sandwiched between me and Sky, Dev sat silent and lost in thought. He'd withdrawn into himself and seemed unaware of Sky's head on his shoulder or her hand rubbing soothing circles on his chest. As for me, I had no fucking idea how to handle this.

The role of comforter was a new one for me. I was usually the sullen one, the angry one.

Is that really true?

I thought back to all the years of our friendship. Sure, Dev had been there for me through some pretty rough times, but… I'd been there for him too. When his parents had insisted Dev attend Saturday morning maths classes instead of the piano lessons he'd wanted to take, I'd sat hours with him coming up with a plan to change their minds. And it had worked. I'd helped him find ways out of every restriction his parents had tried impose on him.

I snuck a glance at his face out of the corner of my eye. This situation wasn't so different, was it? When Dev's parents had wanted him to leave the band, I'd fouled that up. They'd wanted him to marry an Indian girl, and I'd fouled that plan too. And now, they wanted Dev to feel the weight of what they perceived to be his betrayal, his shame. I was damn well going to foul that plan up as well.

Dev was a good man. The best man I knew. The shame was on his parents and any of his siblings who couldn't, or *wouldn't*, I corrected myself, accept him and love him for everything that he was.

I could never do that to him. I could never try to change Dev, because he was perfect exactly as he was. And if that meant keeping our relationship, our triad in the closet, then that was exactly what we would do.

When the car stopped in the private garage under my building, I opened the door and took Dev's hand in mine. Dev looked at me. His eyes were hooded and so lost, I felt my own fill with tears. "Come, babe. We're home."

He blinked and looked around, his gaze clearing. "We're at your place."

I kissed the back of his hand. "Consider it ours. Yours, mine"—I smiled at Sky—"and Sky's. Ours."

She sent me a watery smile of her own. "Let's get inside, Dev."

Like an automaton, he exited the vehicle and headed for the lifts. Sky and I exchanged a look. She was as worried about him as I was. I placed my hand at the base of her spine and we hurried to catch up. I swiped my key card and pressed the button that would direct the lift to my penthouse. It covered the entire top floor of the building and had an enormous terrace overlooking London's downtown core.

I loved this place. When King's Cross had started to earn us serious cash, I'd sunk all my money into it. It was my home, the only place on this big earth where I belonged, the only place where I didn't have to hide my heart or put up a front. Even though Mum and my siblings loved me just as I was, I still kept Hot Rod on a leash around them.

But in my own home? He was free to play.

The lift dinged and the doors opened up into my foyer. I ushered Sky and Dev inside, and a thrill tightened my gut. The two most important people in my life were in my private space, and all I felt was elation. Sky had spent the week with me, except for the hours I'd been in the studio rehearsing for the tour and laying down vocal tracks for the album. And in the past, Dev had spent a lot of time here, mostly, I suspected as a way to get away from his family.

What neither knew was that other than my family and the maid, they were the only two people to step foot inside my sanctuary.

Instead of making me feel ill or scared or anxious, all I felt was glad.

I wanted Sky and Dev to be happy too. But how? How could I turn this sorry situation around?

My instinct was to take them both to bed and let the chemistry between us and the euphoria of a few good orgasms take care of matters. Sex had always worked for me before. It was how I expressed myself best.

Yet, when I took Dev and Sky's hands and led them to the living room, I knew that sex wouldn't be the answer this time. Dev had been disowned by his family, likely kicked out of the Indian community he'd been a part of his whole life. Hell, he'd even been stripped of his name.

I took off my rhinestone-studded suit jacket and black waistcoat and draped them over a chair. They looked divine, but they were a bit constricting.

Sky and I sat Dev down on the couch, once again between us. "How are you doing, Dev?" she asked in a soft, hesitant voice.

Dev stared straight ahead, his hands clenched together in his lap. He closed his eyes briefly and exhaled loudly. "I knew this was going to happen. It's why I put off coming out for so long."

"We're here for you. Whatever you need." Sky placed her hand over his and raised her brows at me. "Aren't we, Rod?"

"Yeah." I coughed to clear my throat. "Of course."

Dev snorted. "Don't strain yourself, mate."

Fuck. I was about to step my foot in it, wasn't I? "I'm sorry, Dev. I'm not very good with..." I trailed off as I searched for the best way to express how hopeless I felt.

"Not good with what, Rod? Words?" His face was twisted into a scowl, but at least the numbness in his eyes was gone.

"Yeah. Words." It was as good an answer as any. Or so I thought.

Dev's scowl deepened. "You're a sodding lyricist, you dolt."

My face split into a grin.

"What the fuck are you smiling about?" He practically spat the words, steam billowing out of his ears.

"You," I said, laughing now. "You're swearing at me and calling me names."

"And that makes you smile?" He rolled his eyes. "Your sainted mother certainly dropped you on your noggin when you were a child."

"I'm smiling because I know you're going to be all right." I caught him around the neck and pulled him against me. I kissed his lips. It started out as a friendly peck, but who was I kidding? Anytime I had Dev in my arms with his mouth on mine, an inferno was sure to follow.

Hands went around my sides, another gripped my hair and tugged my head back. Dev's lips left mine and nipped at my jawline, nibbled on my chin, and licked my exposed Adam's apple, chasing it up and down my throat when I swallowed.

I heard the sound of a zipper being lowered, then another. I opened my lids and looked into Dev's dark brown eyes and Sky's lighter brown ones. So much love was shining on me. My throat tightened and tears burned the backs of my eyes. Again. What the fuck was wrong with me? Tearing up, much less twice in one day? I blinked rapidly to get rid of them. I had to be the strong one today. Rod Taylor did not cry. Not when my father had beaten me, even less when he'd fucked off never to be heard from again.

I had to be strong for Dev, who'd lost everything, and for Sky, who was making a lot of concessions to be with us.

I leaned forward to capture Sky's plump lips. I looked at their fullness and delved inside to taste her mouth, to feel the sensual slide of her tongue against mine. When my chest was about to explode with the need for air, I pulled back and studied Dev and Sky's nearly identical lust-filled expressions.

"The two of you are fucking beautiful together."

Dev licked his lips and bent to kiss Sky, then me.

"Were all beautiful together," she said.

That's when it hit me—what I had to do. What I wanted to do. The only mystery that remained was why I hadn't thought to do it sooner.

I extricated myself from them and stood with my back turned. I removed my nan's gold wedding band from my pinky along with the black tungsten ring with the notes to the opening bar of "Summer Fun." The two rings that meant the most to me.

When I went to slide them into my pocket, I realized that my trousers had been unzipped and were now barely hanging on at my thighs. Laughing, I let them fall to the ground, toed off my boots, and kicked the lot aside.

Standing in only my gray silk dress shirt—the tie had long since been rolled up into the pocket of my jacket—black boxers, and socks, I turned to face the two loves of my life.

They studied me with curiosity. But the questions on Dev's face did nothing to hide the pain in his eyes. I'd do anything to rid Dev of his misery, but even I knew he'd have to work through it on his own.

Slowly, with my eyes on them and the rings clutched in my palm, I lowered myself to my knees between them.

One of Dev's brows arched, and he began to grin as the bulge between his legs grew, pushing through his open zipper. "If you want to suck my dick, Rod, you need only ask. Or better yet, just do it."

I placed a hand on his thigh and squeezed. "There will be plenty of time for a sneak attack later," I said.

Sky laid her hand on my shoulder. "What's going on, Rod?"

Trust Sky to know when I was trying to be serious. I hemmed and hawed and cleared my throat. Dev sat up straighter. "Rod?"

"Sky, when I look back on the past three months and see how much my life has changed, I know it's all thanks to you. Even if I didn't recognize it at the time, I fell for you, hard, during that magical week we all spent together in Palm Springs. You've made me a better person. A more open one. I hope that in time, I'll prove that this foul-mouthed, dirty-minded rock singer is worthy of your love and kindness."

Sky's eyes filled with tears. Her hand moved to my jaw. "Oh, Rod. You already are. You always were."

I turned my face and kissed her palm. "I love you, Sky."

"I love you too."

My eyes sought out Dev's. "Dev, you're smart and loving and selfless and fucking perfect, no matter what anyone says. You were put on this earth to make music and to sing. And I'll spend the rest of my life proving to you that what you do and who you love doesn't make you less of a man. Being honest with yourself makes you more of one."

Dev scoffed lightly, but the corner of his mouth kicked up in a small smile. "You have your work cut out for you, mate."

"We've been together for twenty years," I said. "I'm not giving up on you. Not now, not ever."

Dev placed his hand on top of mine on his lap. His eyes softened and his half-smile expanded into a full one. "You've always been my rock, Rod. Do you know that?"

My head jerked back. "No." He had it all wrong.

"It's true. Every good thing in my life is because of you. The music, the band. Hell, you helped me buy my first axe. Remember? We found that old Takamine at that scrotty music shop on Denmark Street." He turned to Sky, his eyes bright with humor and the memory. "It was scuffed and scratched, and the shopkeeper told us it had once been owned by John Squire of Stone Roses. Rod gave me all the money he'd socked away so I could buy it."

"I remember. The piece of shite cost us two hundred quid and was probably worth less than twenty."

Dev chuckled. "We composed our first song with it."

"'Summer Fun,'" I said, smiling at the memory.

"I hope you'll sing it for me some time," Sky said.

Dev put his arm around her and kissed her temple. "Anytime, sweets." He turned back to me. "Above everything else, Sky is the single best thing in my life, because of you."

"Because of me? You have that backward, mate." I looked at Sky, hoping she understood the depth of my regrets. "We almost lost her because of me."

"No," Dev insisted. "We almost lost her because of me and my inability to accept myself. We won her back because of you."

"Boys, boys," Sky interceded. "You got me back because in my heart, I never let you go. You guys are my world. My life."

I rose onto my knees and kissed her, then Dev. "You two make me whole. I can live without you, but I don't want to. I tried it, and I was sodding miserable. I'm a better man with both of you in my life. I hope I do the same for you. I want you, I need you, and I love you."

I paused for a moment, took a deep breath, then plunged ahead. "You've given me so much, and well... I don't have much to give. Except...." I held out a ring in each hand, my nan's for Sky, the other for Dev. "Dev, you may have been born into the Prakesh name, and"—I looked at Sky—"I know your mum doesn't believe in the whole patriarchy, but I'd really like it if we all had the same last name. We can't get legally married, but maybe this can work for us instead? My old man wasn't much, but my grandfather was stellar, and I would be honored if you both took my name."

"Sky Taylor, Dev Taylor, and Rod Taylor." Dev grinned. "It does have a nice ring to it. What do you say, Sky?"

A happy tear rolled down her cheek. "I love it, oh my God." A sob escaped through her sappy smile. My heart grew two sizes just to contain all my feelings. "I so want us to be Rod, Dev, and Sky Taylor."

I put the rings on their fingers, then Sky launched herself at me at the same time Dev did. They tackled me to the floor. I lay there, beaming, exploding with love, my arms full of the two people who were my everything.

They crawled over me, one on each side. Dev's hot, hard cock prodded my hip, and Sky's firm full breasts pressed into my chest. Her fingers went to work on the buttons of my shirt while Dev kissed every inch of skin she exposed. I shivered and arched into them. Christ, they had a way of making me lose my sodding mind.

When he reached my boxers, Dev pulled them down my legs, then he straddled my thigh. Pre-cum pooled on the tip of my cock and dripped onto my thigh. Sky swooped in and licked it up, making an appreciative sound in her throat.

"How does he taste, Mrs. Taylor?" Dev asked.

"Amazing." She licked her lips and winked. Hearing Dev call her by my name made it all so real. We belonged together. Forever was within my reach. She gripped my cock and I couldn't help thrusting into her tight fist. More cum collected in my slit.

"Fucking Christ."

She angled the head toward Dev. "Would you care for a taste, Mr. Taylor?"

"I so would." He sucked me into his mouth, swallowing me down to the root. I roared out my pleasure. Dev's hot mouth was heaven. But I wanted to be connected to them both.

I sat up, reached for Sky's hips, and swung her over me as I lay back down. This position put her wet pussy right above my mouth.

"Jesus, Mr. Taylor," she cried. "Give a girl some warning."

"Nope. Dev said I didn't have to ask."

And before she could argue, I sealed my lips over her clit and sucked.

"Oh!" she moaned and widened her thighs. Her heat and scent enveloped me. Filled me. I didn't want Dev to be left out though. We were a family now, exactly how I'd dreamed.

I rolled us so we were all lying on the same side. Dev positioned himself with his cock near Sky's mouth and mine in his.

"Oh fuck," I murmured as he lashed his tongue along my shaft.

We were all connected, giving each other pleasure, and I never wanted it to stop. My balls began to tingle, drawing up tight against my belly. I thrust into Dev's mouth and groaned when his throat fluttered around my cockhead. My groan vibrated into Sky's pussy. Her thighs trembled against the sides of my face, and my mouth was flooded with her taste. I gripped her waist and held on, knowing she was as close as I was.

She moaned and thrust against me, doing something wicked to Dev because his answering groan vibrated from the tip of my cock to my heart. I pistoned into his mouth, sucked Sky's clit, and my orgasm hit me like a fucking tidal wave, dragging me under into sweet ecstasy before I could even attempt to stave it off.

Sky's legs clamped onto my head and I felt her pussy pulsing against my tongue. Dev's breath caught and then he too was tossed over the edge. He continued to suck on my cock, light lazy strokes that I mimicked on Sky and she no doubt reciprocated to Dev.

It seemed like forever before our breathing return to normal. I looked at us, daisy-chained as we were, and grinned. "We're a circle," I said.

"No beginning," Sky said.

"And no end," Dev finished.

Chapter 15

SKY

After six long months of us seeing each other only intermittently, Rod and Dev had insisted on San Francisco as the final date of the King's Cross tour. That way I could check in with my parents, who I also hadn't seen much of now that I was headquartered in Miami, and then Rod and Dev and I could take a vacation, and I could show my two loves where I'd grown up.

I'd barely had any time with Rod and Dev before tonight's show, which I'd been watching from the wings with Mom and Dad. The guys were about to play their final encore, "No Strings," which had become a monster hit and always made me smile and sometimes cry happy tears whenever I heard it.

I twisted Rod's ring around my finger. I loved the weight of it on my left hand, loved looking at it when my men weren't with me. And I loved telling people I was Sky Taylor now.

Our relationship had been hinted at in the press—along with the videos from Tahiti, some pictures and video from Aahna's wedding had ended up on the internet—but Rod and Dev had decided to let things lie for a while. Dev still felt bad about how he'd stolen his sister's thunder and "wrecked" her wedding, as he put it.

Indira and Patag had both been keeping in close touch with Dev, and to her credit, Aahna had even called him once and told him she'd forgiven him even if she didn't understand our relationship. Indira was still working on their parents, but she worried that Dev's father was too afraid of what everyone else would think and wouldn't bend on the matter, but it was still early days.

Rod and I felt bad for Dev, but he seemed okay. At peace, at least. And as Rod had mentioned to me during a private moment between the two of us, Dev was writing songs like crazy, music practically pouring out of him now, and Rod thought that was a good sign.

Dev was finally free.

Crossing the stage, Rod approached the mic, looking like pure sin in a black vest with nothing underneath, skin-tight leather pants, the St. Jude medallion around his neck and the rings on his fingers—including the gold Harry Potter-inspired "Always" wedding ring Dev and I had had made for him—catching the stage lights. Rod's eyes were lined in kohl, giving him that predatory, slightly sinister look I loved so well. The man was sex on a stick, and as he hooked a hand on the oversized silver buckle of his belt and thrust his hips at the mic stand, it was clear he knew it too. His skin gleamed from exertion, and a smile of pure joy lit up his features.

The band was about to launch into "No Strings," and I took a deep breath, my heart speeding up, anticipating the serenade I was no doubt going to get. My foul-mouthed rocker with the tender heart. I loved him so.

"I have a special treat for everyone," Rod announced, his voice soaring out to the crowd.

Special treat? He hadn't mentioned anything.

He turned and gestured to me, and like a dolt, I pointed to my chest and mouthed "Me?"

He laughed and nodded. "Sky, get your gorgeous arse out here. And bring your parents."

I looked at Mom and Dad, and they seemed as mystified as I was.

Was Rod intending to sing to me while I was onstage? I should have guessed. He wasn't exactly known for his subtlety.

We walked out to center stage, and I shielded my eyes against the glare. I looked around as Dev and Rod put their arms around me, and the crowd roared its approval. Jesus, there were a *lot* of people out there.

"What's going on?" I asked Rod.

"You'll see," he said, a smile in his voice and lighting up his eyes.

Damon stepped up in front of us, a Bible in hand.

What. The…

I looked from Rod to Dev to Damon, all of them grinning like idiots.

Rod took my left hand and Dev my right, and Damon took the mic from Rod. Damon turned to the crowd. "Dearly beloved, we are gathered here today to join these three people in, well, not quite holy matrimony."

A lump filled my throat. We were getting married! Well, probably not in the legal sense, but we were expressing our intentions in front of all these people, and even if the law never caught up to us, that had to mean something, right?

The audience cheered and my mom hugged me from behind. "I'm so happy for you, honey!"

Damon chuckled. "Looks like the mother of the bride approves!"

Laughter rippled through the crowd.

Clearing his throat and putting on a semi-serious face, Damon eyed us each in turn. "Do you all take each other as husband and/or wife?"

Rod and Dev squeezed my hands, and I squeezed theirs back, our gazes meeting. "We do," we said in unison.

Damon couldn't keep the smile off his face any longer. "By the power vested in me by absolutely nobody, I now pronounce the three of you husband and husband and wife."

The audience went nuts, shouting and screaming and whistling their joy for us.

I looked at Dev, then Rod, then Damon. "Are we actually married now?" Had the guys managed to find some obscure San Francisco law that covered situations like ours?

Damon laughed. "Yeah, no."

Rod broke into a grin. "Mate, what the fuck does that mean?"

"Sod off," Damon said.

The three of them looked at each other, and then I remembered Dev telling me about the day they'd gotten their tattoos, and we all burst into laughter.

Okay, it wasn't legal, but I couldn't be all that disappointed. Leave it to King's Cross to plan the perfect wedding in every other respect.

Damon gestured to Rod and Dev. "Aren't you supposed to kiss your beautiful bride now?"

And then my two men, my two hot British rock stars, took me in their arms and snogged me for all they were worth. And I snogged them right back.

CONTINUE THE ADVENTURE!

Hello, Vanessa here! Want to be part of our VIP Readers list and get all the behind-the-scenes scoop about what *really* happens at Total Indulgence? Want to be part of our ARC team? Sign up at www.totalindulgencetours.com.

If Facebook is more your style, join our Total Indulgence VIP Readers' Lounge!

www.facebook.com/groups/
totalindulgencevipreaderslounge

We hope you enjoyed traveling to Tahiti with King's Cross as Sky challenged Rod and Dev to get their act together… along with challenging the whole band to take some out-of-their-comfort-zone adventures, like crossing that rope bridge or the Turkish oil wrestling competition, which I personally enjoyed maybe a little too much! (Maybe I enjoyed this whole trip a little too much. Seriously, Damon is a hottie McHotPants!)

If you loved our little romp, please give us a thumbs-up review. We're not on Yelp yet, but we are on Amazon and Goodreads!

Next up on Total Indulgence's schedule: a trip to Sonoma for our three execs! That's right, Daniel, Arianna, and Javier are going to get some R&R and experience some challenges of their own as they explore what their relationship is outside of business.

Keep reading for a special preview of *Her Two Men in Sonoma*!

A SPECIAL PREVIEW OF
HER TWO MEN IN SONOMA
(TOTAL INDULGENCE, BOOK 3)

When the past crashes into the present…

My heart has always been split between two men: my childhood friend and my ex-husband. They've been my everything, and we run a successful travel company together, but our love lives are a shambles. As the one-year anniversary of my divorce looms, can a couples' retreat in Sonoma fix everything that's gone wrong between the three of us?

ARIANNA

My battered heart can't take it any longer—I want a baby and the man—men?—of my dreams, but how can I have that when my ex has made it clear he won't share?

DANIEL

Everyone thinks they know me, but no one knows my terrible secret.

If my ex-wife and my best friend discover the truth, it will ruin everything. Or will it?

JAVIER

I've loved both of them for what seems like forever. I lost her to him once before, but I'm not letting her go again. I know he's not into me, but can he learn to share the woman we both love?

Warning: Contains an abundance of alcohol, secrets upon secrets, sexy shenanigans where they shouldn't occur, and the only truth that matters: love will find a way.

ARIANNA

Twenty-nine years old, divorced, and childless. Not exactly my happiest birthday ever. But I pasted on a wide smile for both sets of grandparents, for Mamá and Papá, and for my sisters, Mariposa, Isabel, and Seleste, as I hugged and kissed them and everyone else in the Rodriguez clan goodbye. They'd thrown me a lovely party, and I'd even forgotten about my troubles for a while.

But now it was time to go home, eat a pint of ice cream, drink a bottle of wine, and cry my eyes out. Alone.

As I walked down the driveway of my parents' home, a light breeze cut through Miami's humid air and cooled my face. Night had fallen a couple hours ago, and the sound of laughter behind me was cut off as someone shut the front door. I'd just reached my pearl-white Lexus parked in the drive when I heard a light step behind me. "Arianna."

I closed my eyes. Only Javier Cordero, the man I'd loved all through my teenage years, could make my name sound like a caress. His rich, velvety voice curled around me, leaving me both warm and bereft at the same time. I'd grown up believing that Javi and I would marry one day. And then he'd crushed my dreams by telling me he was gay.

Pasting on another smile, I turned to him. "What is it, Javi?"

He leaned against my car, his broad frame partially blocking the glow from the motion-activated light mounted above my parents' garage door. "You managed to give me the slip." He reached out and touched my elbow. "That's not like you, *corazón*."

Corazón. He'd always called me that, and I'd never told him how much

216

it hurt to hear it. *Sweetheart.* Like we were lovers.

"I'm just really… tired." My voice shook a little, and I looked away.

He frowned. "You look like you're going to cry."

Fuck. He read me so well. I sucked in a breath, unable to look at him. "It's been a long day, Javi."

"A long year, you mean. Well, almost a year."

He was alluding to my divorce from Daniel King, Javi's best friend and our partner in Total Indulgence, the high-end travel company the three of us ran together.

"I *really* don't want to talk about this. I just want to go home and wallow in my misery and not have to smile for anyone."

"*Corazón*—"

"*Don't.*" I raised a hand, fighting for control. "Javi, just don't. I'm not your *corazón*. I'm not anything to you, other than a friend." The words came out sharper than I'd intended, and he looked like I'd slapped him.

He held out his hand. "Give me your keys."

"What?"

"Arianna Rodriguez, you are in no condition to drive."

How dare he tell me I was drunk? "I'm perfectly fine." I'd only had a few drinks, and that had been a while ago. Well, except for that last one I'd downed right before leaving.

"You had at least three mojitos that I saw, and you haven't snapped at me like that in ages. And the last time you did, you were furious. So even if you're not drunk, you're too upset to drive."

Heat flashed up my neck and over my face. Javi hadn't pissed me off this badly since he'd told me about his sexual orientation. And yeah, I had been furious that time. This time, I was just… imploding. "Don't treat me like a child."

Javi leaned closer, his delicious spicy scent washing over me. "I'm not. I'm treating you like someone precious to me. I'd be gutted if anything happened to you." He held out his hand again. "Let me drive you home."

He was killing me with this kindness, and he didn't even know it. "I just really, really need to be alone right now, Javi." I couldn't keep my voice steady any longer.

Reaching out, he smoothed my long black hair out of my face and cupped my cheek in his warm palm. "What you need is a friend. Your best friend in the whole world. And that's me." He pulled me into his arms, and a sob rose up in my chest. "Let me take you home, put you in a warm bath, and listen to how much you hate life right now."

He hugged me tight, and I burst into tears. After I sobbed all over his white silk guayabera, I finally wiped my eyes and stepped back. "O-okay," I hiccupped and handed him my keys.

I was done putting up a front; if Javi wanted to deal with me in this state, who was I to say no?

When we pulled up to my house in Coconut Grove—the house I'd shared with Daniel during the five years we'd been married—Javi shut off the car and hurried around to my side, opening the door and giving me a hand out. "*Mi reina*," he murmured. *My queen.*

I smiled up at him and shook my head. "Damn it, Javi, why do you have to be so wonderful?"

He grinned at me. "Ruining you for other men?"

"Yeah." It was the truth. "And it's really not fair, because I can't have you, can I?"

He offered me his elbow and I took it. That last mojito was starting to hit me, and I was wobbling a bit in my stilettos. No sense breaking an ankle on the flagstone path that led to the house.

Ignoring my question, he unlocked the front door, but before I could step inside, he scooped me off my feet and carried me over the threshold like I was his blushing bride. The way Daniel had when we'd bought this place. My heart started pounding, and I stared up at Javier. "What are you doing, Javi?"

"Turn on the lights," he said, carrying me over to the switch plate on the wall.

I did as asked, then he carried me through the dimly lit living room and down the shadowy hall to the master suite. "Javi?"

"Lights," he said, motioning with his head to the switch inside the bedroom door. I complied.

"What's going on?" I asked again.

He carried me into the spacious master bath and paused by the doorway, waiting for me to turn on the lights again. Once they were on, revealing the gorgeous white bathroom that Daniel and I had designed together, Javi took me over to the plush white vanity bench in front of my sink and set me down. "Stay there," he said, the commanding tone in his voice warning me not to argue—and turning me on at the same time. Damn him. Why did he have to be everything I wanted in a man?

Outside of Daniel, that is.

Grabbing a tea rose bath bomb from the canister on the edge of the huge tub, Javier turned on the water. He really was drawing me that bath. Steam swirled up from the tub, the rushing of the water echoing off the tiles.

I looked around, taking in the travertine marble Daniel and I had chosen for the shower, the granite we'd chosen for the countertops, the chrome fixtures we'd argued over before settling things with a sloppy kiss in the middle of the showroom floor, a kiss that had led to us barely making it home before we'd had wild sex just inside—and against—the front door, and then again on the kitchen table, and then on our brand-new sleigh bed, and then on the old black and white bathroom tile floor that we'd hated…

My bottom lip started to tremble. I missed him so much.

But it was his fault we'd divorced. He'd lied to me. We never should have married in the first place. He could have saved us so much heartache, if only he'd been honest with me.

"Hey." Javier crouched down in front of me, placing his hands on my knees. The heat of his palms seared through the fuchsia linen sundress I was wearing.

I looked into his handsome face, with its high cheekbones, my gaze traveling over those dark eyes framed in thick black lashes, down to his perfectly straight nose and full lips. Sometimes I thought *Dios* had peered into my dreams and fashioned a man just for me.

But in the ultimate cruel joke, *Dios* had also made him gay.

Tears formed in the corners of my eyes. "Why is life so fucking unfair?" I asked.

"If we got everything we wanted, our lives would be downright boring." He used his thumbs to wipe away the tears sliding down my cheeks.

"I was supposed to have a baby by now," I said, the ache in my chest threatening to turn into a wail. I swallowed it down and tried to smile. "Remember when you promised me that if I was thirty and single you'd marry me? And we'd have babies?"

"I remember."

"Why? Why did you say that, when you knew it wasn't going to ever happen?"

His gaze dropped to my lips for a moment, then his eyes locked on mine. "I said it because I wanted to make you happy." His gaze dipped to my mouth again, and a tingle of electricity ran through my body. "I wanted to make us *both* happy."

"But… but you're—"

He leaned in, his forehead touching mine, his warm breath washing over my lips. "About that. I might have left something out."

"You're gay. What exactly did you leave out?"

He cupped my jaw in his hands, angling it just so, as if he were going to kiss me. "It's a little more complicated than that."

"Complicated how?"

He touched his lips to mine, the kiss so gentle, so tender, I had to pull away, shaking my head. "Javi, you can't do that. You can't kiss me like that. I can't take it."

He reached back behind him and shut off the tub's faucet before it overflowed. The sudden quiet revealed the harshness of my breathing. The harshness of his as well. Was he… was he turned on? I looked down between his legs to see a sizable bulge tenting his slacks. I gestured to it. "Care to explain that?"

"I was trying to." He slid a hand down to cup the nape of my neck. "When I told you I was gay back in high school, I thought it was true. But I've come to realize it's not the full story."

I narrowed my eyes at him. "Is this some kind of riddle?"

One corner of his mouth lifted up into that lazy half-smile I knew so well. "I'm bisexual, Ari. It took me a long time to sort out who I am, and by the time I realized it, you were already dating Daniel."

"So, you're saying those women you brought as your dates to family parties weren't just cover? They really were dates?" He nodded. "Does Daniel know?"

"Yeah."

I frowned. "Another thing he never told me. No wonder our marriage was doomed. So why didn't *you* tell me sooner?"

"There really wasn't a point, once I'd figured it out. You and Daniel were getting serious. High school and college were a confusing time for me. I believed that if I was attracted to men, that meant I was gay. It took me doing some reading and talking to other people who felt like I do, to realize that it's okay to be bi. I'm not in denial about being gay. I really am attracted to both men and women, and I enjoy having sex with both." His eyes dropped to my lips again. "And I've wanted to have sex with you for a very, very long time."

I could only stare at him. Had I fallen asleep? Was this some kind of crazy-ass dream fueled by too much alcohol and too many nights alone?

I held out my arm. "Pinch me."

He leaned forward. "I'd much rather kiss you." Then his lips were on mine again, and this time they weren't gentle. This time they were demanding, and my own parted for the invasion of his tongue. It twined around mine, and slick heat pooled between my legs. A helpless little whimper slipped out of me.

Cristo, the man could kiss. If this was a dream, I didn't want to wake up.

He drew me to my feet, then began unzipping the back of my dress, and I started unbuttoning his shirt. I pushed his shirt down his arms as my dress began to fall, and we released each other for a moment so we could drop the offending garments to the floor.

I took in the rich tan of his ripped torso with its sprinkling of black hair across his chest, his chiseled eight-pack, the perfect V of his obliques pointing down to the bulge still tenting his slacks. Javi had been a gym rat since college, but I hadn't known just how much time he'd put in there. I whistled. "*¡Ay, papi chulo!*" He grinned at me, making his pecs dance and flexing his biceps.

Then his eyes fell to my breasts, lingering there, and I couldn't get my black bra off fast enough. I let it fall from my fingers, and he dipped his head down, sucking one of my nipples into his mouth, his strong fingers tugging on the other and making electricity arc from each hard peak to my pussy. I hadn't been this turned on in a long time. When his mouth left my breast, I took his face in my hands. "Is this really happening?" I asked in all seriousness.

Javi broke into a grin. "*Sí, princesa*. It's really happening."

"Let's take this show into the bedroom."

Placing a hand on his shoulder for balance, I stepped out of my black stilettos, then I took his hand, giving it a little tug. He followed me into the bedroom, where he kicked off his shoes and went to work on his belt, the buckle jangling as he unzipped his slacks and left them in a heap on the floor.

Then he stepped forward, backing me into the mattress and urging me up onto it. I lay back, clad only in my lacy black panties, which he proceeded to strip off me. Dropping to his knees, he parted my legs, his lips traveling up the inside of my right thigh. I was quivering all over, and the closer he got to my pussy, the less I could control it. How many times had I fantasized about this? About Javi, the man I'd loved forever, making love to me? Being mine, in ways that went far beyond friendship?

He parted the lips of my sex, his tongue finding my clit and circling it. A throaty moan rushed out of me, and he gently sucked on that little nub, his tongue teasing me and making me writhe. He licked down to my entrance, spearing his tongue inside me, fucking me with it until I moaned. "More." He slid two fingers through my juices, coating them, before sliding them inside me, the sudden fullness making me gasp and rock my hips into his hand.

Keeping his fingers where they were, he rose up and leaned over me, cupping my neck with his other hand and drawing my mouth to his. I could taste myself on his lips. His tongue plunged into my mouth, mimicking what his fingers were doing below, and I cried out, coming apart on his hand.

I'd slept with three men since Daniel and I had broken up, and not one of them had made me feel like this, like I was shattering into a million pieces, but safe at the same time.

JAVIER

Arianna gasped into my mouth, her luscious body writhing beneath mine as she came, and I felt like the king of the world. I'd finally, finally done it. Finally manned up and gone after what I'd wanted for so many years.

I'd let Daniel have her because I'd convinced myself that I couldn't make her happy. I was gay after all. A gay man who weirdly lusted after his female best friend. And other women too.

By the time I'd realized what I really was, it had been too late. Daniel had swept her off her feet, and I couldn't even be that upset because at least the two people I loved most in the world were happy.

Even if I wasn't. Even if I secretly pined for them both. But I'd known when I'd met Daniel in college that he wasn't gay. He'd had a different girl in bed practically every night of the week. And after what had happened between us in Cancun... I knew he'd never go there with me.

For a long time, I'd resigned myself to never having what I wanted. But after Ari and Daniel had divorced, I'd vowed to myself not to lose her again.

The time hadn't been right for me to approach her; I'd wanted to wait until she was over Daniel, until the two of them had settled down and found a way to be around each other without tension filling the room.

But seeing her tonight, seeing her so damn miserable, broke something inside me. Ari was suffering, and it was time to make her see that losing Daniel wasn't the end of the world.

I just hoped I hadn't miscalculated. Was it too soon?

My heart pounding in my chest, my fingers still inside her, I released her mouth and waited for Ari to open her eyes, to look up at me, to let me know if this was going to go further. My aching cock was telling me to just keep going, but I wanted to be sure this was truly what she wanted.

She panted softly, her long, thick lashes fluttering against her tan cheeks, and I held my breath. Finally she looked up at me. "Well, what are you waiting for?" she asked.

"Just making sure you're still with me." My cock pressed into her hip, and she shifted against me, deliberately rubbing it through the thin cloth of my snug black boxer trunks.

"I'm with you. And I'm not done yet." She looked up at me at the same time she slipped a hand between us, her slender fingers grazing my cock.

I inhaled at the contact, and she started working the trunks over my hips. I pumped my fingers in and out of her again, and she moaned, the sound going straight to my already straining cock. Letting go of her, I stood and whipped off my briefs. I motioned to the nightstand. "Condoms in there?"

She opened her mouth to respond, then hesitated. Shit. She was reconsidering, and rightly so. I'd pushed too far, too fast.

Why did I think my being bi wouldn't be an issue? I should have given her time to think it over before taking her to bed.

"I'm sorry. I fucked up, didn't I?" I said, reaching for my boxers.

She sat up and shook her head. "No. I just—" Tears welled in her eyes again.

Oh *Cristo*. I promised myself I'd never hurt her, and look what I'd done. "Arianna—"

"I don't want to use a condom," she blurted.

I froze. "Why is that making you cry?"

"Because... because I want a baby, and I know it's not fair to ask you, and it's completely stupid, and I'm going to be thirty next year, but I wanted to have one by now..." The words poured out of her in a rush, punctuated by sharp inhales as she tried to suppress her tears.

"Shh." I folded her in my arms, rocking her gently. "*Corazón*, I really fucked up."

"No," she whispered against my chest, her warm tears sliding down my right pec. "I'm the one who's fucking up." She pulled back and wiped at her eyes, then she gave me a shaky smile. "The condoms are in the nightstand."

"You sure you want to do this?" I asked.

She nodded and reached down, wrapping her delicate fingers around my still-rigid shaft, which twitched in her hand. Jesus, the damn thing had always had a mind of its own. A one-track mind. And right now, it wanted to be buried inside this woman who made my heart want to beat out of my chest with one of her smiles.

Arianna Rodriguez was fucking luscious, from her bouncy tits to her curvy hips, and when she stroked my cock, her fingers squeezing me just right, every bit of common sense I had flew out the window. This beautiful, wonderful woman who I loved with all my heart wanted a baby. *My* baby. And it wasn't like I was planning to let her go.

What was the harm in making her happy?

What about Daniel? a voice in my head whispered. *She still loves him; he still loves her. What if they make up? Where does that leave you,* pendejo?

It's been almost a year. And Daniel was adamant that he didn't want children.

He'll never give her what she wants. What she needs.

But I can.

"You want that baby, *corazón*?"

She looked at me, her eyes lighting up. "You don't think I'm crazy?"

I laughed. "Maybe we both are. But I would love to have a baby with you."

She lay back on the bed, tugging me forward by my dick. And I was happy to follow.

I crawled up beside her. This *was* crazy. And stupid. And I couldn't stop grinning.

She smiled at me, then she wrapped her fingers around me again, stroking up and down, making me hiss this time. I wouldn't last long if she kept this going. How many nights had I beaten off to the thought of her touching me like this, back when we'd been teens and I'd had no idea what to make of my desire for her alongside my lust for Jack Anderson, the captain of the football team?

I grabbed her hand and pinned her wrist to the bed. "Enough, *corazón*, or that baby will have to wait a while longer." Grabbing the base of my cock, I moved over her, rubbing myself between her pussy lips, coating the tip in her juices. She gasped at the contact, spreading her legs and arching her hips, and then I was inside her, all that tight, wet heat making me groan. She fit me like we'd been made for each other, and I forced myself to go slow, to savor the feeling of her surrounding me. Then she crossed her legs behind my back and pressed down, forcing me back inside her with surprising power.

Apparently, all that yoga and Pilates hadn't just toned those muscles. She was a lot stronger than she looked.

And then she flexed the muscles surrounding my cock, and I about saw stars. "*Cristo*, woman," I panted.

She laughed and did it again, the sensation rippling from my shaft up my spine. "I like to keep in shape. *All* over."

"I'll show you in shape." I snapped my hips forward, thrusting into her hard, and she groaned, her fingernails digging into my back.

"Oh yes," she panted. "Harder."

I let myself loose, plunging into her without mercy, making sure I was pressing against her mound, and she arched, rubbing herself against me, her little gasps in my ear the fuel I needed to keep thrusting harder, faster, the tingling in my balls telling me I was close, so close, and then she shuddered beneath me, crying out my name, and I erupted inside her, my whole body stiffening.

I hadn't come that hard in years.

Collapsing on the bed beside her, I pulled her onto my chest and kissed her softly.

"You're the best thing to ever happen to me, Javi," she whispered.

"Same here, *corazón*." I wrapped my arms around her, enjoying how she snuggled into me like she'd always belonged there.

I'd held her a million times, but never like this.

Never like she was mine.

I'd finally manned up, finally claimed the woman I'd always wanted.

I was going to have everything I'd ever longed for.

Everything except Daniel.

A stone formed in my stomach. Daniel was probably going to hate me for this.

And it was probably going to destroy the company we'd spent the last decade building. The company that had been our dream way back since we'd organized that crazy spring-break trip down to Cancun for us and our entire college dorm. The trip that had made us campus legends.

The trip that had cemented our future.

That stone in my gut grew larger, and I hugged Arianna closer.

The future I'd just blown to smithereens.

DANIEL

Angry bees festered in my veins as I exited Miami International Airport. Or at least that's how it felt to me. I was riled up. Agitated. And horny as fuck. And who could blame me? I'd just spent two weeks in Tahiti with six insanely hot rock stars, two of whom were banging my new partner at Total Indulgence Tours. There'd been sex all around me, and I was going out of my mind with need.

I trudged through the parking lot and dumped my suitcase and laptop bag into the trunk of my silver Lexus. Inside, it was an inferno. I clawed at my tie, tearing it off and flicking open the buttons on my shirt while I waited for the air-conditioning to kick in. Beads of sweat snaked along my hairline, and I knew they weren't only due to the outside heat.

No. I was burning up inside. I angled the jet of air so it hit my face and leaned against the leather seat.

Get a hold of yourself, King.

I didn't want to give in to my need. I wouldn't.

Men didn't interest me. They never had, and they never would. Except when I got like this. When the memories from the past snuck up on me, tried to pull me back into that darkness. The only way I could breathe was to control them. To prove to the demons in my mind that I was no one's bitch. That I wasn't a scared kid anymore. That whatever I did, I did on my own terms.

Divorcing Arianna had only made things worse.

Had only made the nightmares more frequent. The loneliness more debilitating. What choice had there been, though? Once she'd started pushing for a baby, my brain had started to short-circuit, and all the insecurities of the past came back with a vengeance. I loved her more than life itself, but to survive, I'd had to let her go.

She could never know why.

Tomorrow, I'd have to go to the office and face her again. Face them both again. Arianna and Javier, my best friend and business partner since college. The man who'd introduced me to my ex-wife. The man who'd been in love with her all along. They'd grown up in the same Cuban community. Their mothers were friends. I didn't understand why he'd never gone after her. Sure, Javi was bi, though I doubted Arianna would have cared. The two of them were tight as ticks. But I was grateful that she'd picked me.

Javier didn't know that I knew, but it was hard not to notice the way he looked at her. The way his eyes lit up when she walked into a room, and the way his gaze traveled her generous curves and tanned skin.

I'd found it mesmerizing. Confusing. Fucking addictive.

And maybe I was a fucking masochist for continuing to work with both of them.

Today was her birthday, and for the first time in eleven years, I was missing her party. I could call her, but should I? I didn't want her to get the wrong impression, because we were never getting back together. I wouldn't hurt her that way. Not again.

She would be with her family tonight. With Javi. Happy.

He still looked at her like she was a goddess walking among mortals. And sometimes it pissed me off. Even though I couldn't have her, I still loved her. Other times, it *excited* me. I'd picture them in bed, their sweat-slicked bodies sliding together, their faces contorted in pleasure. His hands on her full breasts, her hands on his long, *hard* cock.

And then the fucking festering bees would return.

Goddamn it.

I fished my cell out of my back pocket and made the call that was the only solution that ever worked, even though it helped for only a while.

"Hello," a perky female voice said. "Diamond Escorts. How may I help you?"

"This is Daniel King. I'd like to book one of your escorts for a few hours this evening."

"Of course. Both Brandon and Diego are available. Any preference?"

I hadn't been with either man before, but… Javier's dark eyes and plump lips filled my mind. Fuck. I should pick Brandon. I knew from his photo in the company's online catalogue that he was the complete opposite of Javier, from his blond hair to his slim, small body. I also knew that he wouldn't do it for me. I cleared my throat. "Diego, please."

"Time?"

I checked my watch. It was eight. "Nine thirty at the usual place."

For years, I'd maintained a small bachelor pad in Fort Lauderdale. It was a place neither Arianna nor Javier knew about. My real home, the one I'd purchased after the divorce, was in Coconut Grove, only a short drive from TI's headquarters and minutes away from the home I'd shared with Arianna. She still lived there, because I'd insisted she keep it. It would be perfect for her and Javier when he finally swept her off her feet and gave her the family she deserved.

"Very well, sir. I'll charge it to the card on file?"

"Yes."

I ended the call and drove the short distance to Fort Lauderdale, stopping only to pick up some pizza and a Coke. My fingers tap-danced on the steering wheel as I turned into the parking garage. I quickly found an open spot, and leaving my bags in the trunk, I headed up to my home away from home.

Since I always left some spare clothes here, I jumped in the shower and changed, then sat on my balcony to eat my dinner. I never drank when I was meeting with an escort. The scent of alcohol on my breath would make him think I wasn't in control when nothing could be further from the truth.

At nine thirty on the dot, the buzzer sounded. I walked over to the keypad. "Yes?"

"It's Diego."

"Come on up." I pressed the button to unlock the main entrance door.

A couple minutes later, there was a soft knock on my door. I opened it, and the breath left my body. *Jesus, fuck.* The man could be Javier's younger brother. He looked to be about twenty-five, five-ten, with a slender swimmer's build. His dark eyes shone brightly. He smiled, and the bees hummed louder.

I stepped back. "Right on time. Come in."

He walked into the living room and shrugged off his worn jean jacket, leaving him in a rib-hugging white tank top. His faded jeans sat low on his hips, held up by a black leather belt. There was a thick gold chain around his neck. My cock jumped at the sight of all that golden skin. I wanted to fall to my knees and kiss his stomach. Follow his treasure trail to what I was sure was a generously proportioned cock if the bulge in his pants was anything to go by.

But that wasn't how these encounters went. Not with me.

"Do you understand what's going to happen here?" I asked him.

He nodded. "Velma informed me."

Velma was the manager of Diamond Escorts. We'd ironed out the details long ago, and since they valued my business, they made sure to follow them to a T. "Let's get started then." I pressed Play on the playlist I'd created for these encounters. Liszt's "Dante Symphony" began to play, dark and brooding and matching my mood exactly.

Diego's smile dimmed a bit, but his fingers went to his tank top, tugging the hem out of his jeans and pulling it over his head. He placed it on the back of the couch as per my instructions. Next, he undid his belt, kicked off his shoes and socks, then slid his jeans off his hips, slowly to match the dramatic music. Each inch revealed more of him: his taut belly, his curved cock, his heavy balls.

My mouth watered even as my insides roiled. I wanted this, yet I hated it. I hated that I wanted it.

Like Dante, I was trapped inside my own inferno.

My life was like the nine circles of Hell. Only there was no chance of escape for me. No chance of Paradise. Because I was a wrecked, ruined man.

When Diego stood completely naked in front of me, I said, "On your knees."

He obeyed me. His eyes were wide, but he didn't seem afraid. And rightly so. I'd never hurt an escort. It was just that things had to go a certain way.

I stepped closer. I remained fully clothed. I lowered my zipper and freed my cock. It was achingly hard and already dripping. "Open your mouth."

His eyes on me, Diego parted his lips. I fed him my cock, the only part of me that would be touching him. My hips snapped forward, and I sank into his mouth. Fully. His eyes watered, but he didn't pull away. That was another requirement. The escorts had to be able to deep throat.

I thrust into his mouth as deep as he could take me, over and over. He reached out to touch me. I shuddered and froze. My stomach dropped.

"Hands on your lap!" My command was sharp. Desperate even.

Diego's eyes filled with concern, but his hands returned to his thighs, gripping them. Shame filled me. I hated that I'd let my desperation, my fear, slip into my voice. My erection flagged.

Damn it. I focused on his face, pictured someone else's. Someone I cared about. It was wrong and I knew it, but right now that didn't matter. All that mattered was exorcising the demons inside me.

When I felt I was getting close, I pulled out of his mouth and stepped away from him. "Bend over the armchair."

He rose and walked behind the chair, then leaned over it. His fingers clutched the threadbare fabric. I could no longer see his face, and that was exactly what I wanted. I picked up the condom I'd left on the coffee table after my shower and rolled it onto my cock. Then I tore open the packet of lube and slathered it onto my shaft. My instructions included that the escorts prepare themselves before coming over. An opportunity I'd rarely been afforded.

I stepped behind him. "Part your cheeks," I said.

He reached back and gripped one ass cheek in each hand, then pulled them apart. His puckered hole glistened. I gripped my shaft and positioned the head at his entrance.

"Brace yourself." It was my only instruction before I let loose. I rammed my cock into his tight ass, relishing in his gasp. The half-pained

228

moan. I thrust back and forth until he relaxed enough that I could sink in all the way. I couldn't use the seatback as support because the risk of coming into contact with his arms was too high. Instead, I widened my stance and pistoned into Diego. His back arched, and I enjoyed the ripple of his muscles, the tightening of his glutes as he took me. Every inch of me. I wanted to slide my hand down his spine, feel the movement beneath his skin, but I didn't dare touch him. The one time I'd tried, years ago, before Arianna, the evening had ended with me heaving up my dinner in the bathroom.

So, I did what I always did: I used my imagination. In my mind, I ran my fingers over those sleek muscles, the narrow waist and slender hips. I dug my fingers into his hair and pulled his head back. Though it wasn't Diego in my mind. No, it was Javier. My best friend. But I could never do to him what I did to these men. To Diego.

I pictured myself kissing Javier while my cock drove into Diego's tight body, giving no care to his pleasure, only to mine. He was mine to do with as I pleased. Right now, he was an object. A sex toy. Someone who existed only as a receptacle for my cock. For my cum.

The thought set me off. Electricity jolted down my spine, through my balls and out the head of my cock. I rocked my hips into him as my body spasmed, releasing all the tension that had been building up inside me since the last time I'd fucked a man. Fucked anyone really.

When the aftershocks were done, I wrapped my hand around the base of my cock, holding the condom in place, and withdrew. Diego moaned softly, panting against the couch. He released his ass cheeks and pushed himself up. His cock was still hard, but I was done. That was also part of the instructions. The escorts weren't allowed to come. I'd learned over the years that the sight or scent of another man's cum could throw me into a flashback. And no one wanted to see that shit.

I grabbed some tissues off the kitchen counter to clean myself up and dispose of the condom while Diego got dressed. I reached into my pocket and pulled out a twenty. I handed him the tip. "Thank you."

"Ever thought about loosening up a bit?" Diego took the money, a sad expression on his face. "You might have more fun if you did."

After closing the door behind him, I grabbed the bottle of vodka stashed in the freezer. On my way to the balcony, I glugged down several mouthfuls and wiped away the drops that spilled onto my chin with the back of my hand. I sat in the cheap plastic chair and stared at the evening skyline as I drank more vodka and hoped it would numb the pain in my heart. Diego was right, but I couldn't loosen up, couldn't risk losing control. I already hated that I couldn't suppress this fucking need. The need I had to control another man sexually. The need that had been put there by the sick fuck who'd warped me.

I needed help; I knew it. But how could I ever tell anyone what had happened to me when I didn't entirely understand it myself?

END OF SPECIAL PREVIEW

ABOUT DANA DELAMAR

Dana Delamar is the author of erotic romance, LGBTQ romance, and the "Blood and Honor" romantic suspense series, which is set in Italy among the Calabrian Mafia. Her first book, *Revenge*, received 4 stars from *RT Book Reviews*, was a Top Pick at The Romance Reviews, and was a double-finalist for Best First Book and Best Romantic Suspense in the 2013 Booksellers Best Awards.

Her second book, *Retribution*, received 4 stars from *RT Book Reviews* and was a semi-finalist in the Kindle Book Review's 2013 Best Indie Book Awards. Her book *Malavita* was a quarter-finalist in the 2014 Amazon Breakthrough Novel Awards, and her book *Redemption* was a finalist in the 2014 Maggie Awards and a semi-finalist in the Kindle Book Review's 2014 Best Kindle Book Awards.

Dana is also an editor with over thirty years of editing experience in both fiction and nonfiction and has worked with everyone from newbie writers to experienced pros. The books she's edited have won numerous awards and critical acclaim, including two Top Picks from *RT Book Reviews*.

www.danadelamar.com

ABOUT KRISTINE CAYNE

Kristine Cayne is the author of erotic romance, LGBTQ romance, and romantic suspense. Her books have won numerous awards and acclaim. Her first book, *Deadly Obsession*, was an *RT Book Reviews* Top Pick and won Best Romance in the 2012 eFestival of Words Best of the Independent eBook Awards. Her second book, *Deadly Addiction*, won two awards at the 2014 eFestival of Words and 1st place in the INDIE Awards, Romantic Suspense Category (a division of Chanticleer Book Reviews Blue Ribbon Writing Contests).

Her book *Under His Command* won Best BDSM Romance at the 2012 Sizzling Awards and was a finalist in the 2013 eFestival of Words and 2013 RONE (Reward of Novel Excellence) Awards, and her book *Everything Bared* was a finalist in the Erotic category of the I Heart Indie awards.

www.kristinecayne.com

ALSO BY DANA DELAMAR AND KRISTINE CAYNE

BY DANA DELAMAR

Blood and Honor: A Mafia Romance Series

Malavita (Prequel)
Revenge (Book One)
Retribution (Book Two)
Redemption (Book Three)
Reckoning (Book Four)

BY KRISTINE CAYNE

Six-Alarm Sexy Series: A Firefighter Erotic Romance Series

Aftershocks (Prequel)
Under His Command (Book One)
Everything Bared (Book Two)
Handle with Care (Book Three)
Lover on Top (Book Four)
Baby, Be Mine (Book Five)
Stripped Down (Book Six – coming soon)

Seattle Fire Series
(Six-Alarm Sexy Spin-off)

In His Arms (Book One – coming 2018)

Men of Boyzville: A Gay Romance Series
(Six-Alarm Sexy Spin-off)

Going All In (Book One)
Wrangling the Cowboy (Book Two – coming soon)

Deadly Vices: A Romantic Suspense Series

Deadly Obsession (Book One)
Deadly Addiction (Book Two)
Deadly Betrayal (Book Three)

Other Works

Guns 'N' Tulips
Un-Valentine's Day
Origins: Men of M.E.R. in *Shadows in the Mist*

BONUS CONTENT: SONG LYRICS

"No Strings"

You're just a waif of a girl
But you shook up my whole damn world
Though you're not "just" anything
Oh no, you're everything

You said "no strings"
And I hoped you were lying
You said "no strings"
I said "yes" but inside I was dying

The day you came into my life
You brought along a ray of light
But ever since you up and left
It's only been eternal night

You said "no strings"
And I hoped you were lying
You said "no strings"
I said "yes" but inside I was dying

You own my heart
You are my life
Won't you let me be part
Of your lovely light?

You said "no strings"
And I knew you were lying
You said "no strings"
I said "yes" but I knew I was dying

Oh I knew I was lying
Oh I knew I was dying

"Unfinished"

There are things I want
There are things I have
There are things I can't
There are things I crave
And then there's you...

You left, you think you won
But I have to tell you
We're far from done
You walked away from all of this
But you and I, we're unfinished

You're in my heart, in every beat
You are the life I long to keep
But life's not fair, it's never been
And you and I, we'll never win

You left, you think you won
But I have to tell you
We're far from done
You walked away from all of this
But you and I, we're unfinished

My heart is heavy
I think I'll drown
I need your help
To turn it 'round

You left, you think you won
But I have to tell you
We're far from done
You walked away from all of this
But you and I, we're unfinished

"Just Friends"

So many years
You've been by my side
So many tears
I've tried and tried

You claim we're "just friends"
A bigger lie there's never been
'Cause you and I were born to sin
Take my hand, jump on in

Both our hearts you'll deny
You're too afraid to even try
What will it take to make you see
Your heart is empty without me?

You claim we're "just friends"
A bigger lie there's never been
'Cause you and I were born to sin
Take my hand, jump on in

Take the risk, make that leap
Be the one I want to keep
But you say no, you run away
You can't see another way

You claim we're "just friends"
A bigger lie there's never been
'Cause you and I were born to sin
Take my hand, jump on in

Made in the USA
Columbia, SC
16 March 2019